KNIGHT'S
CROSS

OTHER TITLES BY CHRISTINE KLING

KNIGHT'S CROSS

A Shipwreck Adventure Thriller

CHRISTINE KLING

THOMAS & MERCER

Published by Thomas & Mercer, Seattle

www.apub.com

Amazon, the Amazon logo, and Thomas & Mercer are trademarks of Amazon.com, Inc., or its affiliates.

ISBN-13: 9781503944633
ISBN-10: 1503944638

Cover design by Jason Blackburn

Printed in the United States of America

To Wayne
who showed me I *don't* have to be alone to write

What is objectionable, what is dangerous, about extremists is not that they are extreme, but that they are intolerant. The evil is not what they say about their cause, but what they say about their opponents.

—Robert F. Kennedy

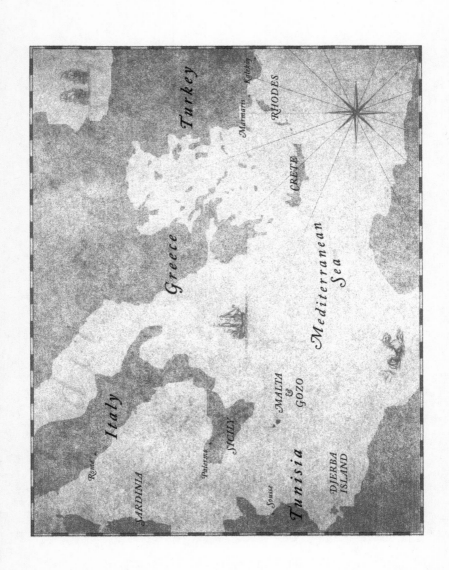

AUTHOR'S NOTE

I enjoy using real historical ships as the basis for the Shipwreck Adventure series. For each book, I look for a ship that went missing but whose wreck has never been found. Since no one knows for certain what happened to the ship and her men, I get to let my imagination take over. In each case I try to show the utmost respect for the real men whose lives were lost when their ship went down.

Just as in *Circle of Bones* I created an imagined ending for the real French submarine the *Surcouf*, and in *Dragon's Triangle* I envisaged what might have happened to the American submarine the USS *Bonefish*, here in *Knight's Cross* I've conceived a unique ending for the HMS *Upholder*.

To this day, the HMS *Upholder* holds the record for the most tonnage sunk of any British submarine. I have attempted to tell her known story as close to true as possible. Lieutenant Commander David Wanklyn was the real skipper of the *Upholder*, and I have tried to portray him as accurately as possible. Captain Robert "Tug" Wilson was a British commando with the Special Boats Unit who did go on that final patrol aboard the *Upholder*. Tug was the last man to see the captain and crew of the *Upholder* before they disappeared. On April 11, 1942, *Upholder* followed orders to patrol east of Djerba Island. Orders were later sent for *Upholder* to form a patrol line with HMS

Thrasher, but those orders were never acknowledged, and she was never heard from again.

The story of the Siege of Malta in 1942 is an amazing tale of the courage and tenacity of the Maltese people and the sailors in the Royal Navy's Tenth Submarine Flotilla, who together saved Malta from falling into the hands of their enemy. I encourage my readers to learn more about this incredible chapter of world history.

—Christine Kling, June 2015

KNIGHT'S
CROSS

CHAPTER ONE

Aboard the Ferryboat
Approaching Rhodes Harbor

April 9, 2014

Riley leaned over the side of the boat, holding her diamond engagement ring at arm's length, and imagined dropping it. The ring was just bits of metal and rock—if you took away all the sentiment. And sentiment seemed to have gone AWOL from her life lately.

The cabin door creaked open behind her. When she turned to look, the wind blew her hair into her face, blinding her.

"Riley?"

His voice calling her name still fired up that warm tingle at the back of her neck. She pushed the strands of hair out of her eyes. Cole stood in the open doorway, holding his forearm in front of his face as a windbreak.

"What are you doing out here?"

The Mediterranean wind called the *meltemi* had started to fill in that morning just as the ferryboat pulled away from the dock. The weather had driven all the other tourists inside as soon as they'd cleared Marmaris Bay, but Riley loved the feel of the wind and spray on her cheeks.

She slipped the ring into the pocket of her jeans. "It's beautiful out here." Reaching out, she took Cole's hand and said, "Come with me." The heavy door shut behind him. She grabbed the railing with one hand and pulled him against her back with the other, pressing the two of them forward into the wind.

When she turned her head to look at him, she couldn't help but laugh at his pout. "You won't melt in a little spray."

He pulled his hand back. "Riley, cut it out." He flattened himself against the side of the cabin, swiveling his head to look fore and aft.

"Cole, it's okay. We've got the deck all to ourselves." She pressed her body up against his and slid her hand behind his neck. "I miss being alone at sea with you."

"You don't get it." His eyes were focused on something over her shoulder. "I'm telling you, I'm not crazy. I know what I saw. The threat is real."

She ran her fingers over the stubble on his cheek. "Okay," she said. "I want to believe it, but it's not logical. They said he couldn't possibly have survived. That was all a long time ago."

"I want you to believe *me*, not what the authorities said."

Riley struggled to find the right words. What he claimed to have seen was impossible. Her military training, her very nature, got in the way when it came to acting on faith.

"It's too open out here," he said. "They might be watching."

They. "Cole—"

"You stay out here. You're probably safest if you keep well away from me." He pushed her off him, and, with his head still swiveling to look up and down the deck, he headed for the door.

He didn't even look back before he went inside.

Riley stood there, one hand holding her hair out of her face, and stared at the closed door. She couldn't bear the thought of going back inside the cabin with all those chattering tourists. For some reason, Cole felt safer in a crowd. One more thing they didn't agree on.

Riley turned and walked forward, toward the open foredeck. When she reached the forward railing, she watched the crew working one deck beneath hers, readying the big dock lines. Already she could feel the wind easing. They'd entered the lee of the island. The ferry was a big catamaran, and, with her speed, they'd crossed from Marmaris to Rhodes in an hour.

Her brother, Michael, would have been able to tell her in a second how fast the cat had been traveling. They'd learned to sail together as kids, at whatever foreign diplomatic post their father had been assigned to. Michael had been a whiz at navigation—a true math prodigy. And he'd always been able to explain things so that she could understand.

Mikey, she thought, *I wish you'd lived long enough to help me to figure out Cole.* She closed her eyes and listened for her dead brother's voice. All she heard was the dull roar of the boat's engines.

When she opened her eyes, she saw the port appear as the ferry rounded the point. After a month in Turkey, a person could get jaded about one more set of ruins, but the ancient walled city of Rhodes, with its medieval saw-toothed turrets and white-domed mosque and minaret, looked magical—like a place where King Arthur's knights would lunch with Aladdin.

The city held something even more potent than magic for Riley, though. She was meeting her best friend, Hazel, there—seeing her for the first time in more than a year.

When the ferry entered the inner harbor, the captain made for an empty dock, where a small group of people clustered together along the seawall. It was easy to pick Hazel out of the crowd, since she was the only black-skinned person in the bunch. And, being Hazel, she was dressed in her best resort wear, which in this case amounted to high-heeled white sandals and a skintight tropical-print dress that revealed her generous cleavage and clung to her curves like it was glued to her skin. Few of the men in the crowd were watching the approaching ferry.

Riley leaned over the rail and waved. Hazel jumped up and down and swung the straw hat off her head. Riley grinned and waved harder. Relief flowed down her arm, and she felt some of the tension leave her shoulders.

Hazel would know what to do. She always did.

All week, Riley had been looking forward to this day trip to Rhodes. After the latest setback in the boatyard, she'd hoped this getaway would cheer Cole up. He was understandably frustrated. He'd ordered his dream boat to be built in Turkey over a year ago, while the two of them sailed her boat, *Bonefish*, from the Philippines to the Med. Things had been great while they were sailing together, but once they'd arrived in Turkey, the problems and boatyard delays had started. Cole had already sold his old boat, the *Bonhomme Richard*, in Manila, and most of his possessions were in a shipping container in the corner of the boatyard. The new eighty-three-foot exploration vessel, the EV *Shadow Chaser II*, was now more than six weeks past the contract delivery date, and the longer he was boatless, the more Cole seemed lost, adrift.

But she knew it wasn't only the problems with his dream boat.

Cole Thatcher, the man she had, a mere six months ago, agreed to marry, now appeared to be losing his mind.

CHAPTER TWO

Aboard the Ferryboat
Approaching Rhodes Harbor

April 9, 2014

He crouched down behind one of the big canister life rafts on the top deck, but it did not provide much wind protection. He pushed up the collar of his black raincoat and held it closed at his throat. Icy tentacles of wind found their way up his sleeves, around his bare ankles. His tolerance for cold had diminished significantly after the accident. That was what he called it. *The accident.* Even though it was no accident at all.

He'd heard her voice just a few minutes before, but since she stood on the deck directly under him, he couldn't make out the words, nor could he see her. She was talking to a man. The tone of their voices sounded angry. That pleased him. Then the door had opened and closed beneath him.

Should he risk leaning over the edge to see if she was still there? It would be very unlikely she would see him. Most people never look up. But then again, she wasn't most people.

He glanced ahead to check the distance to the island's harbor, and he saw her on the foredeck, elbows leaning on the side railing, her face in profile, auburn hair whipping in all directions in the wind. She was wearing a red jacket that came only to her waist, and her tight blue jeans showed off the curve of her ass. The hair was longer, but other than that, the years had not left any marks on her. She still had that compact, athletic body, the smooth, suntanned skin, the aura of strength in one so small.

She turned to look aft, and he saw her full face. He turned aside. Then he opened his right hand and slowly, one by one, closed the fingers and squeezed the hand into a fist.

On the top deck, a gate blocked him from going any farther forward. He didn't need to get any closer. Besides, that was where the navigation-bridge windows were, and he didn't want to be seen watching her. No witnesses. He had spent too many years living in the shadows to risk that.

He had changed so much since the last time he had spoken to her. A new name to go with his new appearance—and a new life. Not a better one, but a life. For a long while he hadn't been sure he would ever have even that.

Years gone, years lost. Her fault. Whatever happened, he was glad he had crawled out of that hole. Glad he had found her. Once again, he closed the fingers of his right hand into a fist, only this time he held his fist up to his eye. He looked through the hole it formed—like a rifle scope. Her head in the center of the circle. His other hand squeezed an imaginary trigger. He saw her head jerk, the puff of red spume, the body falling limp to the deck. A thousand times he had imagined it.

No, that would be too quick. He wanted to take his time. He stretched out the fingers of both hands and then formed fists. His strength was returning.

He stood straight and the wind caught his coat, making it flap loudly round his legs. She couldn't hear it. She wouldn't look back. She never looked back.

Her mistake.

CHAPTER THREE

The Ferryboat Dock
Rhodes Harbor

April 9, 2014

"Congratulations!" Hazel lifted her off the ground in a big bear hug, then held Riley's neck in the crook of one arm while she threw the other around Cole. "I can't believe this guy actually put a ring on it. Let me see!"

Riley was thankful she had wriggled the ring back onto her finger as she'd walked down the gangway.

"I'm so happy for you," Hazel said and squeezed them again.

Riley grinned at her friend, but Cole didn't say a word. "So tell us more about what you're doing in Greece," Riley said. "Is it work or pleasure?"

"A little of both," Hazel said. "I have the pleasure this spring of hanging out in the Med with rich folk, trying to convince them to donate to the Kittridge Foundation. Crete, Capri, Cannes—the usual."

"Very cool."

"Look, it's a bit of a walk to the museum from here," Hazel said, "but there are no cars allowed in the Old Town, and I told Dr. G. we would meet her at eleven. I don't want to be late." In a second, she had turned businesslike and hustled them off toward the center of the old city.

"I really appreciate you setting this up," Cole said.

"When it comes to the Knights," Hazel said, "Dr. Günay is a world-class authority."

"Don't tell me you share Cole's obsession," Riley said.

"No, I met her at a conference on educating girls a couple of years ago in Istanbul. I was there representing the Foundation, and she was a guest speaker. She's fascinating. I had to meet her afterward. You'll understand." Hazel pointed to an arched doorway through a wall. "This way."

At the pace Hazel set, they soon arrived at the Palace of the Grand Master, on a back street in Rhodes's Old Town.

"It doesn't look like much from the outside," she said, "but when I was here yesterday, I was blown away by the museum inside." She pointed at another arched stone doorway. "Through here."

She led them across a huge stone inner courtyard to an unmarked wood door. Hazel knocked, and a short, heavyset, matronly lady squealed with delight when she opened the door.

Hazel laughed. "This is my friend, Dr. Najat Günay."

The woman's glasses magnified her sparkling eyes. Her childlike joie de vivre was startling and unexpected, given her profession and staid appearance.

"Najat works for Heritage Malta," Hazel continued, "but she's here in Rhodes doing research. Najat, this is my best friend, Maggie Riley, and her fiancé, Cole Thatcher."

The woman shook Cole's hand first. When she turned to Riley, she said, "Hazel has told me so much about you. I can't believe a little thing like you was once a US Marine."

"Yes, ma'am. Seven years."

"And now you're engaged to this fellow! You're the lucky girl. He's hot!" And then the renowned historian giggled like a schoolgirl, with her hand in front of her mouth.

Cole flushed, and Riley could not help but laugh with her. "I agree."

"Please, come along to the office they're letting me use here," she said, rubbing her hands together. "I have some tea and cakes for you."

The office turned out to be a conference room with a long table surrounded by high-backed chairs. On the center of the table stood a silver samovar and a plate piled with baklava, halvah, and colorful Turkish delight.

"Sit down, please. And call me Najat." She served them, then sat across from Cole.

"That samovar is magnificent," Riley said.

"Yes, the Maltese have been famous for their silver work for centuries."

Riley took a sip of the black tea. It was good and strong, just as she preferred.

"So what sparked your interest in the Knights of Saint John?" Najat Günay took a big bite of pastry and made little moaning noises as she ate it.

Riley looked at Cole, then back at their host. "I thought we were talking about the Knights of Malta."

Najat swallowed, then threw back her head and laughed. "Oh dear. I do have to start at the beginning for you, don't I?"

"Not really," Cole said. "I'm the one with the 'obsession,' as she put it." He inclined his head toward Riley. "See, my father, he wrote about the modern Knights—the Sovereign Order of the Knights of Malta—a sovereignty with no territory, which issues passports, has an embassy, and has been granted observer status at the UN. A very wealthy secret society with a number of powerful men and women who make up its ranks. It all piqued my curiosity, so I'm here to learn more about their origins."

The woman's eyes twinkled as she rested her index finger on her chin and stared at each of them in turn. "Ahhhh, I see. What you want to learn about are the *naughty* Knights."

Cole's lips lifted in a half smile. "I guess you could say that."

"Okay, well." Najat wiped the corners of her mouth with her pinky fingers, then smoothed her skirt. "The Order didn't start out naughty. They actually started as a monastic brotherhood doing charity work. During the Crusades, they provided care for sick and injured pilgrims in a Jerusalem hospital dedicated to Saint John the Baptist. The work resulted in bequests of land in Palestine, Syria, Italy, and France, and they grew into a military order as they had to defend their possessions. The brotherhood began the transition to the chivalric order when the pope granted them exemption from the paying of tithes. That would be like getting tax-exempt status. Best way to get rich fast. So what had been solely a monastic order grew into the Knights of Saint John of Jerusalem."

"How were the Knights of Saint John different from the Knights Templar?" Riley asked.

"Ah, you've been reading Dan Brown! Good question. During the Crusades, both orders fought to free the Holy Land from the 'infidels.'" Najat made air quotes with her fingers. "While the Knights of Saint John took on their role as Knights Hospitallers, the Templars developed a rudimentary system of banking. That's how the Templars amassed such great wealth."

"Interesting," Riley said. "Never thought about how banking got started."

Najat reached for another piece of Turkish delight. "When the Holy Land was lost to the infidels, both orders were homeless for a while. The Knights of Saint John eventually moved to Rhodes, but the Templars wandered. In 1305, Pope Clement the Fifth asked the two orders to merge, but they refused. Then King Philip the Fourth of France, who was deeply in debt to the Templars, ordered the Templars arrested. Nice way to get out of debt, eh?" Najat giggled into her hand again.

Riley found herself smiling, too. The woman's enthusiasm for this history was infectious.

"The church accused the Templars of everything from heresy to idolatry. Eventually, Philip got his way. The Templar leaders were burned at the stake. In 1313, the pope ordered all the Templars' property transferred to the Knights of Saint John, and the Templars were dissolved. Then the Knights of Saint John got kicked out of Rhodes by the Ottomans, and they moved to Malta in 1512."

Hazel said, "Part of what makes Najat such a fascinating authority on all this is her own background. She was born in Turkey to a Muslim family. Her parents were killed when she was seven years old, and she was adopted by a Christian family in Malta."

"They were the only parents I remember," she said. "But I always knew that in my blood I had one side of this old conflict and in my heart I had the other." She laughed again. "*Both* sides see me as an infidel."

"When I heard Najat speak for the first time in Istanbul, she talked about how her life changed when she went from a culture that rarely educated girls to one where she had the opportunity to learn and excel. Her personal story is just as fascinating as her Knights'."

"Ah, but your friends are here to learn about the Knights. So, today, they are called the Sovereign Military Order of Malta, or SMOM, and their headquarters is in Rome. Last year the Order celebrated its nine hundredth anniversary at Saint Peter's Basilica. They are always granted an audience with the pope. They remain the only surviving chivalric order that can date its origins back to the Crusades."

Hazel stood up. "Listen, Najat, fascinating as this is, I heard most of it yesterday, and I am dying to catch up with my best friend here. So

I suggest you and Cole stay here and visit the museum exhibits while I take Riley to lunch. We'll be back to meet you in"—she glanced at her watch—"say, a couple of hours?"

Cole shrugged without looking up. He muttered something that might have been the word "Fine."

Once they exited the palace courtyard, Hazel linked her arm through Riley's. They strolled the narrow stone-paved streets in silence until they came to an unpainted wood building. The sign over the door was written only in Greek, but Hazel turned through the doorway. Riley followed.

The room inside was no bigger than fifteen by twenty feet, dimly lit from the glow of the soft-drink fridge against the back wall. A teenage girl behind the counter smiled shyly and nodded at Hazel, then turned and passed through a curtain into the back of the store.

"You ready for a picnic?" Hazel asked. "I thought we'd find a quiet place where we could talk, away from the noisy, touristy restaurants here."

The girl returned and hoisted a heavy fabric shopping bag onto the counter. Hazel paid her and they left.

The route she led them on was not haphazard; Hazel had planned it all out. It appeared she knew exactly what Riley needed. At last they climbed a narrow set of stairs and found themselves in a sheltered alcove with a clear view across the harbor from the top of the Old Town's walls. A table was set up there with two chairs. The sounds of the city faded away on the fresh breeze.

"What do you think?" Hazel said.

"My friend, you know me so well."

The bag held cheese, bread, tomatoes, olives, and a foil dish of fish cooked in a slathering of vegetables, as well as a chilled bottle of white wine and glasses.

When they were both seated, Hazel took out the bottle and poured them each some wine. She handed a glass to Riley, then raised her own glass. "Cheers, darling."

Riley smiled as she stared into her friend's eyes and their glasses clinked.

"So?" Hazel said. "Now can you tell me what the hell is going on with Cole?"

Riley looked away and took a long, deep breath.

"I'm scared, Hazel. I know, he appears to be a conspiracy nutjob sometimes."

"Okay, but that's not news to you."

"This goes way beyond his usual conspiracy theories. This is like serious crazy. Hazel, Cole insists he's seen a ghost."

CHAPTER FOUR

Lazaretto Royal Navy Submarine Base
Manoel Island, Malta

April 3, 1942

Captain Robert "Tug" Wilson loved the clanking noise of metal hitting metal, and the ringing vibration of it traveling up his arm. His opponent parried, spun, and jumped atop a fragment of a stone wall. Tug gave chase across the crumbling rocks, but when Lieutenant Commander David Wanklyn whirled around, one of Tug's boots slipped off the broken stones. It was only thanks to his slender frame that he was able to turn aside and avoid being impaled.

"Ha!" Tug shouted as their sabers clanked, and Tug brushed aside his opponent's thrust. "Good try, Wanks."

While he knew that the tall submarine commander's reach exceeded his own by several inches, Tug could also count on the navy man to play fair. Not so, Tug himself. With a quick disengage, he flustered Wanklyn with a lunge, piercing the other man's shirt with the tip of his saber. He ripped his blade free from the cloth.

"My point!" Tug said.

"Bad form!" the commander shouted with a grin on his face. He held his sword aloft and walked around his opponent, his other hand behind his back. "This is the last good shirt I've got, Captain Wilson. You'll owe me one." He lunged.

Tug's saber brushed Wanklyn's aside, and the music of metal on metal rang out in the courtyard as their swords crossed.

"And you'll have to find me to get me to pay up," Tug said. "I got my orders. They're calling me back home."

Tug backed up, fending off Wanklyn's onslaught. The navy man's confidence drove him on as it did at sea. Tug was beginning to understand why this man's boat had sunk more enemy ships than any other submarine in the British Navy.

"I wonder how they plan to get you out of here," Wanklyn said.

Their fight took them closer to the seawall and the glittering harbor. Commander Wanklyn's face appeared even more pale in the bright light, especially given the contrast with his dark, V-shaped beard. These past months the man had spent more time beneath the sea than out in the daylight.

Both men were sweating and breathing heavily when the slow windup of the air-raid siren sounded from the loudspeakers hanging outside the arched galleries of Lazaretto Submarine Base, home to the Royal Navy's Tenth Flotilla. Out in the creek, one of the moored sub's Klaxon horns sounded as she prepared to dive. The bottom of the creek had become the big boats' only safe refuge from the constant aerial attacks.

Their sabers crossed and both men leaned in, Tug looking up into the face of the tall submarine commander. "You're not going to let a few planes put a stop to our fun, are you, Wanks?"

Wanklyn's eyes shifted skyward as both men heard the distant drone of planes approaching.

"Hey, you two!"

Tug turned and looked into the arched galleries that fronted La-zaretto Creek. The only other man on base wearing army khaki was waving at them.

"Are you fellows mad?" he yelled. "Another minute and the two of you'll be flying about like farts in a colander."

The engine noise grew louder. Then they heard the first whine of the bombs dropping.

"What do you say, Wanks?"

"Much as I'd love to stay and ram my saber right through that gap between your teeth, Wilson—"

They saw the plane at the same time. It was coming in low from the west and headed straight for them.

"Shit!" Tug said. Both men dropped their swords and bolted for the cover of the old stone hospital building.

The explosion knocked them off their feet, and they landed half inside the old building's gallery. They lay still on the ground, hands covering their heads while rocks and wood debris clattered onto the stones around them. The bomb, meant for the submarine tied farther along the catwalk that connected to the seawall, had fallen a hundred feet short and taken out one of the hospital's outbuildings. It would have killed the two fencers if they hadn't run for cover.

Lance Corporal Charlie Parker of the Beds and Herts Regiment walked out of the hall that led back to the officers' mess. He stood, hands on hips, shaking his head as he looked down at the two men at his feet.

"Looks like they almost smoked you two musketeers."

Tug sat up and brushed off dirt and debris. Lieutenant Command-er Wanklyn stirred.

"You all right, Wanks?" Tug asked as he grabbed Charlie's extend-ed hand and allowed himself to be pulled to his feet.

Wanklyn stood and dusted off his trousers. He looked back at the crater in the side courtyard, where they had been fencing minutes ago, and slowly stroked his dark beard. "Thank God Jerry hasn't got better aim," he said.

Tug smiled at Charlie. The two army commandos had come to understand these submariners a bit during their stay here in Malta. Wanks hadn't been worried about his own safety. The sub tied up to a floating catwalk just off the Lazaretto Base was Wanklyn's own, the HMS *Upholder*.

It took a bit of digging to find their sabers. Charlie was the most enthusiastic excavator of the lot. Back home he'd been something of an amateur archeologist, and he'd once told Tug, as they walked the streets of Valletta, that he was thrilled to find himself stationed on Malta.

"Parker," Tug had said, "it's a little rock in the middle of the Med. The bloody Luftwaffe bombs are reducing the place to rubble, and the rationing is so bad the whole island's run out of beer. Who the hell *wants* to be here?"

Charlie had replied, "Every time a bomb drops, what's left is an archeological dig. For thousands of years people have been building on top of buildings here." His eyes glowed with an inner light. "This city is an absolute world treasure. Think about it. We may be the last ones to see all this culture still standing."

Watching Charlie now, as he turned over rocks and sifted through the rubble, was like watching a kid digging through presents under the Christmas tree.

"What do you think you're going to find, anyway, Parker?"

"You never know, Tug. Maybe some kind of treasure."

"It better be my saber. Do you realize I took that off the *Arta*?"

"The *Arta*?"

Tug sat down on the low stone wall and wiped his face with his sleeve. "That German troop transport that grounded on the banks off

Kerkennah Island. I was in the boarding party. I found some Jerry's saber, and I mean to hang on to it, so you keep looking."

Charlie stopped digging and looked up. "You might help."

"What? And spoil all your fun with your rocks?"

"It's not just rocks, Tug. There are layers upon layers of history here. You realize this base is an old hospital built in 1643 to house plague victims who arrived on sailing ships? That's one layer, three hundred years ago. This is a fantastic natural harbor. With Manoel Island right in the middle, certainly people've been living here as long as there have been people in Malta."

"And how long is that?"

"Nobody knows for sure. The Phoenicians, the Romans, the Ottomans—they all fought over this rock and settled here for a time."

Tug reached into his pocket and pulled out a crumpled package of smokes. Two left. He shrugged, stuck a bent cigarette in his mouth, and touched a match flame to the end. He pulled the smoke into his lungs and held it before blowing a perfect smoke ring. "Where'd you learn all this?"

"Always liked history. Been reading about it since I was a kid. Aha!" Charlie held a bent saber aloft. "Found one!"

CHAPTER FIVE

**Atop the Ramparts
Rhodes Old Town**

April 9, 2014

"You, my friend, are the bravest woman I know. If you're scared, something is seriously wrong."

Hazel served them up plates of fish, cheese, and olives, and they settled back to watch the small boats skittering back and forth across the harbor.

"I don't know where to start, Hazel."

"Do you love him?"

"Yes, but—"

"No buts. That's your starting and ending point."

Riley looked across at her friend. "Remember all that business more than ten years ago when I was stationed down in Lima?"

"Darling, of course I do. That bastard Priest almost blew you to bits."

Riley took a long drink of her wine. "Right." The food didn't look as good as it had a few minutes ago. For a long moment, she couldn't figure out how to go on.

"Honey, I'm confused. What are you trying to say?"

Riley touched the stone wall surrounding their little picnic spot. "There's a fine line between love and hate. Maybe the only reason I can hate him so much now is because I once loved him."

"That sick son of a bitch—all that horror in Lima, your burn injuries, and then there was what he did to you later in the Caribbean."

"Actually, it started even before that. That day I watched Diggory Priest break my father's neck, he confessed that he had killed Michael, too. Diggory was my father's Skull and Bones protégé."

"Oh Riley, I hate that this is making you relive all that. It was horrible, yes. But it's old history now. You've pressed on, and now you have this new life with Cole ahead of you."

"It seems Diggory won't leave me alone."

"You've never said much about that boat explosion in the Caribbean, but I gather there wouldn't have been a piece of him big enough to find."

"Right." That was what made it so difficult to say it out loud. It sounded so crazy. She'd just have to blurt it out. "Cole claims he's seen Diggory Priest in Turkey."

Hazel choked on her wine. "What?"

"I know. It doesn't just *sound* crazy, it is crazy, right? Diggory Priest is dead."

Neither woman said anything for several minutes as they drank their wine and stared out over the rooftops at the sea.

Riley put down her glass and clasped the edge of the table with both hands. "Hazel, we had such a great time sailing my boat here. We'd sold Cole's old boat. The new boat was on order. Cole and Theo had already flown out to Marmaris and met with the designer and builder."

"And how is First Officer Theo?"

Glad for the momentary change of subject, Riley narrowed her eyes and examined her friend's face. "You've been asking about him quite a bit lately."

"I find him interesting."

"Well, he's gone far beyond being just Cole's first mate. He's been living in Marmaris the whole time we were out sailing, and he's taken all of Cole's ideas and made them happen. All the tech on the boat is Theo's design, and it's brilliant. *He's* brilliant. This new expedition vessel is going to be the perfect workboat for Cole's archeological expeditions."

"So he's back to treasure hunting?"

"Not exactly. See, in his field, there are people who just want to get rich—treasure hunters. Cole calls them poachers and con men. There are others who want to preserve history. They're the archeologists. After Cole found the submarine *Surcouf* in the Caribbean, he had a difficult four years on the run, feeling as though he had joined the dark side."

"You've never told me exactly what he and Theo found on that submarine."

Riley smiled at her friend. "And I never will."

"There really was gold?"

Riley laughed. "Now what did I *just* say?"

"Not a crumb for your dearest friend?"

"Let's just say that Cole doesn't want or need to look for treasure, but he is looking for a little personal redemption. He needs to find windmills to tilt at."

"So that's what sparked his interest in the Knights of Malta?"

"Hazel, I don't know. I thought it was just more of his fascination with conspiracy theories and secret societies. But he's started acting so paranoid again."

"I thought things were much better between you two. Darling, you're getting married in a few months."

"*I know.* And things were better for a while. In the Philippines, when his Full Fathom Five Maritime Foundation brokered that agreement and the government repatriated so much of the Japanese war loot, he seemed to feel better about himself for a while. He wasn't a treasure hunter, he was a real archeologist again."

"And how was he while you two were sailing your boat halfway around the world?"

Riley nibbled at an olive. "He occasionally mentioned the Knights of Malta, and he was reading books about them, but he didn't seem obsessed anymore. No more mention of conspiracies. I thought we were done with that." Riley lifted her chin and surveyed the deep-blue horizon. She nodded to herself. "We had a year of fantastic sailing, swimming and snorkeling over tropical reefs, and making love. We laughed all the time, Hazel."

"You deserved it, girlfriend, after all you've been through."

"So Theo took an apartment in Turkey near the boatyard, and he oversaw everything while we went cruising. By going public with the treasure find in the Philippines, Cole had become too much of a public figure. He eventually believed the organizations he had thwarted, both in the Caribbean and in the Philippines, would finally leave him alone."

"So, what changed?"

"When we got to Turkey, he wasn't happy about several things on the new boat. I won't bore you with all the details, but Cole started making changes. Change orders are the tar pits of construction projects. The launch date kept getting pushed back. We've been living aboard *Bonefish* on a mooring off the boatyard, and he started coming home from the boatyard and spending hours reading his father's journals. The paranoia came back. Every time he went into town, he swore he was being followed. I can't even remember the last time I heard him laugh."

"Oh, Riley."

"I set a date for the wedding in Malta, the weekend after Mother's Day."

"And that's a problem now?"

"It was my mother's idea. She and her husband are supposed to fly into Malta for Mother's Day, and there will be a week of wedding prep before the ceremony on Saturday. It's all been booked. My mother has turned into a crazed wedding planner, inviting half of France and Washington, DC. And then, last week, Cole said it was Dig who was following him."

Hazel refilled Riley's glass. "Drink up, honey."

Riley shook her head. "He won't even talk about the wedding now. He says I'd be better off without him."

"I'm so sorry. I know that must hurt."

"I haven't said anything to my mother. Hazel, he's not being rational. I don't believe in ghosts."

"Oh really? Aren't you the one who talks to your dead brother?"

"But I don't claim to have seen Michael walking around. There's no way Diggory Priest could have survived that day."

"But didn't they say the same thing about Cole?"

"That's different."

"Different how?"

"Cole had scuba gear, for one thing. Hazel, I dove off that speedboat just before Pinky rammed it with a big sportfishing boat. I left Diggory standing on the deck. I swam down as hard and fast as I could. Then I felt the concussion through the water. It was a massive explosion. Afterward, I swam all around *Shadow Chaser* searching for Cole. I would have seen Diggory if he had been there. It's just not possible." Riley crossed her arms and leaned back in her chair.

Hazel reached over and patted Riley's forearm. "You were there, I wasn't. But I just want you to remember all the times Cole said somebody wanted him dead, and it turned out to be true. You say you love him. Maybe you should consider the possibility that there is some-thing there. That he's not just being crazy."

"Hazel, I'm not like that. I need concrete evidence. I was a marine for seven years. We drilled over and over that we don't operate on hearsay or shoot at shadows. You make decisions based on the intel you have—not on conjecture."

"Sounds like you need to figure out just exactly what it is you want."

"What do you mean?"

"It's simple. What do you want?"

"I want Cole to get over this craziness so we can figure out how to make a life together."

"And what if it's not craziness?"

"Come on."

"You said you love him. Then stand up for him. You want to mar-ry this man, right?"

Riley closed her eyes and saw a black-and-white image of two fin-gers holding her engagement ring over the ferryboat's frothing bow wave—*just bits of metal and rock,* she remembered thinking—and felt herself flush. "More than anything," she said.

"Then help him with whatever it is that's causing him grief. Sounds like you've got some research to do. Get with it and find some of that rational marine intel. Hell, protection's your racket—or at least it was while you were an embassy security guard. Help him figure out what's going on, and keep the nutcase safe—because, girlfriend, if you marry him, then he'll be your nutcase."

Riley laughed. Looking across the harbor, she watched a dark thunderstorm on the horizon. The gray film of rain stretched from the clouds to the sea.

"You're right, as usual." When she looked back at her friend, Hazel was pouring the last of the wine into Riley's glass.

Lifting her own glass, Hazel said, "To love."

CHAPTER SIX

**Aboard the *Ruse*
Vittoriosa, Malta**

February 6, 1798

Alonso Montras paced the aft deck of his sailing ship the *Ruse* as he watched his men unloading the fruits of his latest prize. They had encountered the Arab merchants in a sailing dhow off the coast of Tunis, and, thanks to his vessel's outstanding maneuverability, he had felled the dhow's mainmast with his second cannon blast. Having disabled her thus, he'd gladly accepted the captain's surrender and was now lightening the *Ruse* of her cargo of wine, olives, and silk. Once he paid the grand master his percentage and the crew theirs, his little ship should still show a very nice profit from this latest voyage.

"Congratulations, *L'Angel*, you are going to be a very wealthy young man."

Alonso turned around, grinned, and clapped his pilot and mate Nikola on the back. "You shall do very nicely as well, my dear friend. If not for you, we never would have prevailed in that battle. She was twice our size."

The older man laughed out loud. "And since when is L'Angel a modest man?"

The Maltese had started calling him by this nickname when they'd first met, and it had stuck.

Alonso glanced at his friend out of the corner of his eye and smiled. "Rarely."

"Ha! That is more like it, my friend."

"It was a good prize, but nothing like in the days when my great-grandfather sailed as a Knight corsair."

"L'Angel, when *Le Rouge de Malte* sailed these waters, they were aboard the great galleys and xebecs, with hundreds of men and three times the guns our little ship can carry."

"There is a reason why the only remaining corsairs on the island are Maltese. All the riches now are to be had on the land caravans."

"L'Angel, my friend, do not worry about what once was," Nikola said. He pulled a pipe and a pouch of tobacco out of his trouser pocket and began filling the pipe's bowl. "Celebrate today. You are young and handsome, and though your boat may be small, your pockets soon will be full. You go. I can watch over these scoundrels."

Alonso continued watching the men, who had fought so hard at his side, now working to unload the cargo. Carrying only six cannon and sailed by a crew of ten men, his little two-masted xebec was designed to be swift and nimble, but deadly. She was his home now, and he thought he should stay to see his cargo ashore.

"I have to work on the accounts," Alonso said.

Nikola struck a flint over his pipe bowl and puffed until he had a lungful of smoke. He exhaled and said, "That can wait. Surely you have a lady to go visit."

Alonso thought back on the ball he had attended, at the home of Chevalier Boisgelin, one week before he'd departed on this voyage. Boisgelin had recently returned from a caravan to the east, and he entertained lavishly. At the ball, Alonso had met many lovely young women who had clamored for the attention of the Knight corsair.

But now that he had the funds to pursue one of the young ladies, he thought sadly that not one of them stood out in his mind.

"No, my friend, I do not."

"What about that Spanish black-eyed beauty who walks the quay with her chaperone and flips the lace of her mantilla while she watches you work? What is her name? Montalban?"

Alonso remembered her from the ball. "Yes, Maria Montalban. I danced with her once."

"Then go, buy her a trinket and pay her a visit. Get out of here. You are too young to spend all your life at your work."

Alonso climbed the steps that led away from the quay up to the shops of the city of Vittoriosa. He wondered what sort of trinket he should buy for the lady. He had a few coins in his pocket, but he had not yet been paid for his most recent prize. He passed by a tavern, and several fellow Knights called out to him when they saw him pass. They invited him to join them in their drinking. Alonso waved them off. He had no time for such nonsense.

None of the shops captured his interest until he found himself in front of a silversmith's workshop. Perhaps a piece of jewelry would be appropriate. He pushed his way through the heavy wood door.

Inside the dark, low-ceilinged room he saw shelves of gleaming cutlery, platters, coffeepots, and oil lamps. All the pieces were elaborately decorated with engraved designs—shells, scrolls, leaves, flowers. These were the work more of an artist than of a craftsman.

He reached for a tall *lampier* on a raised fluted base. It was so elaborate compared to the simple oil lamps he used aboard the *Ruse*. Implements such as tiny scissors, tweezers, and a snuffer hung from chains, while a cartouche-shaped reflector was suspended from a branch. As he ran his fingers over the shell-shaped handle, he heard someone enter the room behind him.

"Don't touch that."

He withdrew his hand and spun around.

The female voice had been stern and deep. Alonso expected to see an older woman, perhaps the artist's wife. Instead, the person standing before him was a girl of no more than twenty years. Her almond-shaped green eyes glowed beneath arched eyebrows. She placed one fist on the slender turn of her waist and brushed a lock of brown hair back from her eyes.

"So, are you going to tell me what you're looking for?" She spoke in French, which, although it was not his native tongue, he had learned to speak during his years in Malta.

Alonso opened his mouth, but nothing came out. No one ever spoke to him in this manner, much less a shopgirl.

"Are you mute?" she asked.

"No, I am not."

"Very well, then, what do you want?"

"Mademoiselle, I am surprised to hear you speak so boldly to a Knight of Saint John. Did your mother teach you no manners?"

"Sir, my mother is dead."

"I am sorry."

"I have no need of your pity. But I do have work to do, so if you will tell me what you seek in this shop, I will do my best to help you."

"I was looking for something for a lady."

The girl made a little *hmph* sound and reached for a drawer in a bureau against the wall.

"What did you mean by that noise?"

"Sir, who you choose to buy silver for is no business of mine." She pulled at the heavy wood drawer.

"Exactly," he said.

The short sleeves of her blouse exposed the strength in her bare arms as she wriggled the drawer from side to side to pull it free.

"Certainly all of us Maltese are aware," she said as she drew out a tray covered with medallions, necklaces, and tiaras, "that our Knights, who have taken vows of chastity, poverty, and service to the pope, would never break those vows." She lifted out a pair of elongated pear-shaped earrings made of delicate silver filigree. When she held them up for him, he saw in her face a hint of a smile. "Would the lady in question like these, perhaps?"

"Mademoiselle, you have a very bold tongue." As he said it, Alonso glanced at her mouth—and then he could not stop staring at her lips.

"Sir, I have been working in my father's shop for more than ten years, and I have seen many of your kind."

Alonso forced himself to look at her eyes. The shape of those green eyes gave her an exotic appearance.

She brushed the loose lock of hair off her brow again as if unaware of his study of her features. "When my father first came to this island from France," she continued, "the Knights were respected as warriors, sailors, and clerics. When Papa married my English mother, there was still an *auberge* for the Knights' English *langue*. Now the grand master plays religious politics, and what I see in the behavior of your brothers does not command respect."

"How dare you judge men in this way."

"Oh, pardon me, sir. I forgot that trousers make you better than me."

A man's voice shouted from the back room. "Arzella! *Enough*, please. For your father's sake."

The girl glanced back over her shoulder and called out, "*Oui*, Papa." When she turned back to face Alonso, it was as though a dark cloud had passed over her glittering eyes and dimmed their glow. She sighed. "My father is ill, and I need to return to his bedside." She held up the earrings again. "So you'll take these?"

Outside the shop, Alonso crossed the street, then turned to look back at the door. Aloud he whispered, "Arzella." He'd learned enough of the local language to translate her name. The word meant *shell* in Maltese. He'd never met a young woman like her. Nor a man, for that matter.

Alonso folded back the neatly creased paper and examined the delicate filigree work of the earrings he had purchased. The craftsmanship was exquisite. He dangled one between two fingers and wondered what they would look like on Arzella.

CHAPTER SEVEN

The Palazzo Magistral
Via Condotti, Rome

April 9, 2014

Virgil Vandervoort leaned against one of the pillars framing the doorway of the Max Mara store and spit out a piece of tobacco from his hand-rolled cigarette. The man he was there to meet didn't permit smoking in his office, and Virgil was early. He pulled smoke into his lungs and held it for several seconds before exhaling. *Civilians think soldiers spend all their time fighting. If they only knew.* Virgil had spent thousands of hours waiting. The skill was to spend all those hours ready to act.

The sun burned hot for early spring. Virgil had rolled up his cuffs to bare his forearms, but he still felt his underarms growing damp. He wanted to make a good impression today. Knowing he had this meeting, he'd worn khaki slacks instead of his usual blue jeans. He was determined to rise in the ranks.

He heard the purr of a powerful engine. He leaned forward just in time to watch the black Bentley turn through the archway between windows for Jimmy Choo and Hermès. The tourists on this street had no idea what lay behind those gates in the middle. The concierge stepped out of his little office and smiled as he waved the car inside.

The Sovereign Military Order of the Knights of Malta had first come to Virgil's attention when he'd heard that General McChrystal was a member. Virgil had been out of the service for a while by then, and, while the money was good in the private security sector back home, he didn't get to see much action. He was bored. But he thought he needed the money to keep the wife happy. That didn't work out. Bitch divorced him and then refused to let him see his daughter. Left him no reason to stay on that side of the Atlantic.

When he went back to Iraq as an independent contractor, Virgil was tired of the indecision-makers. He'd seen them on both sides, government and private. He was bored, and he wanted to see some action. Then he'd gone to work for Mr. Prince at Blackwater. There, they weren't bothered by all those rules of engagement. The means didn't matter much as long as you got results. Virgil always got results, and they'd paid him well for doing what he enjoyed.

But when this new American president got elected, he brought in an entire administration of indecision-makers. They started prosecuting men for getting the job done. *Winding down the war*, they said. Even though he didn't need the money, Virgil tried for a couple of jobs with other private military firms. The fellows interviewing him looked like they hadn't started shaving yet. Their questions were all about technology. He never heard back from them, which was all right by him. He wasn't going to do his job by sitting in a room playing with a joystick.

So when he'd first learned about the Sovereign Military Order of the Knights of Malta from Mr. Prince, Virgil was able to afford to buy in. There in the Order, he'd found his third career and a real home. Ever since the Crusades, they'd hated the fucking ragheads as much as he did.

He took a long last drag on the cigarette, then dropped it onto the sidewalk and ground his heel on the butt as he stepped into the street. Time to get this done.

The fat little concierge stepped out of his office again. This time he insisted on seeing Virgil's ID. The man was an asshole. It wasn't like Virgil'd never been there before, or like, in a place like Italy, Virgil's white-blond hair made him easy to forget.

"I know the way," he said, turning his back on the greasy bastard and crossing the courtyard inlaid with the image of the eight-point Maltese cross.

When he stepped into the foyer, Virgil was struck again by how quiet it was. Rome was a noisy, dirty city, and yet this palace kept all that outside. Tapestries covered the high walls, and on opposite sides of the door stood matching suits of sterling-silver armor engraved with fancy designs, including Maltese crosses on their breastplates. Virgil reckoned everything in the whole place was an antique.

At the top of the stairs he knocked on a door, and a deep voice said something in Italian. Virgil assumed it meant *Come in*.

The man seated behind the heavy, carved desk was the Order's executive director. Signor Oscura. While the grand master was the public face of the Order, this was the man who got things done. The large window behind his desk looked out across the rooftops toward the Spanish Steps. The backlighting meant the face of the man at the desk was always in shadow.

Signor Oscura looked up and nodded. "*Salve*, one moment." He went back to writing on a piece of fancy stationery.

Virgil recognized the Montblanc pen in the man's hand, and he wondered what it would feel like to write with something that cost more than Virgil's first car. He clasped his hands behind his back and stared straight ahead. He was prepared to wait. Always.

Finally, the man set the pen down. "So, what do you have for me?" Signor Oscura spoke perfect colloquial American English, yet the hint of an Italian accent remained. Virgil had heard that the man spoke more than a dozen languages.

"One of my men is keeping a watch on them, sir."

"Salatino over at NSA warned us there had been lots of traffic. Enough chatter to raise a red flag. I want to know why. Especially considering this man's history."

One of the things Virgil most appreciated about this outfit was their access. Since they had so many members who were CIA and NSA, and Brit members with MI6 or GCHQ, they had ins with all the agencies.

"This guy's interest in the Knights continues," Virgil said. "Salatino was right to flag him. My man has been following them whenever they go into town, listening in whenever possible. The reason I called is because this morning they took a ferry from Marmaris over to Rhodes." Virgil saw the man's posture straighten.

"And your man followed?"

"Yeah. They didn't talk much on the trip across. My guy said they met a black woman there, and the three of them went straight to the museum at the Palace of the Grand Master. My guy couldn't follow them inside."

"Why not?"

"The black chick knew people, and they went back into a private office. When he called me, it wasn't clear who they were meeting yet."

"I see."

"After about half an hour, the two women left. The guy stayed behind, and my guy stayed with him. They're still in Rhodes. The last ferry leaves in a couple of hours. I thought you'd want this intel right away."

Signor Oscura put his elbows on the desk and made a tent with the tips of his fingers tapping each other in front of his nose. His manicure was so perfect, his hands appeared feminine. "We need to know what he knows, Virgil. What he's after."

"You want me to tell my guy to engage?"

The man turned in his swivel chair to look out the window. "Yes, but carefully. You and some of your friends go in hot and either spook him or kill him, and you'll blow our chance."

"You know me better than that."

"Do I?" He said the words slowly, as if asking himself the question and unsure of the answer. "Virgil, what is your rank?"

"I am a Knight of Magistral Grace." When he'd joined the Order, Virgil had been surprised at his pride in the rank. The first time he'd read the title, he thought he'd feel like a puffed-up asshole whenever he said it out loud. Now, after a couple of years as a member of the Order, titles like that sounded normal to him.

Oscura swiveled back to face Virgil. He rubbed his chin. "Tell me again about that tattoo on your arm."

Virgil lifted his arm and looked at the tattoo on his forearm. It was a blue triangle, but one leg was jagged in the shape of a lightning bolt. Through the middle of the triangle was a red-handled knife. "It's the insignia for Delta Force. That was my unit in the US Army. I served for fifteen years."

"Yes. And now I take it you are interested in advancement in the Order."

Virgil nodded.

"The grand master was very impressed when you were the first to bring this Thatcher to our attention."

"I'm happy to be of service, sir."

"We have a need for a man of your talents, Virgil. What I am going to tell you should never be spoken of outside this room. Do you understand?"

"Yes, sir."

"Within the Order we have always had divisions, sometimes called *langues* or *auberges*. Each division has its own responsibilities, but as an organization, we have shared one single goal: to free the Holy Land from the infidels."

Virgil nodded.

"There is a mark that a select few from all classes of the Order have worn. These marked men started as guardians of our order's most precious relic." Signor Oscura loosened his tie and unbuttoned the top buttons of his shirt. He pulled open his collar to reveal a small red Maltese cross tattooed high on the left side of his chest. "It's called the Knight's Cross, and the men who wear it are members of *I Guardiani della Croce di Cavaliere*, the Guardians of the Knight's Cross. They are sworn to protect the Order's treasure."

"Treasure?"

"Yes. I can see what you are thinking. Today, our wealth is in our properties and investments, not in chests of gold or ancient scrolls. And managing our wealth is a large part of what I do. However, the Order's most valuable treasure was lost over two hundred years ago. The Guardiani have sworn to get it back. I am taking this occasion to invite you to join us."

"I'm honored, sir."

"With this honor comes duty."

"I understand, sir."

"Have you heard the Maltese folktale they call the Legend of the Silver Girl?"

"No, sir."

"It is the only clue we have as to what happened to this treasure, sometimes known as *the Religion*."

"I see."

"We've followed thousands of leads through the years—most recently, this claim in Turkey. They've all turned out to be fake. Two hundred years ago, the Religion departed Malta in the hands of the Guardiani. We are left now with little more than hearsay and legends about a key to the hiding place. It was the lowest point in the history of the Order. You will learn more at your initiation, but for now, know this. I have made recovering this treasure my life's ambition. I will return it to the Order, and with it we will return to our former position of power and change the face of the world."

Virgil was liking the sound of this.

"There is a great battle coming, Virgil. We'll be fighting for the pope, for Rome, but most of all for the return of the Holy Land."

This was what he'd been told they were all about. Virgil didn't give a damn about religion, but he sure as hell wanted to go back to the desert and kick ass.

"The Religion will give us our reason to fight. Recovering it must be our first priority. I follow every lead, no matter how thin. James Thatcher, the father of the man you have been watching, has been a person of interest to the Guardiani since his first visits to Malta after the war. We are aware the son has inside information from the father. If there is even the slightest chance that what he seeks is the Religion, we must pursue it. The question is whether or not he's crazy."

Virgil shook his head. "Our contacts in other organizations say they underestimated him."

"Do you think he knows what he's looking for?"

"I'm not sure."

"Virgil, if he really can find it after all these years, you need to be there. Time is short."

"We could pick Thatcher up. Interrogate him."

"No. If this trip to Rhodes tells us anything, it's that he doesn't have all the pieces. Tell your man to stay close. Perhaps befriend them, plant something so we can listen to the conversation between him and the woman. I need to know everything."

"Yes, sir."

"Virgil, our enemies are gathering. This time, we intend to finish what we started one thousand years ago."

Virgil made the call from the palace courtyard. "Is he still in the museum?"

"No, the two women returned, and the three of them are walking through town, heading toward the ferry dock."

"We want you to engage. Get close enough to get a wire in their car."

"Not possible."

"But you said you know her."

"Yes, but—"

"Don't give me that shit."

"It was a long time ago."

Virgil had no patience with disobedience. "What the fuck's the problem?"

"It's not a good idea."

"I took a chance hiring you, and I expect you to follow orders."

"The thing is, she thinks I'm dead."

CHAPTER EIGHT

Driving to the Shipyard
Marmaris, Turkey

April 9, 2014

Cole was glad to see his rental Hyundai parked exactly where they had left it, apparently undisturbed. You never knew, though.

"Wait up a minute," he said. Riley stopped, and the look on her face said she thought he was acting crazy. She always seemed to have that look these days, but at least she did stop.

He walked over to the car and looked through the window. If there was a bomb or something, he wasn't quite sure what it would look like.

"Cole, do you want me to check it out?"

"No, I'm okay doing it."

"Look, they trained us for this kind of thing."

He looked at her face. She looked serious. "I guess," he said.

Riley approached the car. "As Marine Security Guards, we often had to check cars entering the embassy grounds for explosives and listening devices." She walked around to the back end and dropped to the pavement. She checked under the rear bumper, rolled to a crab-walk position, and slid under the midsection. "Looks okay to me," she called out from under the car.

When she stood up, she smiled at him. The I-think-you-must-be-crazy look was gone.

"Thanks," he said. He felt her smile warming him. "I guess I can be pretty difficult sometimes."

"Yeah," she said, dusting off her hands. "You've got that right." Then she slapped him on the butt cheek. "But you're worth it."

He inserted the key into the door. "Come on. Let's get out of here."

As they negotiated their way through the traffic leaving the docks, most of the cars turned toward downtown Marmaris. Cole kept watch on the rearview mirror. A beat-up silver Renault had pulled out of the ferry-terminal parking lot at the same time they did. It held back to let a couple of cars get into the right-turn lane behind him. After Cole pulled out onto the road to Adakoy, he kept seeing the Renault in the line of cars behind him. Never right on his tail. Always lingering behind just enough so he couldn't get a glimpse of the driver.

"What's up?" Riley asked. "You keep looking in the rearview."

"It's nothing."

"So tell me about the museum and your time with Dr. Günay."

He turned to look at her face. "Really? You're interested?"

"Of course I am."

"Well, I learned a lot. The museum is amazing. I mean, there was a sign outside that said the EU had given a couple of million euros for the renovation, but there is no way that covered what they've done there. There must have been some healthy donations from individuals, too. Dr. G. said that's not out of the question. The Knights want these places kept up and their history preserved."

"That makes sense. And I suppose they have lots of wealthy members."

"You don't know the half of it." The car immediately behind him slowed and pulled off to the side of the road. Tourists with cameras, no doubt; the view of the bay along this stretch was spectacular, especially this close to sunset. Now there was only one car between him and the Renault.

The houses and businesses had thinned out, and the road twisted over rocky and scrub-covered hills.

"So tell me more about these Knights of yours," Riley said. "Brits get knighted by the Queen for being artists or inventors these days. What's it take to become a Knight of Malta?"

"In the early days, Knights were soldiers. During the Middle Ages, noble families would send their third- or fourth-born sons off to become Knights. See, the eldest always inherited the title, the castle, the whole shebang." Cole checked the mirror again, and now the Renault was right on his bumper. He continued talking, but his mind was on that car behind him. "And second sons were usually encouraged to go into the priesthood. They could stay local and the family would benefit from having a member in the clergy. Third sons were a problem. So they sent them off to fight the infidels as Knights of the cross."

The driver was wearing a hat pulled down very low, and in the twilight, Cole couldn't make out his features. He pressed down hard on the accelerator.

"What's wrong?" Riley sat up and glanced over her shoulder just as he went into a deep curve to the left. She braced her arm on the dashboard. "Hey, slow down."

"Sorry. There's this guy who's been following us since we left the ferry terminal."

"Cole, come on. It's a single two-lane road out to Adakoy. Maybe he's just going to the same place we are."

He looked into the mirror after he'd straightened out the car, and he saw that the Renault had speeded up, too.

"I don't think so, Riley. He's staying right on my tail."

Riley held on to the door handle. "But it's not safe driving like this on these roads."

"Don't worry." The road climbed up the hill, and the dark-blue water on their right dropped lower and lower as Cole maneuvered the car through a series of hairpin curves. It took all his concentration just to stay on the road.

In a sharp turn, Riley was thrown against her door. "Cole, this is nuts. You're going to get us killed."

Cole took his eyes off the road for a second. She was rubbing her right shoulder, the injured one, and he knew he had hurt her.

"Sorry, Riley."

The car crested the top of the ridge, and for several hundred feet the road traveled straight, with trees on one side and a rocky bluff on the other. They topped a shallow rise, and that was when he saw the herd of goats in the road.

Cole slammed on the brakes, and the Hyundai's tires bit the pavement. The car had just come to a stop when they were rammed from behind.

The impact threw him against the seat back and then snapped his head forward. His nose collided with the steering wheel. Though his eyes were closed, he saw an explosion of white light. Warm blood trickled into his mouth.

Cole opened his eyes. In the rearview mirror, he saw the driver of the car behind him. The man had lost his hat in the collision. The car door flew open, and the man staggered out of the car into the slanting sunlight. Cole saw his face in profile.

"It's him!" he shouted. Cole turned and grabbed Riley's good shoulder. She looked dazed. She reached out and touched his cheek.

"You're bleeding," she said.

Cole shook her arm and pointed. "Riley, look, it's him."

She winced as she turned. The man had run around behind his own vehicle. Now Riley's head was in the way, and Cole could no longer see him.

"See? Riley, it's Diggory Priest!"

She struggled with the handle on the door.

"Riley, unlock it!"

She pushed the rocker button, tried the door again, and nearly fell out of the car when it flew open. She ran to the edge of the cliff. Cole jumped out of the car and followed her. The rocky embankment plunged several hundred feet to the dark water. He saw no sign of the man.

"Did you see him?" Cole asked.

The look on her face when she turned to face him felt like a punch to the gut. "Cole, we need to get you to a doctor," she said.

CHAPTER NINE

On a Hillside
Adakoy, Turkey

April 9, 2014

His feet slipped out from under him on the hard, dry dirt. He danced with windmilling arms for a second before he went down and landed hard on his coccyx. Hot pain exploded in his lower back and buttocks, and he knew his legs would not support him if he tried to stand.

There was a ledge fifteen feet below him. The long raincoat wound around his legs as he rolled like a runaway log down the dirt hill. The turning made him dizzy. He had no idea how far the drop ahead was, but if he couldn't see over the ledge, they wouldn't be able to, either.

When his body shot into the air, he felt the most amazing sensation. His pain ceased as he hung weightless. He'd always wanted to know what it felt like to fly, but the reality was bittersweet. Since the accident, through all those years of skin grafts and rehab, pain had come to be his companion, the one constant in his life. It was what made him extraordinary. He missed it.

A couple of seconds later, he landed backside-first into a clump of dry, prickly bushes. The shrubs broke his fall, but the cotton pants and shirt, along with his coat, were easily pierced by the sharp thorns. His companion was back.

He heard voices above him. He did not move. He waited.

The voices faded, and the next noise was the popping and crunching sound of tires on gravel. The engine revved up and then the noise receded as the car moved on down the road.

This was simply another test. There had been so many, these past six years. Lesser men would never have been able to endure, of that he was certain. His body had been damaged, but his will had been hardened by the fire. That he survived could only be seen as a miracle.

All those years ago, his mother had read stories to him from her Bible. She told him that only God performed miracles. Dig knew better. He was the one who'd been burned over half his body when the gas in the bilge of that speedboat exploded in a fireball. He'd clung to consciousness and avoided Riley as she swam around the boat, searching for Cole. The first boat on the scene had been manned by a paramedic who had agreed to secrecy at the promise of a bribe. And later, the French doctor who treated him told Diggory he was lucky—that it was the immediate immersion in cool salt water that had saved what little skin he had left.

Diggory knew it was neither luck nor the hand of God. As Nietzsche had said, he was of "a higher sovereign species . . . Not merely a master race whose sole task is to rule, but a race with its own sphere of life, with an excess of strength." With every test life had thrown at him, Diggory had proven his superiority.

But just because he had acquired the strength to overcome the damage from the accident, that did not mean he forgave her. It was because of her that people now stared at him, and not for his good looks. She'd have to pay for what she had done to him.

At each step of his early recovery, he had eliminated those who nursed him, helped him, rehabilitated him—and he felt no remorse.

Those who felt bound to a moral code proved only that they were weak and not fit to live.

The supreme ruler was coming back to purge the world of his enemies and all the barbarians. These Knights of Malta were weak with their religious zealotry, but they served his intentions well for the moment. They sure as hell knew how to start up a good war.

CHAPTER TEN

**Aboard *Bonefish*
Adakoy, Turkey**

April 10, 2014

Riley crawled out from under the chart table and squirmed to her feet in the tight little galley. Compared to the new boat Cole was having built, her sailboat had started to feel small and cramped. It hadn't always been that way. Eight years earlier, when she was newly discharged from the Corps and trying to figure out what to do with the rest of her life, she had stopped to see a broker in Annapolis on a whim. He'd shown her several boats at Jabin's Yacht Yard on Back Creek, but the Caliber 40 had felt like home. She'd fallen in love with the stout vessel, in spite of the fact that it was bound to be a handful to manage solo. Her offer had been accepted that afternoon.

Riley closed her eyes and rolled her head around, bending her neck as far as she could in each direction. Her hand went to the right side of her neck and massaged the sore muscles there. She felt the ridges of the old scar tissue through her thin T-shirt. The chronic pain from the old burns continued to haunt her.

It was time for an exercise break. She'd been pulling wire all morning for the new electronic chart plotter she was installing at the nav station, and her shoulder and back were killing her.

In the companionway, she leaned her back against the head door and slid down into her isometric squat position. She tightened her muscles and breathed deeply. It wasn't always easy keeping fit on the boat, but she had developed a routine of exercises that used the boat's interior furnishings as her gym.

All morning, Riley had been going over her memories of yesterday's car crash. She relived the concussion of the collision, how she'd felt momentarily disoriented. But her seat belt had held, and, though the wind was knocked out of her, she hadn't hit her head. She realized they'd been rear-ended, and she'd turned when Cole had told her to look. She'd caught only a brief glimpse of the man. He was wearing a long overcoat, so she could make out little of his body or frame. Tall, with long, stringy, salt-and-pepper hair that hung to his shoulders. His face looked scarred, like maybe he had suffered a severe case of teen acne, and he ran with a herky-jerky motion that suggested a limp. The man looked decades older than Dig.

Cole had refused her suggestion of a trip back to town to see a doctor. She thought his nose might be broken, and, if she were honest with herself, she thought he might need a doctor to look at both the outside and inside of his head. *Seriously? Diggory Priest?* After all they had been through with Skull and Bones and the Enterprise, she just wanted to put it all behind her.

But Cole had tried their car, found it would start, and driven it on to the boatyard. He'd insisted he didn't want to get involved with the Turkish police, and besides, they weren't at fault.

Now she was on her back with her legs in the air, doing the hundred-breath exercise, when she heard the familiar noise of the dinghy's outboard engine approaching. She jumped to her feet.

It was early for Cole to be returning to the boat. She checked the brass clock on the bulkhead. Only 4:00 p.m. More often than not, these days, he was late getting back. She had learned not to think about dinner before 7:00.

She climbed the steps into the cockpit and watched as he tied the dinghy painter to the radar post and climbed the transom steps.

"What's up?"

Cole slipped the backpack off his back. "Nothing." Both his eyes had dark circles under them—a pair of shiners from their rear-end collision.

"This is awfully early for you. Is your nose bothering you?"

When she saw those dimples framing that smile, the old familiar heat bomb went off in her core. Heart, tummy, and everything south of there reacted to this man, and it had been the same ever since the first time she'd plucked him naked out of the sea off Guadeloupe, six years earlier. It was physical and beyond her control.

"No, actually, things went really well in the yard today. I feel great. Theo and the guys are going to finish up early this afternoon, so they'll be ready to tackle the generator problems tomorrow. I think we might actually be able to launch next week."

"That's great news!"

"Yeah," he said, nodding, "it is." He set his backpack on the cockpit table. "But there's something I've been wanting to talk to you about. Is now okay?"

"Hey, I'd much rather spend my time with you than bent up like a contortionist under the chart table. You want a beer?"

"Sure."

Riley went below to get the brews out of the fridge. When she returned and sat next to him on the cockpit seat, he took a long drink from the chilled bottle before speaking.

"Riley, I had hoped to put all this behind us. I couldn't bear it if something happened to you because of me."

"I'm not sure what you're afraid of."

"That's what I'm here to explain. I told you that I'd become interested in the Knights of Malta because of my father." He reached into the backpack and withdrew a leather-bound journal.

Riley recognized the book. She'd been in possession of the last one of the three books during the four years Cole had disappeared from her life. The journal had become a treasured link to the man she thought she'd lost, and she spent many nights reading through the pages, looking for some link to Cole.

"My dad started writing in these after my folks divorced and he returned to England. A way of talking to his son across the ocean. The first one was mostly written when I was just a kid. He wasn't so opinionated then."

"Yeah, 'opinionated' is putting it mildly."

"Opinions that got him killed."

"Don't forget they killed my father, too."

CHAPTER ELEVEN

On the Docks
Vittoriosa, Malta

February 9, 1798

Since her father was having a good morning, Arzella seized the opportunity to get out and walk down to the market. How she longed to smell the sea air. She slung her shopping basket over her arm and slipped out the door.

As she descended the stepped street, she heard singing and laughter from the many balconies that overhung it. Everyone had their shutters thrown open on this warm winter morning, and the joy in the sunny day was infectious.

Soon she began to catch glimpses of the deep-blue water of Grand Harbour between the stone buildings. Arzella wished she could go sailing, as she had done when she was a girl. At least she could stop by the wharf to visit her uncle aboard his fishing boat, the *Emily*. She hoped he'd have a nice fish for her to take home for her father's supper. It was growing more and more difficult to get him to eat, but her father loved his fish.

After purchasing some vegetables, she strolled over to the fish market and located the *Emily*.

"Arzella, I was just thinking about you! I swear, you are more like your mother every day."

"Good morning, Uncle Edward," she said, enjoying the feeling of the smile on her face and the English language on her tongue. "How am I like my mother?"

"Whenever I would think of my dear sister Emily, she would appear as though she knew I needed her. Clairvoyant, she was."

"Oh my. Now that's funny, Uncle Edward. Your *dear* sister. I remember Mum telling me how the two of you used to fight all the time. You don't have to make her out to be something she wasn't. I won't forget her."

Her uncle jumped from the gunwale of his boat to the wharf and landed in front of her. He kissed her on both cheeks. "I have no fear of that. She's been gone eight years now, and I miss her more each day. She was an extraordinary woman." He patted the top of Arzella's head. "Like her beautiful daughter."

She brushed his hand away. "Uncle, please. I am not a child anymore."

He laughed. "That is evident. Come aboard. You can have the pick of my catch. Take my hand."

Arzella lifted her skirts several inches and jumped across the water. "Too late!" Her feet landed on the fishing boat's wooden rub rail. *"Min jorqod ma jaqbadx hut,"* she said in Maltese. It was an expression used by the locals: *Those who sleep late do not catch fish.*

She pivoted and scooted her backside onto the gunwale, lifted her feet, and swung them over and onto the deck.

Her uncle shook his head. "I should have known," he said. "I'm the one who taught you not to depend on me when we went to sea. I said you needed to be able to get around the boat on your own."

"And now I can!" Arzella spread her arms wide and twirled in the middle of the deck. "Oh, Uncle, how I miss those days. I got to wear trousers instead of these stupid skirts." She brushed at the folds of fabric that surrounded her legs. "And no one told me that I couldn't possibly sail because I was a girl."

Edward leapt to the top of the gunwale and swung from the ratlines to the deck. "That's because, given the way you were dressed, no one knew you *were* a girl. But those days have come to an end, Arzella. Now you must act like a lady, or you will never find a husband."

She walked to a large wood box and opened the top. Inside, layers of fish rested on leaves of seaweed. "Who says I want one?"

"Do not speak like that. Your father wants more than anything to see you married. You must grant him that."

"Hmm. We shall see." How she hated that word *must*.

Edward stepped over to the box and pointed to a large monkfish. "That one. Your father will love it."

Arzella nodded and her uncle wrapped the fish in seaweed. She placed it in her basket.

"I should get back to him."

"Take your time. I was just about to deliver this last box of fish and then go pay my brother-in-law a visit myself. I'll stay with him until you return. You deserve some time off."

She kissed him on the cheek. "Thank you, Uncle Edward. I won't be long."

Arzella climbed up onto the gunwale and leapt across to the dock.

"Don't hurry. Enjoy your freedom!" Edward called after her.

Arzella wandered down the quay in the direction of Fort Saint Angelo, the Knights' main armory and the place where local legend claimed they kept their treasure in a vast round room at the center of the fortress. She didn't think much of legends of that sort, nor of the Knights.

Most of them she had met had little money, yet lived above their means. Gossip, gaming, and dueling seemed their favorite pastimes—other than lounging about the taverns in Valletta and Vittoriosa. They really were good for nothing, as far as she was concerned, yet they treated anyone not of noble blood as though they were dogs.

Take that Knight who had come into their shop a couple of days ago. What right had he to scold her for speaking her mind? Didn't he know that, after the events in France, the world was changing? She pictured him standing there, his open mouth gaping like a black cavern in the midst of his red whiskers. Normally, she thought redheaded men looked weak and silly, but that man's hair and beard were more the color of chestnuts than of carrots. It was not wholly unpleasant to look at.

Several of the fishermen called out to her as she ambled along, enjoying the heat of the sun through her shawl. She took a deep breath and savored the smell of the sea and the docks. How she missed those days when her mother was alive and she got to roam these docks every spare moment she had. With her mother gone and her father's illness causing him to grow blind, there was no more time for sailing with her uncle. She'd had to learn her father's trade to keep food on their table.

Still, she was proud of the work she did. There was very little in the shop that remained of her father's work, but few people knew that truth. Every piece she made carried the stamp of Pierre Brun.

"Bonjour!" Another voice called out from the water's edge.

Arzella smiled and shaded her eyes from the sun. She could not see the man on the boat who called out to her, but she assumed it was someone she had known as a girl on the *Emily*. She raised the hand at her brow in a brief wave and kept walking.

Behind her, she heard the thudding of boots running on a ship's deck, and then someone leapt onto the quay, so close she felt the wind on the back of her neck. Laughing, she turned around, but her laughter broke off. The reddish beard was unmistakable.

He was out of breath from running. "I recognized you from the silver shop the other day."

She stepped back and stared.

"I didn't mean to frighten you."

Silly man, she wasn't frightened. But confused? Perhaps. Arzella stepped to the edge of the quay and examined the vessel. "A xebec," she said. "That is a corsair's boat."

"You have some knowledge of boats."

She stared into his eyes for several long seconds, then pressed her lips together in a false smile and said, "Hmm. Yes. *Some knowledge.*"

"This vessel is the *Ruse.*"

Arzella noticed an older Maltese man sitting on a barrel on deck and smoking a pipe. He was watching the young Knight intently.

"*Sir għodwa t-tajba.* Do you know this Knight?" She spoke in Maltese.

The man removed the pipe from his mouth and rubbed his chin. He replied in Maltese. "Good morning to you, madam. Yes, I have made his acquaintance. I sail as first mate and navigator on this ship."

Alonso looked at the man and called out in French, "Nikola, what are you saying to her?"

"So he is a naval man?" she asked the first mate.

"No, mademoiselle, the *Ruse* here is his own ship. He is the last corsair Knight in Malta, and, if I may say, the best. He is Chevalier Alonso Montras from Aragon, the great-grandson of *Le Rouge de Malte.* We have just returned from a successful sortie."

"How successful?"

"We took an Arab dhow twice our size."

Arzella raised her eyebrows.

Alonso tried to step between Arzella and the man. "What is he saying to you? My friend likes to joke. If he is saying terrible things about me, don't believe him."

She turned back to the Knight. "He says you have *some knowledge* of boats," she said.

From the Maltese she heard a low chuckle.

The red-bearded Knight raised his eyebrows. "Some knowledge? Ha! You are an impertinent girl."

Arzella took note of the rope work, the paint, and the canvas. The xebec had been maintained in superb condition. There was no indication she had just been in a battle.

The Knight continued. "I would like to show you my knowledge of boats and the sea. Nikola and I must move the *Ruse* off the wharf now that we have finished unloading. You may watch as we depart for the anchorage."

Arzella reached up and plucked a hair from her head. She held it aloft. "The winds are freshening from the west. You'll have no problem getting out of Dockyard Creek here, but you will have to tack up Grand Harbour to reach the anchorage. You could use a third hand on a boat this size."

Alonso turned to Nikola. "Did you hear that? Have you ever heard such things from a maid? She thinks she knows something of sailing!"

Nikola replied, "She merely repeats the same facts I have just finished telling you. It will be a difficult beat up the harbor."

Arzella said, "I would be delighted to spend a bit of time on a sailing boat."

Alonso turned, bowed at the waist, and swung his hand through the air toward his vessel. "Mademoiselle, you are welcome to come watch us work."

She was amused by the look on the Knight's face when she hiked her skirts above her ankles and walked across the narrow gangplank unassisted.

"Let's go," she told the Maltese. He reached for her hand. She shook her head and jumped to the deck. *"Min jorqod ma jaqbadx hut,"* she said.

The expression caused the older man to laugh out loud. "L'Angel, I think we are the ones who are going to be watching!"

CHAPTER TWELVE

**Aboard *Bonefish*
Adakoy, Turkey**

April 10, 2014

"We both know who killed your father, Riley. You were there."

She closed her eyes for a moment and fought against the images from that day that popped up on her mind's screen every time she thought about her father. Again she heard her father saying there was nothing he could have done to stop his Skull and Bones from killing her brother, Michael. She wasn't sure which man disgusted her more—her father or the man who had killed him. "Please, Cole. Let's not get started about Diggory Priest again."

"Okay," he said.

When she opened her eyes, he was holding up both hands in surrender.

"Riley, I didn't come to talk about what happened yesterday. Or, at least, not just about that."

She reached over and took his hand in hers. "Okay. What did you come to talk about?"

He slipped his hand from hers and rested it on the book. "I want to tell you about some things he wrote in here. This is the second journal. This one covers from 1991 to 1999. It's the shortest term, but it actually explains the most about his life. I was eighteen when he started it, and it was like he thought I was a man and he could now talk about these important things."

"You are well aware that I read all of the third journal. Over and over. Or at least all that I could. There were parts that just didn't make any sense."

"Yes. I remember getting his letters. After that one time he came to Florida to visit, when I was just a kid, I really longed for more attention from him. I thought he was so cool. Being British and all. He was James Bond in the flesh to me. In every letter, he included some enciphered message, and there's nothing more fascinating to a boy."

"I can imagine."

"But later, when he started ranting about the failures of the intelligence community, how all government is a sham, the world is really controlled by the military-industrial complex—I got disgusted with him. I stopped reading his letters, and I didn't save them. I'm furious with myself for that now."

"Don't blame yourself. He sounded pretty crazy."

Cole took her hand this time. "He was right about the *Surcouf.*"

"Yes, but when I think back on those wild days in the Caribbean, trying to make sense of his elaborate riddles and ciphers, I'm amazed we were able to figure them out."

"You do understand why he did it, though? He was trying to protect Henri Michaut. If those men from Skull and Bones had known there was a survivor who could pinpoint the location of the submarine's wreck and all the secrets inside, they would have killed him."

"I know," she said. *Just as they would have killed Cole in the years following, when he'd gone into hiding—and let her believe he was dead.* She and Cole had already lost so much precious time together. Hazel was right. Riley needed to find a way to understand this man she loved. She pointed to the journal he was holding. "Tell me more about the other journals. Are the entries in that volume any more coherent?"

He didn't answer right away. He appeared to look across the bay, but his eyes were unfocused. Then he turned to her and said, "Yeah, I guess. But the important thing in here is that you can see how he grew to believe the things he believed. You get the background."

"Like what?"

"I told you that my father was a lot older than my mom. There was almost twenty-five years' difference in their ages. So he tells in here about what it was like when he was a teenager during the war, watching the bombs dropping on England, everybody terrified the Germans were about to invade. He was only seventeen in 1941 when he faked some paperwork and signed up for the Army."

"He was just a kid."

"Yeah. He went into the infantry but ended up serving with the British Army Special Forces Second Commando Brigade. They trained him as a paratrooper, and in late 1942 he was captured when he parachuted into Southern Italy to blow up an aqueduct over the River Tragino."

"I had no idea."

"He was a complicated guy, my dad. Back when I got so interested in the *Surcouf* submarine, I didn't pay much attention to his earlier writings. But in those years when you and I were separated, I had lots of time to study these." He held up the leather journal. "I realized that there's often more to his writing than what's on the surface."

"What do you mean?"

"Well, first he writes about his wartime experiences."

"Okay, so what happened after he was captured?"

"He's got that usual British understatement, and he doesn't go into any details about how he was treated. That's not his point in telling this story. He says he was sent to a POW camp in Sulmona, Italy, and while he was there he met another army officer—also a commando—who had been stationed at Malta."

"Ah, now I'm beginning to understand where you're going with this."

Cole grinned and nodded. "I always said you were smarter than me. When I first read these stories, right after he died, I didn't see anything special in them. Now I've realized that my dad was sending me messages in these journals, long before his last years when he was obsessed with the *Surcouf.*

"So this other officer was the first one to talk to him about the Knights of Malta." Cole opened the journal and began to read aloud.

Dear son,

My friend whom I met in Campo di Concentramento 78 in Sulmona introduced me to an old chivalrous order of the moneyed aristocracy once based in Malta. He told many stories about the missions he served on out of that island. There was one mission where they found something long lost, an artifact of legend and lore. But alas, that which was found was lost again.

In the years that followed our internment, he and I continued to exchange correspondence. You see, today many in the military and intelligence communities are members of this secretive religious order with roots going back to the 12th century. The Sovereign Military Order of Malta has its own constitution, passports, stamps, and public institutions. It is not a country, but rather a recognized sovereign state without territory. This gives its members certain diplomatic privileges, including the ability to bypass customs by transferring items via a diplomatic pouch. Today, their headquarters is in Rome, a few minutes' walk from the Vatican and the ears of the pope.

The Order once guarded its holy treasures and religious relics with spiritual zeal. Today, it has evolved from a spiritual and chivalrous order to a political powerhouse of elite leaders who have one goal—the eradication of Muslims and the takeover of the vast natural resources their countries currently possess.

Cole stopped reading.

"Wow," Riley said. "It's weird thinking about what's going on in the world today, and he wrote that in 1991?"

"No kidding. I've been doing a little research whenever we've had good Internet connections. I decided to find out who exactly these modern Knights of Malta really are. Riley, you wouldn't believe what I've found. The first head of the OSS, William Donovan, was reputedly a Knight of Malta."

"I lose track. Was he the one who interrogated General Yamashita's driver?"

Cole nodded. "Not only was he in charge when they started finding the Japanese war loot hidden in caves in the Philippines, but he founded the Enterprise. He started everything that led them to their Dragon's Triangle. And lots of sources claim that several CIA heads— Allen Dulles, George Tenet, William Casey, George Bush Sr., and John McCone—were also Knights."

"Why would leaders of the American intelligence community want to be Knights?"

"It's not just that they want to be chivalrous good guys. Today the Order's website claims they're simply a humanitarian organization. And they still call themselves *Knights Hospitaller*, but in fact, most of their medical and humanitarian 'missions' tend to be in places where all the alphabet agency spooks need to go. Humanitarian aid makes a great cover. And places that aren't political hotspots? No matter how great the need, you won't find SMOM doing any work there."

"So it's another secret society, like Skull and Bones?"

"Yes and no. These guys are something even more. See how my father wrote they are a 'sovereign state without territory'? I don't think they want to stay that way. They're tired of being homeless. These guys think they're still fighting the Crusades, and they want to take over all the territory in the Arabian Peninsula."

"Cole, that's a pretty far-fetched accusation." She wanted to both believe him and understand him, but she knew how entranced he could get with inflammatory websites about conspiracies, from Roswell to the Kennedy assassinations.

Cole nodded. "I know, but listen. When I first read these journals, back in 2008, I thought the Skull and Bones guys were the only ones. Then I realized there were these other guys, the ones I came to know as the Enterprise, the guys who nearly killed Theo in the Caymans. Remember what my father wrote about secret societies in that last notebook?"

"Sure. I read the words in that journal over and over during the four years I was searching for you. Your father said that these secret societies had been around forever and gone by different names, from the Masons to the Illuminati. That they'd infiltrated what he called the whole 'alphabet soup' of intelligence agencies—the CIA and NSA and all the rest. So what you're saying is the Knights of Malta are a part of this network."

He nodded. "There's lots of membership crossover. I mean, geez, the copies of the Order's membership roster on the Internet read like a who's who of right-wing Christian extremists. Guys like Rick Joyner. Even Erik Prince, former chief of Blackwater, is an alleged member." He held the journal in front of her. "But take a look at this last part my father wrote. You have to see the words as I read them, because I can't pronounce the names of these towns. Maltese is a very odd language." He read the last section.

The last time I saw my friend was in Malta. He was at the end of his shift. We visited Mqabba, Cirkewwa, Naxxar, and Gwarda-manga. I learned there is an object of great power frozen inside Vyipmmlu. My friend told me, I must get it for your birthday.

"Strange names," Riley said.

"The Maltese language has been influenced by all their conquerors, and the Arabs were there the longest."

"'An object of great power'?" she said. "But then up here he refers to it as something long lost. 'An artifact of legend and lore.'"

"Yeah. See, there's something more I discovered in Rhodes. I showed this last passage to Dr. G., and she got this very strange look on her face. That last name on the list? She said there is no place in Malta with that name."

"She's positive?"

He nodded again. "You know what that means, don't you?"

She reached for her beer and downed the rest of the bottle. Her eyes met Cole's.

"Riley, it's a cipher."

CHAPTER THIRTEEN

Villa del Priorato di Malta
The Aventine Hill, Rome

April 11, 2014

Four men sat at the table, their hands folded around steaming cups of coffee. They had removed their jackets, and each man wore a close-fitting black T-shirt that hid neither his size nor his firm physique. The rough wood dining table tucked into a corner of the large kitchen was where the house servants usually took their meals, but these men weren't servants. There was an unusual chill in the air after the previous night's thunderstorms, and the view of the ancient city out the kitchen window was breathtaking. But these men weren't tourists, either. They didn't care about social protocols or by which door they entered the villa. They were there on a job, and all that mattered was whether or not they got paid.

Virgil pulled over a chair, turned it around backward, and sat with his hands folded atop the chair's back. Unlike the four men already seated there, he wore a black polo shirt. On the breast pocket was a small insignia of a red eight-point cross on a white field.

He knew these men. They no longer fought for country or beliefs. But that didn't mean they were immune to any sort of emotional appeal. These men would fight for each other. For their brothers.

"I appreciate you men agreeing to work for us for the next few weeks. Most of you I haven't seen since Mosul, but I assure you, these folks here think like we do. For now, this will mostly be a protection detail. We've got some VIPs visiting the villa starting just before Easter and then staying through both big events. Some of these men you've heard of—hell, some you may even have served under."

One man, with an enormous, downward-curving nose and sharp, prominent cheekbones, glanced up at Virgil. "You going to name names, Virg?"

"Honestly, Hawk, I haven't seen the guest list. But I bet every one of you guys has got a smartphone in your pocket, and you're all smart enough to Google the Sovereign Order of the Knights of Malta. Although the actual membership is secret, there are speculative membership lists floating around the web. You'll likely find most of the brass from the Joint Special Operations Command there. Granted, there are thousands of members, and they don't *all* feel the way we do about the *hajjis*. But enough do to get the job done in the end."

Virgil saw the men exchange glances. Mention of the JSOC got their attention. All of them had once worked for what some called America's secret army, the antiterrorism unit that takes orders directly from the president or secretary of defense and has no congressional oversight.

"And what job's that?" Jacko asked.

"In due time. I'm not free to give you details at the moment, but I can tell you this: it's going to start out quiet, but this mission will ramp up. These people know how to make decisions and take action." He paused and looked around at the men before him. "I know that every one of you lost at least one guy over there. I know I did. More than one. In coming to work for the Order, I offer you danger, the chance to get back at those killers, and possible death."

"So what else is new?" Hawk looked at the other men, his lips curled into a half smile.

"Listen, I get it. You've heard it before. And this Easter meet-up is a strategic planning session, that's all. But I can tell you that this is big. This is 9/11 kind of big. Pearl Harbor kind of big. These guys want to take the leash off guys like you and me. They're looking to finish what these fucking Knights started about a thousand years ago."

The men at the table laughed, nodded, and exchanged looks.

"In the meantime," Virgil said, "Mrs. Ricasoli is waiting for you in the foyer. She'll show you to your rooms. Stow your kit and check the place out. Walk the grounds. For a treat, be sure to check out the cars in the carriage house. Meet me back here at 0100."

The four men pushed back their chairs and filed out of the kitchen, nodding to Virgil as they passed. There was no chitchat between them.

Virgil slung his jacket over his shoulders and slipped out the kitchen door into the villa gardens. High atop a hill in the distance, he saw the dome of Saint Peter's. While staring at it, he reached into his jacket pocket and took out his tobacco pouch. He was about to unzip the pouch when his cell phone buzzed in one of the pockets of his cargo pants.

"Yeah?" he said into the phone.

"It's me."

"Okay, report." Virgil walked across the gravel, distancing himself from the villa.

"There was an incident. I followed them from the ferry like you said. It's just a narrow two-lane road. I had to stay close."

"Did they make you?"

"I don't think so. But it was close."

Virgil heard the regret in the man's voice. "What happened?"

"There were goats in the road, and he stopped on top of a ridge. I rear-ended him."

"Oh shit."

"It's not so bad."

"How so?"

"They were pretty shook-up. I got out of the rental and managed to attach the magnet before they got their shit together. I was gone by the time they came to look for me."

"And your rental?"

"I left it. It's clean."

Virgil didn't speak for several seconds as he gathered his thoughts. He'd given this man a chance. They'd met many years before over in Iraq, when they were in different circumstances. The guy had done him a favor back then. Virgil owed him for that. And when he showed up with this information about Thatcher's interest in the Order, Virgil had been able to use it to his advantage. But he just wasn't the same guy now.

"Look, man," Virgil said, "do you comprehend what's riding on this? This whole op falls apart if we don't get that piece. That's the linchpin."

"I understand. I have history with this guy. Don't ask me how he does it, but he's got a nose for this shit. And he's lucky. If anyone can find it, he can."

"Yeah, that's what I've heard."

"Trust me. He finds it, we'll get it."

"I vouched for you. I said you were up for this. If you're not, tell me now."

"I'm good. You know that. I'm the one who trained you, Vandervoort."

"Yeah, but times have changed."

"I wouldn't think you'd forget what I did for you."

Virgil hated the way this guy always brought it up. Okay, so he owed the guy. And this guy knew something that Virgil didn't want to see the light of day.

"That was a long time ago."

"Things might look different now, but I'm the same man. It's like we agreed back in Iraq—I'll stand by you as long as you stand by me."

"I'm counting on it," Virgil said, but already he was starting to think about how to get rid of this problem. Nobody blackmailed Virgil Vandervoort.

"Look. They didn't get into the car all day yesterday, so the wire did me no good. But it will pay off. And when these two find whatever it is you're looking for, I'll be there to take it away from them. Believe me. I've got a pretty good idea of what this means to you." The man tried to laugh, but it caught in his throat. "But you have no idea how motivated I am. When it comes to fucking with these two, just look at my face. I'll get you what you want. Then they're mine."

Virgil opened his mouth to speak, but through the phone he heard nothing but dead air.

CHAPTER FOURTEEN

Adakoy Shipyard
Adakoy, Turkey

April 11, 2014

Theo used his red-tipped cane to point out the bulkhead at the forward end of the engine room. "We started to mount the watermaker here but we ran into trouble right away."

Cole smiled at Theo's pronunciation of the word "watermaker." Even after all their years together, he still loved listening to Theo's melodic British-Caribbean accent. They were standing on an aluminum-grate catwalk that allowed them to walk around the two big John Deere six-cylinder diesels. There was enough headroom that even Cole's tall, slender first mate could stand with his usual straight-backed posture. Cole and Theo had designed this new boat to have the engine room of their dreams.

Theo continued, "I didn't realize you'd changed the specs on the unit you ordered. The membrane and the pumps are bigger than I thought. There won't be enough clearance to walk around the starboard engine if we do it that way, and we're certainly not giving that up. I told Tony we're going to have to find someplace else to mount it."

"So what's the problem?"

"It's going to take some time. There's a lot to be considered, and he'd already routed some of the plumbing. Now we have to rip that out and start over. Plus there's an issue with some of the electronics on the bridge that I want to see to first. We're having trouble getting everything onto one network. I need all my data in our local cloud to run this boat. The manufacturers are on board with ubiquitous Wi-Fi these days, but half of them design their units to generate their own separate clouds. That won't do. And then some of what I want still only comes with NMEA 0183."

"Theo, could you speak English, please?" Cole said.

In fact, Theo was from the island of Dominica and his grasp of the language was much better than Cole's. He was brilliant. With the help of the Internet, online videos of university lectures, and TED talks, his first mate who had never attended a single university class was a first-rate electrical and mechanical engineer as well as an inventor. Not a day went by when Cole didn't feel intense gratitude for having met Theo that day in Ocracoke.

"Bottom line, Skipper, is you said you wanted everything up and running before we launched. This is going to delay us another week or so."

"Shit."

"We could put her in the water tomorrow and do this work dock-side, if you want."

"Once we launch, we have to go. It's the element of surprise."

A shadow passed over Theo's face. Cole looked up and saw Riley peering down through the engine room's aft deck hatch.

"Hi, boys," she called out. "How's it going?"

"Theo's telling me there's another week's delay."

"Oh no."

"Oh yes," Cole said.

"Well, climb up out of there and tell me about it."

Theo said, "Let's go up to the bridge. I want to show you some of the cool stuff I've got working now."

Cole remembered his first time working on the Ocracoke Shipwreck Survey, when he was still getting his doctorate. The maritime archeology department's boat was more than fifteen years old then, but he thought the bridge was so cool with all its little boxes and circular dials, some with digital readouts. Engine RPMs and oil pressure, depth sounder, radar, sonar—all that data displayed on the dozens of dedicated instruments on the panel in front of the wheel.

As Theo had explained to him, times had now changed. They worked with a Brazilian designer on their new eighty-three-foot expedition yacht, and everything was state of the art—from the easily driven hull that should motor at twelve knots with the twin diesels, to the new array of screens on the bridge.

They had chosen to have her built in Turkey after they discovered the country's terrific boatyards and craftsmen. The Adakoy Shipyard mostly catered to yacht repair, but their builder had rented the big shed on one side of their yacht and then had arranged to have access to the yard's personnel and shops. A big open area separated their boat from the rest of the yard's tenants, and theirs was the biggest boat in the yard.

The engine room occupied the aft half of the lower deck inside the hull. Forward of that were two guest cabins, and in the bow was a cargo hold for dive equipment, accessible with the big hydraulic crane on the main deck. They exited the engine room by climbing steps that took them up to the aft main deck. There, double doors led into the salon, with a dining table to port and a lounging settee and coffee table to starboard. The furnishings were all covered with plastic, as there was still work under way. Forward of the salon was the enormous galley, a head, and stairs that led down to the guest cabins and up to the "sky lounge."

That was what the designer called it, and while Cole and Riley had laughed the first time they'd heard it, it turned out to suit the space. They took the stairs up and entered the master stateroom that would become Cole and Riley's when the boat was finished. It was huge, with a queen-sized berth, double computer-desk stations, built-in cabinets, and a head with a full tub. The cabin had large windows of twenty-millimeter glass around three of the four walls—the same as was used in the wheelhouse, which occupied the forward end of the sky lounge. Cole pushed open the door, and they entered his favorite place on the boat.

Riley plopped into one of the two cream-colored Italian-leather seats facing four large screens mounted below the polarized windows, which provided 180-degree views. She sighed, "This looks like a movie editor's work desk with a great view."

Theo's guide dog, a yellow Lab named Princess Leia, nuzzled Riley's hand. Cole said, "She's missed you. You haven't been coming around the boat much lately."

Riley cradled the dog's head between her hands and scratched the silky ears. "I've missed you too, Princess."

Theo said, "I can hear those puppy groans. Don't spoil her. She's supposed to be a work dog."

"Oh please, Theo, when she's home, she's family. And now that the two of you have moved into your cabin on board, this *is* her home. Besides, it's not like you need to be guided around this boat. You helped design every square inch of her."

Theo smiled but didn't say a word. There was no arguing that point.

Riley said, "Okay, I see four twenty-inch screens, but where are the instruments?"

"Those are the instruments," Theo said.

"Wait till you see this," Cole said. "Show her, Theo."

"Yoda?" Theo said.

A deep male voice answered from built-in speakers at either side of the wheelhouse. "Yes, Theo?"

"Show me engine instruments on Bridge Display One."

The far-left screen lit up with an array of dials and gauges showing temperature, oil pressure, RPM, flow meter.

Cole saw Riley's eyes widen in delight.

Theo said, "SOG, wind speed, water temp, and heading on Bridge Display Two." Images appeared on another one of the screens.

"That's brilliant," Riley said.

Cole said, "So you don't need all the individual dials and stuff anymore. You can configure these screens to show any instruments you want to see."

"Exactly," Theo said. "That's why we need all the data—from the lights to the freezer temperature to the TVs to the engines to the depth sounder—on the ship's network. You will be able to see it on your smartphone, a tablet, or on these screens. Actually, all the screens in the staterooms, too. Right now, the last two there aren't connected yet, but they will be soon. And for those of us who are visually challenged, I can have Yoda read aloud any data I ask for."

"But Theo, 'Yoda'?"

"He's a total geek, Riley. What do you expect?"

"I am not! If I expect to run this boat, I need certain assistive technologies. So you can speak to Yoda in any space anywhere on this boat."

"Even in the master stateroom?" Riley pointed aft.

"Sure. If you're lying in bed and you want to turn the lights off, you don't have to get up. Just ask Yoda to do it for you."

"Does that mean he'll be listening in on us?"

Cole looked at the concern on Riley's face. Lately, the only noise anyone would hear coming from their bunk was snoring. Since they'd arrived in Turkey he'd been working late and coming to bed exhausted.

"Riley, he's not a person. He's a computer," Theo said.

"Yeah, but he can talk, which means he can tell you what we're doing."

Or not doing, Cole thought.

"So you want me to program a privacy mode?"

"Please?"

"Okay. Yoda?"

"Yes, Theo."

"Yoda, add 'privacy mode' to the punch list."

"Yes, Theo."

Cole flopped down into the chair next Riley. "The longer that list gets, the more I start to believe I'll never make it to Malta."

"Look, guys," Theo said. "There's not a whole lot either one of you can do to help out with these last-minute jobs. To be honest, the work will probably go faster if you leave it to us."

"I've got skills," Cole said. "I might not be an electronics guy, but there are a dozen other ways you can put me to work."

"I'm not questioning your skills, Skipper. The thing is, every time you two come aboard, something else gets added to the list."

Cole glanced at Riley, and she shrugged. They both knew Theo was right.

"So here's my suggestion," Theo said. "Why don't you two take off on a nice getaway. Fly to Malta for a few days. Scope it out. Didn't you say that the woman you met in Rhodes, the history expert, was going back to Malta? Go spend some time with her. Visit the museums. Find a nice little bed-and-breakfast—"

"And get the hell out of your hair?" Cole finished his sentence for him.

Theo grinned. "Not to put too fine a point on it."

CHAPTER FIFTEEN

Alex's B&B
Sliema, Malta

April 12, 2014

Cole opened the door and peered out into the hall. "I don't see anyone around."

"He said he only rents out two of the rooms. What were you expecting?"

"No idea. But this is the strangest B and B I've ever stayed in. I mean, it's just some guy's fourth-floor, three-bedroom apartment, and he rents out two of the bedrooms?"

"Welcome to the new sharing economy. I love it. And he said last night to make ourselves at home. Let's get dressed and go see what's for breakfast."

When they entered the dining area, Riley was pleased to see the table was set with fruit cups, pastries, juice, and an insulated coffeepot. Cole would be fine once he got some food in his stomach.

They hadn't had much time to chat with their host the night before. Their plane had been late, the taxi got lost, and they'd arrived after ten o'clock. He'd introduced himself as Alex, shown them the room, and wished them good night.

"This looks yummy," Riley said as she slid onto one of the high stools around the breakfast table. Through the lace curtains on the window she saw a patch of blue sky, and a shaft of sunlight poured onto the carpet.

They were nearly finished with their meal when Alex appeared in the entry.

"Good morning!" he said, his voice booming. He spread his arms wide. "Welcome to Malta!"

His curly black hair clung to his head like a poodle's coat, yet his eyes were a surprising pale blue. He wasn't handsome in a conventional way, but his enthusiastic personality seemed to fill the room. Riley guessed he was in his forties.

"Thanks," she said. She noticed that Cole was hunched over with his nose practically buried in his coffee mug.

"You have come to one of the most fascinating places in the world."

"So we've heard," she said.

"Malta is where north meets south and east meets west. It has been at the center of European history." Like most Maltese, he spoke flawless English with a lovely, lilting accent.

"I can tell you love your country very much."

Alex bowed to her. "Pardon me. Yes, I do. Are you finding everything you need?" He pointed at the breakfast table.

"Yes." Riley raised her coffee cup in a salute. "It's delicious."

"So what brings you to Malta?"

Cole shot her a look that said, *Don't encourage him!*

Riley ignored him. "Cole is a maritime archeologist. He's interested in the Knights of Malta."

"Ah," Alex said, placing his finger alongside his nose. He smiled. "The Knights. As perhaps you know, they reigned over these islands for more than two hundred years. In the beginning, the Maltese people were happy to see them arrive. They were fierce in battle, and they fought off the Ottoman invaders for thirty years before defeating them soundly during the Great Siege. The Ottomans put the heads of the dead Knights on posts to demoralize their opponents. The Knights fought back by using the heads of dead Turks as cannonballs."

"That's gruesome," Riley said. "They were men of God on the one hand, and brutal killers on the other."

"They weren't *all* men of God," Alex said.

"Really?"

"Well, there were quite a few naughty Knights."

Riley laughed. "That's not the first time we've heard that." She noticed Cole was watching Alex now.

"At the end of their stay here in Malta," Alex said, now speaking to both of them, "most of the Knights ignored their vows of celibacy. You have heard of our neighboring island of Gozo?"

Cole nodded.

"When a Knight found out his mistress was pregnant, the Order sent her to a convent on Gozo to bear the child out of wedlock. The child could take the Knight's name, but it would have the word *de* added. So, for example, if the Knight's name was Niro, the child would be named DeNiro. He is of Niro, but not a real Niro."

"I can't believe they just sent those women away," Riley said.

"They were not very nice, the Knights. They were fierce pirates, also called corsairs. When they first arrived here from Rhodes, they had only these great galleys with oars. They were rowed by hundreds of slaves. While they were here in Malta, they modernized and added sails to their galleys. They attacked the Ottomans and the Arabs down on the Barbary Coast. It is said that they amassed a great treasure in Fort Saint Angelo. There was in the center of the fort a great room filled with all the gold, silver, jewels, and parchments they stole throughout the centuries."

"What happened to the treasure?" Cole asked.

Alex laughed. "Ah, the archeologist is interested in treasure after all."

Riley glimpsed Cole turning aside and rolling his eyes. She knew how he hated it when people thought he was just a treasure hunter.

"Napoleon stole most of it. There are many stories and legends, but no one knows for certain. Have you heard the Legend of the Silver Girl?"

Riley saw Cole glance at the outside door. "We don't have a lot of time here," he said.

"Oh, please, I'm sorry," Alex said. "I've been talking too much." He reached for their dishes to clear the table.

"We can do that," Riley said. "It's just that we're anxious to get to Valletta. There's so much to see."

"Valletta is an extraordinary city. Yes, many museums and architectural wonders. But if you really want to understand this fortified city, you should take the trek around the outer walls. You see, I am a trekker. And this is one of my favorite treks. Sometimes the trail will get narrow, but continue on. You can circle the entire city."

"That sounds fabulous," Riley said. "What's the best way to get to Valletta from here?"

"You can take the ferry or the bus. If you take the ferry across from Sliema, which is my suggestion for you, don't go up into the center of the city right away. Instead, turn left and walk around at the level of the sea. It is a beautiful trek that will take you two to three hours, but you will see the city of Valletta in a very special way."

Lazaretto Submarine Base
Manoel Island, Malta

April 6, 1942

Tug Wilson tapped on the open door and said, "You sent for me, sir?"

The base commander, Captain "Shrimp" Simpson, looked up from the paperwork on his desk. He ran his hand through his close-cut wavy hair.

"Come in, Tug. Have a seat." He gestured toward a rusty metal folding chair opposite his desk.

Tug didn't like the sound of this. He sat down on the offered chair with every expectation that his home leave was evaporating.

"I know you've got your orders, and you're awaiting transport back home."

"And looking forward to it, sir."

"I have a favor to ask of you, Tug."

"I'm listening."

"There are two agents. We need to land them on the coast as soon as possible. I know I've got Charlie, but just one of your little folding boats won't be enough. I need a second man. The agents will be carrying radio gear, but all you have to do is get them on shore. Then you'll be on your way home."

"Right," Tug said. Shrimp always had a way of making these missions sound like a piece of cake.

"This isn't a cancellation of your leave, Tug. Just think of it as a slight detour. I've worked it out so you'll be able to rendezvous and transfer onto the *Unbeaten*. She's headed to Gibraltar for some repairs. Once you're at Gib you should be able to find a ride on home. What do you say?"

"I capsized the last time I tried to land an agent."

"Yes, Tug, I know."

"And my canoe was so broken up we had to sink it."

"Yes. But the mission was still a success. I wouldn't ask if it wasn't important."

"And whose boat will I be on for the mission?"

"That'll be Wanklyn. The *Upholder*."

Tug pulled at one end of his mustache. "Wanks, eh?"

"Parker will be going, too."

Tug enjoyed drawing out the moment and making Shrimp wait. At least he could pretend like he had a choice in the matter. "What time does she sail?"

"At 0400."

Finally, Tug rose and slid his hat under his left arm. "Seems I owe Wanks a new shirt, and he's determined to collect."

"He did ask for you."

"I'll be there, sir." Tug saluted.

Tug and Charlie stood on the forward deck, watching as Wanklyn climbed up to the conning tower and saluted his first lieutenant.

"Thank you, Number One," he said, relieving the officer of command and assuming his place.

Tug could see the lines of stress in his old friend's face. He'd heard this would be the twenty-eighth patrol for the *Upholder*. She held the record for the largest tally of enemy shipping sunk: some 125,000 tons, including three U-boats, a destroyer, and numerous troopships. But so many subs had failed to return to base since the start of the year. It was tough to keep up the infamous British good cheer around the Lazaretto. Every man on Wanks's crew knew the *Upholder* was pushing her luck.

The captain began issuing orders for their departure. The crew pulled in the lines, and the sub started to drift away from the catwalk.

"Slow ahead, port," Wanklyn said. The prop wash churned at the stern of boat. The skipper turned to wave to the men standing just inside the old hospital galleries. A good crowd had gathered to see the *Upholder* off.

Captain Shrimp Simpson stood leaning on the stone wall of the second-floor gallery. He called out, "Good luck, David, and good hunting."

As the sub headed for the booms that protected the harbor entrance off Dragutt Point, Tug and Charlie made their way belowdecks and checked on their gear. After all the organized chaos of men returning to the sub with their seabags and loading the last-minute stores and equipment, the scene below was remarkably orderly. As they passed through the control room, they saw the helmsman, the asdic rating, and the second officer leaning over the chart table. Tug found the familiar odors of sweat, oil, and stale food rather comforting. What would he do with himself on leave back home?

Earlier that afternoon they had seen to the loading of their folding canoes, called folboats, as well as an inflatable RAF rubber dinghy. They also checked over the radio equipment they would send ashore with the agents.

They found the two Arabs squatting in the torpedo room just forward of the ratings' mess. The rest of the crew had no clue what to do with the two, and they were in the way. Tug could understand. When he and Charlie had first started coming aboard subs, the crew didn't know what to do with two army men, either. As an officer, Tug's lot had always been a bit better. He got to hot bunk with another officer, while Charlie often found himself in a hammock above a torpedo.

They were a superstitious lot, submariners. They believed that having "guests" aboard was bad luck. It was only when they saw the results—after Tug and his mates in the Special Boat Service had succeeded in their missions to sneak ashore and destroy the enemy's supply lines—that the submariners grew more friendly to him. Also, he learned how to stay out of the way of the crew as they did their work, and that was equally appreciated.

Tug directed the agents to the ratings' mess and showed them how to make themselves some tea. He confirmed that they knew where and when they could sleep.

"If you hear this sub go to battle stations, the best thing you can do is stay out of the way. I suggest you come here to the mess."

Once he had them settled, he wanted to find out what this mission was really going to be about.

"Let's go see if the skipper's in his quarters," Tug said to Charlie.

Submarine commanders were always issued their orders in writing. They picked them up in a confidential envelope before sailing. Tug hoped to learn their destination, and that it wouldn't be too far, so they could get rid of the Arabs as soon as possible.

They found Wanklyn in the wardroom, pouring himself a cup of coffee. A couple of officers were already playing a game of cribbage.

"Follow me," the commander said. "Sorry, Parker, no room for three, but Captain Wilson will fill you in."

"No problem, sir. I'd rather like to chat with those Arab blokes about their county's history." Charlie cheerfully doubled back to where they'd left the agents.

Once inside the captain's cabin, Wanklyn pulled the secret orders out of his jacket pocket and slit open the envelope.

"Let's see what we're up to this time round," he said.

"I know *what* we'll be doing," Tug said. "Just not sure where."

On the bulkhead above the bunk was a nautical chart of the central Mediterranean. After reading his orders, Wanklyn put his finger on the chart in the Gulf of Hammamet along the coast of Tunisia. "About here," he said. "Four kilometers north of Sousse."

"And we're just to land the agents, right?"

"No, there's more."

"Ha," Tug said. "Why am I not surprised?"

CHAPTER SEVENTEEN

Aboard the Marsamxetto Ferry
Valletta, Malta

April 12, 2014

The little Arab grocery Alex had directed them to sold everything they needed, from cheese to salami to bread. The only thing missing was wine, and they'd found a bottle at a small wine shop opposite the ferry ticket booth.

Riley chose the sunny foredeck seats on the cross-harbor ferry so they'd have a spectacular view of Marsamxett Harbour, including Manoel Island. Cole pointed out the ruins of Fort Manoel, and the old lepers' hospital that had served as a sub base during World War II. Now, as they approached the wharf, Riley watched as the crew picked up the mooring buoy, swung the ferry around, and eased her stern in to the dock.

"Nicely done, eh?" she said.

Cole was already on his feet, staring up at the enormous stone ramparts of the city of Valletta.

"Yeah," he said.

Riley knew he was on another wavelength, but that was okay. She was used to it.

Cole shrugged on the backpack that held their picnic supplies. "Shall we?" He pointed toward the stern of the boat, where the passengers were already disembarking.

They followed Alex's directions. While all the other ferry passengers turned right and started up the hill to reach the city atop the walls, Riley and Cole turned left. At first, they followed a road along the base of the walls. They saw cars parked along the berm close to the rocky edge of the peninsula. Down on the rocks, fishermen with long cane poles nursed their lines in the heaving blue water.

Cole trailed his fingers along the cut-stone wall. "This place is an archeologist's dream. I've been wanting to come here for years—long before I read about it in the old man's journal."

She was happy to see Cole acting more like his old self. "It is an amazing natural harbor."

"It's two harbors, really. You'll see when we get out to the point up here. The city of Valletta is built on a peninsula with two massive deep harbors, one on each side."

At that point, the road petered out and turned into a path across the rocks. Not boulders, but great, flat expanses of weather-beaten rock. The whole base of the peninsula appeared to be solid rock, worn and cracked by the constant battering from the sea.

Some of the swells coming in the harbor entrance were big enough to send up great plumes of spray, which the wind carried across to Riley and Cole. The sun was warm and the spray felt good. Around the point, they found a pier and partial breakwater enclosing a third of the other harbor entrance.

"See," Cole said. "This is the entrance to Grand Harbour on this side. We're just leaving Marsamxett Harbour on that side. Each harbor's big enough for dozens of ships. Lots of smaller creeks, too, for boatyards and docks. This pier was originally built to narrow the entrance. During the war they put booms across the entrance to protect against enemy subs sneaking in."

"So how old is all this?" Riley waved her hand around the horizon.

"It all varies. But when the Knights sailed in here in 1530, after having been booted out of Rhodes by Suleiman the Magnificent, there were less than twenty thousand inhabitants between the two islands of Malta and Gozo. They were mostly subsistence farmers who barely got by, with a few noble families sprinkled among them. Like Alex said, the islands were always getting attacked by the Ottomans, who took away the Maltese as slaves."

The rock foundation had been flat out on the point, but as they made their way along the rocks farther into Grand Harbour, their footing grew more precarious. Cracks opened up into shallow ravines, and Riley jumped from stone to stone, picking her way over the uneven ground. The deep-blue water of the harbor heaved against the stones about fifty feet below them. She stopped when she saw the sunlight shining through a natural arch in the rocks.

"Look at that," Cole said, coming up behind her.

She leaned back into him. "Alex was right. This hike is amazing. I'm really glad we came." She looked across Grand Harbour at the old buildings along the waterfront and the many newer buildings that covered the land as far as she could see. "It's so built up now. Hard to imagine what it must have looked like way back then."

Cole stepped back, but he rested his hands on her shoulders. "Well, the Knights really changed things for Malta. When they arrived, the capital wasn't even here. It was at the only real city, Mdina, in the center of the island. The Maltese thought they could protect themselves better from that city built atop a hill, but the Knights were seafarers. They made their headquarters in Birgu, over there by Fort Saint Angelo." He pointed across the harbor at the high-walled fortress on the end of a point of land. "Over here on this side of Grand Harbour, there was nothing, just a bare mountain. Nothing in Marsamxett Harbour, either."

"So when did the city of Valletta get built?"

"Not until after the Great Siege."

Riley turned and pointed ahead, where a sandy path framed by flowers led along the base of the wall. She started walking but asked over her shoulder, "The Knights always fought against the Ottomans?"

"Yeah," Cole said. "The same old rivalry had chased them from Jerusalem to Rhodes to here. It was the Christian world fighting against the Muslim Ottomans for control of the Mediterranean. During their first twenty-five years in Malta, the Knights saw the need for protection from the other side of the harbor. This peninsula was an uninhabited mountain, but they started work on the fort above us here." Cole turned around and pointed up at the high walls. "Fort Saint Elmo. It's now at the seaward end of the city of Valletta. But it wasn't until they elected Jean de Valette as grand master that things really started to change. Bigger fortifications around Birgu and a growing navy. The Turks noticed that the Knights were getting it together in Malta, so Suleiman decided to use Malta as a stepping-stone to invading Sicily and on to Rome."

"But the Knights held out?"

"Barely. It was a long, brutal, four-month siege. Jean de Valette called it the great battle of the Cross and the Qur'an. Christians fighting the infidels. Thousands died, but after four months, the Turkish fleet withdrew."

"It's odd that we have this word *inhumane*," Riley said. "When I think about using human heads as cannonballs . . ." She shivered in spite of the warm sun. "War, murder, torture are all very common human pastimes. Such actions aren't inhuman at all."

Cole tapped her good shoulder. When she turned around, she saw he'd stopped walking and was looking at her with one eyebrow raised. "You're starting to sound like me."

She pointed her finger at him. "Now that's frightening." She turned and kept on walking. "I take it that Valletta is named for this Grand Master de Valette guy, so he must have built the city."

"He started it, anyway. He only lived for three years after the Great Siege. Birgu got renamed Vittoriosa in honor of the victory, but the place was a wreck. The grand master ordered the mountain on this side of the harbor to be leveled off and a new city built. The next several grand masters continued the construction project."

"So these walls are almost five hundred years old."

"Yeah, well, some parts are. This place got pounded in World War II. They called it the *second siege*. So lots of this has been repaired and rebuilt. They probably were able to use some of the same stone, though—so yeah, these walls are about that old."

They clambered over more rocks, and suddenly the broad expanse they had been walking on petered out. The rock foundation had crumbled into the harbor, and someone had built a small metal bridge right up against the fortress walls. There was an outside guardrail, but the drop to the water was more than fifty feet straight down.

Riley slowed and turned. "Are you going to be okay?"

Cole swallowed. "Sure."

Back in the Philippines, when they'd had to rappel down into a cave, Riley never would have guessed that Cole had this fear of heights. He'd managed then because it was only about a twenty-foot drop. But before they'd left Indonesia to cross the Indian Ocean in her boat, *Bonefish*, she'd wanted to check the rigging. Her mast had been over fifty feet off the water, and when she'd asked him if he'd like to go up, since the view was great from up there, she had seen all the color drain out of his face.

Now Cole started across the bridge after her, holding on to the railing with a white-knuckled grip. He crossed slowly, but he made it.

The path widened, and she waited for him. She took his hand. "I'm proud of you."

"Please. It's bad enough that I feel like such a wimp over stuff like that. You don't have to go on about it."

"Sure."

Even though the air was cool, the sun felt hot when they were sheltered from the wind. All the hiking and fresh air was having an effect on her appetite.

"I'm ready for a picnic," she said. "How about you?"

"Sounds good. Let's try to find a spot off the path, though."

Riley chose her words carefully. "So far we haven't seen a soul out here besides us."

"I just don't want to be too out in the open," he said.

Cole found a spot where they could get off the main trail. A U-turn led them to a path that angled back down the hillside leading to some stone steps and a deep ledge. She could see it was difficult for him, even though both the path and steps were broad and even. It was the drop to the water below that unnerved him. Finally they reached the ledge, and they sat with their backs against the rocks, their feet stretched out in front of them. Riley would have preferred to dangle her feet over, but she knew Cole wouldn't be comfortable so close to the edge.

She took the backpack from him and began to spread out their food. Cole opened the wine.

"This is a Meridiana Cab-Merlot blend," he said. "It's local. The guy in the wine shop recommended it."

"Terrific. Cheers." They tapped their plastic glasses. "Now dig in."

Riley took out her Swiss Army knife and cut a piece of salami, then she ripped off a piece of the hearty Maltese bread.

Cole ignored the food and stared across the harbor. He pointed his finger at the fort on the opposite shore. "Dr. G. told me that the Knights of Malta recently signed a ninety-nine-year lease on Fort Saint Angelo over there. They're back in Malta again."

"I wonder why."

"Not sure, but that used to be where they kept their treasure."

"Hmmm. Come on, Cole, eat something."

He picked up a piece of cheese and nibbled on the corner.

Riley knew what he was thinking about. What was it Cole's father had written? *There is an object of great power frozen inside.* And here he was, staring at the Knights' fort. "Have you been working on the cipher?" she asked him.

"A bit."

"You told me once that your father taught you a bunch of ciphers."

"Most of his letters included some cipher text. He'd sent me a kids' book on codes and ciphers, and I loved working out the cryptograms."

"I don't suppose you still have that book?"

He turned to look at her, the corner of his mouth lifted in a half smile. "In that container in the corner of the boatyard? No, but I do remember lots of them. I've been working my way through them."

"Like what?"

"The usual. Anagrams and word scrambles. Substitution ciphers like the pigpen or the checkerboard."

"I'm not even going to ask what any of that means."

"Don't. None of it's working, anyway," he said. "But I got an idea last night. I think it might be a shift cipher. My father mentions the word *shift* in that passage in the journal, and I remember he really liked those."

"You're staring at Fort Saint Angelo. Our cipher word is eight letters. If you think about it, S-T-A-N-G-E-L-O"—she spelled out the words—"is eight letters, too."

"Yes, but the Knights didn't have their lease on the fort when my father wrote that bit in his journal."

"Perhaps they leased it because of something they think is hidden inside? I read in a tourist brochure that it's now closed to the public. Maybe we could break in?"

He picked up a piece of bread and gnawed off a mouthful. He didn't say anything while he chewed.

Riley poured them both more wine. "I suppose it's not a very sci-entific method to find a solution and try to make it fit."

"You wouldn't be the first." Cole sipped his wine, then softly re-peated the phrase from the journal. *"I learned there is an object of great power frozen inside V-y-i-p-m-m-l-u. My friend told me, I must get it for your birthday."* Instead of trying to pronounce the capitalized word—the presumed cipher text—he spelled it out.

"Well," Riley said, "I suppose we must assume that he wasn't re-ally talking about finding some historical thing of great value for your birthday. It wasn't a shopping list for your presents."

"Definitely not."

"Maybe your birthdate is some kind of key."

He grinned. "Miss Maggie Magee, former US Marine, now noted code breaker."

Riley punched him in the arm. "So you'd already thought of it. If you'll recall, I came up with a few solutions last time we were working at this. I'm a natural."

"Oh really?"

Riley smiled and rested her head on his shoulder. She closed her eyes with her face tilted up to the sun. "It's been a long time since you called me Magee. I've missed it. I've missed you."

She felt Cole straighten his back and go tense. He looked skyward. "What the hell?" he said.

Riley opened her eyes and followed Cole's stare. She had gradually grown aware of a soft buzzing sound, but she thought it was some kind of distant construction. It wasn't. There was a tiny white device with four whirling propellers hovering about ten feet over their heads. "It's a nano drone," she said. "I heard about them in the service, but they were just a DARPA daydream back then." The drone zoomed off, fast as a hummingbird.

Cole scrambled to his feet and started scanning the hillside above them. At that moment, a shower of gravel and rock rained down on them from somewhere above.

Riley covered her head. A rock hit her wine glass, tipping it over.

"Shit!" Cole said.

"Cole—" She was about to tell him the wine didn't matter. He was standing, shading his eyes, staring up the rock wall. The look on his face stopped her.

"It's him, Riley. It's Diggory Priest."

CHAPTER EIGHTEEN

The Silversmith Shop
Vittoriosa, Malta

March 11, 1798

Arzella sat down in the chair next to her father's bed. More than a year ago he had ceased to be able to climb the stairs to their apartment over the shop. Arzella had built a small kitchen in the shop's back room and placed beds inside for the two of them. Now their old apartment was rented out to a nobleman's widow who'd lost her husband during the revolution in France.

"Papa, the rest of the stew is on the stove, and there's bread in the cupboard." She placed her hand on her father's forehead to check his temperature. "You're certain you will be fine if I leave you alone?"

"Daughter, I have been taking care of myself for over sixty years."

"If someone comes into the shop, Madame Benier's grandson, Pierre Antoine, is out there to help them. He is sitting by the window now, doing his lessons. He says he will enjoy the quiet."

"I wish the shop were *not* so quiet these days."

"We get by, Papa." In all the ten years Arzella had been doing her father's work, she had not seen such lean times. Right after the revolution, the Republicans had seized all the Order's commander-ies in France and Italy, and one of the Knights' major sources of in-come had dried up. Soon after, however, Grand Master De Rohan had brokered deals, and finances improved in Malta. But in the last six months, all the Knights she saw could barely feed themselves. The one notable exception, of course, being a very successful young Knight corsair.

"Are you seeing *him* again?" her father asked.

It was as though her father could read her mind. "He has a name, Papa."

"Yes, but we *simple* people are supposed to call them *Chevalier*."

"Times are changing, Papa. I keep trying to explain this to you. Also to Alonso. He is just as old-fashioned as you are."

"I doubt it," her father said.

Arzella brushed her father's white hair back off his forehead. "I can take care of myself, Papa. You don't have to worry about me."

"Ha! A father not worry about his daughter? The world has not changed that much, *ma petite*."

She kissed his forehead. *"Au revoir."*

After giving Pierre Antoine some last-minute instructions, Arzella picked up the picnic basket she had prepared earlier and left the shop. Winter refused to let go of the island that morning. Walking the nar-row streets in the shadow of the buildings, Arzella wrapped her cloak tightly around her body. Frosted fingers of wind slid down her neck and sent shivers dancing down her spine. The idea that such shivers were brought on by her impending meeting with Chevalier Alonso Montras, *her* Alonso, was not something she allowed herself to con-sider.

Surely it was only the sailing that made her heart beat faster when-ever she was with him. Since that first time she had sailed the harbor with him and Nikola, she had been back aboard the *Ruse* several times. Alonso believed that Bonaparte had set his sights on Malta, therefore

he insisted that his men train often rather than sit in the taverns growing soft.

Arzella adored the *Ruse*. Since none of the men had ever seen a
woman who liked to sail, they had been suspicious of her at first. Su-
perstitions had it that a woman aboard meant bad luck for the ship.
But once Alonso began to give her the wheel and she demonstrated
her prowess at the helm, even the crew jumped to her orders when she
called on them to increase sail. To her surprise, Alonso began to teach
her some of the more refined techniques for sailing the xebec. Her
previous experience had been only on the crude sailing rigs of fishing
boats. She hadn't yet been so bold or unladylike as to climb the rigging, but she was not certain how much longer she could resist.

Two days earlier, when he'd stopped by the shop to invite her,
Alonso had told her today's sail would be a surprise. Now, she was in
such a hurry she nearly tripped on the last flight of steps that led down
to the quay.

Since Saturday was market day, the quay was overcrowded, and
Arzella had to jostle her way through the throng. She saw the masts of
many vessels over the heads of the crowd, but none that she recognized
as that of the *Ruse*.

She was standing atop a box belonging to a fisherman friend,
searching the length of the quay, when she felt a pair of hands slide
around her waist from behind.

"*Bonjour, mademoiselle,*" Alonso said as he lifted her off the box. "I
thought perhaps you got lost."

"I am not the one who is lost," she said. "What have you done with
the *Ruse*?"

"She is out at anchor in the harbor. The crew is aboard doing some
painting and rope work. The launch is over here."

He steered her by her elbow over to the small wooden boat. Normally, if they traveled out to the boat at anchor, some members of the
crew rowed for the captain. On this morning, the boat was empty,

and, in addition to the oars, a single mast was rigged with a red-and-white-striped lateen sail.

She turned to face him. "You rigged a sail?"

"That is your surprise. We're going sailing in this boat today. I'm going to show you Saint Julian's Bay."

Arzella took a deep breath. Sailing the small boat out to sea would be exciting, but it also meant she would be alone with Alonso for the very first time.

The northeast wind forced them to tack out of the bay. With only the two of them on board, Arzella took the tiller while Alonso handled the sail. The breeze stiffened when they finally cleared Tigné Point and turned onto a broad reach. Her fingers looked like frozen talons wrapped around the tiller, but since she'd lost most feeling in them, she didn't care.

The sail was glorious. The cloudless sky and sea were broken only by the white froth of their wake and the golden sandstone walls of the fort atop the cliffs.

"I've never been to Saint Julian's," she said. "What is there?"

"On the south side of the bay there is a small fishing village, but to the north is a sheltered creek with a little beach. Last year about this time we took the *Ruse* there to careen her and paint the bottom. I hiked inland and discovered an abandoned house with a small orchard of fruit trees. There were figs, black mulberries, and pears. I've never told anyone about it. That is my secret place where I like to go with this sailing launch. Someday, I'd like to buy the house and fix it up. Perhaps even start a family there."

"It sounds beautiful."

"You will see."

They covered the couple of miles to the entrance to Saint Julian's Bay in what seemed like mere minutes.

"The entrance will be dead downwind, but we will soon veer to the right into the creek," Alonso said. He spoke over his shoulder, his eyes shifting from the water to the sail. "Be careful not to gybe."

"Don't worry, Captain." She glanced at his profile. His reddish-brown beard was neatly trimmed to follow the angle of his jaw. His hair fell in waves that would have touched his shoulders were it not blowing back in the fresh breeze.

Chevalier Alonso Montras of Aragon was a nobleman, Arzella a shopgirl. Though the revolution in France was supposed to be changing such barriers, she did not delude herself into believing that this man would consider a life with her in the house in the orchard. Did he have plans to compromise her virtue? She laughed out loud at the idea. Alonso had always been such a gentleman; if anyone were to put her virtue in jeopardy today, it would be her.

They slowed once they entered the creek, and by the time it shallowed at the headwater, their boat was barely moving. Alonso jumped into the knee-deep water and walked to the stern to remove the rudder. He saw her struggle to peel her hands off the tiller.

"Why did you not tell me your hands were so cold? Your skin looks nearly blue!" He pulled the boat up onto the sand with her still in it. Then he came and lifted her out of the boat. "Can you stand?"

"Of course," she said. But when he set her on her feet her legs nearly buckled—whether from the cramped posture in the boat or the dizziness she felt from being in his arms, she was not certain. She smiled at him as she struggled to stay on her feet. She did not want him to think her weak.

Alonso tied up the boat and brought the basket and a large woolen blanket. When he saw her face, he wrapped the blanket around her shoulders, threaded the basket onto his arm, and took both her hands in his. "I shall warm your hands as we walk."

Arzella liked seeing her small hands in his. That surprised her. As did the tingling in her hands that continued long after her skin had warmed. She'd never felt anything close to affection for a man—but then again, she had never been alone with a man before. The sensations she was feeling were entirely new, and, though he kept the pace very slow, she found it difficult to breathe. She knew her father would not approve, but she made her own choices now.

Alonso was right. The empty stone house, with plants growing from the rafters where the roof had caved in, was lovely—like a place out of a folktale. Several of the trees were in bloom, and the fig tree already had fruit weighing down the branches. The sun was warmer there in the clearing, which was protected from the sea wind. Alonso spread the blanket on the grass, and Arzella knelt and began to set out the meal she had prepared. The stew in the porcelain pot was still warm.

As they ate, she felt him watching her.

"Why do you look at me so?"

"I have never met a lady like you."

"You know very well I am not a lady."

"In my eyes you are."

"Dangerous talk for a Knight."

"Says one most familiar with such talk."

She laughed. "As a Knight you have certain expectations to fulfill, certain vows."

"And I suppose you have noticed how well my brothers in the Order remember their vows."

"We are from two different worlds. While that prevents us from courting, it does not prevent us from being friends," she said.

He put his hand on top of hers. "I should like very much to be your friend, Mademoiselle Brun."

She had no memory of making a decision to do it, but she found herself leaning in and kissing the mouth in the middle of the beard.

Alonso sat back and scooted away across the blanket. "Excuse me," he said. "I'm sorry. I don't know what—"

"Why are you apologizing? You did nothing. It is I who kissed you."

Alonso pulled at the collar of his coat, his eyes darting from the food to the sky. He seemed to be looking everywhere but at her. At last he spoke. "Arzella, in these past weeks, you have amazed me with your wit and skill. The more time we've spent together, the more often I have thought of just such a kiss. But I have seen many Knights steal the virtue from a young woman, only to send her off to Gozo when she grew large with child. I could not bear to see that happen to you."

This time she took his hand in hers. "It is because of that respect that I choose to be with you. I understand that we could never marry. So let me choose this day of happiness."

Alonso grasped her hand and pulled her to him. He wrapped his arms around her and buried his face in her neck. "Arzella," he whispered.

After holding him tight against her body for several long minutes, Arzella grew uncomfortable. Out of the wind, the sun was very warm. There were so many thick garments separating them. She untangled herself from his arms and slid his coat off his shoulders. Beneath it he wore a white shirt. She pulled the tails of the shirt out of his trousers and lifted the shirt off over his head.

His skin shone like polished ivory in the sunlight. She reached her fingers out and touched the mark above his heart. It was red ink on his skin in the shape of the eight-point cross of the Order of the Knights of Saint John.

"What of this?" Arzella had seen such ink on the bodies of sailors before, but never on a nobleman.

"It is nothing."

She slid her fingertips across the skin to see if the mark felt like a scar. Alonso closed his eyes. She heard a deep moan from inside his throat.

"The skin is smooth. This was done years ago."

He reached up and took her hand in his. He brought her fingers to his lips and kissed them. "Arzella, please, let us talk no more of this. I have taken an oath. I do not want to lie to you."

"If Napoleon does come to Malta—"

"He will. And I will be called to fight, perhaps to die, in service to my order."

She touched the red mark again. "You are my marked Knight. I, too, carry secrets and scars in my heart, but mine are not so visible."

"You are my silver-shop girl, and if I were allowed to choose, I would marry you and move into this cottage in the orchard. Together we would heal your heart and mine."

"The future is not ours to choose, but today belongs to us. I care little what others might think of me. I know only that today I want nothing more than to be here now with you."

Alonso lowered her shoulders to the blanket and pressed his lips to hers.

CHAPTER NINETEEN

Outside the Walls
Valletta, Malta

April 12, 2014

By the time Riley got to her feet, Cole had already started back up the steps, chasing the man he said was Diggory Priest. The problem was that the steps angled up the hill to the right, taking him farther away from the man on the path who was running off to their left. Riley preferred the more direct route. She started to climb the rock cliff. Back at MSG school at Quantico, she'd trained in rappelling, should she as a Marine ever have to rescue embassy personnel by exiting out an upper-story window. She'd found she had a knack for it, and it had led her to the sport of rock climbing. She was rusty, but even so, she made good time, finding suitable hand- and toeholds. The fifty-foot drop to the surging blue water didn't faze her.

She pulled herself up onto the path less than a minute later, just in time to see the man's back vanish over the top of a hill of rocks about one hundred feet away. Riley started to run.

When she crested the top of the rocks, she saw the terrain was changing. A long path led down to a cluster of buildings. They looked like fishing shacks now, but maybe they had been homes or even some kind of defense system at one time. There was a launch ramp, and several of the buildings had dories resting on their roofs. She didn't see the man anywhere, so she ran down the path, swiveling her head, searching for him around corners and through the open doorways of buildings that appeared deserted. Somewhere ahead she heard music.

Riley leapt over a stone wall and cut through a courtyard in front of one of the shacks. A clothesline held brightly colored T-shirts and several pairs of cotton pants. She was startled by a loud voice, then saw the cage and a green parrot eyeing her distrustfully.

There was movement inside the house. She stepped to the door and peered into the shadows. A toddler in a baggy diaper looked up at her with big, dark eyes, his thumb in his mouth.

"Excuse me," she said, backing out into the yard.

There was only one route the man could have taken to get out of there. The fishing shacks were nestled right up against the walls of the city, and they marked the end of their path down on the rocks. But there was a perimeter road fifty feet above her head, and a long, narrow staircase at the far end of the buildings that led upward. There was no way he'd had a good-enough lead to make it before she got there. He had to be around here somewhere.

She jumped back over the wall and checked around the back of the house. Where the heck were the kid's parents, she wondered. It was spooky how quiet it was. The music had stopped. All she heard was the breath-like swells surging up the sloping rocks. She could see the seaward side of all the buildings ahead. They were built up atop a rock promontory. There was nowhere to hide there.

She ran from house to house, but most of the doors were locked, and those that opened to her hand were empty. At the top of the launch ramp, she saw a concrete wall topped by a rusty railing. A chair leaned against the wall, and a cigarette still burned in the ashtray on the ground next to it. All the shacks on that level had padlocks on their doors. At the far end, though, she saw a house with a little red awning. It was just before the stairs that led up to the road. Hanging from the awning poles were three little birdcages that held finches flitting behind the bars. The door to the house stood open.

"Hello," she called out as she crossed the courtyard.

As Riley reached the doorway, a very large woman burst from its shadows with her mouth open and her arms spread wide. Her ample breasts and belly plowed into Riley and knocked her onto her back, with the screaming lady on top of her. Birds screeched, a child started crying, and, though the woman's hair covered Riley's face, she saw the shadow of a man run out of the door and turn to head for the long stone stairs. The only detail about him that registered was the gun in his hand.

Riley shoved the woman aside and leapt to her feet. "Get inside," she shouted, then she planted one hand on the rusty railing and vaulted over it. The man was already at the base of the stairs. His back was to her, and she noted his long, stringy brown hair. He was over six feet tall and slender. But he was slow, and she was going to catch him before he made it to the top.

She was almost to the base of the stairs when the man stopped and half turned. She saw the rough skin of his cheek. The first thing that flashed through her mind was that she had seen him before. He was familiar. Then she realized he was the driver of the car that rear-ended them.

He was also lifting the gun and pointing it at her. She heard the sound of running feet behind her.

"Cole! Gun!" she shouted as she dove behind one of the shacks.

The gun boomed.

Riley lay on the ground, curled into a fetal position, gritting her teeth. She had landed on her bad shoulder. The pain from the old burn injury, even after months of skin grafts at Bethesda, could feel like it was still on fire if she hit it just right.

The sound of the swells rising and falling against the rocks seemed much louder. She knew it was the adrenaline making all her senses more acute. "Cole?" Her voice was barely more than a hoarse whisper. "Are you okay?" She struggled to her knees behind the shack, and then, with one hand on the wall, she lifted herself to her feet.

The pain in her shoulder caused her right arm to hang useless at her side.

When she peered out from behind the building, the man on the stairs was gone. She started back down the path, calling Cole's name.

She heard scratching noises, then what sounded like her own name. It seemed to be coming from behind the houses. Around the side of one house she saw a length of clothesline tied to an eyebolt on the side of the shack. Just before it trailed over the cliff, there was a child's pink dress pinned to the line with clothespins. The rope moved, sawing back and forth on the cliff edge.

"Cole?"

"Down here."

When she reached the edge and looked down, she saw him hanging, clutching the line with white-knuckled hands, more clothing wrapped around him and lying on the rocks below. His eyes were squeezed shut, his skin deathly pale.

"Stop wiggling," she said. "You're chafing the line on the rocks."

He made a whimpering noise.

"You weigh more than I do, so I can't pull you up alone." Especially not with this shoulder, she thought. "I'll take a look around."

Behind her she heard footsteps on gravel. When she turned, she saw the same large lady—who was now eyeing her distrustfully—and a small, wiry man.

"Could you help me?"

Together, she and the man pulled Cole up the cliff. He stood and dusted himself off.

"How'd that happen?" Riley asked.

"When I saw the gun, I ran for cover behind this house. I ran through the hanging clothes, not realizing there was a drop-off right on the other side."

"You're lucky you broke the clothesline."

"I'd consider myself lucky if I hadn't fallen at all."

Riley turned to the man. "Thanks for the help. Are you folks all right?"

The woman said, "That crazy man forced all of us into the house with his gun."

"I saw a baby all alone back there." Riley pointed.

"He took her mother first. She's back home now. She called the police."

Cole glanced at Riley. "We need to go back and retrieve the backpack." He turned to the Maltese couple. "We were having a picnic. We need to go get our things."

The man and woman nodded.

Cole took Riley by the arm and steered her toward the path. "I really don't want to get involved with the cops."

"Me neither. We don't have enough time here to do half of what I want to do. That doesn't include spending all afternoon talking to the police."

When they returned to their picnic spot, they packed up and headed back, retracing their steps. Cole walked ahead, keeping up a brisk pace. Neither of them attempted to make conversation.

Riley thought back to those few short weeks when she and Cole had first met. Riley had rescued him swimming out at sea, but he was gone again before she ran into Diggory Priest in Pointe-à-Pitre. She walked herself through those weeks in her head. There was only one time that Cole and Diggory had met face-to-face. It was at the mouth of the Indian River, when Dig told her that her father was ill and she needed to return home. Cole had only seen Dig for about five minutes, six years ago.

But if it wasn't Dig, who was it?

Once they got to the road, they found a shortcut into the city through a tunnel. They made their way to Republic Street and started walking uphill toward the center of the old city.

"I can't believe that bastard was spying on us with a nano drone," Cole said.

"I didn't think anyone outside the military had access to drones that small yet. I've heard they have even smaller ones now. They literally look like little mosquitoes."

"So you did see him, didn't you?"

"See who?"

"Diggory."

"Cole, I saw a man."

"Oh, don't start. What's the matter with you?"

"It was the same man who rear-ended us back in Turkey, Cole. But it wasn't Dig. What about all that scar tissue all over his face?"

"What are you talking about, scars? Other than the long hair, the man I saw on those rocks hasn't changed one iota since the day I first met the bastard in Dominica."

CHAPTER TWENTY

The Palazzo Magistral
Via Condotti, Rome

April 12, 2014

When Virgil entered the office, it was as though Signor Oscura had not moved since their last meeting. It was always like that. Virgil suspected that if he ever saw the man out on the street, he might not even recognize him. He seemed to exist only in this office.

Virgil nodded when the man looked up from his desk.

"So, how are things going out at the villa?"

"My men are settling in, sir. Getting the lay of the place. It's a big property for four guys to cover, but they are some of the best in the business."

"While the guest list is not the same as the Sovereign Council, this group is more controversial. We certainly don't want anything about the meeting leaking to the press. And it's possible some of our more outspoken members may attract unwanted attention. Threats could come from many different directions."

"I understand."

"Easter Sunday is the twentieth of April, and some guests will only be staying for that. Others will stay on for the dual canonization mass the following week. And not all of our guests are Catholic. Many are Protestants and actively anti-Catholic, but they like to come look at all the pomp and ceremony. We need to make sure we can keep the peace within the house as well as without."

"Not sure we can do that, sir. If an actual fight breaks out, you can count on us to break it up, but my men and I aren't trained to be diplomats."

Signor Oscura wore a half smile when he said, "I guess not. Frankly, I don't know what to expect from many of our newer members. Back when acceptance to the Order required proof of noble blood, we could count on a certain level of decorum."

Virgil stood silent with his hands clasped behind his back and stared out the window behind the executive director.

"No insult intended, Virgil."

"None taken, sir."

"Before the weekend of the canonization, on Friday evening, we are going to have the strategic planning meeting of the Guardiani in the villa's chapel. Everything else, having all the other guests in for the Holy Week celebrations and the canonization, these are all excellent camouflage for this event. There cannot be any evidence that this meeting took place. I'd like to have all your men on hand to secure the chapel."

"Yes, sir."

"And what's happening with the search?"

"Thatcher and the woman flew to Malta last night. My man arrived in Valletta this morning. He phoned me a couple of hours ago to check in."

"And?"

"He was using a drone for surveillance. He recorded them discussing some code or cipher that Thatcher's father left in his journal. We have the cipher text now, and I've texted it on to a pal of mine who's a hacker. He's got password-breaking programs that might be able to crack it."

"You know the Order has many resources. If your associate has no luck, I can put you in touch with our talent pool."

"Thank you, sir."

"This is all excellent news." The man reached forward and awakened his computer. He began to read on the screen.

"Is there anything else, sir?"

The man lifted his hand and made a motion as though shooing him out of the office.

Virgil stepped slowly down the stairs, his eyes staring straight ahead. He hadn't told the story of his man being seen, the couple chasing him, and his man getting a shot off in Malta. His guy had had to lay low for a while after that. The Malta police had been all over that part of the island. He'd lost the couple and was heading back to the apartment where they were staying.

Dude was a fuckup. Virgil would have to do this himself. When he'd hired his old buddy, he hadn't realized how important this mission was. He still might be able to use him at the villa for security. He'd bring him back to Rome.

Once out on the street, he turned right and walked down to the intersection, where he hailed a taxi. He checked his watch. He was supposed to call her at 7:00 p.m. That didn't leave much time. He handed the driver his card with the address of his apartment. It was the only way he could communicate with these damn cabbies who didn't even speak English.

The traffic was bad at that time of the evening, and it was already after seven by the time the driver let him off. Virgil unlocked the door and hurried up the stairs. His apartment was on the third floor. Once inside, he turned on the laptop computer on the table in his small kitchen.

While it was booting up, he went into the bathroom to take a piss. When he was finished, he paused in front of the mirror. The black shirt was okay. He'd adjust it so she couldn't see the cross on the pocket. His white-blond hair was sticking straight up. He didn't want her thinking he looked like fucking Einstein. He leaned over the basin and wetted his hair, then grabbed a comb and combed it straight back. He stared at the mirror. The ex always said she fell in love with his blue eyes. At least, she used to say that, before she started screaming at him and calling him a monster and a murderer.

Virgil hurried out to the computer and sat down in the straight-backed wooden chair. He clicked on the icon for Skype and felt his heart rate increase at the familiar sound of the program starting up. He had been practicing for this call for a week. The video image on the screen cut off the top of his face, so he pressed a finger against the top of the screen to adjust the internal camera. There was only one number in his contact list. When he was satisfied with how he looked, he clicked on it.

She answered almost immediately. Her face filled his screen. "Hi, Daddy."

"Hey, sweetheart. Happy birthday." He wondered if he should have said something about it being her sweet sixteenth. It had been so long since he'd been around kids; he had no idea if that was cool, or if she'd think he was stupid.

"Thanks."

Neither one of them spoke then. There was always a time lag with this computer stuff, and he didn't want to interrupt her in case she started talking. He could see her mother in the shape of her face, but she had his icy blue eyes and blonde hair. She had grown into a beautiful young woman.

"So, where are you?" she asked.

"In Rome. I've been working here for a while."

She had reached out to him. She'd found an old email address on her mom's computer, and they'd been writing back and forth for just over a month now. Bonnie had been the one to suggest Skype.

She appeared to be squinting at her monitor. "You know, Mom never says much about you. Well, nothing nice, anyway. And you weren't around much even when you and Mom were still married. And I was pretty little when you left. I don't really remember you."

"I remember you, Bonnie. Real well. Cutest baby I ever saw, even if you did cry all the time, and sometimes that crying made me crazy. I remember teaching you to ride a bike with training wheels. And carrying you on my shoulders to go to the Fourth of July parade in Charleston."

"That's it? That's all you remember?"

"No, I just don't want to do all the talking. Tell me about what you're doing for your birthday."

"Not much. Mom said I couldn't have a party because I'm failing two classes at school, and she doesn't like my boyfriend. She can be such a bitch sometimes."

Virgil had no idea how to respond to that. While he agreed with his daughter about her mother, he thought he ought not to tell her that.

"Which classes are giving you trouble?"

She rolled her eyes and flipped her long hair over her shoulder. Virgil reckoned there were lots of boys showing plenty of interest.

"Health class and English. Coach Nader is such a perv. He stares at the girls' boobs all the time. I can't stand going to his class. Me and Jenny skip seventh period and go over to Circle K, where the clerk likes us. He sells us cigarettes. And the other class is English. I'm good in English, but the teacher hates me. Just 'cuz I was late turning in two assignments, and she caught me texting in class, she failed me."

Again, he had no idea how to respond. He'd always known this wasn't going to be easy, but he hadn't realized she would sound like she was from another planet. And Coach Nader? He didn't like the sound of that.

He heard a muffled voice in the background, shouting, "Bonnie! Who's that you're talking to?"

She looked over her shoulder, then turned back to the screen. He saw fear in her eyes. "Shit, Daddy. Mom'll kill me if she catches me talking to you. Gotta go. Bye."

He opened his mouth to say good-bye to his daughter, but the computer chimed and the video window closed.

Virgil sat there staring at the screen showing his Skype contacts page, the sound of her voice seeming to echo in the empty room. Over and over he heard her voice say, "Daddy."

CHAPTER TWENTY-ONE

The Grand Master's Palace
Valletta, Malta

April 12, 2014

Dr. Günay came running down the hall, her flats slapping the marble. Her hands flopped through the air like a pair of birds trying to alight on her shoulders. "Oh, I'm delighted to see you!" she called out. The girl who stood at the base of the staircase directing tourists giggled behind her hand.

"Great to see you, Dr. Günay," Riley said.

Riley extended her hand, but the stocky historian brushed it aside and moved in for the embrace.

"It's Najat, remember?" She stood on her tiptoes and smacked air kisses at both cheeks.

Cole she embraced even more enthusiastically, and from the color of his face, Riley reckoned the woman had a good grip on him.

"We had another delay in the boatyard," Riley said, "so we decided to fly over here for a couple of days." As they had walked the streets to the Grand Master's Palace, Riley and Cole had agreed to say nothing to Dr. Günay about the shooting.

"How wonderful! Now you are on my home turf, I would like to show you around."

"We'd like that, too. Nothing like having the museum's boss as your tour guide."

"Come upstairs. We'll start with the armory."

Judging from Cole's reaction, the collection here in Malta was far more extensive than what he had seen in Rhodes. They walked through halls with paintings, tapestries, suits of armor, swords, and jewels.

But after a while, Riley listened with only half her attention to the conversation between Cole and Najat. Riley was thinking about the cipher. Cole's background was archeology, and he retained all this history stuff, but after twenty minutes Riley's eyes started glazing over.

She thought about Hazel's words. *Stop doubting him and start helping him.* She couldn't figure out who the shooter was, but maybe she could solve the cipher.

She had memorized the letters: VYIPMMLU. Cole had mentioned a shift cipher. If she remembered correctly, that was where you wrote out the alphabet and then wrote out the alphabet again on top, but you shifted over a few places so the second alphabet might start with the letter *A* written above the letter *E*. Since *E* is the fifth letter of the alphabet, that meant the key to that cipher was the number five.

Dr. Günay's voice droned on in her ear. "The Maltese armorers became fabulous craftsmen as the Knights demanded more and more battle and ceremonial armor. You see, this suit of armor for Grand Master Adrien de Wignacourt is inlaid with gold over the steel."

"It's a work of art," Cole said.

"Indeed. Many craftsmen came to Malta from other parts of Europe. Often, they followed a Knight here, stayed on, married, and then taught the trade to their children. By the eighteenth century, Maltese metal craftsmen were renowned throughout Europe."

Riley tuned them out and thought about a number key. Cole's birthday was November 19, 1973. She pulled her iPhone out of her pocket and opened the calculator. If she wrote out the date numerically as 11-19-1973 and then added up all the integers, she got 32. With 26 letters in the alphabet, an offset of 26 would result in no change— but if she were to offset 32 times and overlap, the result would be 32 minus 26, which is 6.

"Are you okay, Riley?" Dr. Günay asked.

Riley looked up. The others were more than thirty feet ahead of her, looking back in concern. She realized she had stopped walking.

"I'm fine, but a bit tired. We've been walking around the city since early this morning. I really would like to sit down for a bit."

Cole hiked the backpack up higher on his shoulder, and she heard a long sigh from his direction. He was still angry over her refusal to accept that the shooter had been Diggory Priest.

"I understand." Dr. Günay waved her hand at the docent standing by the gallery door. "Peter," she said. "Would you please take this young lady to my office?"

The young man nodded.

"We'll finish up in less than an hour. We'll join you then."

The young man led Riley down the main hallway that overlooked the courtyard. He opened an unmarked door to a beautiful room with sunlight pouring in through the high windows. The furnishings—a desk, armoire, chaise, and chairs—looked like they should have been on display rather than put to everyday use.

Peter pointed to the liter bottle of water on a side table with several glasses. "There is water there. Can I get you anything else?"

She shook her head. "No, this is great. Thanks."

He slipped out the door. Riley settled down on the chaise with a glass of water and took her notebook and mechanical pencil out of her shoulder bag. She needed to see what she was doing.

Cole thought it might be a shift cipher, so she'd begin with what she knew about those. She wrote out the cipher word at the top of the page in all caps. VYIPMMLU. Then she wrote out all twenty-six letters of the alphabet. Above the letter *F* she wrote the letter *A* and continued through *U*, then started back at the beginning with *V* all the way until she wrote *Z* over *E*. Then, in soft pencil, she wrote each of the corresponding letters above the cipher text letters. She tried using both alphabets as the cipher text, but the results QTDKHHGP and ADNURRQZ dashed her hope for an early success.

Over the next half hour she worked her way through different combinations from Cole's birthdate and wore the eraser on her pencil down to a nub. She used the difference between the month and day, tried adding the digits of the year, used just the number of the day he was born on. Nothing looked remotely like a real word. But then again, so many Maltese place names didn't look like real words—how could she tell the difference? She used her phone to Google every combination, but she didn't get any hits.

When Cole and Najat came through the door, she was no further along in solving the cipher. She closed her notebook and asked, "So, are you now an expert on the Knights of Malta?"

"He's barely scratched the surface," Najat said.

"What have you been up to?" Cole asked.

She smiled at him and held up her notebook. "Just playing with numbers." Riley wasn't sure he wanted anyone else to know about the cipher. "It's been a long day."

"If I had known you were coming," Najat said, "I wouldn't have booked this meeting tonight. I would love to take you out to dinner. Some other time, perhaps?"

Riley said, "Next time for sure." She got up and joined Cole by the door.

"Excellent. So what are your plans for tomorrow?"

Cole said, "I wanted to go see the National War Museum at Fort Saint Elmo in the morning. We leave on a six p.m. flight back to Turkey, so we'll have some time."

"Perhaps I'll see you there," she said.

They thanked Najat and headed for the street.

"I'm starved," Riley said. "We never got to eat much of our picnic."

"Dr. G. suggested a restaurant along the way back to the ferry dock. They serve Maltese and Italian food, and they're famous for their rabbit stew."

"Weally? Wabbit stew?"

Cole speeded up his pace. "I think I need to get some food into you."

Riley let Cole try the rabbit, while she had an amazing Sicilian seafood stew, which she mopped up with slices of hot and coarse Maltese bread. Seven o'clock was early for dining in Valletta, and there were only two tables occupied in the restaurant when they arrived. The waiter had tried to steer them to a window table, but Cole insisted on a table in the back.

"At least in here we can be fairly certain no nano drones are going to be cruising by," Cole said.

"I'm worried about where that guy got hold of a drone that tiny. Seriously. I think that means he has military connections."

"Since he is your old boyfriend who used to work for the CIA, I don't think you should be so surprised."

Riley was about to insist again that there was no way that man was Diggory, when the waiter came by to clear their dishes and tell them about their choices for dessert.

Once the waiter returned to his post at the end of the bar, she realized that he had saved her from falling back into the same routine. She was supposed to be trying to help Cole, not criticizing him. She decided to change the subject. She told Cole about her efforts with the cipher text.

"I don't have any idea whether or not I'm on the right course."

"The double letters trouble me."

"I thought about that. I decided to look into common double letters, and which letters were never doubled in English."

"That doesn't help much," Cole said. "Only Q and Z never appear doubled in any words."

"Yeah. That's what I found out. Words like vacuum and glowworm aren't common, but they exist. Still, words that end with double consonants followed by two letters are not uncommon. Get it? UNCOMMON? That one could be our word."

Cole shook his head. "You're getting silly," he said.

"So what's your theory?"

"I remember my dad telling me that he would sometimes introduce double letters like that to throw people off. In fact, the original word doesn't have to have doubled letters. There's another type of shift cipher called a variable-shift cipher. That means that the amount you shift varies for each letter of the cipher."

"Oh, great." Riley pulled her notebook and pencil out of her bag. "Look." She riffled through the pages she had filled that afternoon. "With a simple shift cipher, it took me four pages to get nowhere."

"No, that was good. It's just as important to rule things out. You may not have found the right answer, but you ruled out lots of wrong ones."

"Fine," she said. "So explain to me how a variable-shift cipher might work."

"Okay. Start with a clean alphabet on your page."

"Got it," she said. "Right here."

"And you've got the cipher text on the page, too. Good. The cipher text is eight letters long, so we are looking for a number that is also eight digits."

"So that's like tens of millions, right?"

"It could be. But it could also be several numbers strung together. Have you thought about the distance between the real towns that are mentioned? There are four real towns, and if all the distances are in double digits, that would give us eight digits."

"Great. And we don't even have a map of Malta here."

"You could use a map app on your phone."

Riley took out her phone and opened the browser. She had the entire passage from the journal stored in a note there. Then she set the phone down on the table next to her notebook.

"Wait a minute," she said. "Eight digits. I was just thinking. I was so sure it was going to have something to do with your birthdate, and then I thought—look." She wrote the date of his birthday on the page with no slash marks or dashes between the numbers. 11191973. "See? November 19, 1973. It's eight digits."

"Excellent," Cole said. "So here's how it works. Draw a grid with three rows of eight boxes. Write the cipher text in the middle row and the number key in the top row."

"Okay." Riley drew the boxes. "This is starting to feel rather familiar."

"Now, for the first letter you have the letter V and the number 1. That means you shift one place to the right of V. For Y, you shift one place right to get Z."

"I've got it." Riley counted off the spaces in her alphabet and soon had the letters WZJYNVSX written in the bottom box.

"Crap," Cole said. "That doesn't even look like one of these weird Maltese words."

Riley took a sip of her wine and stared at the boxes. She had felt so sure they were on the right track when she'd realized Cole's birthdate had the same number of digits.

"Wait a minute. Remember when we were in the Caribbean and trying to follow your father's clues to find *Surcouf*? It often turned out that he did things in the opposite way you would expect. The natural thing is to shift right. I've been doing that all afternoon as I've tried different combinations. What if we shift backward? Go left."

"Oh, yeah. That sounds just like James Thatcher. Try it."

There wasn't any eraser left on her pencil, so Riley crossed out the bottom row and drew a fourth row of boxes. She wrote the new letters in the boxes and came up with UVHGLDER. She dropped the pencil into the crease for the book's binding and sighed.

"I give up," she said. "Let's go back to Alex's place and get some sleep."

CHAPTER TWENTY-TWO

**Aboard the HMS *Upholder*
Off the Coast of Tunisia**

April 9, 1942

Tug was resting in the bunk he shared with one of the other officers, when he heard low voices speaking in Arabic. He sat up and swung his feet down to the steel deck. One of the two agents had been vomiting every night when the sub surfaced to run the diesel engines. Tonight, that would be a big problem.

He grabbed a chart of the coast he'd been memorizing and made his way forward to the ratings' mess. He found the two Arabs sitting there drinking tea. Tug slid onto the bench seat, and he made eye contact with the man seated across the table.

"What's your name again?"

"Ben-sheikh Mohammed." The man's accent sounded more like London than Tunis.

"Okay. Ben." Tug turned to the other man on the seat next to him. "And you?"

"Raheeb."

That one kept his eyes averted, so Tug decided the leader was the man opposite him. He turned to face the first man.

"How are you both feeling?"

"We will be fine," Ben said.

"We can't make any noise going in, and these past few nights your buddy there has been making quite a racket in the latrine. Not sure if he just caught the Malta dog or if he gets seasick."

"You do not have to worry about us."

"That's my job."

Ben eyed him with a look that told Tug the Arabs didn't expect any special treatment. Tug liked that.

"What brings you here?" Tug asked.

"I was studying in London. Economics. I saw an advert for native Arabic speakers."

"But you're Tunisian, right?"

Ben nodded.

"And a Muslim?"

He nodded again.

"So why risk your neck sending messages about troop and ship movements to your country's enemies?"

"It is not about religion. I don't care for the French. Or the Germans. Or the Italians. I hope when this is over, my country will be independent. I believe our best chance for that is with the British."

Tug nodded. "Fair enough." He looked back at the chart on the table. "Has either of you spent much time in small boats?"

"As little as possible."

Tug laughed. "I can see why."

"Just get us to shore and keep our radios dry."

"I will. Look, we're going to be landing you on the coast just to the north of Sousse. This afternoon we went in close and had a bit of a look through the periscope. Have you ever been there?"

"Me, no. But Raheeb is familiar with the area." Ben turned to the other man, and they spoke in Arabic.

Tug didn't like them talking and him not understanding.

Ben turned back. "I apologize. Raheeb speaks little English. Only French and Arabic. He grew up in this part of the world. He has an uncle in Sousse. That's where we're going to stay."

"Good." Tug unrolled the chart and spread it out on the table between them. "Can you ask him about this area?" He rubbed his finger over the section of coast where they intended to land. "We saw some buildings there. Are they inhabited? I'd appreciate any help your mate can offer us regarding what we're going to find ashore."

The only charts available to them had not been updated in more than twenty years. The chart showed the village of Sousse as not much more than a dot. Tug had already experienced many inaccuracies between what their charts showed and what he actually found when he got there. This coastline had really grown up in the years between the wars.

The two men spoke some more, and then Ben translated. "There are a few houses that far outside town, but not many. There are families living in the houses. But he says we should be able to find a deserted section of beach."

"And what about the railway line? Captain Simpson suggested you might use that to find your way into town."

Ben translated for Raheeb, who nodded and then traced his finger on the chart as he spoke.

"Raheeb says he likes this idea to follow the railroad. He knows the area well."

"How far inland will you have to walk to reach the tracks? We couldn't see the railway through the periscope today."

Ben conferred with Raheeb again. The other man raised his voice and pointed to an area on the chart. He shook his head. Ben seemed to be trying to calm him down. Then he translated. "It is about two kilometers inland. He says that here in this area"—Ben pointed to the section of the coast that had made Raheeb so animated—"there is a bridge over a ravine. It is a very narrow-gauge railroad, and he says it would be too dangerous to cross at night. Once, when he was a boy, he saw some children playing on the bridge, and another boy his age fell to his death. He says you should be sure to drop us south of that area."

Charlie appeared in the doorway to the mess. "What are you chaps up to?"

"Just going over the mission and the chart. Turns out our friend Raheeb"—Tug nodded at the man—"grew up around here. He's pointing out where the railroad is. They're going to follow it into the town. And he says there's a bridge right about here." Tug put his finger on the chart and then looked up at his partner.

"Does he, now?" Charlie said.

"Says we should drop them off to the south of it and land them about here."

"Good to know."

"Ben, let me explain how this is going to work. We'll tow you two in the rubber boat. We won't be landing with you. We have another mission to accomplish after we set you blokes adrift. As soon as we get close to the surf line, we'll release you. Can either of you swim?"

Ben spoke in Arabic and Raheeb shook his head. Then Ben said, "I can."

"Hopefully, your boat will stay upright through the surf. If not, hang on to the boat. It will carry you to the beach."

Ben nodded. "And once ashore, we bury the boat, right?"

"Right." Tug looked at his watch. "We have about six hours before we launch. Get him to eat some bread," he said, indicating Raheeb. "It might settle his stomach. Then try to rest. We've got a long night ahead of us."

CHAPTER TWENTY-THREE

The National War Museum at Fort Saint Elmo
Valletta, Malta

April 13, 2014

The streets of Valletta were nearly empty of tourists at ten o'clock on a Sunday morning. Cole didn't like the quiet. Though in fact it would have been easier for someone to follow them on crowded streets, the silence felt spooky. On the bright side, he'd certainly notice a drone if it got near.

"Cole, slow down. We've got plenty of time, and I'd like to take some photos."

Ahead of them was a horse and carriage parked in a special taxi stand just for carriages. The driver was asleep on the front seat. He apparently didn't expect much Sunday morning traffic, either.

After she finished taking photos, Riley fell back into step next to Cole. They were following the perimeter road at the top of the fortified walls. The road would lead out to Fort Saint Elmo, where the museum was located.

"You're awfully quiet this morning," she said. "You've hardly said a word since breakfast."

"I'm trying to figure out who's behind this."

"Oh, Cole, it's a gorgeous, sunny morning in Malta." She reached up and stretched her arms toward the sky. The sun shone on the sun-bleached streaks in her hair.

Cole thought she looked great, and in other circumstances he would like nothing more than to stop and kiss her. But these were not those circumstances. They were in danger, and he had to figure out what was going on before something happened to her. "Riley, you saw the drone."

"I did."

"You chased a man, and he shot at you. He could have killed you, and it would have been my fault."

"Cole, you're not responsible for what some crazy guy did."

"But I'm the reason you were there."

"No," she said. "I'm the reason I was there. I make my own decisions, and I choose to be here by your side."

Cole didn't know what to say to that.

"Besides," she said. "If he just wanted to kill us, we'd be dead."

She was right. He'd had plenty of opportunity to kill them. It would have been easy to shoot them and push their bodies into the harbor yesterday. Instead, he had used a drone.

"What would a drone like that be used for in the military?"

"Cole, I've been out of the service for a long time, so I have no idea what sort of tech they have now, other than what I read online. But I don't think something that small would be weaponized. It must be for surveillance only."

"So it was loaded with a camera and microphone."

"Probably," she said.

"What were we talking about just before we saw it?"

"The cipher text," she said. "You spelled it out, and I said that your birthday was possibly a key."

"And you think the drone recorded that."

Riley put the lens cap back on her own camera. "Yup," she said. "Shit."

"I agree."

The National War Museum proved to be better than Cole had expected. When they bought their tickets, it looked like they were the only patrons that morning. At first, the guy in the booth couldn't even find the tickets under his plate of breakfast and coffee cup.

They walked from one exhibit to the next, silently reading the placards and looking at the displays. After all the research he had done in their searches for the World War II ships in the Caribbean and the Philippines, it was fascinating to see what had been going on in Malta during the same period. The museum showed several films with real footage of the terrible bombing raids Malta suffered during the siege. From the time Italy entered the war, Malta suffered constant bombings. Tons of explosives fell on the little island every day, and few supply ships could get through. The population was on the verge of starvation.

"It's difficult to imagine what this island went through," Riley said as they passed from one room of the museum to the next. Here, glass cases showcased uniforms, guns, and bayonets.

"Yeah. And for what?"

Riley shrugged. "I was in the military for seven years, and I'm not sure I can answer that one."

"Power and wealth."

"Which are about the same thing," she said.

Cole nodded. "One buys the other. Look around us. Think about all the uniforms, weapons, and vehicles from cars to planes to ships. It takes millions of dollars to run a war."

"Make that billions. Worldwide, the amount spent on the military must be in the trillions. There was a time when governments made their own weapons and supplies, but with each new conflict, more and more of the business of war has been privatized."

"Yeah. Like my father wrote in his journals, the men who have been pulling the strings behind the scenes cared far more about dollars than ideology."

"But what about the Knights of Saint John and the Crusades? Surely back then it was about religion."

"Riley, I'm not saying that the soldiers, the boots on the ground, weren't fighting for ideals. The Knights saw themselves as soldiers for Christ. But to the pope, it was all about the power of gaining control of Jerusalem. And during the Second World War, there's evidence the pope was on the side of the fascists."

Riley pointed to a photo of a group of young British artillerymen. "I guess these men would have said they were fighting for freedom, for king and country."

"Yeah, but remember, my father was one of those men. While he thought that way when he first joined up, he later had his eyes opened. Throughout history, the fight has always really been about power—to defend it or to increase it."

"What about the Middle East today—what's going on in Afghanistan and Iraq? Surely that's about religious extremism."

"To some it is—just the modern version of the Crusades. Or the continuation of it," Cole said. "The young men strapping on the suicide vests think they are doing it for Allah, but I don't think for a minute that the men at the top on either side care much about that. I don't think it's a coincidence that the lands where we're fighting today are among the richest oil fields in the world."

The next room they entered told the story of the maritime war in Malta.

Cole saw a display titled *The Submarines of the 10th Flotilla in Malta.*

"Great. More submarines," he said.

He heard fast footsteps behind him and a voice called out, "Good morning!" It was Dr. Najat Günay.

"Morning, Dr. G.," he said.

She kissed Riley on both cheeks. "I think it's so cute when he calls me that," she said.

Cole pointed to the photos of subs at anchor in Marsamxett Harbour off the submarine base at Lazaretto, Manoel Island. "It is difficult to be cheerful when reading about this chapter of your island's history."

"The captain of the ferry we take across to Sliema pointed out the sub base the first time we came across," Riley said.

"Yes, the Tenth Flotilla was made up of British U-class submarines. They inflicted great damage on Italian shipping trying to supply the Axis forces in North Africa."

"It says here the submarines even brought in supplies sometimes."

"Yes," Najat said. "The blockade was making things very bad on the island. People were starving. They called it the 'Magic Carpet Service.' Every submarine that was transferred to Malta would arrive loaded with food, medicine, even aviation fuel. Sometimes they even welded external containers to the submarine's casing. But that's not the most fascinating story about our subs."

"What is?" Cole said.

"Well, when the Germans took most of continental Europe in 1940, the British wanted to invade France, but they weren't ready yet. So Churchill organized the first commando units. He gave a famous speech announcing they would 'set Europe ablaze.' These commandos were the first British Special Forces operatives."

"My father was a British commando paratrooper. He parachuted into Italy."

"Really? I'd love to hear more about him," Dr. G. said. "Here in Malta, we had the Special Boat Unit. They had these flimsy little folding kayaks made of canvas and bits of wood. The men and their boats were assigned to the submarines. The sub would surface in the dead of night and these fellows would paddle off in their little boats. They attached limpet mines to enemy ships, blew up railroads, and pulled off all sorts of secret missions."

"Oh my God," Riley said. "Cole—" She yanked her shoulder bag open and pulled out her notebook.

"What is it?"

"Cole, I'm looking at all these dates on the exhibits." She stuck the pencil in her mouth and started leafing through the pages of her notebook. "Your father was British!" she said, her words slurred due to the pencil.

Cole looked at Dr. G. She seemed just as puzzled by Riley's behavior. "Yeah. That's right," he said.

She pulled the pencil out of her mouth and looked at him like he was some kind of dullard. "They do it the other way around."

"What are you talking about?"

"Dates. I'm talking about dates."

"Okay."

"Cole, British people write out dates not with the month and then the day. They do it the other way around. Your birthday wouldn't be 11-19. It would be 19-11."

Cole bit his upper lip then said, "I can't believe I didn't think of that."

Riley set her notebook down on a glass case filled with military medals. It was open to the page with her graph. She changed the numbers to read 19111973.

"It only changes two letters," she said. "The second and the fourth." She counted off the numbers on her alphabet and changed the V to a P and the G to an O.

Cole looked at what she'd written in the box. He read aloud: "UP-HOLDER." He looked up at the two women. "Does that mean anything to either of you?"

Dr. G. said, "Of course! There's a picture of it right there." She pointed to a grainy black-and-white photo in a display on the wall. It showed a black submarine with her crew standing on deck. "That was the name of the most famous submarine in the Tenth Flotilla here in Malta. Her captain was awarded the Victoria Cross."

"What happened to her?"

"She was lost on patrol. Went down with all hands."

"Where?"

"No one really knows. There's no record of her sinking. She simply never returned."

CHAPTER TWENTY-FOUR

The Silversmith Shop
Vittoriosa, Malta

April 17, 1798

The coffeepot represented months of work and was the finest piece Arzella had ever made. The woman in the magnificent embroidered silk dress stood examining the pot, holding it casually and waving it through the air as she spoke.

"This would never happen in Mdina. They have more respect there. The people understand their place there. The Knights have spoiled the people here in Vittoriosa. You understand that merely because my husband is Count Gallego is no excuse to charge this ridiculous price."

Arzella kept her eyes lowered and waited for the woman to finish her tirade. She knew the price was fair. The three cast feet had paws at the bottom and were attached to the pear-shaped pot with delicate leafy foliage. The engraved grapes and leaves were exquisite. She had drawn the design herself. It was not an imitation of the latest styles from Paris, like what so many of the other local silversmiths created.

"You say Pierre Brun is your father?" The woman flicked her wrist and the pot swung by its ebony handle.

Arzella placed a hand on her stomach and thought, *Please, don't drop it*. She said, "Yes, madame."

"Hmm. I have heard the name."

Of course you have. That is why you are here. He is the most famous silversmith in Malta. "Yes, madame." Arzella's stomach contracted, and she swallowed to force down the sour taste.

"Is your father here? I would like to speak to him about this exorbitant price."

"I'm sorry, madame. He is not." She swallowed again. "I am not certain when he will return."

"My soiree is three days hence. This pot would serve me well, I should think. I return to Mdina in the morning, and I will pass by this shop before I depart. I expect to speak to Monsieur Brun himself."

The lady exited the shop with a great swishing of her skirts. Arzella placed one hand on the counter to steady herself. After several seconds the dizziness passed.

"Arzella," her father called.

She straightened her skirts and brushed her hands over her hair. After clearing her throat, she plastered a smile onto her face and walked into the shop's back room, their apartment.

"Yes, Papa?"

"What an awful woman," he said.

"Yes, she was even worse if you could have seen her." She went on to describe the woman, embellishing the tale with details that she knew would amuse him.

He smiled weakly at her imitation of the lady's posture. "I'm so sorry I cannot go out there myself and save you from these indignities."

Her father had not left his bed in more than a week now. Not even to use the latrine. He knew more about indignities than she ever would. He used a pot kept under the bed, and had to ask his daughter's help to bathe himself.

"Papa, please. Stop apologizing. I enjoy working in the shop, but I would rather be working back here—making things rather than selling things."

"Selling is necessary, and the village knows you as a shopgirl. It would be best for you to go back to working only in the evenings when no one will see you."

Arzella sighed. "Would you like a cup of tea?" She crossed to the stove and put the kettle on. "Are you warm enough?" She added some wood to the fire.

"Arzella, I need to talk to you."

"Papa, I am very busy with the shop right now. Perhaps later this evening."

"But that is the problem, my child. You go out every evening."

She started to object, then she thought, *I am not a child.* "I would be happy to stay in one evening to talk to my father."

"Only one evening? I worry about you, *ma petite.* He is a Knight. What decent man will want to marry you if your reputation is sullied?"

"Oh, Father." Again she felt her stomach clench in a spasm. Tea, maybe that would calm her rebellious belly.

"I am serious," her father said. "A good girl does not go out walking alone with a Knight—much less sailing. Please, my child. Before I go, I want to see you happily married to a husband who will care for you."

"First of all, you are not going anywhere anytime soon." Arzella wanted to believe this. She also wanted to tell her father that she would never love another man like she loved Alonso, but he would not understand. "And I can care for myself. You have seen the quality of the work I do. Never has anyone suspected it is not your own. I don't need a husband." She poured the hot water into the teapot.

"Yes, you are the most talented artist I have ever seen. I've had two apprentices in the past, and you learned the trade in less than half the time. But who will buy your work when I am gone? Do you think they will want it if they know it was made by a female artisan?"

"Why not?" She grabbed two cups, and they clanked loudly when she set them down next to the sugar bowl on the silver tray.

"You know very well that you can't change what others think."

She opened the cupboard to get her father a piece of cheese, and the odor enveloped her. Her hand flew to her mouth and she gagged.

"Do not be foolish."

She wiped her mouth. "Times are changing, Papa." Her voice sounded hoarse.

"Not so much that you can be in a Knight's company without a chaperone. I dare not think what you are doing. What would happen if the Order thought you presented a problem for them?"

"I do what *I* choose," she said softly. "Those old stories about shipping girls off to Gozo were just to scare us into doing what our parents wanted us to do." She placed the tray on the small table beside her father's bed.

"Take my hand, my child."

The skin on her father's hand felt loose over the bones. "Yes, Papa."

"They are not just stories, *ma petite*. Do you think, living together here in this small room, I can't smell him on you when you return in the evenings? Do you think I have not noticed the change in you?"

She lowered her eyes. "Papa, please."

"You think I don't see the color of your skin in the mornings? I see more than you credit me for. I will not let them take you from me. You cannot let anyone else become aware of your condition."

"What condition?" The voice came from the doorway at the back of the shop. Madame Benier stood just outside the door, at the base of the stairs that led to her first-floor apartment above. "I'm sorry if I'm intruding, but I was looking for Pierre Antoine."

Arzella let go of her father's hand and stood. She opened her mouth to answer the woman, but she felt it coming. She tried to make it to the sink in time, but she bent at the waist in the middle of the room, and vomit splashed onto the floor.

"Oh," Madame Benier said, stepping back. "*That* condition."

CHAPTER TWENTY-FIVE

The National War Museum at Fort Saint Elmo
Valletta, Malta

April 13, 2014

Riley looked at Cole. "Do you think?"

"Must be."

Najat looked back and forth at them, a tentative smile on her face. "I don't really understand any of this, but I take it this is good?"

Cole stepped over to the door of the exhibit room and looked both ways down the hall. When he returned, he asked Najat, "Is there someplace we could talk? Someplace quiet?"

"Certainly," she said. "Follow me."

She led them through a door marked "Private" to a large work-room. Two people stood at a table, working on some large photographs. The museum workers nodded as the three of them walked through. The door on the far side of the workroom opened into a gray kitchen with a refrigerator, a stainless-steel sink, and a Formica dinette.

She motioned for them to sit. "No one will be coming in here for another hour or two. They take their lunch here."

When they were settled, Cole told Najat the story from the journal, about his father's internment in an Italian POW camp. "He wrote about meeting another commando there from Special Forces. He hid part of the story in a cipher. My father liked to kid around," he said.

Riley liked how Cole downplayed his father's paranoia. Just kidding around.

"I never really knew my father, so I want to learn as much as I can about him. But we have a plane to catch, so we haven't much time. What can you tell us about the *Upholder*?"

Najat looked at her watch. "I can tell you what I've learned working here, but there is someone else who possibly could tell you more."

"What do you mean?"

"One of the volunteers here at the museum is a retired shipyard worker. He is ninety-five years old, but in excellent health. He enjoys telling our patrons his stories about working on the submarines during the war." She pulled her phone out of her pocket. "He lives close by. If he's free, perhaps he can meet with you."

"That would be amazing," Cole said.

"I know he worked on the *Upholder* because I have heard him mention Captain Wanklyn." She swiped her finger on her phone until she found what she was looking for, then she pushed back her chair and said, "Excuse me." She stepped away from the table and began speaking in Maltese into the phone.

"What do you think?" Riley asked.

"If this guy worked in the dockyard here during the war, maybe he'll be able to tell us who my father was talking about."

"Why do you think your father was pointing you to the submarine?"

"I haven't the foggiest idea. What would a World War II submarine have to do with the Knights of Malta?"

"I can't figure it out, either."

From Najat's tone of voice it was obvious her call was ending. She turned around, slid the phone back into her skirt pocket, and announced, "The fates are smiling on you. He's on his way over. He was already close by, so he'll be here shortly. I think one reason he has lived so long is he takes long walks every day. The front desk will call us when he gets here, and we'll join him on his walk."

"Thank you so much for setting that up. What can you tell us about the *Upholder* in the meantime?"

"David Wanklyn was her commander from the day she was launched. He was a career navy man, Wanklyn. He entered the Royal Naval College at Dartmouth when he was only thirteen years old. It was his preference to go into submarines, in spite of the fact that he was quite tall. He was ambitious, and perhaps he thought he would rise through the ranks faster there. It worked. He was appointed to command the HMS *Upholder* in 1940 at the age of twenty-eight. During his sixteen months in the Mediterranean, Wanklyn and the *Upholder* destroyed more ships than any other sub. She became the most successful British submarine of the Second World War."

"No wonder they gave him the Victoria Cross," Riley said.

"Yes, he was quite a remarkable man. We have several photographs in our collection of Commander Wanklyn and his crew. They look so happy in some of the photos. It's heartbreaking." Dr. Günay looked away.

Riley leaned forward and touched her arm. "You've told us so much about him without using any notes."

The museum administrator laughed. "Yes, I've listened to my friend. His name is Gavino Ebejer. I've heard him give his talks about Wanklyn many times. His eyes fill with tears every time, and mine do, too. I believe it is what made me want to become a historian—my ability to empathize with people who are long dead."

"What kind of man was Commander Wanklyn?" Cole asked.

"His men loved him. He was well over six feet tall, and it must have been very difficult for him to live in the cramped quarters of a U-class submarine. The U's had originally been designed as targets for antisubmarine training exercises. They were cheap to build and simple, at one hundred and ninety feet long and only sixteen feet wide. But Commander Wanklyn never complained. His men said he almost never slept."

"I can't imagine the conditions in those boats," Cole said. "I've been in submarines. There sure isn't much room in there."

The phone in Dr. Günay's pocket sang a little tune. "That would be Gavino." She reached into the folds of her skirt, found the pocket, and took out the phone. "Hello? Yes, we'll be right out."

When Riley got her first look at Gavino Ebejer, she was reminded of the other two men of his generation she had met in the past several years: Henri Michaut and the man she'd known as PeeWee, Ozzie Riley. Neither man had been very tall, and here again stood a man no more than five foot six, with a wiry build and a head covered with a flat black cap. He wore blue jeans belted in tight at the waist, a pressed long-sleeved shirt, and brown leather sandals. He carried a jacket folded over his arm. All three of these World War II veterans had worked on submarines in various capacities, and their size had undoubtedly been an asset.

The years had been less kind to Mr. Ebejer than to the other two vets. This man's skin was mottled with dark-brown spots on his face and hands, and his enormous ears sprouted tufts of gray hair. The hand that held his cane was curled into a claw from arthritis. Then again, it was several years since she had last seen Henri Michaut, the last survivor from the submarine *Surcouf.* Riley hoped he was still alive on the island of Guadeloupe in the Caribbean.

The old man embraced Najat. She then turned and made introductions.

"I'm very happy to meet you," he said to Riley, extending his free hand. His English was quite easy to understand, in spite of the fact that his mouth had no more than a handful of teeth.

"Thank you for agreeing to talk to us, Mr. Ebejer," Riley said.

He nodded, smiling. "Call me Gavino. I'm very happy to talk about my old friends with my new friends." He pointed down the perimeter road that would take them back to the ferry landing. "We walk this way?"

"Yes," Cole said. "That would be great. We have to get to the airport later today."

"Tell me about your father," the old man said.

As they walked along the top of the old city walls, more of Marsamxett Harbour came into view. Several sailboats glided across the blue water, and Riley tried to imagine what the harbor had looked like when it was full of submarines moored off the Lazaretto.

Cole again told the story about his father's stay in the Italian POW camp, and the commando officer he had befriended there. He explained that they became good enough friends that they met in Malta after the war. Cole said he believed the commando must have sailed on the *Upholder*.

"There is only one man this can be. Tug Wilson."

"Tug?" Cole said.

"Yes, that was what we called him. I believe his real name was Ronald or Robert or something like that. The British have so many nicknames. Every military man with the surname Wilson is called Tug. There is always some story behind it."

"What can you tell us about this man Tug?" Riley asked.

"He and Wanklyn were good friends." The old man stopped, put his hands on top of the stone wall, and stared across the water. He pointed with a gnarled finger. "You see the Lazaretto over there?"

"Yes," Cole said.

"Seeing it now, you can't imagine what all of this looked like after months of bombings."

Najat said, "I showed them some of the photos at the museum."

"Ah, then you have seen how it was. During the war, this island was not the sunny Malta that you see here today." He pointed at the white sails of a large yacht slowly tacking into the harbor on the light breeze.

Najat started to say something, but Cole cut her off.

"Did you work at the sub base or at the dockyards in Grand Harbour?" Cole asked.

Riley and Najat exchanged a look. Cole and Gavino were deep into their conversation, and Riley knew when Cole got like that, he was oblivious to niceties or manners. She hoped the museum director would understand.

Gavino pointed his walking stick toward the ferry terminal, and they began walking again. "I worked at the sub base under the Tenth Flotilla's chief engineer, Sam MacGregor. They had dug workshops right into the stone behind the old hospital. All the boats came in needing some kind of repair. That is how I was introduced to so many of the sub captains."

"Did you know Tug?"

"Not so well back then, but I saw him around the Lazaretto when he wasn't on a mission. He went on many patrols on different boats."

"Including the *Upholder*?"

"Yes, many times."

"Did you hear if he was ever taken prisoner in Italy?"

"Yes, he was. After the war, he used to come to visit us in Malta. I got to know him better then. We have a Royal British Legion, Malta Branch, and the fellows like to gather there to have a drink or two. Like all of us, Tug loved to tell his war stories. He stayed in the army for many years after the war. He told me once he did not believe the *Upholder* sank as they say."

"Really?"

"He said after they completed their mission near Sousse, he was transferred to the submarine *Unbeaten* out off Lampedusa. He had orders to continue on to Gibraltar. Damn lucky fellow. He was the last man to see the crew of the *Upholder* alive."

"So what does the Royal Navy think happened to the *Upholder*?"

"Wanklyn went off to resume his patrol off Djerba Island. The next day, the *Upholder* was sent radio orders to join two other subs attacking a convoy off Tripoli. One theory has her sunk by German floatplanes dropping torpedoes one hundred miles north of her patrol area. Another theory has her sunk by an Italian torpedo boat that dropped depth charges, also off Tripoli—although there is also record of a plane identifying their target as a dolphin."

"So no one is certain what happened to the *Upholder*?"

Gavino shook his head. "But on one of his postwar visits to Malta, I heard Tug telling some other vets that *Upholder* had been having problems with her radio antenna. There was never any confirmation that *Upholder* received that message to join the patrol line off Tripoli. Tug said Wanklyn was planning to get into the lee of Djerba Island and have his men work on the antenna. Tug always said they were looking in the wrong place for the sub. He didn't think Wanklyn ever got those new orders."

Gavino stopped at the top of the road that led down to the ferry terminal. He put one of his claw hands on Cole's forearm. "I am going to leave you here. My house is close to the church ahead."

"Thanks so much for spending this time with us," Cole said. "You've been a huge help."

"There are a couple of others at the legion who knew Tug, too. I will ask what they remember. If I find out more, I'll pass it on to our friend Dr. Günay."

Riley shook the old man's hand, too. "Thanks, Gavino. I hope we'll see you again when we return with our new boat in a month or so."

Gavino nodded. "Yes, yes," he mumbled, then he turned back to Cole. "I can hear Tug now, talking to the boys over a glass of beer and saying, 'Someday, somebody is going to find the wreck of Wanks's sub off Djerba. Mark my words.'"

"Have you heard if Tug Wilson is still alive?"

He shook his head and looked at his feet. "Tug died more than ten years ago now." When he lifted his face again, there were tears in his eyes. "It is both a joy and a curse to outlive almost everyone you know."

CHAPTER TWENTY-SIX

Adakoy Shipyard
Adakoy, Turkey

April 13, 2014

Virgil flipped up the infrared night-vision goggles on his headset when he saw the taxi pull up outside the shipyard's chain-link fence. He had been waiting in a rental car parked in the dirt lot across from the shipyard for several hours. From the photos, Virgil recognized the man who climbed out of the cab's rear door. The man's face was illuminated by the red glow of the brake lights. A woman climbed out of the other door, but her hair obscured her face. He assumed she was the former marine. He'd debriefed his man before departing Rome, and he'd learned a great deal about the backgrounds of these two.

He tapped his fingers on the steering wheel. Finally, some action. He rotated his head, stretching his neck muscles.

Their plane had landed several hours earlier, but the airport was about ninety kilometers away. They probably stopped for dinner in town. There were only a few cars in the lot; one he recognized as the Hyundai belonging to the man he'd just observed.

The driver executed a U-turn and the taxi drove off in a cloud of dust. The scene out the windshield of Virgil's car turned pitch-black. He flipped the goggles back down, and then he could see them lit up clearly in black and white. This Gen-3 version of the goggles no longer showed the scene in green and black. The images were much clearer now with the grayscale. He appreciated an employer who provided first-class gear.

He tapped a button on the side of his headgear to increase the magnification. The couple walked along the chain-link fence toward the gate. His car's window was cracked open several inches, and he was close enough to hear their footsteps on the dirt road. Each carried a backpack slung over a shoulder, making it more likely one of them would block his view. At the gate, the man reached out for the electronic keypad. Virgil increased the magnification once again and held his breath. The man punched two keys from left to right on the middle row, but then the woman stepped over and linked her arm through the man's.

Virgil exhaled. Looked like this one wasn't going to be as easy as he had hoped. At least two digits was better than none.

The gate clicked and the man pushed it open. The couple passed through. He watched them head for the dinghy dock to his right. They disappeared from view. Soon, the noise of an outboard pierced the still night and slowly puttered away into the distance.

He knew from the debrief that they were living aboard a sailboat out in the mooring field off the shipyard.

Virgil pulled off the headset and ran his hand through his short-cropped hair. The straps rubbed his scalp. He took his pouch of tobacco out of his jacket pocket and began to roll himself a cigarette as he examined the fence in front of him. Spiraling razor wire marked the top. He had wire cutters in his kit in the backseat, but he would prefer not to leave such obvious evidence of his presence.

He lit the cigarette and inhaled. It was probably still too early. He reached into his other pocket and pulled out his phone to check the time. When the screen lit up, it showed the Google Maps directions he had used to locate the shipyard. He looked up from the bright screen to the keypad across the street and chuckled. The address for the shipyard was still visible on his screen: 4536 Marmaris Adakoy Yolu. He had seen the man push the first two digits, four and five; he bet the code was the street address. Virgil tossed his cigarette out the window and opened his door.

Two hours later he stood at the corner of a woodworking shop and stared across the wide-open space between him and the stern of the newly constructed steel yacht. He wore his black watch cap pulled down low on his forehead, both to cover his blond hair and to shield his skin from the straps of the heavy headgear. A black turtleneck sweater and black cargo pants completed the uniform. He carried his necessary kit in his backpack.

Virgil could make out the name *Shadow Chaser II* painted in silver letters on the navy-blue transom. It was the biggest boat in the yard and the only new construction. Most of the other boats looked like older sailboats; the large steel yacht was off in a corner by itself, tucked up tight against another big boat shed.

In spite of the lazy use of the site's address for the gate code, the on-site security was more extensive than he'd imagined. CCTV cameras panned the open areas, and two armed guards patrolled the yard. Once inside, Virgil had hidden in a machine shop and scouted out the facility. He'd determined that the guards were very regular in their rounds, and they would be easy to avoid. Likewise, the cameras, once he was familiar with their sequence, were no issue. It was all about the timing.

He kept his eyes on the camera on top of the pole to his right. Both guards were at opposite ends of the boatyard at the moment, and as soon as the camera swung away, he would make a run for it. His backpack hung from his shoulders. Everything he needed for this job was inside, in specially made pockets. Even though C-4 was good, stable stuff, he still treated it and all his kit with the utmost respect.

It took him only six seconds to cross the twenty meters of open space. He crouched in the shadows under the yacht, which was propped up on stands; he was pleased that his breathing had not changed. In his business, it was necessary to stay in top form, even if he was no longer a Delta.

While waiting in the car outside the shipyard, Virgil had made the decision to follow through on this plan. The man he had assigned to tail them had sent him a recording of their conversation in Malta. It seemed to indicate there was a chance this Thatcher knew something. Given his past record, and that of the man's father, they could not afford to take it lightly.

At the rear of the boat they had constructed a rough staircase for climbing up onto the teak dive platform. Virgil climbed the stairs and entered the aft deck. His crepe-soled shoes made no noise as he ascended the steps up to the bridge deck. He tried the door to the wheelhouse, and it opened.

Virgil was not an expert when it came to boats, but he thought the yacht's bridge looked like it belonged on a spaceship. Two plush leather chairs faced what Virgil reckoned was fifteen feet of the best navigation electronics available. The work wasn't quite finished—spools of wire, tools, and debris littered the bridge deck. The electronic screens were set into a wood facing, with a shelf-like desk running along the front. Beneath that were the cabinets that offered access to the back side of the electronics. He reached down, opened one of the doors, and saw some wiring trailing down from the instruments above.

Bingo. That's what he was looking for.

Taking off the backpack, he got down on his hands and knees. He withdrew the detonator in its black cloth pouch, along with the half block of C-4. A GPS tracking device was built into the detonator, so that once they launched the yacht, Virgil would be able to pinpoint their location at all times. He removed the night-vision goggles and set them next to his pack, and then took a penlight out of a side pocket. Sticking the light in his mouth, he squeezed his upper body through the cabinet door and surveyed the rat's nest of instruments and wiring. He picked the closest of the large monitors just above his head because the back of the device was beige. If he put the gray-colored C-4 along the side of the casing and moved some of the wires to cover it, it would take a really good pair of eyes to spot it even if someone did crawl in here.

It took him less than a minute to attach the material to the back casing of the instrument, imbed the cellular-activated detonator, and test it all with his phone.

Virgil was sliding out of the cabinet when his foot struck a small spool of wire on the floor. Someone had left a soldering iron balanced on top of the spool, and it rolled to the deck with a clatter.

He froze when he heard the sharp bark of a dog. In the next second, Virgil grabbed his backpack and jumped to his feet. The dog's barking was getting closer. There were three doors leading out of the wheelhouse. Two doors led to the outside decks on either side and one door led aft into the interior. He listened another couple of seconds. Then he heard a man's voice coming from the interior.

Virgil opened the door on the side of the boat that was closest to a building. A security spotlight hanging from the building's rafters lit up that whole half of the vessel. He flattened himself against the outside of the cabin. That was when he realized he'd left his goggles lying on the floor inside.

He heard a man's voice through the crack in the door, which had not fully closed behind him.

"Listen, Leia, I don't hear a thing." The dog whined as though answering him.

Then the man sneezed. "Geez, girl, what a stench." More scuffling noises. "Hey, slow down. Get out of there."

The dog was whining louder now. Impossible to tell how big the dog was, but the bark was deep. Virgil wanted to take a look through the window in the door, but he didn't dare. So far, he hadn't been seen.

"Okay, okay. If you insist."

The man grunted, and Virgil heard a noise like something sliding across the floor.

"What the—" The man's voice indicated concern, but he still had not turned any lights on. Virgil took that as a good sign. So far the man hadn't seen anything that really bothered him.

Virgil reached inside his jacket and placed his hand on his phone. He had already programmed the number on his speed dial and he could detonate. But he would have to get himself off the boat before that. Better to take the man out quietly and retrieve his headset. Replacing the phone, he instead took out his Gerber combat knife and unfolded the high-carbon stainless-steel blade.

Knife at the ready, he placed his other hand on the door lever. He pulled the door open fast. In the dark interior, he could barely make out a young black man carrying the large electronic display with the C-4 affixed. Wires trailed to the deck. The man looked straight at him, unafraid—not the reaction he usually inspired in his victims, and it made Virgil pause a fraction of a second.

That was when the dog lunged and hit him in the center of his chest, knocking Virgil back against the door and sending the knife clattering to the deck. Before he could get up, the black man disappeared out the opposite door, and the dog tried to sink her teeth into his skin through the fabric of his pants.

Virgil backhanded the dog and sent her flying across the deck with a yelp. He grabbed his knife and goggles off the floor and pushed his way through the doorway the man had passed through. He closed the door between himself and the dog, then leaned over the railing. A good twenty-foot drop, but it would be faster than the stairs. He stuffed the goggles in his pack, folded the knife and pocketed it, then slung the pack onto his back. He threw a leg over the steel bulwark. Grabbing the rail, he hung by his hands, then let himself drop.

He expected to reach the stairs at the back of the boat before the man did, but no one was there. He heard the clattering of the dog's nails on the steel deck, and he knew the animal would be there at any moment.

Time to cut his losses. Virgil turned and began fast-walking in the direction of his car. He reached into his pocket and took out the phone. With a touch, the screen lit up. The gate was directly in front of him. The man had seen him, and the C-4 could be traced. No choice.

He tapped the green key and heard the *whomp* of the blast on the other side of the yard.

CHAPTER TWENTY-SEVEN

Tug and Charlie passed their boats up through the forward hatch, then climbed out onto the submarine's deck. The night was inky black, but Tug could smell the odors of land on the fifteen knots of offshore breeze. The sub rose and fell on the long swells. Both commandos were dressed in black clothing, including black watch caps and thickly rubbered shoes. They'd smeared black grease on their faces. The two Arab agents wore black clothes over their more traditional robes. Tug was already at work on the hand pump, inflating the RAF-type black rubber boat, working slowly so as not to make too much noise.

No one spoke. When necessary, Tug used hand signals to direct the men. The night sky was awash with stars, but no moon would rise during their mission. On shore, lights were visible to the south, but the stretch of coastline directly inshore appeared dark and deserted. They could hear the breath-like rise and fall of the surf on the beach.

Captain Simpson hadn't needed the extra man for the mission of landing the Arabs. But once Tug learned about the second part of the mission, he understood why he was needed. One man would take too long to pack in all the explosives. He couldn't carry it all in one trip.

When the frameworks were secured inside the two folding boats, Charlie passed up the waterproof bags that carried the four charges of plastic high explosive they would need for their mission. Each bag weighed twenty-eight pounds, and that included the cortex and fuses required to connect and set off their charge. Charlie distributed the packages evenly in the fronts and backs of their canoes. Into the Arabs' inflatable boat went their radios—also in waterproof bags, but their bags had arm straps. So as not to lose the gear, they were to wear them on their backs—though if the boat capsized in deep water, the extra weight would carry them under. Ropes tied both canoes to the rubber boat.

Tug checked over the men's work. He was considered a perfectionist by those he worked with, and he was proud of that reputation. With explosives, there were no second chances.

When Tug was satisfied that everything was in order, all four men climbed into the boats, where they rested atop the decks. Tug and Charlie also carried tommy guns on their backs and commando knives strapped to their legs. Both men grasped their paddles, and Tug flashed the "okay" sign. The submariners cleared the decks, and the men heard a soft *whoosh* of air from the vents. Water coursed across the decks, and in seconds, the little boats were afloat. The *Upholder* sank beneath them, and the two commandos started paddling.

The shore always looked and sounded closer than it was. Because their boats were so heavily laden and they were towing the rubber boat, the paddle toward shore seemed to take forever. They were vulnerable at sea. In the clear, dry air the starlight was nearly as bright as a new moon, and they knew their silhouettes were targets against the night sky.

Though Tug and Charlie were small men, they were both immensely strong, and they pulled their paddles through the sea, dragging their cargo through the darkness. As they rose and fell in the large swells, Tug grew worried. The big swells might indicate a change in the weather, and he and Charlie had a long night ahead of them.

Finally, Tug saw the iridescent white of the breakers ahead. He signaled to the Arabs. Ben untied the ropes from the raft and flung them to the two Brits, who coiled them up. Tug and Charlie attempted to push the rubber boat with their canoes up into the surf line without going too far inshore themselves. At last, a swell lifted the rubber boat, and Tug and Charlie paddled backward out of the waves.

The first swell passed under the rubber boat without advancing it much. The next swell was larger, and it picked them up and carried them a distance high on top. Then the boat disappeared like a surfer sliding down the face of the big swell. The next swell rose up and prevented Tug from seeing what happened.

"Can you see them?" Charlie whispered.

Tug shook his head. Another very large swell obscured their view. A mist from the breaking surf hung in the air between them and the beach.

"Bloody waves." Then Tug got a glimpse of an overturned boat sliding toward shore in front of a foamy wave.

He thought about how it would feel with those heavy radios on their backs pulling them under.

After the next wave broke, there was a lull between waves. Tug saw the dark outline of what looked like two men, one half carrying the other out of the water.

At least one of them was alive. Surely the other couldn't have drowned that quickly.

Tug checked his luminous compass, then signaled to Charlie with his index finger. They had business to the north.

* * *

They paddled about a mile to where they believed the river entered the sea, and as they got close, they were able to spot the V shape in the coast outline that marked the river mouth. They planned to follow the ravine overland to the bridge. That way there was less chance of them encountering anyone. Even with their heavy loads, the two folding canoes made it through the big surf with little problem.

They hit the beach running and dragged their canoes and the explosives up to some brush cover to hide them from anyone who might happen by. Such chances were slim, but Tug wanted to be sure his ride home would still be there when he got back.

The river was barely a trickle of water across the sand, but judging from the sides of the ravine that started a few hundred feet back from the beach, there were flood seasons when the river carried a much greater volume of water.

They loaded the explosives into two rucksacks. With their weapons and the explosive charges, each man was carrying close to seventy pounds as they started up the near-dry riverbed.

It was slow going over the rocky terrain, but within twenty minutes, they could see the dark outline of the railroad bridge ahead. The Arab might not have been correct in his estimate of two kilometers. The bridge looked to be about a hundred yards across. As they got closer, Tug could see two concrete pillars and the steel girders that carried the track across the gap. It would have been a hell of a fall from up there. No wonder Raheeb didn't want to walk across it.

The two commandos started to climb up the steep embankment to get to the level of the track. Tug had chosen the south side because above the tracks, the embankment rose to a rocky pinnacle. He hoped to find more secure footholds, not just crumbling sandstone. It meant the explosion would be closer to town, though, and once they set it off, they would have little time to get back to their canoes.

With the heavy weight on their backs, the going was slow. Both men were breathing hard. They moved from handhold to foothold, sometimes grabbing the scraggly plants that had rooted in sandy soil, other times knocking loose a small avalanche of rocks and dirt.

"Amazing to think who else might have traveled here." Charlie spoke softly. "People have been living on this coast and sailing this sea for thousands of years. Wish there was better light to see this place."

"Better light and someone might see us."

When they arrived at the tracks, Tug realized that they wouldn't be able to affix the charges out close to the concrete pilings as he had hoped. Their fuse wasn't long enough. They would work on the steel girders about twenty feet out. Maybe they would blow half the embankment away as well. It should put this railway line out of business for a good while.

Tug hung first over one side of the tracks, then the other, as Charlie handed him the plastic explosives and the cortex for connecting them. These were then connected to the fuse.

Hanging upside down as he was, Tug was starting to feel dizzy with the blood rushing to his head. He blinked to clear his eyes. It was important to do this right. If she didn't blow, he wouldn't relish having to climb back up here again.

"Did you hear that?" Charlie said.

"Yeah," Tug said. "I've been feeling the vibrations through my legs on the tracks. How far off?"

Charlie walked back off the bridge to look around the side of the hill. "Bloody hell."

"I guess I'd better hurry?"

"You can say that again."

Tug finished off the fuse, pulled himself back up onto the tracks, and pushed himself to his feet. He was so dizzy he nearly stumbled on the narrow-gauge track. Even only twenty feet out onto the bridge, he would be looking at a nasty fall. He could hear the sound of the train now.

"Come on!" Charlie yelled. He was walking backward down the track, turning the spool and laying out the slow-burning fuse.

Tug followed him off the railroad bridge, and they started down the ravine, spooling out the fuse as fast as they could. They ran out of fuse halfway down the hill.

"You ready to run?"

Charlie nodded.

Tug lit the fuse.

Both men turned and began scrambling down the ravine. They were doing more falling and sliding than running. Above them, the engine rattled out onto the bridge, drawing the train of cars behind it.

It was a short train—only six cars.

Tug and Charlie had just reached the bottom of the ravine and started to run down the riverbed when they heard the blast. Both men turned to look. Tug saw that the last car of the train was only a few dozen feet onto the bridge, but then he and Charlie both had to duck and cover their heads as the debris rained down on them.

Hearing the creaking, screeching noise as the unsupported steel girders bent under the weight of the train, Tug uncovered his head and looked back at the bridge. The train slowed and came to a stop as the track that was now disconnected at the south end bent downward. Then the train began to move backward, very slowly, like a film in slow motion. The train's engineer must have poured on the steam, as smoked spewed from the engine's stack. There was no room on the bridge for anyone to climb out of the train.

Tug looked around for Charlie. Where the hell had he gone? Had he already started for the boat?

Then he saw a figure running upriver—away from him, and back toward the bridge.

"Parker!" he yelled. "Look out. That train's coming down!"

Charlie stopped, leaned down, and picked up something that looked like the tin lid to a garbage can. Then he straightened up and started to run back toward Tug.

The train's last car slid off the end, and the weight of it made the rest happen so fast the engine was whipped off the track like a toy.

The noise was deafening. The dust cloud that rose from the riverbed engulfed Charlie.

Tug turned and ran. Hard. He didn't slow until he reached the boats. He was dragging his own canoe toward the surf when he heard a voice from the dark.

"Hey, mate, wait till you see what I found!"

CHAPTER TWENTY-EIGHT

Adakoy Shipyard
Adakoy, Turkey

April 14, 2014

The noise of the explosion pulled Cole out of a deep sleep.

"What the hell was that?" he asked, sitting up and throwing off the light sheet.

Riley slept on the half of the bunk next to the hull. She nudged him in the side. "Go," she said.

Cole rolled out of the bunk, sprinted through the main salon, and climbed the ladder. He stood on the second rung, his head poking out the hatch. He reached for the binoculars on the cockpit table.

Behind him Riley said, "Could you move aside?"

"Sorry," he said, but he didn't move. He was too busy trying to focus the glasses through the front plastic window of the dodger. The sky showed a band of pale blue to the east, but the boatyard was still mostly in shadow.

"Smoke," he said. He could see it swirling in the glow cast by the tall yellow lights.

"I can smell it," she said.

He moved aside, but he saw she was already pulling on a pair of shorts. He held out the binoculars. "Whatever it was, it was very close to our boat in there."

"And that means Theo."

"Oh shit." He looked toward the yard again. He felt like someone had just punched him in the gut and knocked the wind out of him. "God no. Not again."

"Get down here and get some clothes on." She grabbed her shoulder bag and edged her way around him. "I'll lower the dinghy and get the outboard started."

"Okay, okay." He felt around the chart table for the shorts he had taken off before going to bed.

"Hurry up," she said. "That smells to me like a bomb."

Cole cut the outboard at the very last minute. The inflatable boat came down off a plane, and he turned it aside so the tube bumped along the floating dinghy dock.

"Go, go!" Riley said. "I'll tie it up."

Cole jumped onto the dock and ran up the ramp. He heard Riley's footfalls right behind him. Hundreds of boats were hauled out for the winter, and he dodged between the wooden cradles and metal stands that supported what were mostly fiberglass sailboats. The wind had cleared some of the smoke, but he was still breathing it in. His throat and eyes burned.

When he came around the last boat before the open work area, he saw a cluster of people, lit up by one of the security spotlights on the wood shop. They were standing around something on the ground. In the middle of the big open area was a crater in the dirt about twelve feet across.

Cole pushed through the group, and he saw Theo sitting on the ground, one arm draped around his dog's neck. He was wearing only his boxers, and his bare chest was mottled with dust and dirt. Bits of debris were stuck in his hair. Blood trickled down the side of his face.

"Theo!"

His first mate turned his head at the sound of Cole's voice. It was still startling to see those undamaged eyes looking straight at him. Theo's blindness had been caused by brain damage, not eye damage, and people often couldn't tell that he wasn't sighted.

"Are you all right?"

"Yeah, mon. Thanks to Leia, here." He scratched the dog's ears and buried his hand in the ruff of fur around her neck.

The people in the crowd were mostly other boat owners who lived aboard their boats while doing the work in the yard. Several people who worked for the shipyard were there, too.

Riley pushed through the crowd and squatted next to Theo.

The night security guard said, "I already called the manager. They're sending a doctor over to take a look at him."

"I told you I'm okay."

Cole didn't think he looked okay.

Riley put her arms around his neck and squeezed. "Shut up and let the doctor check you over when he gets here."

Theo made a face like he was being strangled, but Cole could tell from the smile that he was enjoying the hug.

"What happened?" Riley asked when she finally let him go.

"Can you stand?" Cole asked in a quiet voice.

Theo nodded once. They had worked together for so long, they often understood each other better without saying directly what they meant. Cole knew Theo would understand that it wouldn't be a good idea to discuss it in front of that crowd. Cole looked around at the faces, trying to fix them in his memory. The guy who did this could well be among them.

Riley took one of Theo's arms, and together they helped him to his feet. Theo's dog Leia refused to let him get more than a few inches away from her.

Cole spoke to the crowd. "Look, everybody, we're going to take him up into the boat so he can lie down."

A Brit who had bought a big wooden Turkish gullet boat and was trying to turn her into a luxury charter yacht stepped in front of them. "What the hell happened, Theo?"

"I didn't see a thing," Theo said.

Cole looked at the Brit and shrugged as if to say, *You can't argue with that.*

"If you blokes are using explosives for some job in this yard, I'll personally make sure you're thrown out on your arses. That's dangerous shit."

"We're building a boat, not blowing one up, Colin. When we figure out what happened, you'll be the first to know."

"Right," he said. He turned around and stomped off toward the dinghy dock.

The other onlookers drifted off into the yard. Several of them wandered over and peered into the crater, chatting in a variety of languages.

Riley said, "Come on. Let's get him inside."

"Take me to the site of the blast," Theo said. "I want to feel it."

The three of them walked to the edge of the hole. Theo squatted and felt around on the dirt. "How deep is it?" he asked.

"Two or three feet," Cole said.

They helped Theo back up to his feet, then walked with him over to *Shadow Chaser II*. The sky was brightening and suddenly the lights in the yard clicked off.

"Must be nearly daylight," Theo said. "What a way to start my day." He climbed the steps gingerly, favoring his right side. Riley went ahead to the galley and got a wet towel. Once Theo was seated on a plastic-covered couch in the salon, she cleaned the blood off his head and pulled sticks and bits of plastic out of his hair.

Cole looked at the two of them and thought about how close this had been. He couldn't fathom what he'd do if he lost either one of them.

"That's a nasty gash on your temple." Riley ran her fingers over the top of his head through his close-cropped hair.

"Probably a piece of glass," Theo said. "Ouch!"

"Sorry," she said. "There's an even bigger cut in your scalp."

Cole sat down on the couch next to him. "So what happened?"

"You'd think I'd have learned my lesson by now. When Cole Thatcher starts saying people are out to get him, listen up. Pay attention, Theo."

"Hey, buddy. I'm so sorry. First you end up blind from that mess in the Turks and Caicos. Now this. Again, this was meant for me."

Riley stood up. "Cole, let him tell his story. Once we have the facts, we'll deal with it. Go ahead, Theo."

"Well, Leia here woke me up from a sound sleep with her barking. I didn't hear a thing. She does that sometimes when she hears people walking to the head in the night, but this time it sounded different. Her barking was more insistent, so I got up."

Cole reached over and patted the dog, but she wouldn't take her eyes off Theo.

"She led me up the ladder to the wheelhouse. As soon as I opened the door, I knew someone had been in there. I could smell a stink of cigarette smoke. It was strong—like the stale breath of someone who'd just been standing there."

"In the wheelhouse," Cole said.

"Yeah, mon. But it gets a whole lot worse. See, Leia started pawing at the cabinetry under the instrument panel and whining. We'd been working on installing those last two displays yesterday, and we had one more left to do, so I wasn't surprised to find the doors left open. But

I got down, stuck my head in the cabinet, and the tobacco smell was stronger in there."

"So what did you do?"

"I had a look around. Used my fingers to see. I'd been in there only a few hours before. Just because I can't see doesn't mean I'm no good at wiring. The guys in the yard understand that I've got good hands for it. There's lots I can do. They just have to tell me the color of the wires."

"That makes me feel better," Cole said. "'Cuz recognizing the red wires from the black ones kinda matters."

Riley grabbed his forearm. "Let the man tell his story."

"So what I felt in there was something that hadn't been in there yesterday afternoon when we quit. It felt like somebody had stuck a wad of clay onto the side of that last big display. At first I thought it was a joke, but then I felt some wires going into the clay, and then I found a circuit board. I almost soiled my pants when I realized what it was."

"C-4," Riley said.

"I've seen enough movies, read enough books. All I could think about was all that work we'd put in to make that bridge perfect. It was my dream command center, and I wasn't going to let some tobacco-breathing Neanderthal destroy it. So I climbed out and lifted the display out of the hole she was resting in, plastic explosives and all."

Riley placed her hand on his forearm. "That really took courage, Theo."

"When I think about that crater out there, it feels rather stupid."

"You saved the boat, man. Riley's right. That took balls."

"But wait. The guy was still aboard. I'd just got the monitor out of the cabinet, and the port-side door opened. I thought I was dead for sure."

"What happened?"

"We were face-to-face. I could smell the tobacco on his breath. Leia saved me. She launched herself right at him. I heard her growl, and then the guy crashed against the side of the cabin. I bolted out the starboard-side door and headed aft to get off the boat. I was sure he was right behind me, but the only thing I could do was to keep going. Thank goodness I've walked these decks hundreds of times, and I was able to get down the stairs to the main deck and down the transom ladder with the display tucked under one arm."

"I can see, and I'm always tripping on this boat," Cole said. "You're amazing."

"All I was thinking was, *Get off the boat*. As soon as I thought I was far enough away, I set that thing on the ground and started running. It was only seconds later when it went off. The blast knocked me down, and little pieces of glass and metal flew everywhere. And half the dirt that used to be in that hole landed on top of me."

"Theo, I'm so grateful you seem to be okay," Riley said. "I'll still feel better after a doctor looks at you."

"Definitely," Cole said.

Theo leaned back against the couch cushions. "But why?"

"Because you could have some kind of internal—"

"No, Cole," Riley said, "he means why did somebody just put a bomb in this boat?"

Cole took her hand in his. "It wasn't just somebody, Riley. You know who this was. The same guy who bombed the Marine House in Lima. The guy who gave you those scars on your back."

"Cole!" The word seemed to explode out of her mouth.

"Riley—"

"No. Seriously. I'm not going to argue whether he could have survived that boat explosion or not. But if there is one thing I'd bet my life on, it's that Diggory Priest would never smoke a cigarette. He was an egotistical health junkie. A clean freak. Theo said our bomber had bad smoker's breath. That means it wasn't Dig."

From the stern of the boat they heard the sound of knocking. "Hallo? Captain?" It was a man's voice.

Cole stood up. "That's probably the doctor. I'll go see."

After closing the door, Cole stepped out onto the aft deck. He found not the doctor but a man in a green uniform. A car was parked not far from the crater in the yard. On the side of the car he read the word *Jandarma*.

The officer looked at him with black eyes. "You are the captain?"

"Yes."

The man turned away and looked at the crater. When he turned back to face Cole, he said, "You were lucky. Terrorists usually kill *somebody*."

CHAPTER TWENTY-NINE

Adakoy Shipyard
Adakoy, Turkey

April 14, 2014

After Cole closed the door to the aft deck, Riley sank back into the cushions on the settee. "What are we going to do with him, Theo?"

"What do you mean?"

"He's fixated on the idea that Dig is alive and after him."

"But Riley, somebody just put a bomb on this boat. *Somebody is* after him."

"Yes, of course, but Dig? That's not rational. I can't deal with people who aren't rational."

"Well, you're supposed to be marrying him, so you'd better learn how."

"I don't know, Theo."

"Are you saying you're not coming with us when we launch the boat?"

"Maybe. I don't know what I'm saying. It's just that he's *the captain*. We're putting our lives in his hands. And he keeps insisting he's seeing a ghost."

"So what do you suggest?"

"Let's look at the facts. First, Cole said someone was following him. Then, that guy rear-ended us. The same guy followed us to Malta, where he used a fairly sophisticated drone to listen in on our conversation."

"Cole told me about that when he called last night. I wish I could have got my hands on that drone."

"It was like nano-small and it was no toy—more military. Anyway, when we chased him, he fired a gun at us. But if he'd wanted to kill us, he could have. He probably heard or even recorded us discussing the cipher text in the journals. The next day, someone attempted to plant a bomb on the boat. We have no idea when he meant to detonate it. I think when he saw you take the bomb off the boat, he decided to cover his tracks by killing you and destroying the bomb. So, who is this guy?"

"Riley, if you don't think it's Diggory Priest, then why don't you help Cole find out who it really is?"

Theo was telling her the same thing Hazel had. "How am I supposed to figure out who he is? I don't even know what he wants."

"He wants the same thing Cole wants," Theo said.

"And what's that?"

"Whatever it is that James Thatcher wanted Cole to find. Thatcher wrote, *There is an object of great power inside*—and now that you've solved the cipher text, we know it's inside the *Upholder*. Like us, they want whatever is inside that submarine."

"*They*? You're starting to sound like Cole."

Cole's voice interrupted them when he opened the doors. "Right through here."

The man who entered certainly didn't look like a doctor. He was wearing a green military-looking uniform, and he wore a sidearm. He had a full head of dark-brown, wavy hair, a mustache, and thick, bushy eyebrows that made him look perpetually angry.

"This is Maggie Riley and my first mate, Theo Spenser. Captain Danyal Pamuk here is with the Turkish *Jandarma*. He's here to investigate the bomb."

Theo stood and extended his hand about fifteen degrees to the right of the man. The officer stepped in front of Theo, took the offered hand, and stared at his eyes.

"Yes, I am blind. Until you start speaking, I won't be sure exactly where you are."

"Pleased to meet you," Captain Pamuk said.

"Theo's the one who found the bomb and got it off the boat before it blew," Cole said.

Captain Pamuk's English was heavily accented, but fluent. "So you are my witness?"

Riley stood and offered her hand. "Don't discount him, Captain. He may not be able to see, but he has fantastic observational skills. Why don't you sit down?" She pointed to a chair opposite the coffee table.

The Turkish policeman sat, and the plastic made a loud crinkling noise.

"My apologies for the state of our boat, here," Cole said. "We're still finishing up some last-minute jobs."

"This is a new boat?"

"Yes, and we have been very happy with the quality of the work done here in Turkey."

Riley smiled. Cole was laying it on pretty thick. She didn't think he'd been happy since the day they'd sailed in on *Bonefish* and he had started asking them to change things. None of it was the yard's fault. They had done terrific work.

"Do you have any idea why terrorists would target your boat?"

The question shocked Riley out of her private thoughts. "Terrorists?" she said.

"No, I have no idea," Cole said. "Other than perhaps we appear as rich American capitalists."

Why was Cole not objecting to the idea that this was a terrorist act?

"I hate these Islamists," Captain Pamuk said. "Don't get me wrong. I am a proud Muslim. But these bombings against foreigners? It is ignorance."

"Until this happened, we have found Turkey to be a nation full of warm and kind people."

"Do you know what is the difference between an Islamist and a Muslim?"

Cole turned to look at Riley. He shrugged and raised his eyebrows. She thought he was hamming it up a bit too much, but Pamuk didn't seem to notice.

"No idea. What is it?"

"A Muslim wants to read the Qur'an, go to mosque, and say his prayers many times every day. An Islamist wants *you* to read the Qur'an, go to mosque, and say your prayers many times every day. Turkey is a country of Muslims."

Riley chuckled and dipped her head once. "That's certainly what we've found. We adore Turkey."

"I appreciate your country, too. I have a brother, he lives in Miami Beach."

"Really?" Cole said. "I grew up not far from there."

Captain Pamuk nodded, and his eyebrows danced up and down as he spoke. "He owns a frozen-yogurt store. He makes so much money he drives a Cadillac and lives in a condo with a sea view. He sends me pictures. America has been very nice to my brother."

"I'm glad to hear that," Cole said.

"For this reason, I am very sorry this happened to you."

"Captain, as you can imagine, this incident is very disturbing. We want to work with you, but for the safety of my crew, we would also like to launch and get under way. In fact, we were planning to launch the boat today."

"What?" Riley said. From the look on Theo's face, she saw he was equally surprised.

"Yes, our launch has been delayed for many weeks, and we are now finally ready to go. I understand that you need to do an investigation. Do you think we can complete everything we need by the end of the day today? This is not meant as an insult to your country. As I said, we love Turkey. But for the safety of my crew, I think it best we depart as soon as possible."

"Yes, yes, of course. I will get a crime-scene crew out here today."

"That's very kind of you. I will also have to clear out with Customs and Immigration and make the arrangements for leaving our sailboat here."

"I have another brother who is an agent in Marmaris. He can help you take care of all that."

Captain Pamuk rose and nodded his head at Riley. "I will leave you, then. Within the hour my team should arrive."

"We'll be here," she said.

Cole escorted Captain Pamuk out the aft doors. As soon as the doors were closed after the *Jandarma*, Theo said, "Seriously, Cole? You think we can just launch this afternoon and take off?"

"Assuming the doctor says you're good to go, Theo, that'd be our smartest move. They won't be expecting that."

"That's just crazy. With all these systems, we can't just take off. We've got to break in the engines slowly. I want to test everything. No matter how well we've built this boat, there will be problems."

"Do you really want to stick around here and give them another chance to blow up the boat and maybe kill us all next time? Which is worse?"

"Cole," Riley said. "I don't even know if it's possible. There's so much to do. I'd have to move stuff off *Bonefish*, we'd have to schedule the travel lift, pay up all the bills with the yard. Then you have to un-pack your shipping container. What about things like provisions and dishes and linens and all the crap people need on a boat?"

"Look," Cole said, "I'm not saying it's going to be easy or that we'll get everything done. But if we divide up the chores, and we all go in our different directions, we can get a hell of a lot done." He checked his watch. "It's just a little after eight o'clock. Theo, after the doc looks you over, you go talk to the yard crew and see if you can get them to splash us this afternoon. I'll go move anything that's left in my con-tainer. Riley, you take the morning to work on getting *Bonefish* ready to be left alone on her mooring for a while and pack up whatever you want to take along on the new boat. This afternoon, you and I will go to town and order provisions and clear us out. We'll tell the yard we only plan to take her out for a trial run, but we want to pay our bill in full before we go."

Again they heard a knock on the boat's hull. Cole looked out the window of the aft doors. "Looks like the doctor is here, Theo, and she's quite attractive."

"Roger, roger, Captain." Theo stood up and headed for the stairs down to his cabin. "I guess I'd better put some trousers on, then."

CHAPTER THIRTY

Adakoy Shipyard
Adakoy, Turkey

April 14, 2014

Riley took the dinghy back out to *Bonefish* and started tossing her toiletries into a duffel bag. Her thoughts tumbled like clothes passing the window in the dryer door. She saw flashes of her life down in Lima, sneaking out of the Marine House to go make love with Diggory Priest, carrying her fellow marine out of the fire as the skin on her own shoulder burned through to the flesh. She saw her mother sitting on the couch in their Paris apartment, Mikey on her lap, a picture book open across his knees. Her father in his DC townhouse, sitting by the street window and looking at her as though he couldn't remember her name. As a foreign-service brat, she had grown up in so many different places; she now realized *Bonefish* had been her home longer than any other.

After ten minutes, when she found herself putting her little zippered shower bag into the duffel, she realized she wasn't packing to move into a new home. For a short trip? Maybe. And maybe her packing told her that she'd already decided not to go at all. She'd taken out the sweater her mom had knit for her and the dress she'd worn to her brother's funeral, and then she'd put them back. They stayed here on her boat, because this was her home.

Mikey, help me out here, please? How can I go to sea on this new boat under Cole's command when I think he's losing his mind?

You think, Sis, or you know?

I think.

Then go find out some facts.

Riley walked across the yard toward the front office. Wes and Ellen, an older American couple who were wintering in the marina aboard their cruising ketch, stepped into her path.

"We're so sorry about what happened to your crewman this morning," Ellen said. She wore her usual stretch jeans and plaid shirt. On her collar was a small American-flag pin.

"Theo's going to be fine," Riley said. "The doctor put a couple of stitches in his scalp, is all."

Wes nodded. Thanks to copious amounts of gel, Wes's white hair never moved, even in the wind. The first time Riley had met him, waiting for his wife outside the showers, he had been sure to tell her he was a US Navy man.

"World would be a better place if we could just get rid of all of them," he said.

"Sorry? I don't know what you're talking about," Riley said.

"Muslims," he said.

Ellen leaned in closer. "We heard it was terrorists."

"What?" Riley looked from one to the other.

"Who else do you think is trying to kill Americans?" Wes said.

"We don't know who set the bomb," Riley said.

Wes turned down the corners of his mouth and looked at her over the top of his glasses. "*We know*, Riley. It's not Americans trying to blow up innocent people. It's them. I don't know how Muslims can call themselves religious. It's a cult of death. They stone people and behead them. Blow them up. They hate all Christians and Jews."

"Not all Muslims are extremists," she said.

Ellen touched Riley's arm. "Dear, if you don't know who your enemy is, you are in mortal danger."

Wes seemed to swell beside her. "I hope to hell in the next election we get a new president with the balls to go over there and stick the sick bastards in the ground."

Riley looked from one to the other, struggling to make sure they were serious. She said, "Excuse me," stepped around them, and opened the door to the boatyard office. As she stepped inside, she wondered if Wes and Ellen understood that they were spending the winter in a Muslim country.

The young woman behind the desk looked up and smiled when she saw Riley come in.

"Good morning. I'm so sorry to hear about the trouble you had on your boat."

"Hi, Nejma." Riley shook her head to clear it. "That, in fact, is what I'm here about. The yard's got all those CCTV cameras around. I assume you are recording?"

"Yes, the video is recorded on a hard drive and stored for about one week before it is written over with new video."

"Could I take a look at it?"

"When the policeman left, he told me to prepare to hand over the drive to the police technicians when they arrive."

"Until they get here, could I review the video? I'll see if I recognize the guy. And if not, then at least I'll know what he looks like in case he tries it again."

Nejma looked over at the closed door to the manager's office. "I guess that would be okay." She pointed to a chair and said, "Bring that around behind the desk here, and we'll look together."

The office desk was L-shaped, and there was a second computer monitor there that showed a grid of views from the different security cameras. Riley sat down, and Nejma showed her how the boatyard's security system had a proprietary app for viewing the camera feeds. The quality wasn't very good, and it was difficult to navigate through the folders and hours of video stored on the drive.

"Geez," Riley said, "this is going to take forever."

"I have to get back to work," Nejma said, turning her chair to face the other computer. "Just let me know if you need help."

In the first hour, Riley found nothing. The nighttime video was terribly boring to scroll through. Little changed as the cameras moved and panned across the yard. Riley was running through it at 3X speed when she saw something odd in the last couple of seconds before one camera moved.

She stopped the video, then hit the reverse arrow for a few seconds. She tried the pull-down menus until she saw how to run it in slow motion. When she saw what had caught her attention, she tapped the space bar and the picture froze. The figure of a man dressed all in black stepped out from behind the corner of a building. On his head he wore infrared night-vision goggles. Everything from his build to the clothes he was wearing screamed *military*.

Riley turned around and spoke to the young woman over her shoulder. "Is this guy familiar to you, Nejma?"

"I cannot really see his face. I don't think so."

"He screwed up, getting caught on the video. We could search through the rest of the footage here, but I don't think this guy screws up very much." Riley tapped her fingers against her lips as she thought. "Is this connected to a printer?"

"Certainly. Just select 'Print.'"

Riley did just that, and, as she waited for the laser printer to spit out the photo, she worked out the dates in her head. It was Monday, and Nejma said there should be a week's worth of video on the drive.

That meant there should still be footage on the hard drive from Tuesday. They got rear-ended last Wednesday.

Nejma handed her the paper printout.

"Thanks. I'm just going to try one more thing." Riley went back through the folders until she found the footage from the camera in the parking lot. First, she looked at the footage for the night before. There were no bright lights in the parking lot like there were in the yard, so everything was deep in the shadows. She had to look very hard before she spotted him in the front seat of a dark sedan. He moved, shifting his position to flip up the goggles when their taxi showed up.

She watched the video as she and Cole got out of the cab, and she saw the white of his teeth. He was smiling.

He waited an hour or longer until he got out of the car and went to the gate. He had taken the headset off. His hair was short, white-blond, and gelled into spikes. She printed several more shots of him walking. When she'd got all the prints she needed there, she ran the video back to the beginning and skimmed through the comings and goings from the parking lot on Tuesday. She was disappointed she didn't see anything. It wasn't until dawn on Wednesday that she saw a familiar Renault pull into the boatyard parking lot. It was the car that rear-ended them. The driver's-side door opened, and a man climbed out.

She recognized the long coat and the stringy hair. The skin on his face was badly scarred. Riley froze the video and printed the screen. This time she started it up in slow motion. The man stared at their Hyundai. Another car appeared at the edge of the screen, and the man's face started to turn toward the other car.

Riley inhaled with a gasp and slammed her fingertips onto the space bar. The screen froze. The man's face had just passed the midpoint of his turn. She could still see both sides of the face, and they looked like two entirely different faces. On the left side his skin was pinched and scarred; on the other it was unblemished. Riley recognized the scars now. They were like hers on her shoulder: burn scars. She bounced her fingers on the space bar a couple of times, and his head slowly turned, like a stop-motion film. When he had turned all the way around, she selected the "Print Screen" command again. He'd certainly not aged well, but she would know that face anywhere.

Cole was right all along.

When she spoke, her voice was a harsh whisper. "Goddammit, Diggory Priest. How the hell did you survive?"

CHAPTER THIRTY-ONE

The Silversmith Shop
Vittoriosa, Malta

April 30, 1798

"Papa, please," Arzella said, holding a spoon in front of her father's mouth. "This is a fish soup I am very proud of. You will hurt my feelings if you don't taste it."

She had been sitting on top of his blanket, trying to coerce him into eating, for the last ten minutes. The soup bowl had grown cold on the bedside table. Her father was propped up on a pile of pillows, but his head lolled off to one side. She couldn't get him to take a single taste. He had no interest in food, and thus no strength left. The wrists protruding from the cuffs of his pajamas could have belonged to a starvation victim.

She watched his chest rise and fall with each labored breath. Every time, she was afraid that breath would be his last. After placing the spoon back in the bowl, her hands fell slack in her lap. Her whole body hurt. The morning sickness and the growing child inside her had sapped what strength she had. Her eyelids felt so heavy that it was a pleasure to let them close.

"Arzella." Her father's voice was no more than a whisper.

She pulled her eyelids open. "Yes, Papa?"

"I will leave you soon."

"Don't say that. You are just tired."

The corners of his mouth lifted. "Yes, and I am ready for a long rest."

"It cannot be time. I'm not ready to give you up."

His thin hand slid across the blanket toward hers. She met him halfway and grasped the fingers gently. His skin was cool, almost cold.

"You are stronger than you know, my daughter. I am so proud of you."

"Even with this?" She indicated her stomach—which was still flat, but they both knew what grew there.

"Yes. I'm going, but because of what grows inside there, you won't be alone."

From the front room of their shop, Arzella heard the sound of the door opening.

"Arzella?" It was Alonso.

Her father's head turned away.

"I won't be long. I'll tell him to leave."

Her father didn't say anything.

As soon as she stepped through the door into the shop, Alonso wrapped his arms around her and held her tight to his chest. "You must come away with me. Now."

She pushed him away. "Alonso, I can't do that. I have to take care of my father."

"Please, Arzella."

He appeared changed. Something was contorting that face she loved. She had never seen fright there before.

"It's the grand inquisitor."

"But they say he favors the Knights."

"Some gossip told him that you are carrying a Knight's child. He intends to make a point with *you*."

Arzella glanced up at the beams that supported the floor of the up-stairs apartment and shook her head. Then she reached up and placed her hand on Alonso's reddish-brown hair. Her heart ached, seeing him so distraught. "And what of you? Do they know you are the father?"

He shook his head. "But I cannot stand by and let them take you."

"We can't be certain what the inquisitor will do. And I will not willingly leave my father's side. Papa has little time left now."

"They are not far behind me, I fear." He put his hand on the sword at his waist and started to draw it out. "They will have to get by me."

She placed her hand on his and stopped him. "Alonso, please, go and live to fight another day."

He withdrew his hand from the sword and stared at her. "I cannot stand by. You are here because of me."

She pulled him to her and kissed his mouth. "Do you not remember that day in Saint Julian's Bay?"

"I think of it with every breath I breathe."

"It was I who built the boat that brought me here." She indicated her belly. "And I have no regrets."

"Arzella?" Alonso's voice was hoarse, and his eyes shone.

"Even if they take me to Gozo tonight, it cannot be as bad as seeing you die."

"I would gladly die for you."

"And that would be utterly senseless. We cannot stop them all. In the end, they will do what they want with me."

He pressed his forehead to hers and took a deep breath.

She placed her small hand on the cross at the center of his tunic and began to push him toward the door. "Go, my love. Let me return to my father's bedside. I may have little time left to be with him. We shall see what comes to pass."

"But—"

"Go!"

* * *

Her father's eyes were open. "I heard what he said."

"Alonso is a good man."

"Yes, I see that now."

"Perhaps they will simply try to frighten me. They are well aware I need to be here to take care of you."

"They won't care." His breathing grew more arduous.

"Surely the inquisitor does not want to be seen as a monster, taking away your only source of care?" She wanted to help him breathe, the one thing she could not do. What she could do was give him dignity. Treat him with intelligence and respect. "Papa, you are renowned on the island. There would be a backlash."

She could barely understand him now. His voice was weak and his chest rumbled with the fluid that was attacking his lungs. "This is political. The church wants the shop, the silver."

"What do you mean?"

"They excommunicate you, and then I die? All this will go to them."

"Shhhh." She smoothed back a few hairs on his head. She wanted him to rest, but to stay with her.

"Be brave, my child." Her father coughed several times, and, deep in his chest, she heard the bubbling liquid.

"Always, Papa." Arzella climbed into the narrow bed and lay next to her father. She rested his head against her shoulder.

"Cherish the new life," he said.

"I will love your grandchild fiercely." She felt hot tears on her cheeks, and she was surprised. She had not thought she would cry. "They will not take my child from me."

This time he did not answer her. She held him, listening, certain that her own heart slowed to his rhythm, waiting with fear as the gaps grew longer between each burbling inhale and exhale.

"I love you so much, Papa," she whispered. She was not certain he could hear her. She didn't know if he was even there anymore.

She had lost count of his breaths when it all went silent.

Breathe, she thought. *Please, Papa. Don't leave me now.*

She had fallen into something more like a numb trance than sleep when she was brought back to the present by the sound of boots in the shop.

Her father's mouth was open, his eyes half-closed, but this thing, this body was no longer the man she loved, the man she had known before any other. That man—her family, her father—was gone. This thing in the bed merely bore a close resemblance. But it was growing cool.

The boots came into the back room. No one ever came into the back room, which was now their home. These men didn't care.

"Are you Mademoiselle Arzella Brun?" It was a Knight with a very deep voice.

She swung her legs off the bed, stood, and acknowledged that she was the woman they sought.

Most of the men before her were Knights of Saint John, the Hospitallers. They wore the same eight-point cross as her beloved Alonso. But one of them stood apart. He wore the robes of the church. He unrolled a parchment and handed it to a handsome young Knight, who began to read aloud.

"By proclamation of the church, the grand inquisitor has decreed that you, Mademoiselle Arzella Brun, are to be transported to the Convent of the Holy Sisters in Gozo, where you shall remain for a period of three years."

"I cannot leave my father." The calm she felt stemmed from the numbness. She could not conceive of a world without her father in it.

The man in the robes went over to her father's bed. "It appears he has already left you."

"Yes, but there are arrangements to be made. The funeral . . ."

The man walked over to her workbench and picked up the silver pilgrim flask she had just finished for a Maltese nobleman. "Hmm. That is not possible. The church will see to your father." The flask disappeared inside his robes.

The numbness burst like a soap bubble, and pain washed over her. She threw herself across her father's body. "No, you'll not touch him."

The man in the robes walked to the door, then turned and pointed to one of the Knights. "Take her to the boat. Carry her if you must, but see to it she makes no noise." He pointed to a pair of Knights across the room. "You two, get rid of the body and put a lock on the shop door. Bring the key to me."

CHAPTER THIRTY-TWO

On the Road to Marmaris
Adakoy, Turkey

April 14, 2014

Riley stared out the car window as Cole drove them toward Marmaris. They had not said a word to each other since they'd left the yard. She was trying to figure out a way to tell him about what she had discovered on the tape, and how sorry she was for not believing him, but the car didn't seem like the time or the place. They had so much more to accomplish before they could leave.

The phone in her pocket made a soft *ping*, indicating she had a text message. She pulled the phone out and checked it.

CELESTE VILLENEUVE: *How was your weekend in Malta?*

Riley groaned.

"What is it?"

"It's my mother. She wants to know about our weekend in Malta. She thinks we went there on wedding business."

Riley typed: *We had a great time.*

Did you choose a florist?
We were there 1.5 days. Played tourist.
Have you found a dress yet?
No.
This is important! You can't keep putting it off.
Got to go Mom.

Riley turned off the phone, slipped it into her pocket, and crossed her arms. She stared out the window.

Cole's voice was very soft when he finally spoke. "You know, I decided I wanted to be a maritime archeologist when I was in the eighth grade. I never wavered on that."

She turned to look at him, then reached over and ran her fingers up the side of his neck and into his hair. "I know," she said. "You told me all about that one night when we were anchored in Raja Ampat. Remember?"

He took his eyes off the road for a few seconds and looked at her. Working in the boatyard, he had kept his tropical tan, and his green eyes appeared to glow in contrast to his sun-browned skin. Looking into those eyes still gave her whole being a jolt.

"I know I've been a pain these past weeks," he said.

I'm the one who should be apologizing, she thought. "I guess we both have."

He made a little noise that was almost a laugh. "We had a great time in Indonesia, didn't we, Magee?"

Riley smiled. "Sure did."

"I've been thinking about all the wonderful people we met there, and in Malaysia, and here in Turkey. They're Muslims, not Islamists, like Captain Pamuk said."

"I liked him." She thought about the conversation she'd had ear-lier with the xenophobic American cruising couple, Wes and Ellen.

"Me, too." He was quiet for a while as he negotiated the traffic on the outskirts of the city.

"Going to Malta and learning about the old-world fight between the Christians and the Muslims for control of the Med," Riley said. "It sometimes makes me wonder if we've learned anything in the last few thousand years."

"Wars, terrorism. I understand that it's all scary stuff. Taking the life of another human being should not be taken lightly by anyone."

"Cole," she said, "you're not suggesting you really thought it was an Islamist terrorist who tried to blow up the boat?"

"No, not at all. My father's journal directs me to look into the Knights of Malta, and the next thing I know you're getting shot at, and Theo's almost killed by a bomb." He braked for a red light and turned to face her. "Part of me wants to forget about this message from my dead father. I'm so afraid that either you or Theo is going to get hurt as a result. But then I think about the man, James Thatcher. He knew what I was going to university to study. Even though I was just an eighteen-year-old kid when he wrote that in the journal, he trusted that one day I would find this thing, whatever it is, that we now think might be on the *Upholder*. And I trust him to be sending me on a search for something that *matters*. I know this sounds crazy, but I don't want to disappoint him."

A car behind them honked its horn. The light had turned green. Cole accelerated through the intersection and turned into the parking lot for the market.

"Yeah, it does sound a little crazy."

He pulled to a stop and turned his face toward her again. He looked like a frightened little boy.

Her throat felt tight. "But it's the kind of crazy that made me fall in love with you." She swallowed hard. She wanted to tell him how sorry she was that she hadn't believed him, hadn't trusted him—but she couldn't find the words just yet. She wondered when she would.

He reached over, took her hand, and squeezed it tight. "Subconsciously, I think I've been trying to push you away. But then I don't know what I'd do without you, Magee."

"Let's hope neither one of us ever has to find out."

"After what's happened in the last few days, I'd understand it if you decided to stay on your boat here in Turkey while Theo and I go off to find the *Upholder*."

"What—and miss out on all the fun? No way!"

"These modern Knights of Malta are an incredibly powerful group. They're no joke—still fighting the Crusades against the infidels. My old man, he had no idea what he was asking. It's like playing Whack-a-Mole trying to stop these guys. It doesn't matter if they call themselves Skull and Bones or the Enterprise or the Knights of Malta. They all want the same thing."

"Yeah," Riley said. "You."

CHAPTER THIRTY-THREE

Adakoy Shipyard
Adakoy, Turkey

April 14, 2014

Riley stood to one side of the boat, watching the hull as it appeared to fly through the air. Their new boat was hanging in the canvas slings as the driver maneuvered the travel lift to the launch slip. Cole and Theo were talking and walking on the other side of the flying boat, Theo's hand on Cole's arm as Cole described everything in detail for his friend.

Riley kept herself separated from the guys on purpose. She scanned the faces of the people who had come to watch, looked around at all the places someone could be watching from. The blond man or Diggory—was one or both out there? She'd have to tell Cole soon, but she didn't want to ruin this moment for him.

Besides, she needed a few moments alone to let it all sink in. She and Cole hadn't really talked about their future much, silly as that sounded. Marriage, yes, but they hadn't really got into the logistics of it. He hadn't sought her opinions on the build of the new boat. Only in the last few weeks had she started adding furnishings like linens and outfitting the new galley with cooking utensils and tableware. This boat was now supposed to be her permanent home. How would she feel about saying good-bye to her beloved *Bonefish* that had carried her more than halfway around the world?

Everyone from the builder to the yard crew had laughed and thought he was kidding when Theo asked to be launched on such short notice, but one thing Riley had learned was that Cole could be very persuasive when he wanted to be. She and Cole had returned from their trip into town with their clearance papers complete and several truckloads of fuel, supplies, and provisions on the way. They found Theo still arguing with the yard about their launch. But as Riley directed the placement of the supplies on board, Cole got them to agree to put her in the water at the end of their workday.

When the travel lift rolled out onto the finger jetties and began lowering *Shadow Chaser II* into the water, Riley walked around behind the big boat to join the guys.

"We forgot the bottle of champagne," Cole said.

Theo nodded. "With everything we've had to get done today, if that's all we forgot, it will be amazing."

Cole said, "Isn't it bad luck if you don't break a bottle of champagne over the bow on launch day?"

Riley pushed her way between the two men and linked her arms in theirs. "What a waste of wine. We'll make our own luck, Cole."

At that moment, the bottom of the boat touched the water. They had painted the bottom weeks ago, anticipating that they would be in the water by now, but Riley had begun to think the bottom of that boat would never touch water.

"This is it, boys," she said.

The boat's builder, the yard manager, the foreman, and all the crew who had worked on the boat had stayed after work. They applauded when Cole was the first to climb aboard the now-floating yacht. Riley followed, and the two of them helped Theo climb onto the stern dive platform from the ladder. Cole had explained to all the yard personnel how they planned to take their new boat for sea trials around various anchorages in Marmaris Bay. They would be back in a week if all went well. While Theo checked out all the systems, the second fuel truck continued filling the big nine-thousand-gallon fuel tanks. At 9:00 p.m., they fired up the engines and let them run for an hour at the dock.

By that time, the crowds had all gone home. With little fanfare, Riley handled the dock lines, and after the last line was untied, she jumped aboard. EV *Shadow Chaser II* motored out into the night.

Riley headed for the wheelhouse once the fenders and dock lines were stowed. When she passed through the main salon and galley, she marveled at how things had changed. She had spent the entire evening stowing the mountains of provisions and household items she had bought in Marmaris that afternoon. The big yacht had a massive amount of storage space and now, instead of stacks of boxes, the salon looked clear and uncluttered.

As she climbed up the steps from the salon to the wheelhouse, she heard Theo's voice. "For the first hundred hours, we need to take things slow. We can't run up the revs until we break these engines in."

"It's a little over nine hundred miles to Djerba Island. How long do think that's going to take us?"

"For the first few days, I only want to run at seven to eight knots. We'll be doing well under two-hundred-mile days. After the first hundred hours, if everything looks good, we can push her up to ten to twelve knots."

"Do you really think she'll do that?" Riley asked.

Theo sat in one of the big easy chairs at the navigation console, and he swiveled around at the sound of her voice. "*Shadow Chaser II* was designed to cruise at twelve knots, but I think she'll reach fifteen or better. Of course, at that speed she'll be burning more than twice as much fuel."

Cole leaned his elbows on the back of the other chair. "So I'd say five to six days, to be on the safe side."

"Has anybody had a chance to look at the charts?" Riley asked.

"Yoda, on Bridge Display Two, show the chart for Djerba Island in Tunisia."

"Yes, Theo."

The chart appeared on the display.

"It's going to take me quite a while to get used to that," Riley said.

"I took a look at the chart for a couple of minutes this afternoon," Cole said. "As you can see, I put a waypoint on Djerba there off the southeastern corner of Tunisia, close to the border with Libya. It's at the southern end of the Gulf of Gabes. If we're going to figure out what happened to the *Upholder*, we have to think back to what was going on in the North African war at the time. The British occupied Egypt, and that meant they controlled the Suez Canal. The Axis powers wanted the canal. Libya was an Italian colony, and with France having fallen and her colonies of Tunisia, Algeria, and Morocco under Vichy rule, the British in Malta and Egypt were very isolated. The Germans sent Rommel into Libya to attack the British along the coast. The Germans got their supplies from Vichy Tunisia and via convoys coming down from Italy to the port of Tripoli, here." Cole had zoomed out the chart view so they could see the North African coastline from Tunis at the north end of Tunisia to the border between Egypt and Libya.

Riley walked around Cole and sat in the chair he was leaning on. "I remember reading about the North African war at the museum in Malta. The Tenth Submarine Flotilla stationed there was primarily tasked with sinking the ships that were supplying Rommel."

"Right," Cole said. "I dug around on the Internet this afternoon, and I found out a bit more about the *Upholder*'s final patrol. They completed their commando mission up here at Sousse"—he pointed to a spot on the Tunisian coast—"on the evening of April tenth. Captain Wanklyn's orders were to resume his patrol off the east end of Djerba Island here. If our friend Gavino is right, and Captain Wanklyn never got his orders to join the convoy, then he may have been sunk en route from Lampedusa or off the east end of Djerba."

"I suggest we start with the island," Theo said. "That was what Tug's bet was."

"I agree. We'll start from the southeast coast down here, where a boat would go to find cover from the prevailing westerly wind, and we'll work a grid out from there."

"It's a big ocean," Riley said.

"True, but maybe I'll get lucky."

"Hmm," she said with a smile. "It's our first night in our cabin on our new boat. You just might get lucky tonight."

Theo snorted.

Cole pressed his lips together in a tight smile. "I'll take the first watch. You two get some sleep."

CHAPTER THIRTY-FOUR

Leonardo da Vinci International Airport
Rome, Italy

April 16, 2014

As soon as the landing gear hit the tarmac, Virgil pulled out his phone, turned it on, and sent a text: *Landed. Aegean Air. Curbside in 20.*

What a miserable trip. He'd decided it was faster to fly out of Rhodes than the Dalaman Airport that served Marmaris. Flights through Athens beat going all the way to Istanbul, but still it had been seven hours with a whole family of Islamists behind him, including a crying baby and a little kid who'd kicked the back of his seat all the way. Virgil had wanted to reach back and snap the little monster's neck. It would be one less he'd have to kill later. The wife wore the veil, but the designer high-heeled shoes and the heavily made-up eyes peering out of that black cloth were both saying *Fuck me*. She'd brushed her ass against his arm when she'd gone forward to use the head.

Now they had to wait for a Jetway. What else could possibly go wrong? Back in Marmaris, he'd seen the Turkish police arrive on the scene after the explosion. When he learned he hadn't killed the man who'd seen him, he was determined to get back and finish him. By calling the marina and pretending to be a boat owner shopping for dockage, however, he'd got the chatty secretary to reveal the man was blind. The witness wasn't a problem. He'd waited twenty-four hours, then gone back to the boatyard to try again to place a GPS tracker on the boat. The boat was gone. The people at the yard said they were just going for a cruise around Marmaris Bay. He'd hired a boat, searched every cove. He'd lost them.

When the flight attendant finally opened the plane's door, Virgil stood and made sure he'd be first in line out of there. He'd had to check his bag because of his weapon and some of the specialized gear he always carried in his kit. Of course, he never flew with explosives— he'd always found he could buy them on-site. Turkey had been no different. But some things, like the detonators he liked, were more difficult to find. He now held a passport issued by the Order, and his bag displayed the diplomatic seal, but they still wouldn't let him carry the weapon into the cabin. Like that would prevent him from killing if he wanted to.

The officials in Rome showed the most respect for the passport, so in no time he was through Immigration and Customs, where they handed him his bag.

His driver was late. Virgil kept checking his watch as the minutes ticked by. When the man finally pulled up in some Russian-made se- dan, Virgil wanted to pull out his gun and put a bullet in the back of his head.

Virgil threw his backpack into the backseat and slid in beside it.

"Sorry I'm late." From the slight smirk on the man's face he didn't appear to be telling the truth.

"What is wrong with you, man?" Virgil said. "I'm trying to help you out. This is a good gig, working for the Order. But you're doing everything you possibly can to fuck it up."

"I didn't intend to hit anybody in Malta. I just fired to distract her so I could get away. She's faster than I am now."

"It's always excuses with you. I get it. You're pissed about what happened to you. But it's done. Deal with it. Pulling some piss-ant power play, making me wait at the airport, is just stupid. Look at you. You look like a bum. I don't want to take you into the villa and introduce you to my guys with you looking like a piece of shit I found on the street."

Diggory Priest didn't reply. He didn't even make eye contact via the rearview mirror.

"Look, take me to the address I texted you this morning." Virgil took out his wallet and removed several hundred euros. He tossed the bills onto the front seat. "There's an advance on what the Order owes you. Go out and get yourself cleaned up. Get some decent clothes. Come back to the villa at eight and join the other guys for dinner. I'll brief you then about what's happening this weekend. About what will be expected of you."

The man made no move to pick up the money.

Virgil shook his head. He took his phone out of his pocket and checked his messages. He'd just started typing a reply to Hawk's message when Priest decided it was time to talk.

"So what happened with Thatcher and the Riley woman?"

Virgil kept on typing. "That's old news as far as you're concerned. It no longer comes under your purview."

"What happens to her will always be of concern to me."

"Get over it."

"Did your guys have any luck with the cipher text?"

"You don't seem to understand what I'm saying. Maybe I can make it more clear. Priest, your orders are—"

"No, Virg, *you* don't seem to understand. What happened over in Iraq? I've got pictures. You might think 2003 was a long time ago, but trust me, the words *Abu Ghraib* still carry weight. And people think they've seen the worst, but you and I know they haven't. You did some sick shit, Virg. I could open that whole story up again with one email to the right source. With photos attached. I can't make them revoke your immunity, but if this gets out, you'll be like me—nobody will touch you."

"You really don't want to pull this, Priest. You were CIA back then and people listened to you. Today, you're a fucked-up nobody."

The car started up the Aventine Hill. The villa was at the top. This ride would soon be over. Not soon enough.

"I'm just stating the facts, Virg. You'd still be in jail if I hadn't stepped in. You will owe me forever."

"Nothing's forever."

"Really? You know, I made friends with some of the guys in the yard where Thatcher and Riley built their boat. Guy sent me an email yesterday. Told me about the explosion. And they launched the same day?"

The car pulled up in front of the gate to the villa. Virgil opened his door and slid out, pulling his backpack behind him. The front passenger's-side window slid down. Virgil leaned down and rested his forearm on the open window.

"You don't want to try this shit on me."

Diggory Priest smiled that damn half smile of his. "No, Virg. You don't want your daughter seeing those pictures."

CHAPTER THIRTY-FIVE

Aboard the HMS *Upholder*
Mediterranean Sea En Route to Lampedusa

April 10, 1942

The pickup had gone off with the precision that Tug had come to expect from Wanks, even though the weather was deteriorating. The wind was up, and the chop on the surface of the sea made paddling much more difficult. He and Charlie were a bit late, but as soon as they'd paddled their way out to their scheduled rendezvous point, the sub surfaced alongside them. Within thirty minutes, they were aboard, and all their gear, boats and all, had disappeared down the forward hatch. The sub dove and headed out to get some sea room in case the enemy came looking for them in the wake of the blast.

Tug and Charlie joined Wanks in the control room.

"You get our Arab friends safely ashore?"

"At least one of them made it alive. Not sure about the other. We sighted one, probably Ben, carrying the other chap. Both radios made it."

"Every agent we can get on this coast with a radio means more information for our boys. More details about enemy shipping."

"The other mission was a success, too."

"We saw the flash, boys. Well done."

"What you wouldn't have been able to see from out here was that there was a train on the bridge when she blew. Quite a sight. The tracks busted loose from the ravine wall and started bending down. The engineer tried to outrun it but he couldn't." Tug went on to describe how the train had been pulled off the track.

"Would like to have seen that myself."

"Parker decided he wanted a closer look, too."

Charlie bumped his shoe against Tug's foot and shot him a look.

"That's just Tug's way of saying that he ran from that train wreck so fast he almost left me behind."

Tug wasn't sure why Charlie wanted to shut down talk of his find, but he could take a hint. "I'm not one to dawdle when several tons of train cars and a locomotive are raining down from the sky."

Wanks laughed. "I guess we're the first sub in the flotilla to sink a train."

Tug stepped into the wardroom when the cook called his name.

"Saved you boys some cake, if you're interested before you head for your bunks."

"Got any hot coffee to go with it?"

"Always."

Charlie said, "I'll be right back." He disappeared toward his bunk.

Cook passed two plates with enormous slices of chocolate cake through the window from the galley. They were followed by two mugs of coffee.

"Thanks, mate," Tug said.

The cook folded a towel, then stepped out into the companionway to look at the control room. "Guess we'll be surfacing soon to charge the batteries, eh?"

"That'd be my guess, too. At least until daylight. Then we'll head on up to Lampedusa."

"I heard you'll be leaving us there."

"That's the plan."

Charlie returned with something tucked under his arm, wrapped in a towel. "Cake looks great, Cook. Thanks."

"I'll be heading off to be first in line for a smoke, topsides." The man headed aft.

"So," Tug said. "What is it that was worth risking your skin over?"

Charlie set the bundle on the table and unwrapped the disk. It was about the size of one of Cook's large pot lids and looked mostly black, but here and there he could see designs etched on it. "Take a look."

Tug pointed to one place where shiny yellow metal shone through. "Is that what I think it is?"

Charlie nodded. "Now that I've washed it up a bit, I'm pretty sure it's steel with gold and silver inlay."

"What is it?"

"A shield."

It was late and Tug was tired. He just wanted to finish his coffee and get some sleep. "And that's what you ran back for?"

"I'm no expert, but my guess is fifteenth or sixteenth century. I'd have to polish it up for you to really see the design, but you can still make out the cross."

"Where?"

"Here." Charlie traced his finger around the design. "It's a Maltese cross. This is what they called a buckler shield. Must have belonged to one of the Knights of Malta who came to North Africa for trade or something."

"More likely he came to kill Muslims."

"I wonder if the whole suit of armor is back there."

"Believe me, we're not going back to look."

"Of course."

They heard footsteps outside the wardroom, and Charlie threw the towel over the shield.

"Change of watch," Tug said.

"Let's keep this quiet, okay? It must be quite valuable. Hard to keep anything a secret when you're sharing a bunk with three other guys. I don't want it disappearing before we get back to the Lazaretto."

"I'm not going back."

"Well, you know."

"Yeah, yeah, mum's the word. But good luck with hiding anything on a submarine."

"I have an idea."

The next evening, one hour before the 3:00 a.m. rendezvous, a sailor found Tug resting on his bunk.

"Number One wants to see you in the control room."

Tug checked his baggage over to make sure everything was ready, then made his way aft. They had been traveling at a slow three knots all day, whiling away the daylight hours so they could rendezvous with the HMS *Unbeaten* off Lampedusa Island as ordered. Tug had spent the time preparing his gear for the transfer. After all those months in Malta, he had little besides a spare uniform and his souvenir saber to take home in his duffel.

As he passed the wardroom, a couple of off-duty officers were playing a game of cards. Tug nodded at them as he passed. During his stay in Malta, he had grown comfortable with these men aboard the subs of the Tenth Flotilla. He felt a twinge of guilt at leaving them. The crew of the *Upholder* had also been scheduled to return to Britain, but their trip had been cancelled due to the shortage of submarines in the Med. The men he passed looked weary but determined to do their best for their captain.

When Tug arrived in the control room, the first lieutenant pointed upward. "Captain wants you."

Tug climbed into the conning tower. The first thing that struck him was the force of the wind. Conditions were much worse than they had been the night before. The seas were being whipped into a froth.

"Doesn't look good, Tug," Wanklyn said.

"Bit of wind, I guess. You made contact?"

"We made asdic contact over an hour ago. Can't see them, but they're closer than you think. Been trading signals."

"Excellent."

"*Unbeaten* asked for you to take over one of our spare batteries and a few other parts."

"Be glad to."

"Look, Tug, this weather is blowing a hooligan. If you don't feel like getting wet tonight, why don't you just stay and finish this patrol with us. I'm sure Shrimp will find you room on a flight out of Malta."

"Much as I love your company, Wanks, I've paid my debt for tearing up your shirt, I think."

Wanklyn nodded. "They said they'll surely appreciate it if you decide to make the crossing."

"Looks like a fine night for a boat ride to me."

"Your call. We're on target for the transfer at 0300."

"I'll be ready," Tug said.

He climbed back down the ladder and set off to find Charlie. He wanted to say good-bye. He found him in the wardroom with a cup of tea.

"Trouble sleeping, Parker?" Tug slid onto the bench opposite him.

"No, I just felt like getting a brew on. Not that I wanted to see you off."

"Right, mate."

"Feels like it's gone dirty out there."

Tug looked at Charlie. "Would it stop you from getting your ride home?"

Charlie shook his head.

"We've had a good run together."

"That we have."

"Did you get that trinket of yours hidden away?"

The cook appeared in the doorway. "Last chance to get some decent food before you go, Tug. What can I get you?"

"Nothing, thanks."

"Cook here's helped me out," Charlie said. "We've eaten through enough stores in the icebox there, he found room for my trinket. We wrapped it up in oilskin to protect it from any more deterioration until I can get back and clean it proper."

"Got to admit, Parker. Bloody brilliant. But I'd expect nothing less."

Tug stood and stuck out his hand. "See you around."

"Safe travels, Tug."

Tug sat in his boat on the foredeck of the sub. The *Unbeaten* flashed her signal lamp to give him a target. He checked his compass. His canoe would be riding low with the weight of his own gear, the heavy battery, and the box of spare parts. He'd better be ready to paddle fast.

He raised his thumb in the air and heard the familiar *whoosh* as the ballast tanks blew out some air. The water level rose up the side of the sub's hull. Then a wave pushed him into the sea, and he was paddling as fast as he could.

In minutes he could make out the dark outline of the *Unbeaten*. When he got within hailing distance, he heard a voice call out from the darkness.

"Piss off, Tug. We've got two feet of water in the fore-ends and the batteries are gassing. You'll never make it to Gib."

Tug recognized the voice of the first lieutenant on the *Unbeaten*. He smiled. "I'd belay that last message if I were you. I'll make you a real good price on a battery here, as long as you don't send me back to Bells, Smells, and Yells."

Tug heard laughter from the men on deck, who recognized the Royal Navy's nickname for Malta. A line sailed across his boat, and he grabbed hold of it.

He was going to make it home.

CHAPTER THIRTY-SIX

Aboard the EV *Shadow Chaser II*
Mediterranean Sea off Djerba Island

April 20, 2014

Cole was very pleased with the new boat. They had made excellent time covering the nine hundred open sea miles to Djerba. They'd been lucky with the weather. The winds had remained under fifteen knots, the seas no more than three to four feet high. There were still certain things about the boat that would take some getting used to. For example, from the height of the wheelhouse, the glare from the sea surface was so bright, Cole had to wear his polarized sunglasses all the time. It made reading some of the instruments a challenge, but Cole liked the view from up there. There was so much more glass.

Moving up to a boat that size changed the rules and regulations that governed them. Some of the electronic gear—like the radar and the AIS, a system that broadcast their position to other boats within a twelve-to-fifteen-mile radius—were now required to be running at all times. Which made it more difficult to operate "under the radar," so to speak. But their night departure from Turkey appeared to have worked. There had been no indication of any boats taking an interest in them during their five days at sea.

Theo was amazing with the engines, frequently checking on them, telling Cole and Riley what to notice while on watch. But really it was the computer that kept them informed of any systems that needed attention. Theo had set it up so that all the data flowed into the ship's main computer, and he was able to set thresholds, so Yoda spoke up and told them when they needed to service something. It was a truly stunning system.

Djerba Island had been a bit of a surprise when they arrived. Cole hadn't known what to expect, but the beautiful whitewashed luxury hotels along the coast north of Aghir looked more like they belonged in Greece. Farther south, where they were working, the coast was low and brown with what looked like date palms and a few houses set well back from the shallows. He didn't like the fact that there were so many eyes on them from shore. It was difficult to hide his new eighty-three-foot yacht, but so far, after a couple of days of running their search quadrants, no one had come out to question them.

"Teatime," Theo said as he came up the steps from the galley, Leia at his heels. He was carrying a basket with sandwiches and some chips. Riley followed them with three bottles of water in her hands. "Best I could do for an Easter basket for you."

"I'm touched, Theo," Cole said.

Riley came up behind him and handed him a water bottle. "How's it going, Skipper?"

"Not bad," Cole said. "We've been running our grid for a day and a half and we've covered lots of territory. Haven't found our sub yet, but the systems are all performing well, and we're collecting an unbelievable amount of data."

Theo set the basket down on the table in the corner of the wheel-house. "Come and get it," he said. "They're all ham and Swiss."

"Looks good," Cole said. He got up, grabbed a handful of chips, and pushed them all in his mouth at once.

"You're going to make yourself sick," Riley said as she slipped a chip to the dog.

"I'm starving. No lunch, and it's such hard work running this boat."

Theo flopped into one of the two leather chairs and held his sandwich in front of his face. "Yes, this is the way I like to battle the elements." He took a bite. "It's just brutal. You even make us work on Easter Sunday."

Cole strolled over to the table and picked up a sandwich. "Work? The computer does all the work for us."

"I still don't understand all this data collection you guys keep talking about," Riley said. "We're looking for a submarine. Why would we want to collect data about the places where it isn't?"

Theo held one finger in the air. "Because we can."

"I'm serious," Riley said. "I don't get it."

"There are lots of reasons," Cole said, "but mostly it's a pet project of mine. Theo was brilliant enough to make it happen."

"I don't know about *brilliant*."

"Okay, then, persistent."

"No, I'll take brilliant."

Cole came up behind Theo and gave him a thwack on the back of his head with his open hand. "Damn right you're brilliant." He turned to face Riley. She was sitting in the other of the two watch chairs with her bare feet up on the desk, drinking from a chilled glass water bottle. "How's the water taste?" They made their water on board with a reverse-osmosis system and then filled their own bottles.

"Doesn't have much taste. We might have to work on that. So, tell me more about why Theo is brilliant. I know he is, but explain to me why he is this time."

"Okay," Cole said. "We are now towing the magnetometer, which is measuring the iron content of whatever's on the sea floor. We've also got a permanent installation of our bathymetric side-scan sonar now. We no longer need to tow that fish. The side-scan sonar is taking an impression of the shape of things down there beneath us and, depending on the depth, a hundred feet or so off to either side of the boat. There's also a multibeam sonar system that works like a fish finder, but this one reads the nature of the material on the sea floor. It determines whether it's sand, coral, rock, or grass. Then all of this information is tagged with the GPS location, so we are collecting all this geologic, magnetic, and bathymetric data for every precise section of the grid we are surveying. Later, if and when we launch the ROV and send our new little robot down to take video, that too will be added to the GIS survey data."

"GIS?"

"Geographical Information System," Theo said. "See, Cole told me that he wanted to collect all this data whenever we were working a grid. I mean, we've got all the gear. Why not store the data? So part of this boat's systems is a massive storage array that can store up to one petabyte of data."

"Again, though. What's the purpose of storing all this data?"

"As Cole says, we are going to be searching for 'archeological residues of the past.'" Theo turned to Cole. "You're better at this than I am. Explain it to Riley."

"So far, we have mostly been looking for World War II ships, but there's much more to maritime archeology than that. These residues of the past aren't always going to be big hunks of metal like a submarine. It might be pottery or wood. If we save the data, then we can give it to the preservation authorities of the country whose waters we're working in. From that data, they may learn much more about the sea's secrets."

Riley said, "Wait a minute. So here we are off the coast of Tunisia searching for a wreck—without permission from the Tunisian government, by the way—just so we can give them some data? Heck, we haven't even cleared through Customs and Immigration."

"That's just a technicality," Cole said.

Theo choked on a piece of his sandwich and started coughing.

"Yeah," Riley said. "A rather important technicality. And I have a feeling the longer we stay out here driving up and down their coast-line, the more likely it is someone is going notice."

"Not a problem unless we get caught—entering a wreck, that is. We haven't gone ashore in Tunisia. We've just come in here for shelter. If and when we find this wreck, we'll take a quick look and see if we can figure out what it is we're supposed to be looking for. We will disturb the wreck as little as possible, and then we will turn over all our data to whatever government or university group is in charge of historical preservation. If we can find the *Upholder*, that will be a pretty significant find."

"Did you just hear yourself? Cole," Riley said, "you don't even know what it is you're looking for."

A high-pitched tone sounded from the speakers on either side of the wheelhouse dash.

Theo jumped out of his chair. "That's a hit," he said. He pulled back on the throttle. "Do you see anything on the side-scan sonar?"

"Negative," Cole said.

"The magnetometer's on too long a tether."

"So the boat's already past it," Cole said. "Probably not a very big piece of metal. Some junk, maybe."

"Yoda, take us back to the position of the hit."

"Yes, Theo."

"Reel in the magnetometer fifty feet."

The big boat made a wide, slow circle. Cole and Riley stared at the center display that showed the sonar image of the sea floor. It was mostly a flat, sandy bottom.

"What's our depth?" Theo said.

Yoda and Cole answered in unison. "A hundred and forty feet."

"Approaching our target in thirty seconds," Yoda said.

Theo said, "This is when it sucks to be blind."

Cole rested his hand on his friend's shoulder, but he didn't take his eyes off the screen. The screen image looked like an old sepia-tone photo of the surface of the moon. Mini craters dotted the sea floor—homes to crabs, probably—but there was little else to distinguish the scene.

"There." Riley pointed to a dark image in the corner of the screen. "What's that?"

"It looks long and dark. Not very big."

"Maybe a log? It looks like it's got branches."

"That's no log, Riley," Cole said. "I think that's a deck gun."

"Seriously?" Theo put the engines into neutral, but the boat was still moving at about two knots.

"Oh yeah," Cole said. "There we go."

Theo grabbed the hand resting on his shoulder. "What is it?"

"Hey, mon," Cole said, imitating Theo's accent. "We found ourselves a submarine."

"What time is it?" Theo said. "Yoda, record the time of the sighting."

"It is four thirty-seven, Theo."

They could only see what looked like the bow of a ship in the upper-right corner of the screen. Cole jogged the autopilot to take them closer to the area where the submarine lay.

"Oh crap," Riley said.

"What is it?"

"Well, Theo, we found ourselves *part* of a submarine. The center section of the wreck looks like it was made of glass and a giant hit it with a hammer. It's been blown into hundreds of pieces scattered across the seabed."

"Damn," Theo said.

Cole sighed. "I'll second that."

CHAPTER THIRTY-SEVEN

Villa del Priorato di Malta
The Aventine Hill, Rome

April 20, 2014

Virgil was glad to have the extra man, even if he was an asshole. And like the old saying about keeping your friends close and your enemies closer, Virgil intended to keep very close tabs on Diggory Priest. Never good to be threatened by a man with little to lose.

The main house was shaped like an L around the formal gardens. Signor Oscura had told him the villa had once been the priory of the Knights, but now it was the site of their embassy, home of the grand master, and a great house for entertaining.

On this Sunday, the villa was full of resident guests and many others who were not staying on-site but had driven up for the evening's Easter dinner. The number of international military and political dignitaries at the villa that night would make it a very desirable target for some dumb-ass suicide bomber making a bid for his promised seventy-two virgins.

The Rome police were cooperating. They had set up a barricade at the entrance to the Piazza dei Cavalieri di Malta. No tourists had been allowed to come visit the famous keyhole in the gate since early morning. That made a car-bomb attack unlikely. He'd put Hawk on the front of the estate, his best man. Jacko and Priest were working the hillside perimeter, while he and Dutch were working the main house.

They'd made it through most of the meal, and the twenty-five guests and wives were moving out of the big dining hall into the salon, where they were to be served coffee and dessert. Actually, it was some sort of chocolate fountain. The kitchen at the villa didn't have the capacity to feed such a large group, so they'd brought in a catering crew that had been working for the Order for more than ten years.

The crew was moving in to clean up the dining area. Virgil watched for faces he didn't recognize or workers who had managed to slip through some crack in their vetting process. After all his years in this business, Virgil was at the point where nothing could surprise him anymore.

Signor Oscura had told him to meet the other Guardiani in the Church of Santa Maria del Priorato at ten that night. The small chapel was on the grounds of the villa. He would check in with all his men and then slip off for an hour or so.

When Virgil walked into the church, the only light came from the candles burning at the altar straight ahead. He paused just inside the door to let his eyes grow accustomed to the dark. Catholic churches always felt strange to him. He had been brought up a Methodist, and they hadn't had any sculptures or artwork that showed Christ with blood on him. The Catholics, he'd learned, really seemed to be into that. Virgil smiled. As many men as he had killed, it was odd that it bothered him to see Jesus with his hands nailed to the cross wearing a crown of bloodied thorns.

He walked forward down the center aisle. Before he reached the altar, he noticed more lit candles in a small alcove to his left. Inside the alcove, there was a single man with his back to Virgil.

When the noise of Virgil's footsteps on the stone floor reached the man, he turned and waved a welcome. As he approached, Virgil saw that there were several occupied chairs in the shadows. He counted five men in all.

One of the seated men stood and stepped forward with his hand outstretched. Virgil recognized Signor Oscura.

"Welcome, *Cavaliere* Vandervoort." Oscura introduced him to the other men. One of them, a Frenchman, he had met before at an event at the villa. The other two he had never seen. They all spoke excellent English, and they were dressed in business suits—undoubtedly because they had come for the dinner that evening. Virgil noticed they were all either gray-haired or bald, but they looked fit, confident, and rich. That last part made Virgil wonder why they had picked him.

"The Order has always tried to have Guardiani from the different *langues*. In this way, we ensure that the men of this brotherhood will work for the Order, not for their own nationality. You are the first American to be invited to join."

"I am honored," he said.

"Each man here has been invited because of a certain skill set. We have a lawyer, banker, historian, and diplomat." He pointed at the individual men around him and introduced them. "What we have not had in many decades is a soldier, a warrior, a true military Knight. That is why, after looking at your record, we are now inviting you to join our ranks. What say you?"

Virgil nodded but said nothing at first. He turned around, looking each of the five men straight in the eye, sizing them up. He could smell the power on them, see it in their shoes, watches, haircuts. Teaming up with these guys would mean he wouldn't be eating in the kitchen with the security detail anymore. That sounded damn good to him.

"I'm in."

The German stood up and said, "Take off your shirt." The man reached under his chair and pulled out a large Pelican case. He opened the lid to reveal a tattoo kit with the machine, power supply, inks, needles, and an extension cord.

Signor Oscura went to the small altar that held all the candles and reached into a crevice behind it. He withdrew a fat black garment bag and unzipped it. He handed each of the men a black robe. When they pulled them over their heads, Virgil saw that a white Maltese cross graced the front of each robe while a long black hood hung down the back. One robe remained folded next to the candles on the altar.

"This is going to take some time. While I work, they will talk. Take a seat."

Virgil sat, and the man took a pen from his kit and began to sketch the cross just above Virgil's left breast.

The Brit had a briefcase, and from it he took a scroll and unrolled it. "Every initiation requires that you swear to what is written on this scroll. When the Guardiani were formed, they spoke many different languages, but the common language was that of Rome. Therefore, this is in Latin."

The others had all gone to the altar and taken candles. They now stood around him, their candles illuminating his chest, where the black ink was starting to form the shape of the Maltese cross. Virgil wasn't superstitious and he didn't believe in magic, but he was starting to feel uncomfortable.

"I don't speak Latin, so how do I know what I'm swearing to?" It wasn't really that he was having second thoughts, he just wanted to be informed.

"That is what I will explain to you," the Brit said. "From the beginning, our Order has defined different jobs for different Knights. In Jerusalem, some Knights worked in the hospital, some were clerics, while others were military. The Guardiani were a sect apart: established to guard the Order's treasury and most treasured possessions. Among the treasures were religious relics like the manuscript that has come to be called the Religion."

Over the next two hours, the tattoo machine buzzed close to his left ear and the men around him told him about how the early Crusader Knights had found the relic in the Church of the Holy Sepulchre in Jerusalem. That church was built on top of the site of the cave where Jesus was buried. The ancient manuscript was believed to be one of the earliest copies of a gospel written by one of Christ's disciples. These early Knights were shocked by the words in the manuscript, but they recognized the power it gave them over popes and kings. For seven hundred years, the Knights protected the Religion, but in the late eighteenth century, the Religion disappeared at the behest of the grand master. He ordered a Knight to save the manuscript, to keep it out of the hands of the invading French. He sailed off with the precious relic, but that Knight was never heard from again.

Signor Oscura said, "Without the great source of their power, the Knights were disbanded by Napoleon, and the Order has never regained the status it once held in the world."

Then they told him the Legend of the Silver Girl in Malta. They explained that the Order only knew of her story from her son, who had left his entire library to the Order upon his death in 1882. They believed that, somewhere among the volumes that were currently housed in the Magisterial Library on the Via Condotti, was the answer to what had happened to the Religion. What they did not have, however, was the key that would help them find that answer.

Signor Oscura said, "When you swear to become one of the Guardiani, you will vow to do anything in your power to return the Religion to the Order. Now, more than ever in our history, we need to find this manuscript. Our sources in the intelligence world tell us that there is a new power rising in the world of Islam. This group is even more extreme than al-Qaeda. They follow a literal translation of the

Qur'an, and they will even kill other Muslims for not following their medieval traditions."

The German turned off the tattoo machine for a moment and said, "If only we could count on them just killing each other, it would make things easier for us."

"We cannot wait for that. They are about to appoint a caliph. They plan to take over certain territories in Syria and Iraq that are described in the Qur'an as the place where the End of Days will occur. There they will establish their medieval caliphate, called the Islamic State. There has not been a caliphate since the Ottoman Empire, and even that one is not seen as legitimate by this brand of Islamist, since the Qur'an says the caliph must be a descendent of the tribe of their prophet. And this new chap, al-Baghdadi, is from that tribe. This is going to be heady, powerful for Islamists worldwide."

"I don't understand what that word *caliph* means," Virgil said.

"A caliph is a leader of all Islam, and his arrival is the fulfillment of a prophecy. According to their texts, the prophet Muhammed foretold that a caliphate would be declared sometime in the future, and all the Islamists would rise up and defeat Rome. These Islamists think that time is now." The man placed his hand on Virgil's shoulder. "Son, with your help, we're going to make sure that doesn't happen."

When the tattoo of the small cross was complete, they ceremoniously placed the black robe over his head and cinched it at his waist. Oscura produced a sword that he said had once belonged to a member of the Guardiani.

The Brit read all the Latin off the scroll, and they made him kneel.

When Virgil had first become a Knight of Malta, he had hoped they would make him kneel and tap him with the sword, but it never happened. This night, he would get to live out this little fantasy. They said lots more Latin stuff when the Brit tapped him on both shoulders. Then he rose, and the others all embraced him and kissed him on both cheeks.

Virgil was officially a member of the Guardiani.

CHAPTER THIRTY-EIGHT

Aboard the EV *Shadow Chaser II*
Mediterranean Sea off Djerba Island

April 21, 2014

Cole stood on the aft work deck, preparing to launch the ROV using the aft crane. It had been excruciating to have to wait all night before investigating the wreck with their little robot, but by the time they had finished surveying the wreck site with sonar imaging, it had been nearly dark.

This would be their first launch of Theo's newly designed Remotely Operated Vehicle, and they decided to use it alone for their initial investigation of the wreck. This new underwater vehicle carried the same name as his first effort, *Enigma*, but Theo had outdone himself on this one. He claimed their new *Enigma* could safely travel to depths of fifteen hundred meters. With her four horizontal thrusters she could achieve eighty kilos of forward thrust. The two robotic arms could carry a hundred-kilo payload, and she was currently outfitted with two HD pan-and-tilt video cameras and four bright LED lights. Her cables, one for data and another for power, were spooled onto a drum mounted near the transom.

Cole hooked the lifting cables onto the pad eyes in *Enigma*'s frame, one on either side of her bright-yellow water-ballast tanks. The ROV was neutrally buoyant when the water-ballast tanks were empty, but once they were filled with water, she would start sinking. This trip down to about a hundred and fifty feet would be a good test dive for their new toy. Cole spun his finger in the air. Riley was standing in the shade under the aft deck overhang, holding a metal box with the crane controls. She toggled the switch and *Enigma* lifted off the deck. *Shadow Chaser II* was rolling a bit in the swell, so Cole held tight to the frame to keep the ROV from swinging.

Riley maneuvered the crane around as Cole stepped out to the edge of the aft work deck following the ROV. Theo was spooling out the cable according to Cole's commands.

"Okay, she's loose," Cole said. "Happy hunting, girl."

Theo pulled a phone out of his pocket and spoke to it. "Yoda, take *Enigma* down and hold position five meters above the southern end of the wrecked sub." Thrusters whirred, and the yellow ROV disappeared under the surface.

"I've got a tablet here," Riley said. "I'm logged on to *Enigma*'s video."

Cole joined her in the shade where they could watch the *Enigma*'s progress more easily on the small screen. When the sub reached her hover depth, Cole used the on-screen controls to pan the camera down.

The image on the screen showed the entire surface of the sub covered in algae and sediment. Using short bursts of the thrusters, Cole took *Enigma* down alongside what was left of the forward end of the sub's hull. He took the little ROV down almost to the sea floor.

"It looks like she hit bow-first." It had become Cole's habit to narrate for Theo whenever they were working. "A significant amount of her forward hull appears to be buried in the sand."

Since the ROV lights were fixed, Cole had to turn the entire vehicle to see in a specific direction. He turned it to face the center section of the sub.

"Turning to look aft from here, we can see the sub is basically in two halves and the center section's nothing more than a debris field. I almost wonder if there wasn't some explosion of their own torpedoes."

He turned the vehicle around again and took the ROV along the sea floor to the very front end, then up along the stem and over the top of the bow.

"Got a view now looking down what remains of the deck. The bow section is lying tilted over on her side at about a forty-five-degree angle. There's a tangle of cables that trails off the deck into the sand. Looks like the forward hatch is missing, maybe blown off when the sub exploded."

Trying to find anything in this wreck, Cole thought, would require more luck than even he had.

He maneuvered the ROV back over the side of the sub and began a survey of the port side of the hull. When he panned aft from the bow, the outline of an enormous anchor was visible. Cole was surprised that there were no fish, even in the growth around the anchor flukes.

"I don't know enough about what the *Upholder* looked like to determine if this is her or not. We'll have to compare these images to the file photos we have."

"It looks like there is some kind of marking there on the bow," Riley said. "I can't make it out, though."

"If there's too much growth on the hull," Theo said, "you can try using the thrusters to pressure wash it."

"Yoda, rotate ROV one hundred and eighty degrees," Cole said.

The image on the screen turned dark blue. The headlights of the ROV penetrated only a short distance into the open sea.

"Full ahead thrust. Stop. Rotate one hundred eighty degrees. Ahead slow. Pan camera up ten degrees."

Riley said, "There's too much silt in the water now."

"Give it a minute," Theo said. "It will clear."

No one spoke as they waited.

"Okay," Riley said. "It's almost visible. There. It says U-702."

"Crap," Cole said.

"What's wrong? Dr. Günay told us the *Upholder* was a U-class submarine."

"Yeah, but the Brits didn't number them like that. I'm afraid we're looking at a Nazi U-boat."

Theo said, "Brilliant. We found the wrong submarine."

CHAPTER THIRTY-NINE

The Grand Master's Palace
Valletta, Malta

June 9, 1798

In the courtyard before the palace door, Nikola put his hand on Alonso's arm. "L'Angel, before you enter, may I speak?"

Alonso turned to face his friend. "Of course."

"This morning, when we stood together on the ramparts of Fort Saint Angelo and looked out to sea at that fleet—"

"Nikola, my friend. I understand."

"Please, let me say what I must."

"Yes, go ahead."

Nikola raised his arm and pointed his forefinger toward the mouth of the Grand Harbour. "I have never seen a fleet such as that."

"Nor have I. Masts to the horizon and beyond."

"Yes! And I have a wife who is heavy with our sixth child. It has always been my honor to fight by your side, my friend. We fought against the infidels and to feed those five hungry mouths. But this, a French fleet of warships and troop transports? An army thousands strong?"

"Against a few hundred Knights and a handful of Malta militia who have never fought in battle and rarely ever trained. Against Bonaparte, the most brilliant general the world has seen. I understand, my friend."

"L'Angel, half the Knights are either too old or too drunk to fight."

"This is true." Alonso grabbed his friend by the forearms. "Nikola, this is not your war. Go home to your beautiful wife and children and keep them safe. If it comes to it, fight for them. I do not expect you to fight for the Order."

"Thank you, L'Angel. May that angel namesake of yours keep watch over you and keep you safe."

The two men embraced. Without another word, Nikola walked out of the courtyard heading toward the city's gate.

Alonso watched him go. He hoped the grand master had not called him to prepare the *Ruse* for war. Without Nikola, the rest of his crew would bolt as well.

The sentry at the door knew Alonso well and nodded as he passed. Inside, he met Father Vincent in the corridor.

"He is waiting for you on the balcony outside his chambers."

"How is he?"

The priest shrugged. "I do not think he fully realizes the situation he is in. He talks as though he still believes the Russians and the Bavarians will come to his aid."

Alonso shook his head. "Even now, when the wolf is at the door."

"Yes. Good luck in the days ahead, my son. God be with you."

Alonso found Grand Master Hompesch pacing on the balcony. From that height, with the late afternoon sun turning the sea silver, the fleet looked like a vast winter forest. Without any verbal greeting, the grand master turned and placed his hand above his heart.

Alonso followed with the same salute.

Grand Master Hompesch turned back to the sea. "I wasn't certain you would come, after our last conversation."

Alonso said nothing. He had threatened to leave the Order if the grand master did not intercede between Arzella and the grand inquisitor. Grand Master Hompesch had refused to do so.

The grand master then said, "An hour ago *he* sent a messenger from that monstrous ship of his. Look at the size of her. *L'Orient.*" He spoke the ship's name as though it were a curse.

"What does Bonaparte want?"

"To destroy us, of course!"

"Yes, sir. But what did he say?"

"He asked permission for his fleet to enter the harbor to take on water."

"And?"

"I have convened the Grand Council for six o'clock. I know what they will say. They have been politicking already. They want to enforce the Rule of 1756, allowing only four ships to enter at one time."

"Bonaparte won't be happy."

"No, he won't." Hompesch pointed seaward. "Can you imagine how long it would take to water a fleet of more than five hundred ships only four at a time?"

The two men stood in silence as the sun slipped down toward the island.

At last the grand master spoke. "They aren't coming to save us, are they?"

"The Russians? No, sir, I don't believe they are."

"I am not a warrior. My only armor is purely ceremonial. The men have not trained. I don't remember the last time we fired any of Valletta's guns."

"The city fortress will hold."

"Let us pray that we shall not be attacked."

"Prayer cannot be your only defense."

"I will listen to the Grand Council and play that hand. But if I must, I will negotiate a surrender. The centuries of our Order's accumulated treasure from the strong room in Fort Saint Angelo, as well as the holy relics in Saint John's Cathedral, in exchange for the lives of the people on Malta and Gozo."

"But what about—"

"That is why I called you here."

Alonso put his hand over his heart and bowed. "I am at your service."

"Bonaparte reveres no god. All those French Republicans have taken great pleasure in punishing the clergy. They hate the church. We cannot let our most precious relic fall into their hands. They would only use it to discredit the pope, to show they were right all along."

"Agreed."

The grand master reached inside his blouson and took hold of a gold chain. He lifted the length of it out of his shirt, and Alonso saw the iron key. Placing the chain over Alonso's head, Grand Master Hompesch said, "Chevalier Alonso Montras, Guardian of the Knight's Cross, I charge you to fulfill your pledge. Keep our most treasured relic safe. Sail far and then send back word of its hiding place. Go now, tonight, to Fort Saint Angelo before Bonaparte receives our response. I've already sent word ahead. The guards are expecting you."

Alonso bowed his head. "I am deeply honored."

"And what of your men?"

"They will be gone. The Maltese believe this is not their war. Besides, I cannot ask them to follow me on this journey."

"So how will you sail your ship?"

Alonso met the grand master's questioning look with a wry smile. "I know where I can recruit at least one excellent sailor."

"Go, then. Do what you must. Protect the relic with your life and find a safe hiding place. Someplace no one would ever look."

* * *

An hour later, as the Grand Council met, Alonso shipped his oars and tied his launch alongside the *Ruse*. She was docked at the wharf in Vittoriosa, not far from the entrance to the fort. As he expected, there was not a single man left aboard ship.

He didn't blame the men. This was not a fight for the Maltese. Throughout the past months, they had made it clear they were unhappy with the Knights' rule. They hoped things would go better for them under the French. Alonso knew little and cared less for politics, but he was not sure that trading one set of warring rulers for another would serve them as well as they hoped.

In his cabin, Alonso moved the center table aside, pulled back the rug, and lifted out several short-cut floorboards. The raised afterdeck of the xebec meant the bilge beneath his cabin was always dry. He grunted as he pulled out the gift his grandfather had given him just before he died. His grandfather had inherited it after the death of *his* father, Alonso's great-grandfather. Though it was over one hundred years old, the corsair's box was in remarkably good condition. For four generations, the men in his family had kept their most valuable possessions inside the sturdy chest. The dark wood was crisscrossed with black iron straps that were riveted in place. In the center of the eight-point cross on the front was a keyhole. Two smaller keyholes were cut into the box to the upper left and right of the main lock. Alonso fetched a ring with three keys from the small desk along the bulkhead.

All three keys were required to open the box. Using them in the correct order was the fourth key. When he opened the box, Alonso lifted out a cloth parcel. Inside were several small silver pieces and some tools he had bought when they had auctioned off the contents of the Brun silversmith shop. Then he removed the small, round buckler shield, also a gift from his grandfather, and he set it aside. In the very bottom of the box was a folded black cloth. Inside that was what remained of his spoils from the last sortie—gold and silver coins, and the earrings he had first bought from Arzella. He left the cloth in the bottom, relocked the box, and tucked it under his arm as he exited the cabin and leapt for the wharf.

While the walls of Fort Saint Angelo were not far from his vessel, the entrance to the fort was high above him through the main gates. As he sprinted up the narrow streets, Alonso felt the chill in the city. The residents of Vittoriosa weren't out on their balconies chatting with their neighbors or walking the streets arm in arm. Windows were shuttered and the streets empty. Everyone knew Bonaparte was right outside the harbor. Many had already left to seek safety in the countryside. Alonso wondered if he would ever see these streets again.

At the top of the hill, he turned to his left and approached the bridge over the moat. Two Knights stood guard at the gates, but they knew him well and let him pass without a word. Inside, he entered a world unlike any he had ever seen.

The courtyard had been transformed by the coming battle. Dozens of men moved about the fort, pushing carts and carrying barrels of powder, cartloads of cannon shot, and armloads of rifles. In all the years Alonso had been a Knight, he had never seen either real battle preparations or even training for such an event.

The result of that lack of training was painfully obvious in the scene taking place before him. Two men were arguing; they dropped their loads and began exchanging blows. There did not appear to be anyone in charge, and one fellow was smoking a pipe while wheeling barrels of black powder.

Alonso hurried down the steps that led to the strong room, feeling the urgency of his mission more keenly than ever. There was not a chance Malta would hold out against Bonaparte. The Frenchman would soon arrive, intent on expropriating all of the Order's property, including the vast collection of gold and *objets d'art* that was inside the round chamber deep in the bowels of the fort. Still holding the corsair's box under one arm, with the other Alonso seized a torch from a sconce on the wall and headed into an unlit passage.

After several twists and turns, he arrived at what looked like a stone wall. A dead end. He pressed on a stone, and a doorway seemed to open out of the rock. They had used clay on a steel door and fashioned the clay to look just like the stone walls. A spring latch held it closed until the proper stone was pushed. But even all these preparations would not save the manuscript if Bonaparte began torturing the Knights. Many men not of the brotherhood knew of the treasure strong room. Alonso didn't want to contemplate what might happen if the manuscript fell into the hands of a man like that. *I Guardiani della Croce di Cavaliere* had been sacrificing their lives since the manuscript was first discovered in Jerusalem. He would sail under Bonaparte's nose and keep the manuscript safe.

Two more Guardiani stood in front of the final chamber door. Neither of them had keys to the lock. There was only one key, which Alonso now wore around his neck. He juggled the torch into the hand holding the box, retrieved the key, and fitted it into the lock.

His torch lit the domed ceiling of the round chamber. Big wooden crates covered the floor of the room. Alonso turned to the guards. "I will only be a few minutes, but I must close this door." They nodded.

Once he was alone, Alonso placed the torch in a sconce on the wall and walked straight to the center of the chamber. Several crates were piled on top of each other. He considered asking one of the other men to help him move them, but he resisted. The top crate was not too heavy, and he was able to lift it and rest it on top of another crate off to one side. The next one was much heavier. He opened the top and saw that it contained sacks of gold coins. He pulled out several bags to lighten the box so he could move it. Finally, he slid the bottom crate aside. Even then, most men would not notice the piece of leather nailed to the wooden floor. The fit was so tight, it was impossible to make out the trapdoor. He tugged at the piece of leather and the door lifted open.

As far as Alonso knew, no one had opened the box inside since the Knights of Saint John had first arrived in Malta in 1530—not even during the Grand Siege. The box had been designed with thick ceramic and wool linings to seal out the elements and keep the manuscript free from damage. It was, however, too unwieldy to carry. Inside, the manuscript was wrapped in a silk shawl. Alonso carefully lifted it out and placed it in his corsair's box. He locked the box, then moved the crates back to cover the trapdoor in the floor.

Leaving the room, he nodded at the two brothers as he relocked the door, his corsair's box tucked tight under his arm. Alonso strode up the dark stone corridor, in a hurry now to finish this night's errand before the moon made an appearance. From the dark shadows behind him he heard a voice.

"God be with you."

CHAPTER FORTY

Aboard the EV *Shadow Chaser II*
Mediterranean Sea off Djerba Island

A p r i l   2 2 ,   2 0 1 4

"I've got an email from Dr. G. here," Riley said when the three of them were sitting at the table on the aft deck, drinking their coffee. She was scrolling through the emails on her phone.

"And?" Cole said.

"Just a minute." Riley read the brief note. "Right." She looked up from the screen. "Cole, remember what the old vet Gavino said just before we left Malta?"

"He said he was going to ask around among the other old-timers to see if any of them remembered anything more about Tug."

"She says here Gavino left her a message yesterday. He wants to meet with her this morning to tell her about something he's learned."

"Would be nice if it was the lat and long of the *Upholder*'s location."

Riley shook her head. "*Any* new information could possibly help." She set the phone down on the table and took another sip of coffee.

"We've been out here searching for three days now based on a tiny bit of information and one wild-assed guess."

"It's worked for me before. And we did find a submarine."

Theo said, "I did a bit of work in my cabin last night. I started by asking myself what might have sunk that U-boat down there."

"Good question," Cole said.

"For most of the war, the only Allied warships in this part of the Med were protecting convoys. With one noted exception: the subs out of Malta. They were on the hunt. So I asked myself, if an Allied sub sank that U-boat, shouldn't there be a record of it?"

"And?"

"Nothing. After the war, all sides released their records, and they are available on the Internet. There were no U-boats reported sunk in this area. That doesn't mean it wasn't sunk by a sub, though. It just means that if a sub sank it, and that's a pretty good guess, then that sub never reported the kill."

"I think you're on to something here, Theo. Gavino said that Tug thought the *Upholder* never got that radio message with new orders because they were having trouble with their radio antenna."

"So they couldn't have reported the kill," Riley said.

Cole set down his coffee cup. "And since they never returned to port, it was never recorded. In fact, finding that U-boat could be evidence we're on the right track."

Theo hitched himself forward and sat on the edge of his seat. "I have an even more radical idea that has little or nothing to do with the damaged radio aerial."

"Okay?"

"What if these two subs sank each other? What if the Germans had critically damaged the *Upholder*, but those Brits were still able to deliver a kill shot before they sank to the bottom?"

Riley's phone rang.

"Hold that thought. Don't say another word till I'm done here." She pressed a button on the phone and said, "Hello?"

"Riley, it's Najat."

"I hoped it would be you. Did you talk to Gavino?"

"Yes, I did, but I don't know if this will be of any help."

"Listen, we'll decide that. We'd really appreciate any information at this point. I'm going to put you on speakerphone so the guys can hear what you have to say. Is that okay?"

"Certainly. Gavino said one of the old-timers remembered a story that Tug told about his last trip on the *Upholder*. Tug made him swear not to tell anyone about it because Tug said he had a friend who had a son who was a diver, and this guy was going to go get it."

"Get what?" Cole asked.

"Good morning, Cole. Why don't I tell you the story as Gavino told it to me."

"Okay."

"Tug Wilson told this old-timer that he and another commando had orders to go blow up a bridge down in Tunisia. After the explosion, his partner found an antique that he thought was quite valuable. He thought it might belong to a Knight from Malta. The next night, Tug transferred over to another submarine. The *Upholder* and all the crew were never heard from again."

"Dr. G., did Tug tell this guy what the antique was?"

"No. When the man pressed Tug to tell him, he refused."

"Hmm. Something that might have belonged to a Knight of Malta," Cole said.

"There is one more thing."

"What?"

"The old man said he later overheard Tug carrying on when he'd had too much to drink. He was telling another British vet that before he left the *Upholder*, his partner told him where he'd hid the antique."

"Where?"

"In the galley."

When Riley disconnected the call, Cole said, "That could be very valuable info, but only if we can find the wreck."

"I wonder if that other British vet he was talking to was your father."

"Could have been."

"It sounds like the two of them were plotting how to get you to dive on the wreck for them."

"Yup."

Riley snapped her fingers. "Of course. It was there in the journal all along. Remember? He said in that passage with the cipher text that it was *frozen*."

"Good job. I'd forgotten that."

Theo interrupted. "My guess is neither one of them had any idea just how difficult it is to locate a wreck when you have no clue where it is."

"You're right, Theo," Cole said. "Even a location like 'off Djerba Island' leaves us with hundreds of square miles of ocean to search."

"Which is where my theory comes in. Let's see if we can come up with a battle reconstruction for this U-boat."

"How?"

"Yoda, show a screenshot of the sonar image of the sub on Display Two."

The image appeared on the center screen.

"On Display Three show the chart of our anchorage here in the lee off the southeast coast. Zoom out until you can place a waypoint on the location where we took the sonar image."

Riley looked at the chart and tried to imagine where the *Upholder* might have been patrolling. "It looks like the U-boat wreck is about six miles offshore, Theo. But two miles off the island, it shallows up to less than fifty feet, so the subs probably didn't come in too close to land."

"Okay. Now orient the sonar image to north up."

"What are you trying to do?" she asked.

"When we took the *Enigma* down, you both described the remains of the U-boat as lying over on its side. We're going to assume that the torpedo struck the sub amidships and holed it. Therefore, as it sank, the air inside was blowing out that hole as the water rushed in, resulting in the boat tilting to one side when it hit the bottom. Can you identify the keel in the sonar image?"

"Yes," she said.

"Okay, now that the image is oriented correctly, which direction is the keel facing?"

"I'm not following you."

Cole said, "He can see it all in his mind, Riley. We sighted people are at a disadvantage. Yoda, overlay the sonar image onto the chart in the correct position and match the scale."

"Good one, Skipper," Theo said. "Now can you see what I'm getting at? The kill shot came from the direction the keel is facing."

"It's facing southwest, directly toward our anchorage."

"So that tells me that whatever sank that U-boat was between the sub and the island. World War II torpedoes had a range of about two and a half miles. Yoda, draw a line from the sub waypoint three miles long at a heading of two hundred degrees. Now draw a forty-five-degree angle starting from the waypoint, such that the line we just drew bisects the angle."

Riley said, "It looks like a cone."

"That's where I say we should start our search today."

It was Riley's turn in the galley, and she was preparing a pasta salad for a late lunch when the alarm went off. Cole was on watch. As she secured the dishes and shoved the salad into the fridge, she heard the engine revs drop. Theo had been down in his cabin. She almost collided with him when they both tried to climb the steps to the wheelhouse at the same time.

Cole swung around in the leather pilot chair with a huge grin on his face. He pointed to the sonar screen. "Ladies and gentlemen. Meet the HMS *Upholder*."

CHAPTER FORTY-ONE

Aboard the EV *Shadow Chaser II*
Mediterranean Sea off Djerba Island

April 22, 2014

There'd be no way to know for certain if it was the *Upholder* until they got some video of the wreck. The sonar image was of an intact sub lying on her side in about a hundred and sixty feet of water. Most of the hull below the waterline was in the shadow of the sonar scan. If she were holed, it would probably be down there, as nothing was visible from what they could see of the deck.

During the morning, as they'd been towing the fish back and forth across the grid, Theo had been running Internet searches and had managed to find both photos of the profile of the U-class subs and an interior layout diagram. But it was difficult to be certain if what they'd found was a U-class sub or not by looking at the two grainy black-and-white photos.

The forward end of *Shadow Chaser II*'s main hull was devoted to dive gear and a workshop. Only the *Enigma* was stored in the aft toy garage behind the engine room. Tanks, regulators, compressor, and the long stainless-steel tool bench were in the bow.

Riley followed Cole onto the foredeck when he went up to grab his gear. He pulled his old wetsuit out of the hanging locker and stepped into it. Ever since seeing that image on the screen, he'd been beaming, happier than she'd seen him in months. Nothing like finding a wreck to get her man excited.

She'd brought a printout of the interior layout of the *Upholder*. "I want you to take a look at the layout when you get a minute."

"Okay," he said, but he didn't stop suiting up.

"What I'm worried about," she said, "is if Theo's first guess is right, and they all died down there in the sub as they ran out of air. How will you get in?"

He stood up and zipped the front of his suit halfway up his chest. "As they say, I'll cross that bridge . . ." He grabbed his tanks and tossed a regulator over his shoulder.

"I'll get your mask and fins," she said.

Just before they headed for the stern, he reached over and grabbed a small pry bar.

Theo was already at the reel for the *Enigma*'s cables, and the crane's harness was attached to the lifting points. "Ready when you are, Skipper," he said.

Cole passed through the gate to the dive platform, sat down, and started pulling on his gear. Just before he put on his mask, he said, "I'll take a look at that layout now."

She ran him through it. "Torpedo tubes forward, then the fore ends for crew's quarters and storing torpedoes, then crew mess, officers' quarters, the galley, then the wardroom. Aft of that is the control room. Hopefully, you can enter via the forward hatch here or through the conning-tower hatch."

"Got it," he said.

Riley stood up.

"Hey," he complained, "aren't you even going to give me a kiss for good luck?"

Finding this wreck really has made a difference in him, she thought. She couldn't remember the last time he'd wanted to kiss her. She knelt next to him and made sure to remind him of what he'd been missing all these weeks.

When Cole slipped into the water, Riley took her position at the crane. She lifted *Enigma*, swung the crane around, and lowered the ROV to the surface. In the water, Cole disconnected the lifting harness, and Riley moved the crane back aboard. By the time she got to the tablet to control *Enigma*, Cole was already on his way down to the wreck. She fired up the thrusters and sent the ROV after him.

"Pay it out fast, Theo. Cole's already ahead of us."

"I haven't seen him this cheerful since you two got to Turkey."

"You noticed that, too, eh?"

"Now you have a basis for comparison. The funk he's been in these past couple of months is nothing compared to how he was during those years he felt he had to lay low and let you think he was dead."

She slowed the ROV down as it caught up to Cole and illuminated him with the headlights.

Theo continued. "You know, Cole built this boat to retire on. He was going to live the safe life for all of us. The thing Cole Thatcher doesn't want to admit to himself right now is that he loves trying to outwit these bad guys. And that's got him mad. Mostly mad at himself, not us."

The visibility was excellent on the descent. The water around Cole was growing darker. "You may be right. You've certainly spent more time with him than I have."

"But that doesn't mean I understand him."

Riley watched the screen and felt an eerie sense of déjà vu as Cole approached the submarine.

Theo said, "What's happening down there? Has he reached the wreck?"

"Yeah, he's just arriving. I can see the conning tower now."

She gradually became aware of a strange noise. She wasn't used to all the sounds on the new boat yet.

"Do you hear that?" Theo asked.

"Yeah, what is it? A pump or something?"

"No, that's not a noise on this boat. Is there another boat approaching?"

The noise grew louder. Riley set the tablet down on the table and climbed the ladder to the sky-lounge deck. She scanned the horizon but didn't see any boats.

"It's getting closer," Theo said. "Is it a plane?"

When she shifted her focus to the sky, she saw the helicopter flying south down the coast.

"It's a helicopter," she said. "Mystery solved." Riley started to climb down the steps when she noticed the chopper had turned, and it was now heading directly for them. "Great," she said. "Looks like they've decided to buzz us."

"Have we got a Q flag flying?"

"Yep. I got worried yesterday after our conversation and dug it out. Our yellow quarantine flag is very visible."

Once the chopper had turned toward them, it came on quickly.

"Do you think it's officials?" Theo said.

"Not sure. I can't see any markings."

The helicopter flew straight to their boat, slowed, and hovered overhead. The noise grew superloud.

"What can you see?" Theo shouted.

Riley ran down the steps and stood next to Theo so he could hear her. "Looks like there's only one man besides the pilot. He's leaning out the window."

"What's he look like?"

"He's white with short-cropped white-blond hair. Fit guy. Probably in his forties. He's taking photos with an SLR camera." She couldn't tell Theo she recognized the man. She hadn't yet told either of them about her discovery at the boatyard. He was the one on the security video. The one who'd set the bomb on their boat. "Wait. He just disappeared out of the window."

Through the deck speakers, she heard a voice calling on the VHF radio. "*Shadow Chaser II, Shadow Chaser II*, do you read?"

"Riley, do you think that's them?"

"I don't know. I'll go answer." She climbed up to the wheelhouse and grabbed the radio microphone. She paused briefly before answering. It didn't feel right that they hadn't identified themselves. But if it was officials, it would be better to play along. "To the vessel calling, this is the Exploration Vessel *Shadow Chaser II*."

She waited for them to respond. She heard nothing. She repeated her response, but still there was nothing.

Then the noise of the helicopter began to recede. She ran out on deck and saw them flying off in the direction they had come. She ran down the steps to the aft deck.

"What happened? What did they want?"

"I don't know," she said. "I couldn't get anybody to answer me."

"Let's worry about that later. Right now, we've got a diver down."

"Shit." She spun around and looked for the tablet. She saw it on the table and grabbed it. The video screen showed nothing but dark, blue water. She spun the ROV around and sighted the submarine.

"Riley, what's going on?"

Her hands were shaking as she tapped on the tablet screen, working *Enigma*'s controls. The camera panned up and down the length of the submarine.

"I see the sub, but there's no sign of Cole."

CHAPTER FORTY-TWO

**Djerba Zarzis Heliport
Djerba Island, Tunisia**

April 22, 2014

The helo pilot, a young Frenchman, had been too talkative during the flight. Virgil hated small talk. When he had a question, he wanted an answer. Nothing more.

"What's the range of your chopper?" he asked after they had landed and the pilot turned off the engine.

"About four hundred kilometers, but that is assuming there is no headwind and I am not carrying—"

"Do you fly to Malta?"

"No—it's possible I could make it, but it is just on the edge of the range."

"Thank you." Virgil grabbed his backpack from behind his seat and climbed down onto the tarmac.

The pilot hurried around the helicopter and handed Virgil a business card. "Customer satisfaction is very important to my company. This business is very competitive. I would appreciate it if you would go to our website and leave a review."

Virgil nodded, turned away, and started walking toward the terminal. He crumpled the card in his hand and tossed it onto the ground. So many of these pilots were military trained. Now that they were pulling all the forces out of the Middle East, of course there was more supply than demand for chopper pilots on the civilian side. What was needed was a damn big war. It would solve so many problems.

Before he entered the terminal, Virgil stepped off to a remote corner outside the building and dialed the executive director's personal cell.

"It's me," he said.

"Did you locate them?"

"Yeah. Their boat popped up on the Marine Traffic website when they got here to Djerba. Their AIS signal was picked up by the authorities at the local port."

"I didn't ask you how you did it, Virgil."

"Right. Okay. I chartered a helicopter, and I just flew out to take a look. They had some cables running into the water, and I only saw two people on deck. Thatcher was probably on a dive. If he's diving, I'd say they've found something. I got the GPS coordinates."

"You're sure it was them?"

"I called their boat on the radio just to make sure. The woman answered."

"How long would it take you to charter a dive boat and get out there?"

"Port Houmt Souk is the only marina on the island. I'll find out if they have a dive boat there. If so, I can rent a car and drive over there. It might take a couple of hours."

"Go ahead. Get out there as soon as you can. In the meantime, I'll get in touch with the Tunisian authorities. We'll see if we can get a local patrol boat to stop their diving."

"Good idea. If by some chance they do find something, I don't want to lose them again. They'll figure out how I found them, and I doubt that method will work a second time."

"What about using the helicopter to search again?"

Virgil shook his head. "It doesn't have the range."

"In that case, we can't lose them."

"Agreed."

CHAPTER FORTY-THREE

Aboard the EV *Shadow Chaser II*
Mediterranean Sea off Djerba Island

April 22, 2014

Cole adjusted the fit of the regulator in his mouth and cleared his ears one more time as he pulled his way, hand over hand, down the descent line toward the dark shadow on the bottom. They had dropped their light anchor on nylon line earlier, both to mark the wreck's location and to help hold their position. Visibility was good, but the light grew dimmer the deeper he descended, and the world around him turned a dark blue. He reached up and switched on his headlamp as he approached the submarine, which was lying on her side, the deck facing him. The sudden light changed all the color in the world around him. The surface of the sub, which moments before had looked like black iron, was now revealed to be covered with a rust-colored layer of algae and crustaceans. Some of the barnacles appeared white as they reflected his light.

Cole swam right up to the tilting deck and, with his gloved hand, grasped a riveted piece of metal to steady himself. On the deck in front of the conning tower was an intact deck gun. The barrel of the gun hung down, pointing at the sandy bottom. Even the rails on either side of the gun were still standing.

Behind him Cole heard the whirring of *Enigma*'s little thruster props, and the light from her big LED spots lit up even more of the deck. Aside from the growth, there didn't appear to be any damage all the way up to the knifelike bow. He identified the foredeck hatch through the growth on the deck, but it was sealed and closed up tight.

Cole turned aft. He started to swim around the high side of the conning tower to check out the aft end of the sub, but realized he didn't hear any whirring behind him. He turned and waved at the video camera on the ROV. He expected Riley to waggle the joystick up topsides and make the little underwater robot dance or something. He got no reaction. Maybe they were having some kind of malfunction.

There was no time to worry about it. He checked his remaining air supply, knowing he was limited on bottom time. Determined to find a way into the sub on this first dive, he continued around the conning tower, leaving the ROV behind. Again, he found no deck damage.

A school of sea bream darted through a swarm of bait fish as Cole swam over the high side and then kicked his way down to inspect the hull. It didn't take long to find the hole. The dented area about six feet across appeared almost insignificant until he made out the inward gash in the metal tube that ran up toward deck level. Cole imagined that water would have been gushing in, down in the engine room and probably into the control room as well. Depending on the depth where they were hit, the water pressure could have been pretty intense. As the air poured out that slit and the water gushed in, they must have had enough time to turn and fire off their own torpedo, if they hadn't already done so. While archeologists might never know who fired first or how the battle unfolded, Cole imagined some enterprising doctoral candidate would make his thesis out of trying to figure it out.

He swam back up to the conning tower and, to his great surprise, he found the hatch open. Once the sub had settled on the bottom, the hole in the hull would have continued to fill her with water. Had the last survivors tried to open the hatch and swim to the surface? Had the internal pressure forced it open? There were more mysteries than answers.

Cole put his head down into the hatch, and his headlamp illuminated the iron rungs of the ladder that led into the dark hole. He pulled his second high-powered flashlight out of a Velcro holder on his vest. The water inside was siltier, but he could see the clear passage to the floor below.

Diving in small spaces is extremely dangerous work, and many of the wreck and cave divers Cole had known during his years at university were no longer around to tell their stories as a result. He swam over to the side of the conning tower and looked down at the *Enigma*. They had planned for the video camera to be his backup. If he got into trouble, they'd see it on the video, and Riley could dive down with an extra air tank or two to give him time to figure things out. It wasn't a perfect plan, obviously, but it was the best they could do on short notice.

He swam back to the hatch and looked down into the darkness. Even though he'd been wreck diving for most of his adult life, he always felt that combination of excitement and fear when he was about to enter a wreck for the first time. The hole was small, barely big enough for a diver with double tanks on his back. The possibility of getting his gear caught on something in there was very real. He looked back aft of the conning tower, where he saw *Enigma* hanging in the water, still not moving. His instructors would have called him crazy for taking the risk of entering the wreck—and totally insane for doing it alone.

He went down the hole feetfirst. A spool of hundred-pound-test monofilament on his vest, tied to a carabiner hook, served as his guideline. He attached the hook to the top rung and fed out the line as he descended into the sub. He took it slow.

When his view opened up into the control room, Cole felt a familiar sadness wash over him as he thought about the men who had worked there. The crew of the *Upholder* had cheated death on so many patrols. It was fitting they'd taken a U-boat with them on their last. He would be proud to be able to add that to Wanklyn's record.

Away from any sunlight, there was little marine growth on the chart table or the various instruments. The mysterious dials and pipes and valves looked remarkably well preserved, such that it was impossible not to imagine the men who had last stood on that deck. But he wasn't there to get sentimental.

For an instant he felt a flash of panic when he kicked with one of his fins and raised a cloud of silt. In that moment, he doubted his sense of direction. He'd turned himself around when he'd let go of the ladder, and he couldn't remember which direction was forward. Slowing his breathing, he turned back and grasped the ladder. He remembered the layout of the deck at the top of the ladder. He made sure his guideline was spooling out, and Cole started to pull himself forward toward the wardroom.

The two tables with benches on either side identified the officers' dining area. The galley should be just aft of that.

In the galley, Cole saw the first evidence of the damage the sub had sustained. Broken white crockery and glass bottles littered the floor. The surfaces that had once been stainless steel were holed in a few places by corrosion. The sink was obvious, but it was full of what Cole assumed had once been cooking pots but were now a melded pile of debris. Cole saw the door to the chiller box next to the sink. He thought of his father's use of the word *frozen*.

The handle was gone, either broken off in the explosion or corroded away. The hinges were unrecognizable as such. The door had been made of stainless steel, but when Cole brushed his glove over the surface, he felt only the rough edges of small crustaceans. The door wouldn't budge when he got his gloved hands on the corner and tried to tug at it. He pulled his dive knife from the sheath on his leg and tried to pry it open. No good. He checked his watch, then his air supply. It was time to start for the surface. He reached for the small pry bar he'd hooked inside his weight belt. He wedged the sharp prongs into the crack at the edge of the door. He tried to push on the lever, but nothing moved.

Cole really did not want to have to return on a second dive, but he couldn't argue with his air supply. He needed enough air for a decompression safety stop before surfacing. It was time to go. He floated his legs up, intending to turn around. He wasn't even aware of making the decision to try again, but he braced his legs against the bulkhead and put all his weight into one last effort.

The chiller-box door popped free and sank to the deck, releasing a wave of silt and debris from inside what had been the boat's refrigerated locker. Cole tried to shine his light inside, but the light simply reflected off all the suspended particles. He reached his gloved hand in and felt around. There had been some kind of wire shelving, now tangled and rusted into a mess. He tried to pull the shelving out of the box, but it was hanging up on something, and the water was now so cloudy he couldn't see what. He felt around the bottom of the icebox door and his fingers touched something made of solid metal on the bottom of the box. It moved when he jostled it. With both hands in the gap, he was able to move the object until he could get his fingers around the edge. He pulled it free.

What he drew out was a concave disk about two feet across. It appeared to have been wrapped in some kind of black fabric, which disintegrated and further muddied the water. Cole had to hold the object close to his mask to see anything with all the debris in the water. He rubbed his fingers on the convex side and saw a design in the metal. He rubbed a bit more, and he made out one branch of a familiar symbol. He reached for his guideline and began feeling his way out of the murky galley and back toward the control room and the sub's exit. He held the silver disk tight to his chest with one hand. If his suspicion was right, the object he clutched against his chest was a Knight's shield engraved with the image of a Maltese cross.

Aboard the EV *Shadow Chaser II*
Mediterranean Sea off Djerba Island

April 22, 2014

"What do you mean, no sign of Cole?"

"I can't see anything, Theo."

"What *do* you see?"

"*Enigma* is alongside the conning tower where I left it when I went to answer the radio. I've turned it in a complete three-sixty looking up and down the deck, and there is no sign of Cole."

"He didn't just disappear, Riley. He's probably down examining the hull or back looking at the props."

"He'd better not have gone inside without *Enigma*," Riley said.

"This is Cole we're talking about, you know."

She set her teeth at that and steered the ROV up and over the high side of the sub, shining the lights up and down the hull. "I can see what sank her. There's an open crack in the hull down here, as well as a pretty good dent. It looks like a long rip in the metal."

"What about Cole?"

"Still nothing."

Riley steered the ROV along the sea floor, panning the lights up and down along the hull. She intended to go all the way around the wreck. He had to be somewhere. The lack of fish in the water surprised her. She had grown accustomed to the fantastic diving in Indonesia and the Indian Ocean, where coral and fish were abundant. Aside from a few schools of silvery minnows and the occasional grunts, she didn't see much life at all.

"You're not talking to me."

She jumped. Theo had left the drum with the cables, and he was standing right by her side. "Oh, geez," she said. "You scared the bejesus out of me, Theo." She looked up at the worry lines on his face. "I'm sorry. I'm not as good as Cole at telling you what I see. I've been driving *Enigma* all the way around the wreck and I—" She stopped. Something had caught her attention over his shoulder.

"What? What were you about to say?"

Riley set the tablet down on the table on the back deck. "I think I see a boat headed our way, coming very fast. Hang on a minute while I run up to the bridge and get the binoculars."

She took the steps two at a time and carried the binoculars out onto the side deck. With that much higher altitude now, she could make the boat out clearly. The color was gray, either paint or unpainted aluminum. It was pushing a big, frothing, white wake at the bow. It looked like a pilot boat or maybe police. Either way, it didn't look good.

When she reached the deck, she said, "Theo, it looks like we've got official company heading our way—maybe customs, maybe police." She took one last look through the glasses, and now she could make out what looked like a machine gun on the foredeck of the boat.

"I can see a deck gun on the foredeck, so I'd say either military or police." She set the binoculars on the table and picked up the tablet. She drove the ROV back up to the submarine's deck level for another look around.

"Any sign of Cole yet?" Theo asked.

"I still don't see anything. Wait. It looks like there's a stream of bubbles coming up out of the conning tower."

"Do you remember how to use the robot arms on *Enigma*?"

"I think so."

"Take *Enigma* down to the hull and use one of the metal claws to tap out an SOS. If Cole's inside the sub, he'll hear it."

She maneuvered the little ROV over the edge and alongside the hull. The virtual controls on the screen were not easy to use, but she got the arm moving and rapped it once against the hull. Then again. After the third time she was getting the hang of it, so she was able to follow that with three short taps. Then three long. So she wasn't starting with *S*. He'd get the message eventually if he could hear it at all.

If he couldn't hear the SOS, then may he'd hear the prop noise of the approaching boat. She and Theo could certainly hear the patrol boat's engines now, and the noise grew ever louder.

"How far away are they?"

"Less than a quarter of a mile now. They must be doing twenty-five knots." She set the tablet down on the table. "Theo, I'm worried about Cole's air supply. He's run out of bottom time."

An amplified voice began speaking in French. *"Attention. Attention. C'est la police. Restez où l'on peut vous voir."*

The dog at Theo's heel began a low, rumbling growl.

Theo reached down and touched Leia. "Shhhh," he said, then he took hold of Riley's arm. "What are they saying?"

"They're just telling us to stay on deck where they can see us."

"It sounded like they said 'police.'"

"Yeah. And it looks like they're coming alongside. They've got a guy manning the gun on deck, and it looks like three guys with side-arms on the back deck. Then the boat driver. And he sucks at it, so get ready for impact."

There was the sickening sound of metal scraping against metal, and the three men jumped on board *Shadow Chaser II*. They were all dressed in desert camo fatigues and black berets.

The three men spoke amongst themselves in French. Obviously, they didn't think that the crew on an American-flagged vessel would speak their language. Riley wasn't about to inform them otherwise. This was the time to keep quiet and play dumb.

The tallest and oldest of the group stepped forward. "Where is the captain?" he asked in quite fluent-sounding English.

"He's not here," Riley said.

"Where is he?"

She pointed downward but didn't say a word.

"This vessel has not cleared in with the local authorities. What are you doing here?"

"We have mechanical difficulties."

The man walked up to Theo. "Look at me when I am speaking!" he yelled.

Theo swung his head around in the direction of the voice.

The man turned to Riley. "What is wrong with him?"

"He's blind," she said.

The man waved his hand in front of Theo's eyes.

It never ceased to amaze Riley when people did that. Granted, there was no damage to his eyes, so it wasn't always easy to tell, but when you saw how his eyes didn't track, it was pretty clear they weren't working.

The man pointed to the drum with the cables that passed over the side.

"What are you doing here with this equipment?"

Riley looked at the drum of cables like she was surprised to find it there. "That? We're using it to work on the boat. Like I said, we have mechanical trouble."

"We received a report that you were out here diving on a wreck in our territorial waters. That you are stealing antiquities."

Riley didn't say anything—just glanced at her watch. What if Cole had entered the sub and got disoriented or snagged his gear on something? What if he was down there running out of air?

The man stepped closer to her, invading her space. "If the captain does not return immediately, I will arrest you both and seize this vessel."

She could handle being arrested and forfeiting the boat. She couldn't handle losing Cole. If she told them the truth, they'd allow her to dive down with spare tanks. She was about to confess to the officer when she heard splashing at the stern of the boat.

A pair of black fins flew up onto the swim step. The three officials walked back to the bulwark in time to see a wetsuit-clad Cole stand up and shove his face mask to the top of his head.

"Hey, looky here," he said with an exaggerated twang in his voice. "We got guests." He stepped forward and stretched out his hand. "Welcome aboard, fellas."

CHAPTER FORTY-FIVE

Aboard the *Ruse*
Grand Harbour, Malta

J u n e   9 ,   1 7 9 8

Fortune was in his favor, Alonso thought, as the wind in the harbor was moderate and from the southwest. He had never sailed his vessel entirely alone, but he cast off from the wharf and sculled his ship out past Fort Saint Angelo and into the main channel. There, he unfurled the lateen sail on the foremast and tied it off. With the wind behind him, he would clear the harbor entrance in no time.

As he rounded Ricasoli Point, Alonso got his first view of the sea beyond Grand Harbour. Even with only starlight and the lanterns aboard the ships, the view of the French fleet was unlike anything he had ever seen before. The masts and hulls overlapped in his view in such a way that it looked like a wall of ships, less than half a mile off the harbor entrance.

Alonso spun the wheel and backed his sail. He tied off the helm and ran forward to reset the sail. Then he raised the larger sail on his main mast and set that by tying it off. The *Ruse* was slowly turning up into the wind and starting to head for shore. He ran back to the wheel and set his course to skirt as close to the shallows as he dared.

And that was very close indeed. When he'd first bought the *Ruse*, two of the features he'd liked most about the xebec were her small size and shallow draft. Many times he had thwarted a pursuer by crossing over shoals where his enemy could not follow. Now he sailed so close to the island's cliffs he knew only a very sharp eye could discern the outline of his sails. The French would not be interested in him, in any case. His smaller boat would make him appear to be a fisherman out trolling for fish along the coast.

The night was unusually quiet. He heard nothing but the occasional call of a bird on shore and the gurgling of the water as his wake closed behind the *Ruse*. She certainly was a fast boat, and this night the conditions were perfect, with the wind blowing off the shore. Every other time he had sailed his little ship, he'd had his full complement of crew. Men were loud, even at night—snoring, talking, playing cards, telling tales. If he had known how peaceful it was sailing alone at night, he would have done it sooner. But the truth was, eventually he would need to sleep, so he could not continue alone for days. And he intended to travel far from his island home. He needed crew.

Watching the coastline fly past, he calculated his speed and started to make his plan. The island of Gozo lay about four leagues to the northwest. Mgarr, a small fishing port, lay just across the channel that separated the two islands. Alonso had anchored there several times when he had needed to find shelter from a sudden weather change. He supposed he would arrive several hours before dawn, given the speed his boat was making. At that early hour of the morning, they certainly would not be expecting visitors at the convent.

The half-moon was well above the horizon by the time Alonso anchored the *Ruse* and rowed the launch ashore. He found a horse tethered outside a tavern and took off for Victoria, the capital in the center of the island. If he made it back before sunrise, the horse's owner need never know.

It must have been years since a rider had asked the animal to run. It took all of Alonso's strength, digging his boots into the sides of the beast, to get it to change from a walk to a canter once they had climbed up the steep road out of Mgarr.

The Citadel was a fortified city that adjoined Victoria and guarded the capital. It stood on the highest elevation on the island. For centuries Ottoman raiders had stormed Gozo, taking away its citizens as slaves. The Citadel was Gozo's attempt to build a safe harbor for its people. Just outside the gates to the Citadel stood one of the oldest churches on the island, the Saint Augustine Church. The monastery was quite large, but there was also a small convent, and it was there that the Knights sent their pregnant mistresses.

Sometimes the women went to live with local farmers until their time was near. Alonso hoped he would find his Arzella inside the convent when he arrived.

The horse was breathing heavily when they entered the outskirts of Victoria. Alonso let him slow to a walk while he considered his approach. Asking for her would not do. They sent these girls off with specific instructions to keep the Knights away from them. The nuns were familiar with love-struck Knights who came knocking at their door in the night, and they were instructed to send the Knights packing.

When he arrived at the church, he tied the horse to a tree. A gate in the wall adjoining the church looked promising. He passed through it and found himself in a tree-shaded courtyard.

First, he needed to find the nuns' sleeping quarters, and then, hopefully, he could locate her room. He crossed to a building in the back and entered. It was very dark inside, especially after the bright moonlight outside. Alonso felt his way along a wall until he came to a doorway. The door was unlocked, so he entered.

In the darkness, he heard light snoring, but it was impossible to tell if the sleeper was a man or a woman. Alonso approached the bed. Still it was too dark. He was standing above the sleeper, waiting for his eyes to adjust to the dark, when a fist connected with his chin.

The man in the bed came roaring up. Alonso had fallen from the first blow, and he crouched in the darkness, feeling for the walls. The monk stood now in the center of his cell, yelling in Maltese, one language that Alonso knew nothing of. He heard the man fumbling with something and realized it was the sound of a flint. The monk was about to light a candle.

Alonso found the door and leapt to his feet. Once in the corridor, he could see a shaft of moonlight angling across the floor from the courtyard entrance. He turned and ran but had not yet made it out the door when the monk started yelling behind him. Once outside, Alonso paused behind one of the trees in the courtyard. Where was the building for the nuns? There had to be another door somewhere.

A monk emerged from the dormitory wearing a white nightshirt and holding a lantern aloft. The man's posture was bent and his hair white.

"Who goes there?" the monk asked in Spanish.

Alonso decided to take a chance and answered the man in his native tongue. "It is Caballero Alonso Montras from Aragon."

The monk did not reply immediately. Finally, he said, "What do you seek, my son?"

Alonso stepped out from behind the tree. The monk approached him.

"Father, my request is strange, I know, but these are strange times. You have seen the fleet off Valletta?"

"Yes, my son. Here we do not concern ourselves with the affairs of such men."

Alonso chose his words carefully. "Perhaps you have heard that this war is just between the Knights and the French. But in France, Bonaparte's men killed priests and burned churches."

"I am not afraid to die," the old man said.

"I see that," Alonso said. "But I swore allegiance as a guardian of a religious relic that the Order of Saint John brought back from Jerusalem at the end of the Crusades. The relic dates back almost to the time of Christ. We cannot let it fall into Bonaparte's hands. I have been charged to go to sea, to spirit this treasure away from these islands, but my crew has deserted me. Here in the convent is a young woman who learned to sail as a child."

"You speak of the Brun girl, yes?"

Alonso nodded.

"She has been working in the kitchen with the sisters. I have heard her talk of going to sea."

"If you will permit her to help me, we will sail this relic to safety."

The old man ran a hand through his white hair. "Your story is far too strange to be an elaborate ruse. Go back out through the gate and wait."

Alonso started to turn away, but the monk put a hand on his arm. He made the sign of the cross and said, "May God go with you."

Alonso wondered what could be taking so long. Surely dawn was near. Then the gate in the wall opened, and she stepped out. The gate closed with a slam behind her.

She didn't see him standing under the tree where the horse was tied. She was dressed, but she had not had the time to put up her long hair. A satchel was slung over her shoulder. She looked around the square, then back at the gate. Her face wore a puzzled look.

He said her name softly. "Arzella?"

She spun around and faced in his direction, still unable to see him in the shadows. "Alonso?"

He tried to say more as he stepped out into the moonlight, but the words could not escape his tight throat.

She saw him and ran into his arms with a cry, burying her face in his chest. Lifting her head, she smiled. "You came for me," she said.

"Yes, my love. I came to take you sailing."

CHAPTER FORTY-SIX

Aboard the EV *Shadow Chaser II*
Mediterranean Sea off Djerba Island

April 22, 2014

"You are the captain of this vessel?"

"Yes, sir. That I am." Cole unzipped the front of his wetsuit and began peeling off the wet neoprene.

"What were you doing in the water?"

Cole shook his head. "Well, this is a new boat, you see, and we're doing our sea trials. We put variable-pitch props on her—you know, where you can dial in the pitch that will work for whatever you need to do at the time? And when we went to put her into reverse, the pitch stuck on the starboard engine, and we couldn't get the mechanism to move." He draped his wetsuit over the aft bulwark and Riley handed him a towel. "It just froze and I figured—"

The officer interrupted him. "We got a call reporting that you were wreck diving without permission and stealing antiquities."

Cole was drying his face, but he lowered the towel, an incredulous look in his eyes. "Seriously? You think we'd be that stupid? I mean, look at that coast. We're in plain sight of several thousand people.

My mama didn't raise no fool. And I'm not about to do something illegal in your country, anyway. I have too much respect for you." Cole wrapped the towel around his waist like a skirt, then walked over to the tablet on the table and turned it facedown.

The officer spoke to the other men in French. He explained to them that he wanted them to search the boat. He had some rather un-kind things to say about what he thought of Cole and told them that if he resisted, they had permission to hurt him a little, but not enough to leave marks.

"Monsieur, please bring me all your ship's papers and the crew's passports. Meanwhile my men will search your vessel."

Cole flashed them a wide grin. "Fine with me. I've got nothing to hide. Just so they don't break anything. She is a new boat, after all."

The officer waved his men off, and they went in through the doors to the main salon.

Riley said, "I'll go fetch the papers on the bridge."

"Thanks," Cole said. "Could we offer you fellows a cold drink? Something to eat?"

Riley passed through the salon, where she saw the two guys go-ing through all the cabinets in the galley. She thought about her own training for conducting a search. Clearly these guys hadn't read the same manuals.

When she got to the bridge, she went straight to the cabinet where she had stored her satellite phone just before they left. She stood next to the window and dialed Hazel's cell phone, hoping it wouldn't go to voice mail.

"Hi there, girlfriend," Hazel said. "Where are you?"

Riley covered her mouth and spoke softly into the receiver. "We're off Djerba Island in Tunisia, and we've just been boarded. They're talk-ing about seizing the boat because we haven't cleared in properly."

"I haven't received one of these calls from you in a long time."

"What calls?"

"The sort where you use me as your 'Get Out of Jail Free' card."

"Well, I was hoping you knew somebody who might know somebody."

"I'll see what I can do."

"Thanks, Hazel."

Riley switched off the phone and returned it to the cabinet. She retrieved the pouch Cole used for the ship's papers and went back down the steps.

The atmosphere, when she went out the doors onto the aft deck, was quite strained. The three men sat around the teak table, but no one was speaking.

Riley handed Cole the pouch. He took out the documentation and his clearance papers from Marmaris. Then he set out the three passports.

The officer lifted up the passports and flipped through the pages, comparing the photos to the three of them. He was behaving like such on officious jerk that Riley began to fear that Cole would lose his temper and get them into worse trouble. That fear level escalated when the officer slipped the three passports into the breast pocket of his fatigues.

"I will need those back," Cole said.

"You will get them when I am ready."

Riley saw the train wreck that was about to happen, so she jumped in. "You know, your English is quite good. Where did you learn to speak so well?"

"I have worked in Malta."

"Really?" she said. "What a coincidence. We hope to go to Malta someday."

The man looked at her and narrowed his eyes.

She continued. "In fact, there was a helicopter that flew out over us just a little while ago."

Cole looked at her, his eyebrows arched in puzzlement.

Riley continued. "I could swear that the guy in it was Maltese. Do you know him?"

From inside the boat they heard a loud crash. Cole winced. "Your guys are being a little rough with our stuff," he said.

"Quiet," the official said.

After another five minutes of listening to the noises from inside the boat, Cole shifted his weight and drew a deep breath. Riley knew the signs. The man had no patience. He was about to do something stupid.

Then a cell phone rang with a pop-music ringtone. The official drew the phone out of his pocket.

"Hallo?" As he listened, he stood up and walked to the far side of the deck. Riley could tell from the tone of his voice that he was furious, but she couldn't make out the words. He ended the call and stood for almost a minute with his back to them. Then he lifted his hand and waved to the launch driver who had kept the police boat hovering just off their starboard quarter.

The man turned around and slapped the three passports down on the table. He stepped to the cabin door and barked an order at his men. The two appeared, looking slightly disheveled and sweaty. The leader pointed to his boat and the two men climbed up on the bulwark, ready to jump to their vessel.

"You have one hour. If you are not under way headed away from our shores, I will be back. I will seize this boat. Do you understand?"

Cole nodded.

When the patrol boat was up on a plane and heading back the way it had come, Theo said, "Let's get *Enigma* back on board."

Riley picked up the tablet from the back table and turned it over. On the screen was a clear picture of the submarine beneath them. "Good thing he didn't decide to take a look at this screen."

"What happened, anyway?" Cole said. "Did *Enigma* malfunction? She just stopped, so I left her behind."

Theo told Cole about the helicopter.

Cole reached for the transom bulwark, straightened his arms and looked out across the water's surface. "So, whoever it was had the money to charter a chopper and the juice to sic the local officials on us." He turned around to face her and rested his bum on the bulwark. "What do you suppose made them back off?"

Riley said, "You've got Hazel to thank for that. I called her on the sat phone when I went up to get the papers."

"You foreign-service brats know lots of folks at the State Department, don't you?"

Riley decided it would be diplomatic not to answer that one. "So do we take this threat seriously? Are we done with the *Upholder*?"

"Not quite yet."

"While you're taking your time deciding what to do next, I think it would be prudent to fire up the engines and at least make like we're leaving." Riley picked up the tablet.

Theo said, "Yoda, start both engines."

Cole yelled, "Hold it! Don't put 'em into gear. I really was down there around the props." He scooped his face mask up off the deck and pulled it on his face. He dropped the towel at his waist and jumped off the stern of the boat.

"What the heck is that all about?" Theo asked.

"I have no clue."

Less than a minute later, Cole surfaced off the stern and heaved a net bag up onto the swim platform. They could hear the clank of something metal hit the teak grate. He climbed the ladder and picked up the bag.

"When I heard the noise of that boat's engines, I surfaced and caught the gist of what was going on. So I dove back down and hung this on one of the prop blades. I was pretty sure those knuckleheads weren't going to take their search that far."

He handed the net dive bag to Riley.

"It's heavy," she said. She pulled open the drawstring at the top of the bag.

Cole said, "Direct from the galley of the HMS *Upholder*."

Riley pulled the blackened steel disk out of the bag. It looked like a metal garbage-can lid, and it was covered with slime and growth. One section of it had been rubbed clean, and she saw yellow metal that looked like gold.

Theo said, "Would someone tell me what you're looking at?"

Cole took Theo's hand and placed it on the disk. "Take a look for yourself."

His fingers slid lightly over the surface. "Underneath all this gunk, I think there's some engraving on this metal."

"Yeah. Won't be sure until we get it all cleaned up, but I think there's more than a little engraving. The steel is black, but there is also some gold inlay."

"I feel some pitting, too, but after spending sixty years in seawater, there's not that much damage. Can you make out the designs?"

Cole moved Theo's fingers over to the part of the shield he had cleaned. "Feel this. It's one branch of a Maltese cross. My guess is this is a shield. You know, like knights in armor? I think it's a shield that once belonged to a Knight of Malta."

CHAPTER FORTY-SEVEN

**Aboard the EV *Shadow Chaser II*
Mediterranean Sea off Djerba Island**

April 22, 2014

Riley's and Theo's heads were bowed together as they examined the shield, but Cole figured there would be plenty of time later to do that.

"Hey, folks, those same guys who just chartered a helicopter to locate us are probably on their way back here by boat. I'd just as soon be gone when they get here."

Riley nodded. "You're right. We should get moving."

"Theo, you start reeling in *Enigma*. Riley, ready the crane. I'll get back on the swim platform to attach the lifting harness."

Cole was pleased with how efficiently they worked together as a crew already. By now he had sailed for years with Theo. Then he'd spent the last couple of years sailing with Captain Riley. Sometimes mixing crew together like this ended up causing rifts, and he was glad to see that it didn't seem to be happening with them.

"Theo, go ahead and raise the anchor and take her out. I assume the engines have been broken in well enough now we can go all-out?"

"Not a problem."

"Okay. Let's see what this baby can do."

"So what's the destination, Captain?"

"Malta."

Once Cole finished stowing all his scuba gear and cleaning everything off the decks, he headed up to the bridge. Someone had wrapped the shield in a towel and placed it on the table at the rear of the wheelhouse. Riley and Theo were sitting in the twin navigation chairs with their feet up on the dash, each with a bottle of beer in hand.

"It looks like we're hauling ass. How fast are we going?"

"Fifteen knots, *mon capitan*."

Riley handed him a beer and clicked her bottle against his. "I propose a toast to the two most brilliant men I know."

Theo said, "I'll drink to that."

"How much fuel are we burning?"

"Um, I don't think you really want to know," Theo said. "The good news is it's only about two hundred miles to Malta. We'll certainly be there by morning at this speed, or we could slow down in a bit and conserve fuel."

"It sure is nice to know we're capable of this speed when we need it. Speaking of which, what do you see on the radar or AIS? Do we have any company?"

Riley said, "Not at the moment. And, by the way, I know it's illegal, but I'm running the AIS in stealth mode."

"Good idea," Cole said. "Given that we are also leaving the country with stolen antiquities, I'm not too worried about that transgression."

Riley said, "When we first got under way, I kept an eye on the radar. There is a small marina on the north coast of Djerba called Port Houmt Souk. I saw something start out from there and head south, but we've been moving so fast, I lost him in the sea clutter. That probably means he wasn't very big."

"My guess is it was just a fisherman heading out for a night of fishing."

"So, Mr. Archeologist, are we going to try to clean that thing up and take a look at it?"

"Sure, why not. We'll need a big bowl of water, a soft toothbrush, and several of those microfiber cloths from the galley. Oh, and some baking soda."

"After you," Riley said, pointing to the stairs. "I'm on watch." She swiveled her chair back around and put her feet up on the dash again.

"Really is hard to get good help these days," Cole hollered as he went down the steps.

Cole unwrapped the shield and spread out the towel on the table. He arranged his tools and began the process of dipping a cloth into the water and then gently washing the growth and slime off the metal. He kept up a running dialogue for Theo.

"The shield is round, about one meter across. The way it's resting on the table, the convex side—the side that would face the opponent—is up. Picture one of those conical hats the Vietnamese wear working in the rice paddies."

"I've got it," Theo said.

"In the very center of both the shield and the Maltese cross is a raised knob. Would hurt like hell if you hit a man in the face with it."

"That might be the point."

"Looks like the outline of the cross has been drawn with a thin line of inlaid gold, while the center of the cross is silver inlaid over the steel. The steel around the cross is black from oxidization. This type of work is called damascening."

"That's a new one to me," Theo said.

"You might have seen the jewelry they make in Spain. Gold inlaid into black oxidized steel. Not surprising that the Knights of Malta would have imported this art, given that the Spanish *langue* was one of the *auberges* from the start."

"You lost me there, Skipper."

"The design of the Maltese cross is very deliberate. As a cross, it has four branches. But there is a V cut into the end of each branch, which gives the cross eight points. Originally, the eight points of the cross were supposed to represent the eight beatitudes of the Sermon on the Mount. But as the Order grew, they built hospitals, and, as a charitable order, hundreds of properties were donated to them. By the thirteenth century, they owned thousands of feudal manors, which had to be defended and managed, and which provided income. The Order developed what they called *commanderies* all over Europe. They were somewhat like local forts, with Knights whose job it was to collect money and provide protection to their properties."

Riley said, "That sounds to me like the beginning of their naughtiness."

"I suppose you're right. They were definitely into wealth and power, even back in the Middle Ages when they were still at Rhodes. The Order had grown into a huge international organization, and it required more structure. So they eventually organized themselves into eight branches, or *langues*, which is French for 'tongues,' or languages. The original eight *langues* were Castille, Aragon, Germany, England, Italy, France, Auvergne, and Provence."

"But Castille and Aragon are both in Spain," Riley said.

"This happened in the fifteenth century. What we now think of as countries didn't have the same borders back then. It's the same with France, Auvergne, and Provence."

"Okay," Theo said. "Enough with the history lesson, Professor. Get back to this shield."

"Well, the gold and silver bits look in fairly good shape, but the steel is badly pitted. So thin in this area near the edge, it has corroded all the way through."

"A hole?"

"Yeah, but small. Only about the size of a pencil eraser. The metal is very thin and fragile all around there, though."

Riley was sitting up at the nav station, monitoring the sea ahead, as a good watchkeeper should, but Cole noticed she kept glancing over her shoulder to watch his progress.

"There is a circle, drawn again by a thin line of inlaid gold, around the Maltese cross. That circle and the outer edge of the shield form a band around it. That's where most of the engraving is. There are leaves and vines and little fleur-de-lis shapes. Lots of fancy curlicues. It's going to take some work with the toothbrush to clean it all up." Cole grabbed the box of baking soda and sprinkled some onto the shield. He dipped the toothbrush in the water to make a paste. As he brushed it on, the tarnish turned the paste black, but the metal beneath brightened. He moved the brush in ever-larger circles. *This is going to take a while,* he thought.

The sun was lowering into the western sky, and the light slanting through the wheelhouse windows was a soft gold color. Cole dipped the toothbrush into some more baking soda and brushed it onto the silver cross. The corrosion washed off, and what had been black began to shine. He glanced up at Theo. Cole wished his friend could witness this moment on their new boat, cleaning up their first artifact.

"So how old do you think this could be?" Theo asked.

"No clue," Cole said. "If it truly is from the period the Knights were in Malta, that would be somewhere roughly between 1500 and 1800."

Riley swiveled her chair around to face them. "I wonder why this shield would be important, though. Why would your father want you to retrieve it, and why is there somebody following us and trying to keep us from getting our hands on it?"

"I don't know," Cole said, "but just the fact that they don't want us to have it makes me want to keep it out of their hands. I don't like these guys. They tried to blow up my boat."

"I agree we don't let them have it. So why," Theo said, "would they go so far like that over this shield? Is it that valuable?"

"What if it isn't the antique value?" Riley said.

"Then what?" Cole said.

She got up and walked over to the table. She pointed to the part of the shield where the metal was corroded through. "Right there. Look."

"What?"

"There in the design. It looks like letters."

"Where?"

Riley handed him the magnifying glass she'd brought over from *Bonefish*. His close vision had been deteriorating for years. She wanted him to get reading glasses, but he couldn't bear the thought. Now he held up the magnifying glass and squinted at the part she was pointing at.

"What do you see?"

"It looks like a name."

"Cole! What name?"

"It looks like *Joseph Roux*."

"Who the hell is that?"

CHAPTER FORTY-EIGHT

Aboard the Dive Boat *Odysea*
Mediterranean Sea off Djerba Island

April 22, 2014

Virgil checked his watch for the third time. They'd been down there for thirty-five minutes and the sun was sinking fast. He needed to know if there was something there or not, and he wasn't going to wait until morning.

He picked up his backpack and pulled his phone out of the side pocket. He checked his messages. His daughter had emailed him earlier that she wanted to talk to him. Soon. He'd sent her a brief note saying he was working, he'd be in touch when he could. There were no more messages. He put the phone away.

The boat driver was an Arab kid who spoke no English. He wouldn't be able to get any info from him. He slouched against the bulwark, ignoring Virgil and only occasionally tweaking the controls so they could hold position according to the GPS unit attached to the windscreen above the helm. Virgil hadn't liked giving them the coordinates, but there was no other way to get out here.

This thirty-five-foot dive boat with twin 200 HP outboards was the best thing he could charter when the cab dropped him off at Port Houmt Souk. It wasn't much of a marina—barely more than a man-made harbor cut into the coast and protected with a meager breakwater. The surge in the harbor kept most yachts out. It was only a few fishing boats and the government boats that needed to be in these waters. The little dive boat was owned by an entrepreneurial Frenchman who thought he could pick up business from the many hotels along the beach. Lucky for Virgil, he hadn't been too successful at that, so he jumped at the chance to take Virgil out.

From Virgil's ride out in the helicopter, he had marked the exact GPS coordinates where Thatcher's boat had been when he flew over. He understood from a phone call with the policeman who had boarded them that Thatcher had been in the water when the officials arrived.

That they had left so quickly was problematic. Or were they merely pretending to leave and in fact meaning to return to complete their work? He would find out when Remy and the other diver surfaced—hopefully soon.

About fifty yards away from the boat, the two divers surfaced.

"Hey, kid," Virgil said. "Do you see that?" He pointed to the men in the water.

The Arab kid was sitting on the side of the boat, smoking a cigarette. When he saw the divers, he threw it into the water and walked to the wheel.

Virgil didn't normally find anything wrong with the smell of cigarettes. Hell, he'd smoked since he was sixteen years old. But this kid's cigarette smelled more like sweet spice than tobacco. The stink of it was making Virgil nauseated.

Of course, it might have had something to do with the swells, too. There wasn't much wind, but the boat kept rolling in these long swells. His gut clenched into a tight ball with every roll. It wasn't a natural motion.

The boat pulled up alongside the divers. The men shucked their dive gear while still in the water, and the Arab kid hauled it on board.

Remy was the name of the owner of the dive boat. Virgil didn't know his dive partner's name. He didn't think that guy spoke any English, either. They'd taken a camera down with them, and whatever they found they promised they would record. Both men stood on the aft deck, peeling off their wetsuits, as the young crewman stored the tanks and equipment.

"So talk to me," Virgil said. "What did you find?"

The Frenchman grinned. "It is quite a find. A submarine. Not a modern nuclear one, but from the Second World War."

"Is it British?"

"I cannot say for certain. I don't know them that well, but I took many photos." He said something in French to the Arab kid boat driver. The kid walked over to the wheel and got the boat under way. "It's late. I want to get back to the marina before dark. There's nothing more we can do out here. Let's go inside the cabin. It will be easier to talk in there."

Virgil thought it was an exaggeration to call it a cabin. The forward part of the boat had a hard top, plastic side curtains, and a plywood-enclosed head. They were a bit farther away from the outboards, though, and out of the wind.

As Remy toweled himself off, Virgil asked, "Could you tell if there was any way to get inside the sub?"

"Yes, the main hatch is open, but it is too dangerous to go inside. I would need a team."

"Why?"

"Wreck diving is a very special art. The entrance hatchway to a submarine is so narrow, a diver could easily get stuck and drown. Also, inside, you don't know what you will find. It's too dangerous to go without using an ROV to do a video search of the wreck first."

"And what if a man was really reckless? What if he thought he had one chance and one chance only to find something of value? Is it possible he went in and got it and made it out safely?"

"Of course it is possible. Maybe he'd get lucky, but he'd be a fool to do it."

Virgil thought about what Priest had told him. Too many times people had underestimated this guy. He took chances. He'd probably gone in on his own. The question was whether or not he found something.

Remy was talking, and Virgil focused back on the dive master. "I can do the research for you if you like," he was saying. "Tell you what type of sub it is and even exactly which one. There were some numbers on the side of the hull. Then, if you want, I can set up a dive to enter the wreck."

"Just give me the pictures."

"I know some guys at Cap Monastir who have an ROV. Do you know what this is?"

Virgil nodded.

"We could have it down here in a couple of days."

"Take me back to the marina and give me a flash drive with all the photos. That's all I'll need."

When they got back to the dock in Port Houmt Souk, Virgil went into the head to take a piss. When he came out, the three boatmen were up on the bow, messing with the dock lines and trying to rig the gangway that they used to cross to the concrete dock. Virgil went back to the stern. With the knife from his pack, he slit a fuel line that fed one of the big outboards. Liquid spewed out onto the deck. From his pack he pulled out a small electronic device and armed it.

When he started walking to the bow, he saw the underwater camera resting on a table. He opened the waterproof housing and pulled out the data card from the compartment on the bottom of the camera. When he reached the foredeck, he had his wallet open showing all the colorful bills inside.

"So what do I owe you guys?'

"We agreed on three hundred euros, right?" Remy said.

"You've been very cooperative. Thanks." He handed him a sheaf of bills.

"Are you going to report the wreck? It's a big deal to claim a find like that. That will really change the face of the dive industry around here."

"Not interested."

"Do you mind if I do?"

"What you do is up to you. Look, I'm in a hurry. I've got a plane to catch."

"What about the images of the wreck?"

He waved them off. "I have your card. I'll email you for them."

Remy yelled at the guys to let Virgil pass.

The two Arabs stood aside.

Virgil crossed the parking lot and used his key to open the door of the Peugeot he'd rented at the airport. He tossed his backpack into the passenger's seat, climbed in, and placed his cell phone on the dash. Once the car was running, he backed out of his parking place and headed slowly for the exit. He reached for the cell on the dash and dialed a number. Then he pulled to a stop. He couldn't resist. He turned around in his seat so he could watch. Then he tapped the screen.

CHAPTER FORTY-NINE

Manoel Island Yacht Marina
Marsamxett Harbour, Malta

April 23, 2014

Cole pulled back on the throttle as the big boat came out of Msida Creek, where they had just cleared in with all the authorities. He and Riley were sitting up in the helmsman chairs, where they had spent most of the night.

"We're cleared and ready to dock, and it's not even noon yet," he said. "Not too bad."

"You know, after the last six years of sailing *Bonefish* more than halfway around the world, it's hard to believe we just did two hundred miles in a bit over sixteen hours. We were hauling ass."

"The original *Shadow Chaser* was no ball of fire, either." Cole sat forward and patted the dash. "I'm very happy with the new boat. Now we've just got to make sure we keep us and her safe. I'm not crazy about the fact that by clearing in, we just popped up on the grid again."

Cole heard Theo and Leia come up the stairs behind him.

"It's a bit difficult to hide when you're driving around in an eighty-three-foot expedition yacht," Theo said.

"Look ahead there," Riley said. "It's the old Lazaretto Submarine Base. It's right next to the marina I booked us into."

Cole swung his head to take in the whole scene before them. "Pretty amazing to think of this place with half a dozen submarines in the creek and one or two tied up to a pontoon off that old stone building."

"What does it look like?"

"I wish you could see it, buddy. The Lazaretto, like most of the old buildings here in Malta, is built of this local limestone, which has a beautiful yellow-gold color. At the Lazaretto, they cut small stones like bricks. On the ground floor, there is this gallery with columns of stone that support these arches. The limestone they use here is soft, which makes it easy to cut, but it also erodes in the weather faster than, say, something like marble. So the buildings here, both Fort Manoel and the Lazaretto, are crumbling and eroding away. Some of the damage probably dates back to the bombings during the war."

"I guess the *Upholder* spent a lot of time here, then."

"She did," Cole said. "When I was doing research on the passage down to Djerba, I found this photo of Wanklyn and his crew right after he was awarded the Victoria Cross. They looked so young and happy. I'm looking at the spot right now where those men were standing and smiling. And just yesterday, I dove on their grave."

No one said anything after that. Cole hadn't meant to dampen the good cheer of their arrival, but he felt the weight of the loss of those good men. The big yacht was moving through the water at less than a knot. The harbor was plenty big enough, and there was no boat traffic, so he took the time to appreciate the ruins on Manoel Island.

"Looks like there's a fence between the Lazaretto and the marina," Riley said. "Guess we won't be able to go in and explore."

"Yeah, the Lazaretto and the fort are both in such bad condition it's not safe to let people climb around there now. But there's a plan to develop the island, renovate the Lazaretto complex, and turn it into shops, offices, flats, and a casino."

"I kind of like it the way it is," Riley said. "It's easier to imagine the ghosts of Captain Wanklyn and Tug Wilson roaming around those ruins."

"Hey," Cole said. "Aren't you the one who keeps insisting you don't believe in ghosts?"

Riley sat up straight, but her phone rang just then.

"Hello?" she said after she'd slid it out of her pocket. "Oh, hi, Hazel."

Theo inclined his head in an effort to listen. Cole had noticed it before, the effect that woman's name had on his first mate.

"We're fine. We just got docked at the Manoel Island Marina here in Malta." Riley sat forward in her chair, and her free hand flew up to her collarbones, her fingers spread wide. "Really? Oh my God."

"What is it?" Cole said.

She held up her hand as she listened. "No, I'm glad to say it wasn't us. Sorry that you were worried. Yeah. Okay. You go back to enjoying Corsica. We've got lots to do today. I'll call you later to let you know what's happening. *Ciao*."

"What was that about?"

"Hazel just heard on the news that three people were killed in a boat explosion yesterday on Djerba Island."

With the help of the marina launch to run their stern lines ashore, Riley and Cole had the *Shadow Chaser II* med-moored to the seawall in no time. Cole congratulated his crew when they sat down for a quick lunch of cheese, yogurt, and crackers.

"Thanks, guys. We make a good crew. Eat up, then Riley and I will go see Dr. Günay."

"What with standing watches all night," Theo said, "we haven't really had time to sit down together and go over what happened down at Djerba. And now with this news from Hazel, I think we need to talk about this before you two take off with that shield in hand."

"Are you becoming a mother hen?"

"No, but I am the one in this group who has felt the effects of pissing off some bad guys. Let's not be stupid and go blundering into this blindly, so to speak."

"Theo's right," Riley said. "We've been reacting, and so far, we've been lucky. We need to get ahead of this."

Theo said, "And I'm not even sure what 'this' is. I can't see the big picture here."

"To be honest," Cole said, "I can't, either—but that's only because we don't know what these Knights of Malta are after. Is it the shield or something else?"

Riley scraped the inside of a plastic yogurt cup with her spoon. "Besides the name, did you find any other markings that might tell us something?"

"Riley, wait," Theo said. "Before we get to that, let's start at the beginning. Cole became interested in the Knights of Malta. He started doing some simple research, and the next thing you know, you're being followed. What I want to know is *why*. How did we unwittingly kick a hornets' nest?"

"Theo, they are never going to leave me alone. I'll be on their wanted list forever just for the *Surcouf* incident, let alone for what happened in the Philippines."

Theo reached up and rubbed his eyebrows.

"Don't give me that 'Here we go again' look."

Theo held his hands up in front of his face. "How can a blind man give you a look?"

"You know what I mean."

Riley stood up and walked away from the table. "Boys, boys," she said. "Stop your squabbling." She picked up her shoulder bag, then turned around. "Look. I think I can explain how the Knights of Malta got interested in Cole. And, much as I love your little paranoid, conspiracy-loving self, I don't think it's because the Knights had you on their Most Wanted list."

"Oh really," Cole said. "Would you care to explain?"

"Well." Riley crossed her arms and looked at the floor. "I have a confession to make. I haven't been entirely honest with you guys."

She looked up, but Cole didn't say anything. He just waited. She'd have to spit it out, if he was going to just keep quiet.

"That last day in the yard in Turkey, while you guys were getting ready to launch, I went into the office and asked to go over the tapes from the closed-circuit security cameras." She opened the flap on her purse and pulled out a folded sheaf of papers. "I went back to the night before the explosion. And several days before, to see who might have been following Cole or keeping us under surveillance."

Cole couldn't believe he hadn't thought to do it. "You found something and you didn't tell us?"

"Things have been moving pretty fast."

"Riley, we had a five-day passage down to Djerba."

"And you and I stood opposite watches. There was rarely a time the three of us were together."

"And what about the days we were running the search?"

Theo put his hand on Cole's arm. "Skipper. Do you want to hear what she has to say or not?"

Riley unfolded the papers and set them on the table. "I took some screenshots." She spread out a couple of the pages and pointed. "That's Blondie who was in the helicopter yesterday," she said, and then she slipped out a page beneath it. "And this one is of Diggory Priest."

CHAPTER FIFTY

Aboard the *Ruse*
Mgarr Harbor, Gozo

June 10, 1798

The sky in the east was growing light when Alonso helped Arzella aboard the *Ruse*. She spread her arms and spun around in a circle.

"I cannot believe I am free." The past weeks at the convent, she had dreamed of Alonso coming to take her away. She'd thought of those daydreams as silly indulgences with no hope of ever coming true.

"You won't be for long if we don't get moving." He stood in the launch still. "Pass me that line so we can hoist the launch aboard."

"Where are your men?" she asked as she swung the spar over and he grasped the hoist.

"You are the crew, my dear Arzella. We are going to sail the *Ruse*, just the two of us."

"But why?"

Alonso jumped onto the deck, wrapped the line around a capstan, and began to turn, hoisting the smaller boat out of the water. "The men assumed we would be fighting against Bonaparte's fleet.

Rightfully, they assumed that would be suicide. The fight here is between the Knights and the French. The Maltese want no part of it."

When the launch was above deck level, they swung it inboard and settled it into the chocks built into the wooden deck between the two masts.

"So I gather you and I are not rushing into battle?"

"No, dear. We are taking off on a long voyage. You've often said you wanted to see more of the world than just Malta. This is your chance. Come help me raise the anchor. Let's get out of here before the French notice us."

By the time they had secured the anchor and set both sails, the sun was well up. Alonso came out of his cabin carrying a large wooden strongbox crossed all around with straps of steel. She admired the metalwork, from the beautifully peened-over rivet heads to the elaborate designs around three different keyholes.

"That box is lovely."

"It belonged to my great-grandfather." He set it on the deck with a loud *thunk*. "Even with little gold inside, these old corsair's boxes are heavy."

"No treasure, then?"

"I did not say that."

Alonso lifted the lid of the box and drew out a shield of steel inlaid with gold and silver. As Arzella ran her fingers over the shield's engraved design, Alonso pulled out a large, leather-bound book.

"What do you know of navigation?" he said.

"I can steer by the compass."

"Very well. Steer a course east-northeast for now. There is much more you will need to learn, as there are only the two of us. If something happens to me, it will be up to you to finish our voyage alone."

Arzella sat behind the wheel, one hand on a spoke, holding a steady course. Alonso stood at her side and held out the book he had brought. The letters of the title were stamped into the cover: *Carte de la mer Méditerranée en douze feuilles*, Joseph Roux.

Alonso opened the book and turned the heavy pages. "Can you read a sea chart?"

"I have only ever seen the one that my uncle used. I can see I have much to learn."

For the next hour, Alonso taught her how to read the sea charts, and the way a hand compass could be used to determine a course.

"For now, we are headed to Crete, an island in Greece. Here." He pointed to the chart. "The voyage will be long, but we have food and water aboard."

Arzella looked up to check her course. Even as they passed some two leagues north of Malta, they could see the forest of masts that was Napoleon's fleet.

"I've never seen anything like it."

"There has never been anything like it, I believe."

"Surely the Knights will be slaughtered if they resist."

"I don't believe they will resist. When I last saw Grand Master Hompesch, he already looked defeated. He hoped to negotiate a truce."

"Will Bonaparte let the Knights stay?"

"No one can predict what that man will do. My guess is no. But, my love"—he threaded his fingers through her hair—"we will not be there to see the end of it."

"So where are we going? And why? You don't strike me as the type to run from a fight."

"No, we are not running. And this is not to be an easy voyage, sailing this ship with just the two of us."

"You didn't answer my questions."

"Let me start with why. We are leaving because von Hompesch asked me to. You know the mark I wear above my heart?"

"Yes. You told me you had taken an oath, and you could not speak of it."

"That is true. But these are trying times, and I have no one to turn to but you."

"I am glad of it. With my father gone, nothing holds me to Malta. So tell me about this mark."

"I am a member of a brotherhood of Knights known as the Guardiani. Hundreds of years ago, during the Crusades, the Knights of Saint John came into possession of an ancient manuscript. It is a gospel written by one of Christ's disciples, and it has long been the most valued treasure belonging to the Order."

"That is your oath, then, to guard this manuscript?"

"Yes. Bonaparte hates the church, and he certainly has plans to expropriate all the riches he can find in Malta. The grand master plans to allow him to take most everything, but not this." He tapped the side of the corsair's box. "We have been charged to keep the manuscript not only safe, but hidden as well."

"Hidden?"

"Yes." Alonso paused. "Have you read the Bible, Arzella?"

"Some of it. Not all."

"So you know then that the Bible is made of many books."

"Yes. What are you trying to tell me, Alonso?"

"In the early days of Christianity, there were many different sects, many gospels. These books contradicted one another. Men decided on the four gospels that made it into the New Testament. Many of the other gospels were destroyed."

"But this one wasn't destroyed?"

"Perhaps it should have been. I don't know why it survived. The tale it tells is quite different from the books you know, and it is older than any other texts we know of today."

"How did the Knights come to own this manuscript?"

"During the Crusades, when the Knights of Saint John were assisting with a renovation of the Church of the Holy Sepulchre, in Jerusalem, they found a passage into an underground cavern. The church had been built on top of an old Roman temple to the goddess Venus, and in that chamber, the Knights discovered this manuscript."

"May I see it?"

"It is too fragile." Alonso placed the shield back in the box and closed the lid. "We cannot touch it or let the light of day shine upon it. The pages are animal skin and the ink fades. It was written in ancient times."

"Why do you say perhaps it should have been destroyed?"

Alonso leaned back and gazed up at the sky. "You ask many questions."

"And you have asked me to sail off into the unknown with these pages."

He reached over and slid the back of a finger down her cheek. "My dear Arzella. I do love you more than you will ever know." He cleared his throat. "This manuscript is both dangerous and of great value because it might change everything you *think* you know about Jesus Christ."

CHAPTER FIFTY-ONE

Triton Fountain
Valletta, Malta

April 23, 2014

The cab let them out in the roundabout next to the Triton Fountain at Valletta's City Gate. Neither of them had said a word during the ride from the marina. Cole slung his arms through the straps of the big backpack while staring at the bronze mermen in the fountain. He was still angry with her.

Riley waited on the curb while he paid the driver. Throngs of people were pouring into the city from the bus terminal a ways down the hill and the tourist buses idling at the curb circling the roundabout. Bright, colorful flags snapped in the wind, giving the scene a carnival-like atmosphere.

Instead of joining her, Cole headed straight for the entrance to the city. Riley trotted after him as he crossed the bridge over the moat. She grabbed hold of his arm.

"Hold on, Cole. Let's not go in to see Najat like this." She led him to the side of the river of people, and she leaned on the stone barrier there. The view of the fortifications of the old city was spectacular. "Let's talk about this."

"Okay. But I still don't understand it. Why didn't you tell me sooner? It's been more than a week, Riley."

"I know, and I apologize. I screwed up. I wanted to tell you sooner, but the time never seemed right. Remember that first night at sea, when you were so excited to be under way on your new boat after all that waiting?"

"Of course I remember."

"I planned to tell you then, when we were alone in our stateroom. But then you took the first watch and sent me and Theo to get some sleep. I told myself I'd wait until the morning. And then another day went by and another. I admit, I took the easy way out, but I wanted my laughing, happy fiancé back. I was afraid that as soon as I inserted Diggory Priest into the mix, you'd be back to the quiet, paranoid guy I'd been living with for the last few months—even though I recognize now that your fears weren't irrational."

"And what about these past few nights at Djerba Island? We were alone in our stateroom there."

"Yes, and we slept. We didn't talk, we didn't make love."

"Riley, would you have come on this trip if you hadn't seen those videos?"

"I don't know. I hadn't decided yet. But I knew once I saw him that I needed to be at your side to help you deal with whatever is coming."

"You wanted to protect me?"

"I guess you could say that."

"But I'm the guy—I'm supposed to protect you."

"We don't have to think that way. You know my background. I don't need you to protect me."

"So you don't think I can manage on my own?"

"No, it's not that. You're an archeologist, and you've now got your ideal expedition boat. What about me? What am I supposed to do on *Shadow Chaser II*? Put on an apron and be chief cook and bottle washer? I haven't figured out where I fit in this new life, Cole. I want us to be a team. But we're both trying to figure out how we're going to work as a married couple."

He looked into her eyes for a long moment, and then nodded. "I understand that this new boat represents a big change for you," he said, speaking softly. "And I know it's not just the boat. Believe me, I'm hearing what you're saying, and I know we have a lot to figure out. And we will. It's all going to be fine, I know it. We just have to be honest with each other." Cole adjusted the straps of his backpack and looked around at the crowd. "But right now? To be *honest*, I'm a bit nervous, considering what is on my back. Let's go see our favorite historian." He took hold of her hand. "Together."

Riley had called Najat from the boat and asked for her help with an artifact they had found. The historian had hammered her with questions, but Riley held her off, telling her she would see it when they arrived.

Najat was waiting just inside the entrance to the Grand Master's Palace. "Follow me," she said. She took off at an astonishing pace for such a short woman and led them back to the beautifully furnished office where Riley had worked on the cipher from James Thatcher's journal. "Have a seat." Najat gestured to the two chairs opposite her big desk, then she circled around and sat behind it.

Cole slipped off the backpack and drew out the shield, wrapped in a couple of beach towels. Riley took off one of the towels, folded it, and placed it on the desk. Cole set the shield on top.

Najat's eyebrows lifted, and she made a little yipping noise. Then she clapped her hands. "Bravo! What a lovely piece."

Riley waited for her to say more, then realized that she had not told Najat where they had found it. "Cole found this on the *Upholder*."

"You found the wreck?"

Riley nodded. "This is what Tug and Charlie discovered in Tunisia after they blew up a bridge outside Sousse."

The historian lifted the pair of reading glasses hanging from a chain around her neck and placed them on her nose. She leaned in and examined the curling engraving around the outer edge of the shield.

"What can you tell us about it?"

She shook her head. "I wonder if it is possible?"

"What?" Cole asked.

Najat looked up and blinked several times. The woman's eyes were not focused on anything in the room.

Riley reached over and touched her forearm. "Are you okay?"

"Yes, yes, excuse me. My brain is sometimes working faster than my mouth. Do either of you know the Legend of the Silver Girl?"

"Several people have mentioned it since we arrived in Malta, but so far, we haven't actually heard the story."

"Well, permit me. You'll see why when I am finished.

"Many years ago, a strange young woman wearing foreign clothing arrived in Mdina with a baby boy in her arms. Though she was still young, her long hair was silver colored. She settled in the old city and opened a shop, where she made the most lovely things out of silver. At first, no one would buy her wares, because they had never heard of a woman silversmith.

"One day a noblewoman saw the girl in the market. She exclaimed that the necklace and earrings the girl wore were the most exquisite she had ever seen. The girl took them off and handed them to the lady, saying, 'If you like them so, then please take them as a gift.' From that day on, she was called the Silver Girl, and she became the most famous silversmith in Malta.

"When she was a very old woman and she lay dying, her son asked her why she had always had such silver-colored hair. She told him a story of sailing off to a faraway land with a Knight corsair on the eve of Napoleon's arrival on Malta in 1798. The Knight's errand was to hide the Order's greatest treasure. During a terrifying storm on that voyage, she said, her hair turned silver overnight. Her son asked her what had happened to the treasure. She explained that they'd hid it in a place where no one would look, and that then she'd engraved the secret key to finding this treasure onto the Knight's silver shield. Just as she was about to tell her son how to find this shield, God took her."

"Of course," Riley said. "But it is a great story." She glanced at Cole and then back at the shield on the table.

"I'll bet it's brought boatloads of treasure hunters to Malta through the years, too," Cole said.

Najat nodded. "Yes, it is astonishing the things people will do. We've had attempted thefts here at the museum, and people come with the most flimsy credentials, asking to do research. Of course, they want to examine the shields."

Cole's grin stretched from dimple to dimple when he touched the shield and said, "Do you really think—"

Najat's eyes twinkled and she was literally licking her lips. Riley thought, *Surely this renowned historian doesn't really believe in that old folktale.*

"Well, Cole," Najat said, "I think there is some element of truth in this tale. You see, today, the headquarters of the Sovereign Order of the Knights of Malta is in the Magistral Palace in Rome. Inside the palace is the Magistral Library, which houses the world's finest collection of books, articles, maps, photos, and prints about the Order. As you can imagine, in my line of work, I've been there to do research many times."

"So what does that library have to do with this legend?"

"I'm getting to that. You see, the library was started in the mid-nineteenth century when members and friends began donating their entire collections to the Order. In 1882, a Maltese man by the name of Lukka Demontras died. He willed his entire library and fortune to the Order. A very wealthy man, he lived in Mdina. He claimed that his mother, who had died fifty years earlier, had been the source of the legend. In a letter to the grand master, he stated that his mother had died in his arms when an unexpected illness took her suddenly. He wrote that he believed the Knight with whom his mother had sailed had been his father, therefore he felt a loyalty to the Knights. He hoped the Order would someday be able to recover their lost treasure. I've seen the letter myself. All the material he donated is in a special collection in the Magistral Library in Rome."

"Come on," Riley said. "What are the odds that, after all these years, this mythical shield would suddenly show up?"

Cole turned to her and smiled. "Riley, let your imagination run with it."

"Let's not get ahead of ourselves," Najat said.

Cole said, "Do you have any idea what this treasure is?"

"Again, there has been lots of speculation, but no one really knows. There are those who want to believe it is gold and jewels. Others think it may be a religious relic—perhaps even something that once belonged to Jesus."

"Or," Riley said, "it's all just a folktale."

Cole said, "My father thought there was something to it."

"Let's take a closer look at this shield of yours."

Cole picked up the shield and rotated it so that the section with the hole was in front of Najat. "I've examined it fairly carefully, and the only thing I can find that looks odd is in this part right here. Do you see the letters? It looks like the name Joseph Roux."

Najat put her hand in front of her mouth and began to giggle. Then she opened the center drawer in her desk and began fumbling through the mess of pens, letter openers, scissors, and the like. She reached deep inside and pulled out a magnifying glass. She held her breath as she examined the letters and then straightened up with a loud exhale.

"It's true. Those letters have been engraved on this shield." She giggled again.

"What is it, Dr. G.? What's so important about that?"

"Joseph Roux was a well-known eighteenth-century French cartographer. His sea chart atlas of the Mediterranean was thought to be top-notch in his day. Admiral Nelson carried a set on his flagship, the HMS *Victory*."

"Okay," Cole said. "So what does that tell us?"

"Oh, but I haven't told you the best part."

"Which is?"

"Among the books that Lukka Demontras donated to the Magistral Library in Rome, there is a copy of *Carte de la mer Méditerranée en douze feuilles*, by Joseph Roux."

CHAPTER FIFTY-TWO

**Aboard *Shadow Chaser II*
Marsamxett Harbour, Malta**

April 23, 2014

Riley stood at the sink, rinsing off the last of the cutlery. Cole had tried to get her to use the fancy dishwasher he'd installed on the new boat, but she didn't like it. She'd lived without such amenities for nine years aboard *Bonefish*, where she'd had to be very frugal with water and power, and she was finding it difficult to adjust to the new lifestyle on the big yacht.

Cole was still sitting at the dining table, filling Theo in on what he and Riley had learned at the museum that afternoon.

"I guess that makes sense," Theo said. "If Joseph Roux's atlas of sea charts was in the library of books owned by this Lukka Demontras, there's a good chance it belonged to his mother."

"Right," Cole said. "Especially since, according to Dr. G., there's no evidence that the son was ever a sailor."

"So, the shield is supposed to have some kind of key engraved on it, and what we've found there is the name Joseph Roux. Why not just get another copy of this book from an antiquarian bookseller?"

"Just as there was something written by the Silver Girl on the shield, I think there must be something written in *her* copy of this sea atlas."

Riley stepped out of the galley and both men looked up at her.

"Thanks for cleaning up," Cole said.

"Thanks to Theo for making dinner," she said.

Theo smiled and nodded at her. "My pleasure."

"I think I'm going to go up and take a shower and turn in. Good night, fellas." Riley knelt next to Theo's dog and scratched her ears. "Good night to you, too, Princess."

"I'll be up in a bit," Cole said.

When Riley closed the door to their stateroom, she leaned against it. The cabin looked like it should be photographed for some yachting magazine. At the head of the queen-sized bunk, a stylish fabric-covered headboard ran beneath the large windows along the port side of the boat. All the furnishings, from the partner desk to the cabinets and drawers, were beautifully crafted in cherrywood. Soft blinds now covered the windows, and the lighting from the recessed spots in the overhead was lovely. But Riley didn't know if she would ever be able to feel at home there.

She crossed to the head compartment. While she might not be ready to use a dishwasher, she was happy to take advantage of the big tub and shower and the plentiful hot water. She stripped off her clothes and examined herself in the full-length mirror on the back of the door. Sailing had kept her fit these past few years, and her suntan was just starting to fade. She turned aside and examined her scarred back and shoulders. Even the old injury didn't look quite as bad when the skin around it was brown instead of white.

Riley adjusted the shower flow and stepped into the tub. The hot water stung her skin, but it felt marvelous. She washed her hair and scrubbed her body. The tension of the day sloughed off her like old skin.

After she'd dried off, she wrapped a white towel around her body and carried another with her out through the door to the aft deck. She leaned on the railing as she toweled her hair dry. A change in the weather had left the air warmer and drier than it had been on their first visit to Malta. Her hair, though it now fell past her shoulders, dried quickly as she ran her fingers through the damp waves.

She hadn't heard him enter their stateroom or step out onto the deck. When with both hands she lifted her hair off the back of her neck to dry it in the night air, his warm lips kissed her right at her hairline, and she gasped in both surprise and pleasure.

His hands slid around her waist, and she felt his hot breath on her ear when he said, "My God, Riley. If you could see yourself out here in just that white towel." He rained kisses down the side of her neck and across her scarred shoulder.

Riley's lips parted, but her brain was so overloaded with trying to process the sensations, it was all she could do just to breathe.

He slowly turned her around and ran his fingertips across her forehead to push her hair back from her face. His sea-green eyes reflected the many lights shining on Valletta's fortified walls across the creek. "I came up here to finish the conversation we started in town today, but when I saw you standing out here, looking so soft and sexy, I realized I don't want to be angry. I don't want to argue. I just want to love you." He leaned in and kissed the hollow of her neck, and her knees threatened to give way.

"Cole—" She tried to say his name, but it came out as a long moan. The last thing she wanted to do was distract him at that particular instant, but leaving things unsaid was what had got them here. "You're making it too easy for me."

He didn't pretend not to know what she meant, but his low laugh, and the kisses that were headed for the edge of her towel, gave her his answer. But he *deserved* more. She slipped her fingers into his hair on either side and lifted his head up until they were eye to eye.

"This is important, Cole. I need to say it."

"I'm listening," he whispered.

"Okay." She took a deep breath, then said, "I am so sorry."

"Riley, you don't—"

She shook her head to silence him. "Yes, I do. I should have told you about Diggory sooner. I can come up with a million excuses and reasons, but that's not really it." She found it difficult to speak with those green eyes of his locked on hers, but she needed to say this. "I've never felt such hate for a man. I think part of me hoped that by not telling you, I could continue to believe he was dead."

He pulled her in tight and placed one hand on the back of her head so her face rested against his chest. The rhythm of his heartbeat filled her ear.

Speaking into his chest, she said, "While I was accusing you of being crazy, I was acting even crazier."

"Shhhh." He stroked her hair and kissed the crown of her head. "After all that man has done to you, you have the right to be a little crazy where he is concerned."

"What does he want with us, Cole?"

"I'm not sure this is about us."

"You think this is just another job for him?"

"I'm guessing he's working for the Knights of Malta now. Bones wouldn't have him back."

She leaned back so she could see his face. "He's dangerous."

"I know that. Probably even more so now that he looks like a freak."

"He's not sane, Cole. I don't frighten easily, but Diggory Priest scares me."

He slid the back of his fingers down the skin of her cheek. "Riley, you don't have to take him on alone. We are a team now." His touch raised goose bumps on her arms and made her nipples harden.

She reached up and pulled at the neck of his T-shirt. She ran her fingertips over the two words tattooed on his collarbones: *Carpe Diem*. "Seize the day," she said in a hoarse whisper.

"Yup. That's my motto. Or the night, as the case may be." He leaned in then and pressed his lips against hers, gently at first. Then as his arms tightened around her, his mouth opened, and their tongues entwined in a delicious dance.

Her mind was so focused on his kisses, she was not aware his hand had moved until his fingertips slipped under the hem of her towel. She moaned with pleasure as his feathery touch made little circles on the skin of her thighs. Wrapping one leg around his, she slid her bare foot up and down his calf. His hand kept moving ever higher up under her towel until he touched the spot that sent jolts tingling through her.

She broke off the kiss and inhaled sharply as she gripped him tight to her. Her legs trembled, and she felt as though they might soon crumple beneath her.

Something between a deep laugh and a growl rumbled in his chest. "I think it's time my fiancée and I broke in the bed in our new home." He reached down, lifted her up in his arms, and carried her inside.

CHAPTER FIFTY-THREE

Leonardo da Vinci International Airport
Rome, Italy

April 23, 2014

When the cab pulled to the curb and he saw the driver, Virgil considered waving him off and waiting for a different cab. The scraggly beard, Afghan cap, and long shirt spoke louder than words. Virgil didn't want to be late, though, so he threw his pack in and handed the driver one of his address cards. Then he settled back into the seat, hoping that the driver would just get him home as soon as possible.

But it was still Rome. And it was rush hour. They weren't even out of the airport before they hit the stop-and-go traffic.

Virgil could feel the driver sizing him up in the rearview mirror.

"You speak English?" the driver asked.

"Yeah."

"American?"

"Right."

"I come from Syria."

"Great."

"Damascus. Have you ever been there?"

Virgil's head was going to explode if this guy didn't shut up. "Is there anything you can do to get us there faster? Don't you know any back roads or shortcuts?"

"I don't know these words *short cuts.*"

"Never mind."

"I like American president Barak Hussein Obama."

Oh please. Just take me out and shoot me. Or let me shoot him.

"Are you American soldier?" The guy was grinning like a fucking monkey, like he was wishing he had a grenade to throw into the backseat.

"Just shut up and drive."

Virgil pulled his phone out and checked his email again. They'd set up another Skype call for tonight. She said in her email that her mom was supposed to be out of the house, so she wouldn't have to worry about getting caught talking to him.

He'd decided to fly back to Rome when he'd learned that there were only three flights a week from Djerba to Malta. He couldn't even be sure the boat had gone to Malta. Too much was happening back in Rome, and he was needed there, too.

He hadn't brought his laptop along on the trip down to Tunisia, either, and he wanted to make a video call to his daughter. He hadn't figured out how to do that on the phone yet. It didn't matter. There wasn't any reason for him to have to stay in Tunisia any longer if Thatcher was gone.

The problem was, he didn't know where.

Virgil wondered what he would tell Signor Oscura, if anything. He'd covered his tracks in Djerba. No one knew about the submarine. He had driven down the coast and taken a hotel room and kept watch on the site, but they hadn't returned that night or the next morning. That meant they had found what they were looking for in the wreck. Virgil had checked the Internet on his phone to see if they popped up on the AIS Shipfinder site, but he'd had no luck there. Maybe they headed to Malta or Sicily or even back to Turkey. He knew it would take time for them to arrive anywhere. When they checked in with the authorities, he would know soon after. He had used one of the Order's members who worked at the CIA. And then he would go find out what they'd found on the wreck. In the meantime, he would go home and talk to Bonnie.

The driver was trying to start a conversation again, but Virgil tried to ignore him.

"Mister? Mister?"

"Hey, I'm trying to work."

Virgil wondered what her mother had told her about him. The ex knew about some pretty bad shit, but she didn't know the half of it. He'd told her too many stories back in the beginning.

"Mister? The police are ahead. It is for the canonization. Road-block. You want me to take different way?"

"Just get me to the address on that card as fast as you can. And be quiet." *You stupid raghead.*

Five million extra people invading the city. That's what some in the media were predicting. This new pope had decided to make saints out of two ex-popes on the same day. A double canonization. People were flying in from all over the world, and it was wreaking havoc on the already-bad traffic situation in Rome.

The phone in Virgil's hand started to ring.

"Hello?"

"How dare you contact her without talking to me first."

"What?"

"Don't play dumb, you asshole. You know who this is."

"Hey. She's my kid, too."

"You lost your rights to Bonnie when you signed those divorce papers."

"I think she should know her father's side of the story."

"Oh really? What should I say, that her father is a fucked-up old man? Or maybe I should tell her what a monster you really are."

"You don't want to do that."

"Is that a threat?"

"No, just my opinion."

"Leave her alone, Virgil."

"She reached out to me, Shawny. She's curious. If you try to stop her, you know she'll hold it against you."

"I don't want her to have any contact with you. I'll make it your fault."

"Of course you will. Brilliant. You don't think she'll know you're lying? And what's this she was telling me about some gym teacher who's a perv? Guy named Nader? What is he, an Arab gym teacher? What kind of fucking school you got her going to?" Virgil saw the driver look up at the rearview mirror.

"Shut up, Virg, or I swear to God I'll tell everyone what I know about you."

"You don't know anything that anyone cares about."

"I know what you did in Iraq."

"What do you think I did in Iraq?" Again those eyes watching him in the rearview mirror.

"I think you murdered people."

"You've got that wrong." Virgil stared into the eyes in the mirror. "I killed the enemy before he killed me."

CHAPTER FIFTY-FOUR

Manoel Island Yacht Marina
Marsamxett Harbour, Malta

April 24, 2014

Cole came down the stairs from their upper-deck cabin and found Theo at work in the galley, with his dog sitting attentively at his feet.

"There's coffee in the pot."

"Why do you think I'm down here so early? It smells great." Cole filled his favorite mug—he'd bought it at Ocracoke Island the year he'd met Theo there.

A mechanical voice said, "Beat until creamy two-thirds cup sugar, three-quarters stick butter, three-quarters teaspoon grated lemon zest."

Cole peered around Theo. He had two big mixing bowls on the counter, several bananas, and a collection of other ingredients. His phone was resting in the open pages of a book.

"What are you up to?"

"Making my auntie's recipe for banana bread. I haven't scanned her book of Caribbean recipes into the computer yet, so I'm using the OCR text reader on my phone."

"Need any help?"

"Not really."

Cole exited the galley, went around the corner, and slid onto one of the stools at the breakfast bar, which looked into the galley. "And to think I lost sleep last night worrying about us flying off to Rome and leaving you alone and vulnerable on the boat."

Theo laughed out loud. "That's good, mon. I don't think that's why you lost sleep."

Cole decided to ignore his first mate's comment. There were few secrets on a boat—even one as big as theirs. "Well, you know the big blond guy might be coming around looking for what we found on the *Upholder*."

"And if he does, this time I will have the security system on. With all the workers coming and going in the yard, I got lax. No more. Yoda's now receiving data from the magnetic sensors on all the doors and opening windows, the floor pads under the welcome mat, the rugs in here and in all the staterooms—"

Riley's bare feet appeared coming down the stairs. "Are you telling me Yoda knows when we step out of bed in the morning?"

"Pretty much. See that little white thing, up in the ceiling there, that looks like a thermostat? That's a tri-mode PIR detector. It can—"

Riley was about to fill her cup of coffee, but she stopped, holding the pot up in the air. "Wait a minute, back up."

"Okay. It's a passive infrared sensor that detects motion."

"A motion detector. Why didn't you just say that?"

"PIR motion detectors detect the infrared radiation emitted by an object. In our case we have them all over the boat, inside and out, but they are designed only to detect something as large as a human. Birds landing on the boat, or even the dog walking around, won't set them off."

She slid onto the stool next to him wearing a thin-strapped, form-fitting tank top and boxers. She hadn't combed her hair yet, and Cole thought she looked fabulous.

"Riley, what our resident geek is trying to tell us is that we don't need to worry about going off and leaving him alone on the boat."

The mechanical voice said, "Beat in two large eggs, one cup mashed bananas."

Riley turned to look at Cole, tilted her head to one side, and raised her eyebrows.

"He's making us banana bread."

"Muffins," Theo said.

"He's got this app on his phone that allows him to use the phone's camera to scan text using OCR and convert it to speech. He can read the labels in the grocery store, a posted bus schedule, or a restaurant menu."

"It also tells me the value of coins and bills in twenty-five different currencies."

"And we're supposed to be worried about him?" Riley said.

"She's got a point," Theo said. "It's the two of you I'm worried about. We think Diggory Priest and the Knights of Malta are after the shield to get this treasure, whatever it is. But you two are planning to fly up to Rome, walk right into their headquarters, and steal this valuable old book of charts out of their library's special collection."

"That's more or less the plan," Cole said.

"That's sounds to me like barely half a plan. Cole, you're the one who's always reminding us how dangerous these guys are."

Theo spooned the batter into the muffin cups. At least, most of it was going into the cups. He opened the oven door and slid the pan in. After he closed the door, he turned around. Dabs of flour on the dark skin of his face made him look like he had war paint on.

"Come on. I know there has to be more to this plan."

Cole said, "There is."

"And the rest of it?"

"Okay." Cole didn't want to tell Theo the plan because he wasn't happy with it himself. While he and Riley had chatted in bed that

morning, he'd tried to convince her to let him go in, but she was ada-
mant that it had to be her. Now he told Theo, "We're going to pick up
some odd clothes and a wig, and Riley is going to go in."

"Alone?"

"As she continues to point out to me, my face is better known. I
have actually had my photograph circulated by folks on the lookout for
me. She'll have on makeup. Only someone who knows her well would
recognize her."

"Cole got on the Internet this morning and found a rare-books
dealer in London who has a copy of the same sea atlas. He sent the
info to a printing-and-graphics firm in Rome. They are going to make
a mock-up copy for us."

"That was fast."

"It won't be cheap," Cole said. "The pages inside will be blank, but
the outside will be a decent reproduction. She'll carry it in a big shoulder bag. When she asks the librarian to study the sea atlas, she'll take
it to the farthest table. When the time is right, she'll make the switch."

Theo looked thoughtful for a moment, then said, "But what about
security? Surely these Knights of Malta have some kind of electronic
security system for the books in their library?"

Cole nodded. "We talked about that. There are photos of the Magistral Library on the Internet, and we can't see any system, but if there
is one, then Riley is just going to find a corner and photograph the sea
atlas the best she can with her iPhone. But ideally, we'd like to get a
look at the real thing."

"And what about the shield?"

"I think it's safest if we leave it here with you. You're the one with
the awesome security system."

"Agreed. And that will give me more time to work with it."

"What do you mean?"

"I'll photograph it and then have Yoda search for symbols or text
in the engraved silver. During the eighteenth century they were into

that *trompe l'oeil* and optical illusions. We're just seeing decoration at the moment, but you can't trick Yoda."

Riley got up off the stool and walked to the aft-deck doors that stood open. The stern of the big yacht was tied to the stone wharf. Beyond the wharf were some old stone buildings that looked abandoned. They had probably been part of the Lazaretto complex once. A barbed-wire fence divided them from the marina. There was no one on the dock, not a single person in sight.

Cole came up behind her and rested his hands on her shoulders. "Are you okay?"

"I wonder if we're being watched right now."

"It's possible."

"And will they know it when we fly to Rome?"

Cole had been thinking the same thing. "It occurs to me that if our old friend Gavino Ebejer was able to find other men Tug had told his story to, it's probable the Knights know the story as well."

"What they don't know is that the shield was simply a key to something they've had in their possession all along."

"I hope you're right."

CHAPTER FIFTY-FIVE

**Mercato Trionfale
Rome, Italy**

April 25, 2014

Cole had been checking behind them all morning, and if there was somebody tailing them, he must be good. They had rented a room in an Italian family's home via an app called Couchsurfing that Riley had downloaded to her phone. They'd used fake names, and the father who showed them to their room had not asked to see ID. Cole and Riley were up and gone before any of the rest of the family had stirred. They had taken the Metro and cabs and then walked, separating and meeting up again later. Cole had followed Riley, and she had tracked him. They hadn't seen anyone taking any special interest in them.

They were traveling light, with just the one backpack holding a change of clothes for each of them and a few toiletries. But they intended to buy more things while in Rome, so they'd made sure the backpack was big enough to carry everything home.

Once they were certain they weren't being followed, they took a cab to pick up the replica of Joseph Roux's sea atlas at the graphics shop near the Piazza Cavour. It turned out to be owned by a couple of brothers. Cole had told them they needed the old atlas of sea charts for a commercial they were filming. The brothers had had fun with the job, weathering the leather cover and making it look very much like the edition of the atlas pictured on the web. Whether it could pass for the one in the Magistral Library was something they expected to find out that afternoon.

The brothers had recommended the Mercato Trionfale, up north of the Vatican, when they'd inquired about shopping for clothing. They said it had once been an outdoor market, but that it had recently moved into a big building. There were a few stalls that sold clothing.

Cole was surprised that the building was so ugly. It looked more like a gray concrete box. It appeared very un-Roman. But inside, the place was a feast of colors and smells. Most of the stalls sold food— everything from seafood to sausages and cheeses to fruits and vegetables. The vendors were shouting and laughing in Italian to customers who seemed to shout back with equal vehemence. It was the first place in Rome they could not find anyone who spoke English, but using a combination of French and sign language, they found their way to the clothing stalls.

"So, what do you think I should wear?" Riley picked up a teeny white tank top that said "I ♥ Rome" with the heart made of red sequins. "How about this?"

"Maybe. No man would be looking at your face if you were wearing that."

"I think not." She folded the shirt and placed it back on top of the pile. "You know, I don't know if we're going to find something here. I'm not even sure what to look for."

"Think about what you see on the streets in Rome."

"Yes, but I won't be on the streets. I'm going into a library to do research. I need to look like one of those."

"Okay, but don't stereotype. In academia, I found researchers came in all shapes and sizes." He thought about the characters who had been in the Maritime Archeology program at Eastern Carolina University with him. "In fact, I guess you could say academics are often an odd-looking lot."

"I like this." She held up a man's shirt screen-printed with an image of the Colosseum. It was at least two sizes too big for her.

"Good. Now we need some pants. And keep your eyes open for a wig or a hat. And glasses."

Cole found some imitation Doc Martens boots next, and they settled on denim overalls. They asked the woman who sold them the boots about wigs. She gave them directions to a stall way on the far side of the market. The people there mostly sold their services of braiding hair with beads and shells in it, but they also had a few wigs of long braids. Riley chose a black one. It had a fringe of black hair across her forehead and shoulder-length braids all around. When she tried it on, Cole wasn't even sure he would recognize her if he didn't know it was her. They bought it.

When they left the market, Riley said, "At any other time, I'd suggest we cut through the Vatican and walk through Saint Peter's, but judging from the mobs of people heading that way, I think the Vatican is the last place we want to go this week."

They skirted their way around the Vatican walls and made it to the Piazza del Risorgimento.

"I'm hungry," Cole said. "What do you say we stop in a restaurant, order some lunch, and then you can change in the restroom before we go."

They walked back in the direction of the Piazza Cavour until they found a little hole-in-the-wall pizza place. Cole ordered a seafood pizza, and Riley insisted they have an antipasto plate as well. After walking through all the tempting food in the market, Cole pounced on the food when it arrived. There was too much of it, and he ate too fast, but Cole couldn't resist. When Riley went to change, he belched and waved for the bill. The waiter looked like he'd seen one too many bad-mannered Americans.

The transformation was amazing. When Riley came out of the bathroom, she walked straight out of the restaurant without stopping at Cole's table. She had taken a big shopping bag inside with her, and when she emerged, she looked like some Goth university student. Cole paid the bill and grabbed his backpack and the bag with the fake sea atlas. He followed Riley out into the street.

When she saw him approaching, she shook her head and turned away. He sauntered along the Via Crescenzio, stopping to look in windows and peering up at street signs. He turned down a side street toward the Castel Sant'Angelo. Just before they got to the river, Riley passed him on the opposite side of the street. At the next signal, she crossed over and joined him.

"So what did you find?"

"When I left the restaurant, there was a guy with dark glasses loitering in front of that clothing store across from the restaurant. He ignored me when I came out, but he seemed to take notice of you when you came out. When he didn't follow you, then I wondered if he had just signaled someone else to follow you. But in the end, I couldn't find a tail."

"It's better to be safe, though. We're not stronger, so we have to outsmart these guys."

"In that case, let's pick up the pace. I'd like to get to the Via Condotti before sunset."

Cole saluted. "Yes, ma'am."

"Do you want to take a cab?" she asked.

"I ate too much. Let's keep walking. It's not that far now, and besides, I don't want to be sleepy while I'm waiting for you."

Riley pulled out her phone. The map they had used to find their way to the outdoor market was still on the screen. She tapped and swiped and brought up the pin she had dropped at the Magistral

Palace. "You know you can't be seen waiting for me anywhere near this place, right?"

"I don't like the idea of not being somewhere close by."

"I'll be fine. You stay out of sight, and when I'm done, I'll meet you here"—she pointed to the spot on the map—"at the entrance to the Spagna Metro station at the top of the Spanish Steps."

He knew he wouldn't be able to stay away, but he wouldn't tell her that. He didn't like sending her in alone. Something didn't feel right about it at all.

CHAPTER FIFTY-SIX

Villa del Priorato di Malta
The Aventine Hill, Rome

April 25, 2014

Signor Oscura opened the door to the small security office. "Would you step out here? We need to talk about some details for tonight."

Virgil didn't normally spend much time in the office, but he had brought his own laptop to the villa that morning, and he was trying to get it plugged in and on the network so he could call Bonnie.

He stepped out into the main entrance foyer of the villa. The ceiling above them was over two stories high and crowned by a glass dome. The grand staircase curved up to the second floor. An enormous arrangement of fresh flowers stood in a vase on the table beneath a fourteenth-century tapestry on one side. On the opposite wall was an original Titian painting of Jesus talking to his disciples.

"Virgil, I just got a phone call from the caterer for tonight's dinner. He's got some problem. Will you please call him back?"

"Of course, sir."

"How are things going with security?"

"No problems, sir."

"After the meal, make absolutely certain that none of the regular guests interferes with our meeting in the Church of Santa Maria del Priorato tonight."

"I understand."

"There is one guest, he is not yet a member of the Order. This Italian gentleman has no one to will his fortune to. Signor Carretto. Do whatever it takes to make sure he enjoys his weekend in Rome."

Virgil nodded.

"I'm going back to my office for the rest of the afternoon. Let me know if there are any more problems."

"Yes, sir."

When the executive director left, Virgil was about to return to the computer when one of his men approached from the back of the house.

"Virg, we've got a problem with a guy at the gate."

"Jacko, you don't have to bring every little problem to me."

"It's a tourist, I think. Insists he wants a tour. He's blocking the entrance, and he won't budge. You said white gloves."

"You've got to move him. This is a not only a private estate, it's a sovereign territory. We do get to make our own rules here. Permission to rough him up a bit."

Jacko grinned. "Yes, sir."

When Jacko left, Virgil decided he'd better make the rounds to be certain all was running smoothly. Then he could take a quick thirty minutes to make his call. He walked through the kitchen and the dining room, checking in with staff. He was pleased to see everyone working, and no one jumping to grab his ear with another problem.

When Virgil returned to the foyer, he made the call to the caterer. They wanted to stop by early to check with Mrs. Ricasoli. Something about a dessert. He told them he would inform the gate to let them in early.

Just as he terminated the call, he saw an elderly gentleman slowly descending the stairs. The man smiled and nodded at Virgil, then said, *"Scusami."*

"Can I help you with something?"

"Yes," the gentleman said. "This is my first time here among the *cavalieri*, and I would very much like to visit the Palazzo Magistral."

"I'd be happy to call a car for you, Signor . . . ?"

"Carretto is my name. That would be so kind."

Virgil pulled his phone out and dialed. "Priest? Meet me in the office in the foyer right away. I need you to drive someone down to the Via Condotti."

It was thirty minutes later before Virgil got rid of the old man and sent Priest off in one of the Bentleys to chauffeur the guy around. He went into the office, closed the door, and locked it.

He was getting the hang of using Skype now. He'd ignored Shawny's threats, and he and Bonnie had talked twice more. He couldn't explain to himself what the fascination was. He'd always hated kids. When Shawny first got pregnant, he'd tried to convince her to get rid of it. That was when the real fighting between them started. He'd relented and told her she could have the kid, but she just couldn't let it go. After that, every time he came home on leave, all she did was bitch.

Half the time he didn't even understand what his daughter was talking about. Between her teen talk and the fact that she was smoking-smart, Virgil didn't even know what half the words she used meant. But there were times, watching her, when he'd seen her move a certain way or caught her in a certain light, and he saw himself in her. She was made out of part of him, and at his age, he now found that fucking amazing.

He heard the familiar ringing tones, and then there was her face. "Hi, Daddy."

Something was different about her today. She sounded distracted.

"Hey, sweetheart. Is everything okay?"

She looked off the screen at something or someone he couldn't see in her room. There were questions in her eyes, then he saw her settle on a decision. She looked back at the camera.

"No, everything's not okay. Mom never respects my privacy. It's like she doesn't even know there's a human right to privacy."

He didn't know what to say to her. He said the only thing that occurred to him. "What happened?"

"Like, I should be allowed privacy in my own room, and she has no right to read the diary on my computer. But she says if the government can listen to all our phone calls and that's legal, and the military can torture people, then I can't expect any privacy, either. She says life's not fair, so there. I hate when she says that. It's just stupid." The girl's blue eyes were shining with unshed tears. "She read in my diary that Tony and I have been skipping school and going over to his house and doing it. Like she doesn't have a different asshole boyfriend over here every week."

An arm reached in and pushed the girl. "Okay, enough." Virgil recognized his ex-wife's voice. "Now your father can see what a little slut you are."

"And what about you?"

"Stop whining to him. He doesn't give a flying fuck about you."

"That's not true. He cares more about me than you do."

"Oh yeah? So ask him where he's been for the last sixteen years."

Virgil wanted to tell Bonnie that Shawny had forbade him to contact her, but he couldn't get a word in edgewise.

"You're just mad because your boyfriend hit on me."

Shawny flashed into view and slapped the girl across the mouth. "Get out of here."

Bonnie stood up and ran behind the chair to the door. "I hate you," she said.

"Well you know what? If you think you can run to him, think again. He didn't even want you. He wanted me to have an abortion."

"That's not true!" the girl screamed. "Daddy, say that's not true."

Virgil opened his mouth and then closed it again. He didn't know what to say.

Shawny said, "You go to my bedroom and wait for me there. Your dad and I have to talk."

The girl opened the door, then looked back over her shoulder. He blue eyes looked like they were alight with some inner fire, and her cheeks were wet with tears. "I hate you both!" she screamed. She slammed the door.

Shawny sat in the chair and smoothed her fine blonde hair back out of her face. "Listen, that was the last contact you are ever going to have with my daughter."

"She's *our* daughter, Shawny."

"Not anymore. I found more than just that diary on her computer. I found some old buddy of yours from Iraq has also been emailing with her and talking dirty. Now that's just disgusting. You old men are such perverts."

Virg felt his whole body tuck up into a defensive position. "What was his name?"

"Let's see if I can find that email somewhere." She leaned forward toward the camera. He heard her clicking the keyboard. "Crap, he's sent her another one. Looks like there's a photo attached."

"I said, what's his name?"

She narrowed her eyes. "It's weird. Diggory Priest." He heard the mouse clicks as she opened the email. "Oh my God." Her face contorted into a grimace. "That's disgusting."

He took a deep breath before he spoke. "What is it?"

"This photo."

"Has Bonnie seen it?"

She didn't answer him. She was concentrating on something on the screen.

"Shawny, answer me."

"You dumb asshole, I'm trying to text it to you."

His screen filled with a photo of him holding a sniper rifle in one hand, a dead dog dangling by his back legs from his other hand.

Virgil blew out a sigh of relief.

Shawny said, "He says in his email that he has lots more pictures to send her of all the fun he had with you overseas. You are a sick fuck, Virgil."

The computer made a *boing* sound, and the video window closed.

When Virgil reached up to close the laptop lid, he saw, for the first time in his life, that his hand was trembling.

CHAPTER FIFTY-SEVEN

The Magistral Library
Via Condotti, Rome

April 25, 2014

"Do you speak English?" Riley asked of the tiny woman sitting behind the high desk. Riley had not seen her until the last minute, as the woman's head didn't even come up to the level of the desk.

She tipped her head up to look at Riley, looking more like a baby bird than a grown woman. "Yes, of course."

"Thank goodness," Riley said, her voice half an octave higher than her normal speech, "because I don't speak a word of Italian."

So far, things had gone well. They had transferred her old clothes into Cole's backpack, and she was now carrying the counterfeit sea atlas and her phone in the big shopping bag. Riley had entered the big portico on the Via Condotti and asked for directions to the library from the plump concierge. He spoke little English, but he understood what she was looking for. He walked her across the courtyard inlaid with a mosaic Maltese cross and pointed to the correct doorway.

The concierge's directions led her down a hallway, passing a huge tapestry of a Knight on a horse, to the door of the library's reading room. The long, narrow room was lined with bookshelves. On either side of the central aisle, a row of tables stretched to the back of the room. There were no more than a half dozen people seated at the tables, their heads bent over books. At the rear of the reading room, sunlight shone through the windows onto a graceful, curving staircase. If she didn't know the place was owned by the Knights, she would count it as one of her favorite rooms in the world.

"So," the tiny woman said, "how may I help you?"

"I understand you have an extensive geographical collection?"

"Yes, we have maps and sea charts dating from the seventeenth to the nineteenth century."

"I'm interested primarily in sea charts from the seventeenth and eighteenth centuries."

"Let me see." The little woman stood, slipped on her glasses, and stepped over to the computer on the desk. After tapping the keys and tilting her head back to read through the lower half of her glasses, she wrote a couple of numbers on a paper. "I'll be right back." She disappeared through the door into the rear stacks.

When the woman returned, she was carrying three large books in her arms. She went around the desk and walked over to the closest table.

"The first one is the *Isola di Malta, olim Melita*, by Vincenzo Maria Coronelli." She moved that one aside and pointed to the largest leather-bound volume at the bottom of the pile. "This is volume one of the *Atlante Novissimo*, a four-volume atlas of the world by Antonio Zatta. And this last one is *Recüeil de Plusieurs Plans des Ports et Rades de la Mer Méditerranée*, by Henri Michelot. I will leave you to look these over and let me know when you are finished."

Riley sat in a chair with her back to the librarian's desk and set her bag on the floor next to her. Who knew there would be so many titles to choose from? Not wanting to call too much attention to the one book she wanted, she had decided to try to get the librarian to select the Joseph Roux sea atlas for her. That hadn't worked. She opened the last volume the librarian had given her.

The title page was decorated with an elaborate drawing of mermaids, mermen, whiskered fish, angels, and lots of curly designs. A cartographer in those days was clearly as much fine artist as surveyor. She flipped through the pages of maps, trying to look interested, but feeling the pressure to go back and get the one book she had come for.

Riley slid the three volumes onto the reference desk and said, "Thank you. This one on Malta was especially good. I'm really interested mostly in the Mediterranean. Do you have anything else that covers just that area? Perhaps in a special collection?"

"Not at this time." The librarian pulled the books off the top of the checkout desk and set them on a cart behind her.

"I'm not sure I understand you. Not at this time?"

"There is one volume in our Demontras collection that is out on interlibrary loan at this time. It is *Carte de la mer Méditerranée en douze feuilles*, by Joseph Roux."

"And may I ask what library requested it? Perhaps I could view it there."

The little woman smiled. "That might be a bit of a challenge. Especially this week."

"Really? Why?"

"With the dual canonization and all. It's on loan to the Vatican Library."

Before leaving the Magistral Palace, Riley asked the librarian for directions to the restroom. The door to the ladies' room was just across the hall outside the library. Like the rest of the palace, it was decorated with antique furniture and original art on the walls.

After using the toilet, she set her bag on the fancy antique chair and crossed to the sink. She stood holding her hands under the running water and stared at her own reflection in the small mirror before her.

All this effort to put together a disguise, and it was all for nothing? The Vatican Library? She couldn't wait to see the look on his face when Cole heard this. It was one thing to try to steal a 250-year-old book of charts from the Knights of Malta, but to steal from the Vatican? She wasn't sure she was up for that.

She looked back down at the faucet and turned it off with the back of her wrist.

The hand came out of nowhere, flew past her face, and grabbed the left side of her neck. Her neck was in the crook of his elbow, his bicep pressed hard against her carotid artery. She knew what was happening. She'd been taught the sleeper hold in her training at Langley. As she squirmed and fought against the black that was closing in around her vision, she caught sight of the strange two-sided face leering over her shoulder.

Diggory Priest.

Then she lost the fight against the darkness.

CHAPTER FIFTY–EIGHT

Aboard the *Ruse*
Off the Island of Crete

June 18, 1798

On their second day at sea, Alonso had been watching her drawing designs on a scrap of paper. He remarked on what a good artist she was. Then he disappeared into the cabin. When he emerged, he surprised her with the small collection of tools he'd bought when the inquisitor had auctioned off the contents of her father's shop. It included gravers and burs, a small hammer, and a couple of clamps. But by the third day, the seas and winds had grown so strong, she didn't think she would ever be able to work on board. The powerful winds continued for nearly a week, and Arzella's strength continued to ebb. She worried for the health of the baby inside her.

That morning, the ninth day since their departure from Gozo, when Alonso had awakened her for her turn at the helm, she felt rested for the first time. The sea had calmed at last, and steering the small ship no longer took all her strength and concentration. As the sun climbed into the cloudless sky, she lounged in her pantaloons, steering the *Ruse* with one foot and an occasional glance at the compass. With her hands free, she had started engraving a flower design onto a pewter tankard she'd found in the ship's galley.

Up until now, their meals had been quite simple. Dates and oranges, dried meat and fish, and a hard bread Alonso called *biscuit*. Fortunately, the sea did not make her sick, and any sickness due to the baby had long since passed. But with the bad weather, neither of them had the strength or the desire to cook hot food. Now she was looking forward to preparing a hot meal. Everything looked so much better once the sun came out.

"I'm glad to see you working."

Arzella looked up from her work to see Alonso climbing the steps from the lower deck, their chart atlas tucked under one arm, his navigational instrument in his other hand. "You surprised me," she said. "I did not think I would see you so soon."

"I've had enough sleep. And, as I expected, there is an island there ahead." He pointed off the bow.

She got to her feet and peered through the sails. "I can barely make it out. Is it far?"

"We should reach the coast by nightfall. Assuming my calculations are correct, that is the western end of Crete."

"How can you be so certain after so many days of bad weather?"

He held up the instrument. "Because of this. It is called an octant. With it, I can measure the elevation of the sun off the horizon, and using mathematics, I can calculate our latitude." He set the sea atlas atop a deck box and opened to the page showing the eastern Mediterranean.

Arzella said, "I know from our compass we have been sailing south of east."

He pointed to Malta and dragged his finger across to the southwestern corner of Crete. "Yes, like this."

"So our latitude is decreasing."

"Very good. How quickly you learn."

Arzella reached over and ran her fingers through his hair. "You are an enthusiastic teacher."

"Only you, my dear, would think sailing and navigation are romantic."

When Arzella looked through the sails again, the outline of the island was more distinct. "What do you know of this island?"

"The people here are mostly Ottoman Turks, but I do not think they bear us ill will. The people on this end of the island are farmers and fishermen, and they will be happy to trade some water and fresh food for a gold coin or two."

"I've never met an Ottoman."

"They are not so different from us."

"But in Malta, they have been the enemies of the Knights for hundreds of years."

"Yes, and I have sunk their ships at sea. But I have always respected the men I fought against. We fought not out of a personal enmity, but rather because of power and politics. We were merely pawns. Lately, even the grand master was talking treaties with the Ottomans. We will present ourselves as simple pilgrims stopping only for supplies. I do not anticipate any troubles."

"And after this island, how much farther?"

"This end of the island marks the halfway point."

"If the weather and sailing stay like this, I don't want it to ever end."

"As you know from the start of this voyage, we have no control of the weather. I have never sailed these waters before. But my grandfather told me stories about the Aegean Sea."

"He is the one Nikola always used to talk about? *Le Rouge de Malte?*"

"That was my grandfather's father. His real name was Jacques-François de Chambray."

"French?"

"Umm. He had an affair with a Spanish noblewoman. Their son was my grandfather. He became a sailor, too, in his youth, but he never sailed far. That was his dream, so he used to tell me the stories his father told him, about the Ottoman Turks and the Greeks and the great battles he fought."

"So that is why we sail eastward?"

"Yes, in part. I have a thirst to see new lands. There is a castle my grandfather told me about. It was built in the Middle Ages when the Knights were at Rhodes." Alonso turned over all the pages of charts in his book. He showed her the paper that lined the inside cover of the atlas. There was an ink drawing there of a small castle on top of a hill. The castle walls flowed down the hillside. Just outside the walls, the artist had drawn a half dozen little houses. "This sea atlas belonged to my great-grandfather, and he drew this when he was there. The people in the village knew *Le Rouge de Malte*, and they protected him once. My grandfather recounted to me the many tales he told about their kindness. I hope they will be as good to us."

"You said that was one part of your reason. What is your other reason for finding this castle?"

"Because I plan to take the Religion to the last place anyone would look for it. We are going to sail off the edge of the map."

CHAPTER FIFTY-NINE

The Palazzo Magistral
Via Condotti, Rome

April 25, 2014

Diggory Priest lifted the limp body and held it in his arms. He didn't have much time. She would come around in less than a minute. He cracked open the door and checked the hallway. Empty. He slipped out and walked toward the exit door, his strides purposeful, his demeanor daring anyone to question him. But he encountered no one, neither in the building nor in the parking lot. He pushed the button on the car key fob and the trunk popped open. He dropped her in, closed the lid, and walked around to the driver's door.

He couldn't believe his luck. He'd been up at the villa on the Aventine when Virg had asked him to drive one of the guests down to the palace. They let him take the Bentley that belonged to the Order and was normally used only for driving the grand master or the director. The guy he'd driven was Italian, and he didn't want to talk, so Dig hadn't been the least distracted. If he had been, he might not have seen Thatcher loitering in the doorway of that Jimmy Choo store up the street from the palace. He was wearing a ball cap pulled down over his face, but there was no doubt it was him.

If he was hanging around outside, there was a good chance Riley was inside.

Dig had pulled the big car into the palace driveway and told the guard he was going to park and use the facilities before returning to the villa. He'd dropped his passenger there close to the front door, and then had done a three-point turn. He'd parked in the back corner with the car facing out. Which also meant the trunk was well screened from view.

At first he had looked right past the funky-looking student in the library reading room. The overalls sagged on her body, and she was of no interest to him. The girl was talking to the librarian at the reference desk and patting her hand on a stack of books as Dig scanned the other faces in the room. Abruptly, she'd turned and started for the door. That was when he saw her face.

Dig stepped into the men's room. He'd left the door open a crack so he could watch. And his luck had held when she went into the women's restroom. He'd followed her in while she was in the stall. A screen that blocked the view into the ladies' room had hidden him when she came out. From there, it had been easy.

When he turned onto the Via Condotti, he drove past the Jimmy Choo store. Thatcher was gone. The girl started to move around, then she beat on the trunk lid. She was awake, and it would be dangerous driving around the city with her making all that noise back there, but she couldn't get out.

Virg wouldn't approve. This wasn't on his agenda. But she wasn't the one Virgil needed. Thatcher would find whatever the Knights were looking for. Riley was his.

* * *

He took the Via Tiburtina in the direction that took him away from the city center. When he saw a side street that looked like it had little traffic, he turned and pulled to the curb. When the car stopped, her hollering and pounding grew louder.

"Listen," he yelled.

She grew quiet. He was certain that if he could hear her so loudly, she must be able to hear him, no matter that the car was a Bentley and built like a tank.

"I have a gun, and you know I won't hesitate to kill you, Riley. I'm taking you someplace where we can talk. When I park the car and let you out, I will have the gun trained on you. Then we're going to go for a little walk in a park. And we're going to talk. Afterward, you'll be free to go. I just want to talk to you. I think you're going to want to hear what I have to say."

He turned around, put the car in gear, and circled the block back to the Via Tiburtina. He drove as fast as he dared. He didn't want to attract attention, but he also did not want to be gone too long. Already Virgil didn't trust him.

She remained quiet. Of course, he had no special information to tell her. He just wanted her to think she would have a better chance of taking him out later, while they were walking. He needed to get her underground where it wouldn't matter how much noise she made.

Dig had first read about the Christian catacombs in a book he found at the villa. The idea of several enormous underground cemeteries beneath the city of Rome fascinated him. In the early days, when the Christians were persecuted, they buried their dead in these underground tunnels they'd carved out of the volcanic soil. They'd started as family tombs, but they grew and were opened to others of their faith. There were some special large chambers that had once been used for secret worship, but mostly there were simple tunnels with three levels of crypts carved out of the walls on each side, where once-wrapped bodies and occasionally stone sarcophagi had rested.

When he had a day off, he'd gone and taken a tour of the cata-combs of Saint Callixtus. On the tour, he had learned that there were nearly sixty different catacombs, with so many miles of burial cham-bers that, if placed end to end, they would stretch the entire length of Italy. Though all were considered the property of the Church, not all of them had been excavated, and only a handful were open to the public. Online, he'd found a map showing the locations of all the catacombs, and he'd taken to exploring the nonpublic sites in his free time.

The catacombs Diggory had come to think of as his own were entered via an unmarked stairway that descended within a small park, one block away from a bank in one direction and a big traffic-circle pi-azza in another. Fortunately, there was plenty of parking, and he soon found a spot along the park's perimeter.

Standing next to the trunk, he said, "I've got the gun under my jacket. I'm going to open the trunk slowly. If you make any move I don't like, I will shoot. You know I will."

He stood off to one side, then checked up and down the street. No one close enough to take notice. He pressed the fob, and the trunk popped open a crack.

She lay on her side in a fetal position, her hand shielding her eyes from the sudden brightness.

"Climb out," he said.

She sat up and swung her legs out of the trunk.

"Move."

She stood.

Dig closed the trunk lid and grasped her arm with his free hand. He led her down the sidewalk to the park entrance. He felt her looking at him, but she hadn't said a word.

They passed a woman walking a small, almost-hairless dog, and he tightened his grip on her arm when he felt Riley tense.

He spoke softly, his mouth close to her ear. "You don't want this woman to get hurt. She's nothing to me, you know. Killing her would be so easy."

When they got alongside the old woman, the dog started yapping and pulling at his leash. Its eyes bulged. Dig was tempted to kick the damn thing.

The old woman said something in Italian to the dog, and she and the dog hurried off. Dig guided Riley around the hedge that hid the stairwell. He looked around to make sure no one was watching them.

"Down here," he said.

Riley looked down the stone steps, and he felt her tense and start to move back. She lifted her head and scanned the area. Even the woman and her dog were nowhere to be seen.

"Move it." He jerked her arm forward. "I really don't want to hurt you."

He felt her take a deep breath, then she took the first step.

When they got to the iron gate, he checked the lock and chain. No one had replaced the chain since he'd cut it a couple of days ago. Judging from the amount of rust on the chain and the gate, he doubted anyone ever came down. What was one more catacomb in Rome?

Once they were through, he pushed the gate closed and hung the chain to make it look like it was locked. The stairs continued down into darkness. He took a penlight out of his pocket as well as one of the big plastic zip ties they'd issued the men working security at the villa, for use as handcuffs.

She spoke for the first time. "I haven't resisted you, Dig. You said you just wanted to talk."

"Put your hands out in front of you."

She did as she was told, and that worried him. She was cooperating too much. He knew her well enough to know she was working on some kind of plan.

"Diggory, I don't believe you'll hurt me. Not me. Someone who once thought she loved you."

CHAPTER SIXTY

The Palazzo Magistral
Via Condotti, Rome

A p r i l   2 5 ,   2 0 1 4

He'd waited at the Metro entrance until 5:00 p.m. growing more worried with every minute that passed. When he couldn't stand the wait any longer, he had returned to the Via Condotti, and now he was standing in the doorway to the Max Mara store across the street from the entrance to the palace courtyard. At the street level there were retail shops, but looking at the second and third stories and the rows of shuttered windows gave him an idea of how big the place was. A small stone balcony over the portico was decorated with a ceramic emblem of the Maltese cross, while three flagpoles flew the flag of the Hospitallers with the white cross on the red field. More importantly, two CCTV cameras were mounted on the stone walls, one on either side of the door.

Why had he let her go in alone? His imagination was conjuring up all sorts of scenarios of what might have happened to her. This would be so much worse, even, than Theo's beating that had left him blind.

Cole pulled his baseball cap down low over his eyes, checked for traffic, and crossed the street. He'd only got a few feet through the doorway when the concierge stepped out of his little office and told him to halt.

"I'm looking for my girlfriend. She's in the library."

"No, library closed."

"But she's still in there." Cole started for the door again.

The concierge grabbed him by the arm and spun him around. The little guy was stronger than he looked.

"Signore, no. Library is closed."

"But I know she's still in there."

The guy wouldn't let go of his arm.

Cole saw a tiny woman come out a door, several bags hanging over her arms, her glasses on top of her head. Her car keys dangled from her hand.

The concierge dragged Cole to the entrance. He pointed to the street with one hand while his other hand administered a firm push.

When Cole turned around on the sidewalk, he saw that the woman was now approaching the concierge. She was holding up a black shopping bag. Cole pulled out his cell phone and pushed a button to dial Riley's number. A few seconds later, he heard a phone start to ring.

When the concierge turned and saw Cole approaching, his cheeks puffed out and he started toward Cole.

"Signora," Cole said, "do you speak English?"

The tiny woman said, "Yes."

The concierge grabbed Cole's arm again.

"Please, answer the phone in that bag."

The woman pulled out Riley's phone and tapped on the screen. She held it to her ear.

Cole hit the speaker button on his own phone. The woman's voice echoed in the courtyard from his phone.

"Hello?"

"That phone belongs to my girlfriend," he said. On his own phone he tapped the screen a couple of times to pull up a photo of Riley. He held out the phone to the woman. "This is a photo of her, but today she wears her hair different. Have you seen her?"

The tiny woman said something to the concierge that sounded like she was scolding him. He let go of Cole's arm. The woman pulled down her glasses and balanced them on her face. Little lines appeared in her forehead as she examined the photo.

"Yes, I think that is the young woman who was in the library this afternoon. She looks quite a bit different now, but yes. That is her."

"And that's her bag you're holding."

The woman looked up from the phone screen and looked confused for a moment. Then she said, "Oh, yes, this. I found this bag when I went to the ladies' room after closing the library. Someone had left it on a chair in there. I was bringing it out here to Signor Giancolo in case the owner returned."

Cole said, "Somehow I must have missed her when she left. We were supposed to meet, but it seems she has gone back to our hotel. I'm sure she would be very happy if I returned to the hotel with her bag."

The librarian turned and spoke in Italian to the concierge. He argued with her, throwing several stern glances in Cole's direction, but finally shook his head and stepped away.

"I believe I have convinced Signor Giancolo that I can give you the bag. Tell your lady friend I am sorry about the Joseph Roux atlas of sea charts. It should be returning in two weeks."

"Returning?"

"Yes, as I explained to the young lady before she left, it is out on interlibrary loan at the moment."

"Oh," Cole said. *Please tell me it hasn't gone to Tasmania or somewhere like that.* "What library?"

"The Vatican."

CHAPTER SIXTY-ONE

In the Catacombs
Via Tiburtina, Rome

April 25, 2014

"Be quiet," he said.

Diggory cinched the plastic zip tie so tight around her wrists, it cut into her skin. Her hands were clasped together in front of her waist, her arms straight. It had taken significant strength to force her wrists apart as he'd yanked on the end of the plastic strap, but she needed to make certain he didn't tie her too far up the arms if she was going to work her way out of this mess.

Ever since she'd awakened in the trunk of that black car, she'd been trying to come up with a plan. It was downright embarrassing how easily he had taken her. She remembered assuring Cole that she would be fine by herself in the Magistral Palace. And now look at her.

"Your burns look worse than mine," she said.

He stepped away from her and turned. She remembered how vain he had always been. Looked like that hadn't changed, even with the body he had today. She'd noticed he'd been trying to keep her always on the side with a view of the unscarred half of his face.

"Is it only your face?"

He didn't answer. He rummaged in the bag he carried, ignoring her.

All those years ago in Lima, when she had defied the rules and started an affair with the CIA liaison at the embassy, she had been so young. And he had seemed so gallant and charming at first. When she'd spent nights at his apartment in town, she'd loved watching him shave in the mornings. The way he stroked the razor across his own cheek was like a caress.

"Get moving."

They descended the equivalent of two flights of stairs. The lower they went, the more damp the air grew. At the bottom of the stairs, they entered a small, round room—at least, that was what it looked like in the dim light of Dig's flashlight. Riley shivered. The temperature was at least ten degrees colder than it had been out in the sunlight. Several dark shadows around the perimeter appeared to be doorways. He pointed the beam into the tunnel closest to them.

"That way."

When they entered the tunnel, she realized this was a burial place. That explained the earthy odor of something organic now rotted away. Human-sized slots in the walls were where they had placed the dead.

She heard the uneven rhythm of his footsteps behind her.

"In about a hundred feet there's a chamber off to the left," he said. "We'll stop there."

The material was stone, but it appeared soft, almost more like mud. They wouldn't have needed fancy tools to cut this rock. The builders of this place must have removed the rock and dirt and passed it to others behind them. The tunnel was not wide enough for two men to walk side by side. No wonder the niches for the bodies were so narrow. She counted five rows from ceiling to floor. Each slot was only sixteen to twenty inches high and a little over five feet long. The labor that must have gone into creating this place was staggering.

"In here," Diggory said.

An arched opening to her left led into another round room. On the walls were faded mosaic murals. The murals depicted a scene of some sort, but the colors were so washed out that Riley could make out only a picture of a fish here, some Roman-looking writing there.

"Who built all this?" Riley asked.

"Early Christians."

Riley walked to the wall, reached up with her bound hands, and touched the fish. It was a simple drawing, more like a symbol or a hieroglyphic. "Amazing."

"We're not here as tourists."

When she turned around, she saw there was a camp chair and an air mattress just inside the door. A shopping bag lay on the air mattress. A plastic gallon jug of water rested on the floor next to the mattress. She hadn't seen that when they first stepped into the chamber. Dig bent down and picked up a piece of chain. She couldn't see the other end of it, as he wasn't pointing the flashlight that way.

"You're leaving me here?"

"There are things I have to take care of. We'll talk when I get back."

He picked up the bag and pulled out another plastic zip tie.

She'd been waiting, hoping to see an opportunity to make a move, to get the better of him. Now it was too late. She would have to try, though.

He bent at her feet and set the small flashlight on the ground. He was juggling things, trying to hold on to the gun while he fitted the end of the zip tie through a link of chain. He was starting to wrap the zip tie around her ankle when Riley brought her hands down hard on the back of his neck. He fell onto his side, and the gun clattered across the stone floor. She jumped on top of him, pummeling him with her bound hands. The flashlight rolled away, lighting the frescoes but leaving Dig and Riley in darkness.

The gun had vanished somewhere. The sound bounced off the walls, and she couldn't tell which way the gun had gone. He'd tucked into a fetal position on his side, his arms protecting his head and throat. She wanted to use her bound hands to strangle him, but she couldn't reach around him. He was half again as big as she was. Even with his injuries now, he remained so strong.

His fist slammed into her left cheek, and her head snapped back. He pushed her off, and she fell to the stone floor, landing on her old shoulder injury. The hot flash of pain sapped the strength from her limbs. She wanted to curl into a ball on the floor.

Dig clambered to his feet and retrieved the flashlight and the gun. It had been there within her reach all along. Its light played across the walls. The fish looked like it was dancing. She felt him cinch the zip tie tight around her ankle, and she struggled into a sitting position.

"How did you do it?"

He picked up the bag and turned the flashlight on her, blinding her. "One punch was all it took, Riley."

She held an arm up, trying to shield her eyes. "No, I mean down in Guadeloupe."

"Oh, that."

"You're supposed to be dead."

He made a noise that sounded like *Ha!* She thought he'd meant it as a laugh, but it caught in his throat like a cry. "I am dead, Riley." He walked over to her, yanked off the wig, and threw it into the corner. "Thanks to you." He turned and walked out of the chamber, his limp now more pronounced.

Over his shoulder, he said, "And when I come back, I shall return the favor."

She yanked on the chain as she heard his footsteps retreating down the tunnel. The other end was firmly anchored. It would not budge. The light from the retreating flashlight dimmed until she saw nothing but absolute darkness.

CHAPTER SIXTY-TWO

On the Street
Via Tiburtina, Rome

April 25, 2014

Virgil stood leaning against a building at the corner of the small park, his backpack slung over his shoulder. He was watching the black Bentley parked several cars away. The car was from the fleet kept in the large garage up on the hill. When Virgil had taken over the security at the Villa del Priorato di Malta, he made a number of changes to bring it into the twenty-first century. Among those changes, he had fitted out all the cars in the fleet with a tracking system, so he could keep an eye on his men when they went off in the Order's $300,000 vehicles.

As soon as he'd closed his laptop after that Skype call, he'd checked on the location of the vehicle Priest had taken. Virgil was surprised to see the car on the Via Tiburtina in the northeast quarter, well out of the city. He'd put Hawk in charge and told him he had to go off the grounds for an hour or so. He collected his kit bag, checked to make certain Priest's vehicle still had not moved, then took the keys to the vehicle that would get him there the fastest: the Bugatti Vitesse.

Virgil turned his head to check up the street. When he turned back around, it was as though Priest had suddenly appeared in the middle of the park. He pushed off from the building and started down the street to intercept him. The man was almost to the car when Virgil tapped him on the shoulder.

Priest spun around. His eyes narrowed, and his lips curled off his teeth like those of a cornered animal.

"What are you doing out here, Priest?"

"You're following me?"

"You're driving one of the Order's very fine automobiles. You're a fool if you don't think we'd keep tabs on you. But you didn't answer my question."

Priest's eyes shifted in a quick, furtive glance at the park. "I had to run an errand in this neighborhood."

"What kind of errand?"

"It's personal."

"Show me."

His eyes darted to the park again.

Virgil grabbed his arm and pushed him forward, controlling the desire to kill the man then and there. He needed to know what Priest was up to first. "Let's go. You walk ahead. I'll follow you."

They entered the park, and Priest seemed to hesitate. Then, as though he had made a decision, he started walking toward a six-foot hedge in the center of the park. They turned a corner to the back side of the hedge, and that was where Priest made his move.

Virgil figured he would do it there. It was the place with the best cover. When Priest started to swing around, Virgil batted his gun hand aside, and the weapon flew into the hedge. The two men faced each other crouched over, their hands out like wrestlers. Both men had trained to fight using a combination of martial arts, wrestling, and boxing. Virgil attacked first with a kick to the head, but Priest blocked it, then landed a punch to Virgil's ribs. Virgil was surprised at the strength of the blow. The man might have strength, but his weakness was obvious. Virgil kicked hard at the injured side of Priest's body, and the man went down with a strangled cry.

He lay in the dirt, dazed. Virgil bent down and sighted the gun where it had slid under the hedge. He reached in and retrieved it.

"Stand up, asshole."

Priest didn't move.

Virgil walked over and kicked him in the ribs, not hard enough to break a bone, but certainly hard enough to get his attention.

"I said stand up."

The man slowly got to his feet. His hair hung around his filthy face and a string of drool hung from the corner of his open mouth. He wouldn't look Virgil in the eye.

"What is that down there?"

"Catacombs."

"Like for dead people?"

"Used to be."

"What have you got hidden away down there?"

Priest said nothing.

"Go pick up your bag and bring it to me."

The man grabbed the bag with his good arm and held it out. Inside, Virgil found a flashlight, headlamp, extra batteries, bolt cutters, zip ties, and a length of rope. Whatever had happened today, Priest had been preparing for it.

Virgil pointed to the stairs. "What do you say we go down and see for ourselves?" He handed Priest the flashlight. "After you." Virgil slung the bag over his shoulder, then pulled the headlamp's elastic strap onto his own head.

Priest started down the stairs. When he got to a locked gate, he pulled on the chain and it fell free. He pushed open the gate. As they continued downward, both men turned on their lights.

At the bottom of the stairs they came to a small, round room. There were four tunnels leading off it in different directions. The place smelled like an underground prison Virgil had once visited in Nicaragua.

"Which way from here?" he asked.

Priest said nothing, but in the distance Virgil heard a voice begin hollering, "Hello. Is somebody there? Hey!" It was a woman's voice.

Virgil pointed to the tunnel on the left. "Let's go."

It was tight quarters in the tunnel. Virgil wondered if the man was going to make a run for it. He could always shoot him if he did. What was he keeping a woman prisoner for? The guy was way more fucked up than Virgil had reckoned.

Another room opened up on their left. Priest stepped through the opening and his flashlight lit up the room.

Virgil stepped in next. When he saw the girl, he said, "Oh shit."

She said, "You were in that helicopter."

The girl was wearing overalls and heavy black boots. He almost had not recognized her.

Virgil turned to Priest. "What the hell were you thinking?"

Priest still wouldn't look him in the eye.

"He said he was going to come back and kill me," the woman said.

"Shut up," Virgil said, never taking his eyes off Priest. "Where did you find her?"

"She was at the palace. In the library."

Virgil glanced at the woman. She was watching him with her chin held high.

He reached into the black canvas bag and took out one of the big plastic zip ties. He inserted the plastic end through the pawl and zipped it a couple of clicks, forming a large circle. Virgil held it out toward Priest. "Put your hands through here."

"Hell no. You don't think I'd be that stupid, do you? If something happens to me, an email will be sent to your daughter."

Virgil pointed the gun at Priest's foot and fired.

The man roared and bent forward at the waist, screaming curses.

Virgil spoke very slowly. "I said put your hands through this or it will be your knee next time."

Priest straightened. He put his hands through the loop, and Virgil zipped it tight. He grabbed the flashlight out of his hand.

"Now go sit next to her."

The man did as he was told.

As Virgil tied Priest's uninjured foot to the chain, he said, "I saw the photo you sent her already." He stood and stomped down hard on the man's bleeding foot.

Priest howled.

Then Virgil retreated out of reach of either of them and took off his backpack. From inside, he took out a block of C-4 and a cellular-activated detonator. He took out his own phone and checked for a signal. Nothing. He moved out of the room and into the tunnel. He waited. After about a minute, his phone found a signal.

When Priest recognized what Virgil was doing, he lunged and jerked against the chain. The woman watched him through narrowed eyes, but said nothing. Ballsy bitch.

When Virgil had finished, he reached into one of the pockets of his cargo pants and drew out a knife. He stepped over to the woman and slit the plastic tie on her ankle, then stood back.

"Stand up. You're coming with me."

She was shaky on her feet, but she apparently knew enough to distance herself from Priest. The man's eyes were wild, yet he had grown silent.

Virgil handed her the flashlight. "You go first, but don't try to run." He tilted his head toward Priest. "You've seen what can happen."

The woman looked at Priest. Virgil was surprised to see not an ounce of sympathy in her eyes.

"You want me to beg?" Priest asked.

"No," Virgil said. "I want you dead."

Priest turned his head so that only the scarred half of his face was visible. He spread his lips in a false smile that showed more gum than teeth. Then he said, "She beat you to it."

When they reached the Bugatti, he opened the passenger's door, tossed the bag into the footwell, and told her to get in.

She stopped and looked up and down the car.

"You've undoubtedly never ridden in a car worth more than a million dollars." Virgil might have conceded that he'd never driven one before working for the Order, either. "Maybe this car will help you comprehend the power of the Order. And the special relationship we enjoy with the police here. We have diplomatic immunity. There is very little I would hesitate to do. Keep that in mind when you think about running from me."

She climbed into the car and he shut the door.

He walked around and climbed into the driver's seat. He set the gun on the seat by his outside leg and took out his cell phone.

He slid the key into the ignition, but paused before starting the car. "So you're the one responsible for his scars?"

She faced forward, refusing to look at him. "I'd say *he's* responsible, but he doesn't see it that way."

He extended the phone toward her. "Would you like to do the honors?"

She turned away and did not say anything. He waited. At last, she turned back to face him. "I'm not a murderer," she said.

"But you're not going to risk your life to stop me."

"Would it work if I tried?" she said.

To answer her question, he tapped the screen.

At first nothing happened.

She smiled. "No signal?"

He knew how long it took sometimes. He waited, and finally he felt the car bounce. A second later, he heard the satisfying *whomp*.

CHAPTER SIXTY-THREE

Piazza dei Cavalieri di Malta
The Aventine Hill, Rome

April 25, 2014

Cole stood in the long line of tourists waiting to peep through the keyhole in the big wooden doors. In their room the night before, he and Riley had used their phones to research the two large properties owned by the Sovereign Military Order of Malta. They knew about the Magistral Palace from their talks with Dr. Günay, but they had found out online that the Order also owned this villa and church up on the Aventine Hill. It was a popular tourist spot, mentioned in the guidebooks and lots of travel blogs, because of the mysterious aura of the Knights of Malta and because of the view through the keyhole in the villa's great door.

Down at the palace, Cole had had a feeling in his gut that whoever took Riley wouldn't have kept her there. Even during the time he had been watching the place, he'd seen several cars come and go. She could have been inside any one of them. They'd have had no trouble moving her.

He looked around the Piazza dei Cavalieri. He had taken a cab to the bottom of the hill and walked up. The wide piazza was actually a dead end to the Via di Santa Sabina. The piazza was surrounded on three sides by garden walls, churches, a monastery, and the high stone wall decorated with obelisks and military trophies that marked the entrance to the villa. The large black double doors in the center stood at least fifteen feet high. A carabinieri van was parked at the entrance to the piazza. Cole had no doubt the military police had great respect for the Order, and he would not find a sympathetic ear there. This was a much more secure place to hold someone against her will.

When Cole arrived at the front of the line, he turned his baseball cap around backward and put his eye to the keyhole. It was startling how the seventeenth-century architect had aligned it. The view looked straight down a garden walk rimmed by neatly trimmed hedges. The long green corridor perfectly framed the dome of Saint Peter's at the Vatican in the distance. As it was late afternoon and there was a bit of mist in the air, the sight bore a golden, gauzy look, more like a Renaissance painting than reality. It was difficult to believe that Riley might be in danger in such a fairy-tale garden.

Cole moved his head from side to side, trying to see more. He saw no people. No movement. The Japanese tourists in line behind him began growing restless and chattered among themselves. There was nothing more to be learned, so he moved aside and let the next person take a peep inside the walls of the Villa del Priorato di Malta.

When Cole turned around, he saw a limo with security cars on either end drive across the piazza to a gate at the very back. He took out his phone and pretended to be taking pictures like a tourist, but he also snapped the diplomatic plates on the car.

Next, a large truck arrived and parked close by the entrance the limo had driven through. On the side of the truck were a painting of a chef's hat and the words *La Mela D'Oro*. Two people got out, a man and a woman all dressed in white chefs' outfits. They headed by foot to the same gate as the earlier vehicles. Cole pulled his baseball cap down very low over his eyes and walked closer.

A Japanese couple held up a camera in an attempt to take a selfie with the villa as a backdrop. Cole used sign language to indicate he could take the photo for them. As he lined them up and motioned for them to smile, he watched the couple from the catering truck approach the gate.

A security guard, wearing a tight black T-shirt that strained to contain his biceps, appeared at the gate. The man held a clipboard up in front of his enormous nose to check some list. As Cole approached, he could tell they were speaking English.

"I can't let you in to park now. They don't have you down until seven because our dinner guests have to get their cars in first, but they told me you were coming."

"It is okay, we just need to ask Signora Ricasoli a question about this dessert." The man carried a cardboard box.

Cole smiled, nodded, and handed the young Japanese man his camera. He waved to them as they walked off, then pulled out his own phone again and pretended to take a photo of the monastery gates while he watched the villa entrance out of the corner of his eye.

The big man spoke into a walkie-talkie. Cole couldn't hear the reply, but the guard waved them through.

Given that it was a few days before the double canonization ceremony, Cole surmised that the villa must be full of invited guests. Perhaps he was wrong in his guess that they would have brought her here. He refused to believe they would hurt her. What they wanted was information, and they believed that whatever he and his friends had found on the *Upholder* was the key to something. And they didn't have Riley's bag with the false sea atlas. That was now in his backpack. Chances were they didn't even know about that.

He walked over to examine the caterers' van. He was standing next to their truck when he heard the deep rumble of a powerful engine.

When he turned to look, one of the new Bugattis rolled slowly across the square. The sleek black car looked like a modern version of the Batmobile. The windows of the car were tinted dark, but as it passed in front of him, the driver rolled down his window. The license plate held simply the letters SMOM.

Cole stepped behind the back of the catering van. He had recognized the blond-haired driver from the boatyard video capture Riley had shown him. He moved around to the front of the van and peeked around the hood. He watched as the man leaned out the window to talk to the security guard.

Cole had to force down his impulse to run to the vehicle and drag the man out through the window. There, sitting in the passenger's seat, was a very pissed-off-looking Riley.

The car pulled in through the gate and disappeared.

Cole looked at the size of the guard on the gate, then ducked down and half crawled to the back of the van. He leaned against the doors. If that was an indication of the security inside, how in the world was he going to get in there? There was no way he could pass as a guest. He looked at the wall with the keyhole door. No way he could climb over that. And he had seen when he walked up here that the villa backed onto a sheer hillside.

He stood up, and, on a whim, he tried the latch to the double doors at the back of the catering truck. He pulled the handle down and the door opened. Cole peered inside. There was no access between the cab and the back of the truck. He looked around the piazza. The line of tourists at the keyhole had disappeared, and no one that he could see seemed to be looking his way. He didn't see anyone over by the carabinieri van.

He slipped inside the truck and pulled the door closed behind him.

CHAPTER SIXTY-FOUR

**Aboard the *Ruse*
Off Chart along the Coast of Turkey**

June 29, 1798

The morning was hot and the wind was light. Alonso told Arzella she should stay in the cabin and rest. They had been at sea for eleven days, and they were nearly out of food and water.

For the last two days they had been carefully rationing their water. When he tried to measure their speed with the log line, they had been sailing so slowly, the chip of wood had barely moved when the hourglass ran out. His calculations told him they should have arrived at the coast by now. They had sighted the tip of the island of Rhodes four days earlier and decided against putting in there. They had less than one hundred miles to go, and the wind had been fair. And every time they encountered people here amongst the Turks, they ran the risk that one would decide to rob them. A man and a woman alone on a ship this size presented an easy target. Alonso could not risk losing everything now. Not after they'd made it this far.

He heard the cabin door close and soon saw Arzella climbing the steps up to the aft deck. Due to the heat, she wore only a thin cotton shift. He could see her body through the transparent fabric. The child she was carrying had started to change her shape. Her breasts were more full, her belly slightly rounded. Her hair was piled atop her head and held by a hairpin. He thought she had never looked more beautiful.

"You should be resting, my love."

"The air doesn't move in that cabin. I'd rather find a bit of shade and lounge on deck. May I take a small drink of water?"

He knew he should ask her to wait, but he could not refuse her. "Of course," he said.

She had been stronger of spirit than he had ever imagined possible on this trip. They had seen their share of foul weather, miserable heat, and rotten food. She had never once complained. He'd known men who had attempted mutiny over more tolerable conditions.

She walked over to the water barrel on the starboard side. She scooped a ladle out, drank, and watched the sea passing the hull.

"I feel a bit more wind," she said. "It looks as though we're moving."

Alonso looked up at the sails. She was right. The cloth no longer hung like wash on a line. He had not felt the wind because it had come up from behind. They were now moving through the water at nearly the same speed as the wind. He checked the compass and made a slight correction. There, now he felt it—and their speed increased.

"Looks like you've brought me luck again, Arzella."

She laughed and retrieved his great-grandfather's shield, which she had been engraving with new, flowery designs. "Find me land and then talk to me about luck, *mon chevalier.*"

Two hours later, he did indeed sight what looked like a gray smudge on the horizon. Arzella was napping on a blanket in the shade of the sail. By the time she awoke, it was early afternoon, and he had already turned south to run parallel to the coast. When she sat up, she was facing away from the coast.

"I'd hoped to wake up and see land."

"Turn around, then, my love."

She got to her feet and ran to the port-side rail. "I've never seen anything so welcome and lovely. But why aren't we going in? How do you know this is the way you must go?"

"I intentionally took us to the north so I would know which way to turn when we arrived." He lifted his brass telescope to his eye and scanned the coast. "We've now sailed off our sea maps, and I have no idea what the character of the shoreline should look like. I am only searching for our castle."

"Couldn't we simply go ashore and show some local villagers the drawing? Surely they will recognize it and point us in the right direction."

"Even when we stopped in Crete, I saw the calculus in some of the fishermen's eyes. Such a large ship as the *Ruse* with only one man and one woman aboard? Fortunately for us, the people of that village were not murderous scoundrels. We cannot count on that reception everywhere here on the Ottoman Coast. Every encounter we have with strangers is potentially dangerous."

"You have your pistol," she said.

"But so do they have firearms. I am sorry."

"Two days with only that horrid biscuit and water are not the best nourishment for a growing child."

"I worry, too."

"Let me take a turn at the helm. You've been steering all day. You need some rest."

"Yes," he said. "A bit of rest would be nice."

* * *

Alonso did not know how long he'd been asleep when he heard Arzella calling his name. He sat up and saw her pointing off to port. He hoped to see the castle atop a hill. Instead, he saw the sails of a small fishing boat maintaining a course to intercept them.

"How long has he been there?"

"I just saw him and called to you."

"I'll get my pistol," he said, and then, after looking at her standing at the wheel in her transparent shift, he added, "and some clothes for you."

When he came back topsides, the fishing boat was closer, but not yet close enough to make out the people on deck. Alonso took the wheel, set his pistol next to the compass, and handed Arzella a suit of his own clothes. "I know they will be quite large for you, but let's give it a try. I brought a scarf for your hair as well. If you tie it in a pigtail, that might help."

When she'd changed, he thought she looked like a girl dressed as a man, but perhaps from a distance they would be fooled.

The *Ruse* was moving through the water at four to five knots when the fishermen hailed them. The captain was an older man with a white beard. His crew was a boy of no more than fourteen. The captain called to them in a language Alonso did not understand. He shook his head and held up his hands to show he did not comprehend. Then the captain held his hand in the air and made motions like he was smoking a pipe.

Alonso nodded and made motions as though he were eating. The captain held up a large fish. Alonso nodded again, then said to Arzella, "Go check Nikola's berth below. In a bag hanging on the bulkhead, you will find some tobacco. Bring it to me."

Alonso dropped the larger mainsail. The smaller forward lateen sail was barely large enough to move his ship in the light winds. The fishing boat also reduced sail.

Arzella appeared with the bag of tobacco.

"Take the wheel," he said. "Just hold a steady course so they can come alongside." He picked up the pistol and placed it in the belt that held up his trousers.

As they approached, Alonso saw the fishing-boat captain pick up a net at the end of a long pole. The captain appeared to be accustomed to these exchanges at sea. When he passed the net within reach of the xebec, Alonso placed the pouch of tobacco in the net.

The captain of the fishing boat retrieved the net and passed the tobacco under his nose. Then he nodded to the boy. The young man placed the fish and another parcel in the net. The captain lifted the pole and extended the net back toward the *Ruse*. When it came within reach, Alonso lifted out the large fish and the parcel.

Behind him, Alonso heard Arzella's voice. "Do you know this castle?"

He turned around, and she was leaning over the ship's rails, holding up the book of sea maps open to the drawing.

The fishing-boat captain was still carrying the net, but he narrowed his eyes and motioned for the boy to steer them closer. As the gap between them narrowed, Alonso feared the two boats would collide.

The old fisherman leaned over, then his face broke into a gap-toothed smile. "Kekova," he called out.

Alonso held his hands up in the air to indicate he didn't understand.

The white-bearded captain pointed to the land to their left and said again, "Kekova." Then he moved his other hand in an up-and-over motion. He said "Kekova" again, then pointed his hand straight ahead and then swung it around to the left.

Alonso nodded and waved.

The fishing-boat captain had not had time to stow the net pole before his young crew turned the wheel, and they veered off. The captain raised the sail and their vessel began to pick up speed. He moved to the rail and raised a hand to Alonso.

"What do you think he meant?" Arzella asked. "Do you think he recognized the castle?"

"Yes, we passed an opening in the coast a while back. I think this must be an island next to us. He was trying to say that it's on the other side of the island. When we get to the end of it, we should turn around and sail up into the waters on the other side."

"What was in the net?"

Alonso held up the fish by its tail. "This and two oranges."

"Oranges! How kind! Do you think he was an Ottoman?"

"I guess we will never know who he was, other than a good friend."

CHAPTER SIXTY-FIVE

Villa del Priorato di Malta
The Aventine Hill, Rome

April 25, 2014

Riley realized as soon as the car started up the hill that they were headed to the villa on the Aventine. She and Cole had read about the place the night before. Originally a monastery, the property had passed to the Knights Templar. Then, when Pope Clement disbanded the Templars, the site passed to the Knights of Saint John along with all the other Templar properties. Today, the villa, designed by the famous architect Giovanni Battista Piranesi, was the residence of the current grand master of the Knights of Malta.

She hadn't spoken a word since the explosion back at the catacombs. She'd been trying to sort it out in her mind. As shocking as it had been to discover Diggory Priest was still alive, she was now finding it difficult to wrap her head around the fact that he was dead again. Riley wondered who this blond man was who killed so easily. Hadn't he and Dig been working on the same side? She'd noticed the blue triangle tattoo on his forearm, and she knew what that meant. They would be arriving at the villa soon, and if she expected any information, she'd better get him talking.

"Where'd you serve?" she asked.

He took his eyes off the road to look at her. His blue eyes were unnaturally light. Like arctic ice. They didn't look real.

"Iraq. Delta Force."

"Thought so. Me, Marine Corps, embassy security guard. No combat."

He ignored her.

"What do you want with me?"

"You should be thanking me for saving you from that freak," he said.

"Saving me? I'd call it kidnapping."

"You and your friend have something that belongs to us."

"Who's 'us'?"

The car approached a guard gate, and the driver rolled down his window briefly. The guard waved them through.

"You know what I'm talking about," he said.

Riley got a glimpse of the gardens on the front side of the villa, but their car proceeded down a gravel lane at the rear of the buildings. Three-quarters of the way down the lane, he pulled to a stop outside a door. Beyond, she saw steps leading up to what looked like the entrance to a church.

"Stay here," he said.

Blondie climbed out of the car and tucked the gun into the back of his pants. He unlocked the door, stepped inside, and looked around.

Her chances would not be great if she tried to run for it. Technically, she wasn't even in Italy anymore. This property belonged to the sovereignty of the Knights of Malta. They issued their own passports and made their own laws here. And Blondie had trained as one of the most efficient killers on the planet. The smart thing to do was to sit tight for now and see what she could learn.

He returned to the car and opened the passenger's-side door.

"Come," he said.

She swung her legs out first, then reached forward with her bound hands to lift her weight out of the low seat.

He waved the gun toward the door. "This way."

She entered a dark corridor.

"Second door on your left," he said.

When they passed the first door, it was half-open. Inside was a small, dimly lit dressing room. Various robes and cloaks hung on pegs on the wall. On the far side of the room, she saw another doorway, through which she glimpsed candles burning atop an elaborate altar.

When she arrived outside the second door, he said, "Open it."

Riley entered a small, dark room. Blondie switched on a bare bulb overhead. The room was furnished with a simple wood dresser and an iron-framed single bed. A crucifix—a bronze Jesus on a wood cross—hung on the wall above the bed.

"Sit," he said. Then he pulled another zip tie from his jacket pocket. He squatted and pulled her ankle tight against one claw-footed leg of the bed frame at the head of the bed. He zip-tied her ankle to the metal bar, then stood.

"You found the shield on the submarine."

The statement surprised her, and she knew her face had given that away.

"James Thatcher wasn't the only one who knew Captain Wilson," he said.

"Then why didn't you search for it yourselves?"

"They tried. It seems their 'experts' had them looking in the wrong place. That was before my time."

"And what makes you so sure Cole found something?"

"You're here. In Rome. Otherwise, you would still be searching off Djerba." Blondie checked his watch, then ran his left hand through his stiff hair.

Riley said, "So what now?"

"Priest has given us no choice."

She remembered the look on his face when he'd tapped the screen on his phone. He'd been smiling.

"You will tell me what you found," he said. "Soon."

"And if I don't?"

"You will," he said. "In Iraq, I learned how to be very persuasive."

Riley glanced at the tattoo on his arm.

He walked to the doorway and paused. He looked back over his shoulder. "I take no pleasure from hurting women. But when I come back, you will tell me what I want to know."

CHAPTER SIXTY-SIX

Piazza dei Cavalieri di Malta
The Aventine Hill, Rome

April 25, 2014

When Cole closed the truck's back door, everything went pitch-dark. The quick glimpse he'd had of the interior revealed that the back of the van was almost empty.

He took out his phone and turned it on. The dim screen provided some light, but with a couple of taps, he was able to use the camera flash as a flashlight. The back wall of the cargo area was lined with three floor-to-ceiling storage cabinets. The first one he opened had deep shelves filled with pots and pans in the bottom, china on the upper shelves. The middle cabinet was mostly table linens and uniforms. The last one looked like the "everything" storage area. Cleaning supplies, lighter fluid, candlesticks, a couple of lanterns, and electric kitchen appliances. The bottom shelf was almost two feet high. The only thing down there was a large meat-slicing machine.

The caterers would be returning soon. The guard had said they could take their truck in at seven o'clock. He had to find someplace to hide.

Cole rearranged the upper shelves and made room for the slicing machine on the shelf one up from the bottom. The machine was heavier than it looked and unwieldy, but after several attempts, he was able to get it onto the upper shelf. He was about to climb in when he thought that he would probably have little time on the other end. Might as well have a look now to see what he might be able to use. He opened the middle cabinet and took out a chef's coat. He closed the door.

He took off his backpack and was about to put the coat on when he heard voices outside. Quickly, he got down on the floor, wormed his backside into the space, and curled his arms and legs inside, hugging his pack and the coat to his chest. He was about to close the door when he heard the forward cab doors open. The sound of their voices speaking Italian was now very clear.

The engine started. The noise was loud, but he wasn't sure it was loud enough to cover the noise of closing the cabinet doors, so he held on to them.

The truck backed up. Then, instead of pulling through the gates, as Cole had expected, it made a wide turn and started to accelerate. He felt the incline change. They were heading down the hill, away from the villa.

Cole wondered if he should crawl out, open the back doors, and jump out of the truck at a traffic signal. He had to find Riley. He checked the time on his phone. Maybe they were just going to fetch the food they were supposed to be serving at dinner. He decided to wait, but if the drive was too long, he'd bail and catch a cab back up the hill.

A few minutes later, the truck stopped, then backed up and began a turn. Several voices shouted in Italian, and then an emergency vehicle turned on its siren right alongside the truck. Cole pulled his cabinet doors closed seconds before the truck's back doors opened.

He heard shouting, then music playing from inside a building. There was lots of clattering and the screech of metal on metal. He thought they were pulling a ramp out so they could load the truck.

It took them only fifteen minutes. The truck filled with the aromas of garlic, yeasty bread, and roast lamb. It sounded like they loaded ten or twelve rolling carts into the truck. Then Cole heard a ratcheting sound, like straps being tightened. The doors slammed closed, and the truck started up again.

The ride back to the villa seemed to go much faster. Their business must not have been far from the Aventine Hill. Now he was starting to worry that they might need something out of the cabinet where he was hiding. He was still trying to think of a story in case he was discovered, when the incline changed, and the truck groaned as the automatic transmission downshifted.

No, he told himself, thinking negative thoughts wasn't any help. He would get onto the villa grounds. After that, he would create a diversion, then find Riley. It would be simple.

Yeah, right.

Cole held his breath when they slowed to a stop. He heard the driver say, "Where do you want us to park after we unload?"

He couldn't hear the answer. The truck's engine revved, and they were driving over uneven terrain. The dishes clanked and the heavy machine on the shelf above him bounced, threatening to break the shelf.

The truck stopped, reversed, and parked. The back doors opened before the driver cut off the engine. The ramp screeched out, and Cole counted six different voices, each coming into the truck and taking a cart. Then it went quiet. He tried to open the doors, but the rest of the carts were blocking the storage cabinet.

The voices returned, and they took the remaining wheeled carts of food. Cole opened the doors to his storage area and crawled out. He shrugged into the chef's coat, then picked up a flashlight off one of the shelves. He searched the cabinet for matches, but couldn't find any. He grabbed a package of steel wool off the top shelf and stuffed that in a coat pocket. He grabbed his pack, jumped to the ground, and looked around.

A few stars shone in a sky still tinged with pink. The truck was backed up on a concrete slab at the rear entrance of a weathered stone building. Dark hedges ran along both sides of a dirt lane that ran the length of the property, down to the edge of the hill that faced the Vatican. Light poured out the kitchen door as well as voices. And they were coming closer.

Cole pushed through the hedge and lay down on the ground. Now he regretted putting on the white coat—it wasn't a good color for hiding at night. He heard the rattle of the ramp sliding back into the truck. The engine started, and the truck turned, drove several hundred feet away, then parked next to a cluster of vehicles. The parking lot was on an open, grassy area around what looked to be an old carriage house. The lone driver returned, whistling a tune as he walked. He paused outside the kitchen, then Cole smelled cigarette smoke. The man was so close, Cole could barely breathe. Then the whistling stopped and the kitchen door closed, turning the night dark once again.

Cole let out a long breath, then jumped to his feet.

There had to be security on the grounds. Cameras or guards or both, but Cole didn't see either. He brushed some grass and leaves off the coat, then slipped back through the hedge and walked toward the catering van. Hopefully, anyone watching would assume he was one of their crew. When he stepped between the truck and the car next to it, he ducked down. Keeping his body low, he ran between the vehicles to the open barn doors at the end of the wooden building.

Half a dozen cars were parked inside. Cole assumed they must belong to the Order. He recognized the new Bugatti with the SMOM license plate, as well as a couple of Porsche Cayennes, and a Rolls-Royce Ghost.

What a shame, he thought. Cole had already decided that the best diversion would be a fire.

CHAPTER SIXTY-SEVEN

Villa del Priorato di Malta
The Aventine Hill, Rome

April 25, 2014

Riley did not doubt that a trained Delta would be able to break her, and she wasn't about to give the man the opportunity to try. Why he had left her alone was a mystery, but she intended to make that his first mistake.

Reaching down, she tested the zip tie around her ankle. It was tight, and even if she could lift the bed, there wasn't enough slack in the band around her ankle to slide over the claw-shaped foot at the bottom of the metal leg.

She would need two hands to work on the leg band, so she turned her focus to the zip tie around her wrists. The white pawl that kept the zip tie tight was on the back of her right hand. She brought her hands to her mouth and bit the buckle. By pulling with her teeth, she was able to reposition the zip tie so that the pawl fell between her wrists when she looked down.

Riley stood and reached up high over her head. She brought her wrists down slowly at first to check out where her elbows would hit her body. She was aiming for her pelvic region, so it would require some hunching over. She reached up again, paused, and drew in a deep breath. Then, with all her strength, she brought her arms down. Her elbows were driven apart, one on each side of her body, and the zip tie at her wrists broke away.

Bright-red rings around her wrists showed where the plastic had cut into her skin. The last time she'd tried that move had been in MSG School at Quantico, but there she had protected her wrists with duct tape. She was glad to know the move still worked, but the instructor was right. Without the protection, it hurt like hell.

The hands had been relatively easy, but the leg was another story. Using both hands now, she tried again to push the plastic band down over the claw foot. The plastic dug into her skin when she tried to stretch it over the metal, but she couldn't get enough slack. That wasn't going to work.

Riley stood up and lifted the single mattress to check for any other bits of sharp metal on the bed frame. The springs were strung very tight. There was little chance she'd be able to get one loose, and the ends didn't look sharp enough to make it worth the effort. Nothing else on the frame looked like it would come loose. She dropped the mattress, drew in a deep breath, and bit her lower lip.

"Goddammit," she said. Then she noticed the crucifix on the wall, and she said, "Sorry."

She'd always read that priests and monks lived austere lives, but there was nothing in this room but a bed. She plopped down onto it— then sat up straight, turned around slowly, and looked up at the wall.

A bed *and* a crucifix. The wooden cross was about fifteen inches long, and the body of Christ appeared to be made out of bronze.

She couldn't climb up onto the bed with her foot tied at floor level, but there was bedding on the bed. She pulled the blanket free, wadded it up, and threw it at the crucifix. The blanket bounced off and nothing moved. It would be just her luck that they had screwed the thing to the wall. The second time, she got hold of a corner of the blanket and tried using it as a whip. The crucifix clattered to the floor.

After several tries, she pried the statue off the wooden cross. The crossed feet and each of the hands were literally nailed to the cross. Years of corrosion had fused the metal, and the nails came away with the bronze statue. She started pounding the foot nail on the plastic zip tie where it crossed the edge of the squarish leg. The nail punched holes in the plastic band. She tried being gentle to keep the noise at a minimum. When the foot nail broke off, she used the nail from one of the hands until the plastic was well perforated. Riley slipped the feet of the bronze statue under the plastic band. With one swift movement, she cranked down on Jesus's head and levered up the zip tie. It broke with a pop.

She opened the door slowly and put one eye to the crack. The hall was empty in both directions. She slipped out and started back down the hall the way she'd been led in. When she got to the door to the church vestibule, she stepped inside. She lifted one of the black robes and stuck her arms into the sleeves. She found an odd-looking black hat that looked a bit like a crown with a black pom-pom on top. She stuffed her hair up into that. There was no mirror in the room, so she could only hope she looked all right.

There had to be another exit out through the chapel itself, so she peered out into the sanctuary. The only light came from the candles on the altar, and though the light was dim, the church was small. She couldn't see anyone in there. The door led her into the front of the church beside the altar. As her eyes grew more accustomed to the light, Riley stopped and stared in wonder at the arches and columns of magnificent white stone. Images of cherubs flying around the Virgin Mary made up most of the huge altarpiece.

She skirted around the elaborate wooden pulpit and headed for the back door. When she was at the third row of seats, she heard a creak and felt the air move as the church's front door opened.

CHAPTER SIXTY-EIGHT

Villa del Priorato di Malta
The Aventine Hill, Rome

April 25, 2014

Cole was certain these guys had more security than just the one guard on the gate. He hid in the shadows beside the catering van and watched the grounds around the big main house. It didn't take him long to spot them. The first guy he saw was patrolling the front entrance, from the keyhole doors over to the driveway gate. The second guy he spotted was walking around the garden outside the front entrance to the house. Both were dressed in long-sleeved black T-shirts and black pants.

All that food that arrived in the catering truck must mean that there was some kind of big dinner going on in there. Cole didn't think Riley had been invited to sit down and eat with company. It was more likely they had her holed up in one of the other rooms of the house. The blond guy with her was the same guy who had set the bomb on their boat in Turkey, and who had been in the helicopter that had buzzed them down off Djerba. He was looking for this relic or treasure, too, and it seemed he wanted it badly enough to kidnap Riley to learn what they'd found down in that submarine. With the big shindig dinner going on, Cole hoped they hadn't got around to interrogating her. Not that he was afraid she would tell them anything. He was more afraid of how much pain she would have to endure if they were dishing it out.

He had to get her out of there before that started.

Cole ducked down between the parked cars and ran back into the garage building. He ran past the cars to see what he could find in the rear.

Indeed, the building had originally been a stable and carriage house. In the rear, he could smell horses. Two stalls looked like they had fresh hay in them, but there were no horses inside. Cole found a locked door. The glass pane in the door didn't show much of what was inside—it was too dark. He guessed it was some sort of workroom. All the way in the rear of the structure, he found an old wagon wheel and a large open space. It was big enough for a carriage, and Cole suspected that both the horses and the carriage were off somewhere else on the property.

He dropped his backpack, pulled off the chef's coat, and tossed it over the gate into the stall. Then he grabbed a handful of hay and dropped it in a pile in the middle of the space left by the absent carriage. He pushed one of the hay bales out, close by, and made a trail of hay leading over to it.

On the ground outside the workshop, he found a small gas can. It was nearly empty, but a half cup or so dribbled out onto the small pile of hay he'd made in the middle of the carriage stall, and then he shook the remaining drops on the hay leading over to the bale. He saw a broom and a shovel leaning against the wall, and he brought those over and set them on top of the hay bale.

When he was satisfied with his fire preparations, Cole took the flashlight out of his coat pocket and shaded it with his body. He flicked the switch to make sure it worked. The light flashed so bright it blinded him for several seconds. He closed his eyes and then blinked a few times until the bright yellow dot marring his vision cleared.

Then he grabbed the top of the flashlight and unscrewed the lens. Inside he found two big D-cell batteries. This little trick had served him well back in his days at university. He'd placed many bets with some of the fraternity types to make beer money. Those guys never believed him when he said he could start a fire with a battery and some steel wool. His problem now was that it usually worked too well. He wanted to be out the door long before the fire really got under way.

The trick was going to be to make sure he had enough steel wool so it would burn long enough to ignite his tinder. He opened the package of steel wool. The caterers probably used it for scrubbing pots and pans, and it wasn't as fine as the stuff he had used in college. It should work, though. He pulled the fibers apart, shaping the wool into a long cigar-like shape. It was important to loosen the pack of the fibers to make sure the fire would have plenty of oxygen.

Cole knelt next to the pile of hay. He turned to look at the cars in the front of the garage, hoping that the guards would delay their arrival long enough for him to get out, but not so long as to let those machines go up in smoke. That would really be a crime.

After settling the steel wool on top of the straw, he nestled one end of the battery against the fibers. Nothing happened. He checked his escape route again. Then he curved the other end of the long tube of fibers and touched the opposite end of the battery. The steel fibers lit up bright red and glowed. The hay started to smoke, then a yellow-and-blue flame popped up. Cole smelled the burning gas.

He grabbed his bag and ran.

CHAPTER SIXTY-NINE

Church of Santa Maria del Priorato
The Aventine Hill, Rome

April 25, 2014

She slipped behind a column.

Judging from the footsteps, there were several of them. She kept the wide stone column between her and the new arrivals, so she didn't see them as they passed to the front of the chapel.

"Just take a seat in the first couple of rows," a man said. He spoke English with a very light Italian accent.

Other voices murmured words she could not understand.

She decided to risk a quick look around the column. If they were sitting with their backs to her, she'd be fine. But at least one was probably standing up front. She moved slowly so as not to attract attention. She slid one side of her face out into view.

She counted six men. Five seated and one standing at the front. She ducked back behind the column.

"Welcome, Cavalieri of the Guardiani."

The other men mumbled again.

"My good friend Cavaliere Vandervoort has some news for us. Would you like to share the news, Virgil?"

Riley recognized the next voice immediately. It was Blondie. So that was his name. Virgil Vandervoort.

"I have a good line on the location of the shield," Virgil said. "And we have reason to believe whatever is engraved on it may lead to something inside our own library."

The murmuring voices grew louder.

"Based on what I know at this time, I'd say the Religion will be back in the hands of the Guardiani in time for Operation Barnabas to go forward."

"Thank you, Virgil."

Riley peeked around the column to get a look at the face of the Italian with impeccable English.

"Gentlemen," he continued, "the opportunity is before us to complete what our ancestors started in the Crusades—not just Jerusalem and the Holy Land, but the entire Arabian peninsula will be scoured clean of barbarians and become the new Sovereign Territory of the Knights of Malta."

Riley slid back behind the column. She could not believe what she was hearing.

"I'm sure you have heard the recent news from Syria. The Islamic State has become a reality. They are beheading civilians, women and children, and they have brought back live crucifixions. Slavery and rape of non-Muslims grows every day. They're playing right into our hands. Throughout North America and Europe there is growing outrage. People are calling on their leaders to do something, and our members in the JSOC tell us that they have developed a doomsday plan to present to the Western world when the outcry for blood reaches its crescendo. You see, we don't care if they are al-Qaeda or Palestinians or Hamas or the Muslim Brotherhood. Already social media channels are calling for their extermination. The entire Christian world knows these barbarians must be annihilated."

"How do you plan to do that?" The deep voice sounded British.

"That, my friend, is where the brilliance of Virgil's Operation Barnabas lies. All these years the Guardiani fought to keep the Religion out of the hands of the infidels. Now, the time has come to hand it over to them."

"What?" Several voices spoke at once and the murmuring rose to a roar.

At the rear of the church, a large man burst through the door.

"Virgil!" he yelled. "Come quick. We got a fire!"

CHAPTER SEVENTY

Villa del Priorato di Malta
The Aventine Hill, Rome

April 25, 2014

When the church door closed behind the last of them, Riley didn't move right away. She stood still, stunned at what she had just heard. Extermination? What kind of Kool-Aid were these guys drinking?

She peered around the column to make sure the church really was empty. Her hair was escaping out from under the hat, so she repositioned it and stuffed the stray strands back under the black cap. It was too dark to see the zipper up the front of the robe, so she just held it closed and walked toward the exit with her head bowed, just in case there was still someone in the church she couldn't see.

When she opened the door, she smelled smoke immediately. The odor was a combination of wood smoke and a chemical smell. Something like paint burning, maybe.

She followed a gravel path around to her right and back along the side of the church. The front of the church opened at the end of the property overlooking the city. The lights of Rome spread out to her left, and in the distance she could see the lights on the dome of Saint Peter's Basilica at the Vatican.

At the end of the church wall, very formal gardens opened up on her right. She saw the huge villa and several outbuildings off to the side, stretching the length of the property. The vast gardens ran parallel to them. She was at the back of the villa's property, and the exit out to the square would be on the other side of the gardens, past the villa and the other buildings. It looked very far away.

Keeping her head bowed, trying to look like a pious cleric, she strolled the gravel paths, weaving her way in and out of the hedges. The garden had one straight, long path on the far side that provided the clear sight-way for the keyhole visitors. But between that long, open path and the big house was a garden maze of sorts. Around every corner she found little stone benches, statues, and alcoves with fountains.

She heard a distant siren, and, over the top of the manicured shrubbery, the sky took on an orange glow. The gate she and Virgil had used to enter the villa appeared to be the only access for vehicles. With the fire and emergency vehicles entering through that gate, that escape path would be crowded. Perhaps she could slip out through the crowd, but it would be even better if she could find another way off the grounds.

As her path had taken her wandering through the gardens, she became aware of the high wall that occasionally blocked her progress. When she and Cole had been looking at the villa on Google Earth the night before, she had seen that the adjoining property was the Basilica of Saints Bonifacio and Alessio. She remembered the name because she'd had to do an Internet search to even know who those two saints were. Only in Rome. She was trying to make her way over to the wall when she heard footsteps on the gravel.

Riley froze. She listened, waiting. She began to wonder if she had imagined the noise. Then she heard it again. Very close this time.

Had they discovered her missing? If so, they might also know that certain vestments were gone, and her disguise would do her no good. Her only hope would be to outrun them. Yet, if they didn't know it was her, by running she would give herself away.

It's funny how it works. It had happened to her like that before. So little time elapsed between the moment she decided to run and the time her feet were moving, that she seemed to start running before she'd even made up her mind.

The robes were a problem. She was running full tilt for the vine-covered wall that divided the properties between the Knights' villa and the adjoining basilica, but the voluminous fabric of the robes kept getting tangled around her legs and throwing her off her stride. The crunch of feet running on gravel behind her grew ever louder.

She was almost to the wall when something slammed into her from behind. She stumbled and felt herself falling forward. She dropped her shoulder and rolled to her left. It was only due to years of training that she didn't end up with a face full of gravel—or half-paralyzed with pain from her old injury.

Her assailant grunted as he hit the ground next to her. That was when Riley recognized him. She rolled free and was struggling to get to her feet when she saw his arm pulled back, his fist ready to slam into her face.

"It's me!" she said in a frantic stage whisper.

The fist dropped. "Shit, Riley." He reached over and pushed the pom-pom hat off her head.

Her hair tumbled down to her shoulders.

Cole's body sagged, almost like he was deflating. He said, "Magee, I almost knocked you out."

"You were going to punch a priest?"

"Yeah, I was gonna steal the robes." He looked up and grinned. "I guess great minds think alike."

"Well, I didn't have to tackle a priest." She stood. "Come on. Let's get out of here before they find us."

Riley tucked the robe and hat under her arm and led him toward the high wall at the edge of the property. They both heard the footsteps at the same time. Cole stepped behind the waist-high hedge and Riley followed. They lay down and rolled their bodies up tight against the stems of the shrubs.

The earth beneath them had been turned over recently in preparation for more planting. Someone had added manure to fertilize the soil, and the stench was making Riley's eyes water.

A man started talking, and she nearly gasped. The voice was so close. There were two of them. Riley could see their pant legs through the bushes. Jeans and work boots.

"I could have sworn I heard something this way." The man's voice wasn't a whisper, but his voice was so low, no one could hear him outside ten feet.

"Man, it stinks here." That one was a different voice.

"She's got to be here somewhere. Virgil said he'd only left her alone for thirty minutes."

They must be part of a security detail. They were standing right next to the shrubs where Cole was. Riley couldn't believe they didn't see him.

"Wouldn't take you or me that long to break out of zip cuffs."

"She ain't us."

The other man chuckled, and they moved on down the path. Riley waited until she could no longer hear their footsteps on the gravel.

She sat up and motioned for Cole to follow her.

The wall looked like it was just a bigger hedge. She tugged hard on one of the vines, then gave Cole the thumbs-up sign. She wrapped the black robe around the back of her neck and placed the hat on her head. She leaned close to his ear and whispered. "There's a big church on the other side."

Cole pointed to the robe. "You think you're going to need that over there?"

"No, but if we leave it here"—she pointed in the direction the guards had gone—"it'd be like leaving a sign saying, 'They Went Thataway.'"

"Good point." Cole grabbed a vine with both hands and put one foot on the wall.

The climbing wasn't that difficult—trying to do it without making any noise was the hard part. There were almost no footholds, so it required upper body strength. By the time she got to the top, Riley was winded. She knew better than to sit up on the wall. She didn't want to present that outline against the night sky, so she rolled over the top. To her surprise, there were no vines on the other side of the wall, and she fell the twelve feet to the ground. She landed feet first, but lost her balance and rolled to the ground. A few seconds later, Cole dropped next to her. He stayed upright. He stuck out his hand.

Riley reached for his hand. He pulled her to her feet and then wrapped her in his arms and squeezed.

"I need to breathe," she said.

He eased his grip on her. "Sorry. I just thought—" He didn't finish the sentence, but rather just tightened his grip again.

"I'm okay."

"Yeah, but I didn't know that for the last five or six hours. I was so afraid they'd hurt you."

"You set the fire?"

"Yeah." He glanced back at the wall. "Those guys, they said you broke out of zip cuffs?"

She lifted her shoulders and let them fall again.

Cole said, "Damn right you ain't them. If you'd been the one searching, you'd have found us."

She nodded. "Probably."

A bright light clicked on. Cole and Riley stepped away from each other. They turned to face the light, squinting and attempting to shield their eyes with their arms.

The silence dragged on. The person holding the light didn't say a word. Finally, Cole took a step toward the light.

A deep voice said, "Stop. Put your hands on top of your head."

Riley didn't recognize the accent.

"Now follow the trail to your left. Head toward the yellow light on the corner of the building. I will be right behind you."

They followed orders.

CHAPTER SEVENTY-ONE

**Aboard the *Ruse*
At Anchor off Kekova**

June 30, 1798

Even before she opened her eyes, Arzella marveled at the boat's stillness. No creaking from the wooden hull, no gurgling rush of water, no moaning of the wind in the rigging. Her head was nestled into the crook under Alonso's shoulder, and, though she saw daylight through her eyelids, she didn't want that sublime moment to end.

"Good morning, my love," Alonso said. "I feel you wakening."

"I refuse to open my eyes. This is our first night spent together in bed, and it can't be over yet."

"I could grow accustomed to awakening with you by my side."

"Last night was lovely." They had sailed round the island at sunset, feasted on fresh fish, and found the castle under the light of a near-full moon. Best of all was setting the anchor and falling into each other's arms in bed.

"But we were both so exhausted all we did was sleep."

"Sleep was what we needed."

"I am a man, my dear Arzella, and this morning I have other needs."

He wrapped his arms around her and began to pull up her nightdress. She kissed his throat, aware that she, too, had needs.

They both jumped at the sound of loud knocking on the hull. Then they heard a man's voice shouting words in a language they did not understand.

Alonso leapt to his feet and grabbed his trousers. He had one leg through and was hopping toward the cabin door as he tried to get the other leg into the right hole. When he was successful, he buckled his belt, grabbed his shirt off the peg, and disappeared through the door.

Arzella arose and looked out the windows in the high transom. She saw brown, rocky hillsides turned golden by the morning sun, but no boats. Their visitor would be alongside.

From the cupboard she took out a frock. She had not worn ladies' clothing since their short visit at Crete. On the boat it was far easier to wear only undergarments and go barefoot. She looked at her shoes and sighed. She supposed it would be necessary to wear stockings and lace her feet into leather again.

As she dressed she heard voices, but she could not make out what they were saying. At least it sounded civil. She hoped the people here would be kind. It would be ridiculous to find she had sailed all this way only to exchange one prison for another. She combed her hair, and, when she was satisfied that she was presentable, she ventured out onto the deck.

A man and a boy were seated in a wooden boat tied alongside. They were chatting with Alonso.

"Come, my dear. Meet our new friends." He put his arm around her waist. "This is my wife, Arzella."

She looked up at him in surprise.

He pointed to the older man, "This is Turan. He worked as a sailor on French boats for several years and speaks the language well.

And this is his son, Kadir. They were kind enough to bring us a loaf of bread and some goat's cheese."

"Thank you very much," she said.

"Welcome to Kekova Roads, Lady."

Arzella turned to Alonso. "Kekova—that is what the fisherman said."

"Yes, Turan has been explaining to me that Kekova Roads is what they call this stretch of water inside Kekova."

Turan smiled at her. "We have invited you and your husband to come ashore with us. My wife will prepare a midday meal, but before we eat, we would like to show you around the village of Kaleköy."

Arzella looked at Alonso. He nodded and said, "That is very kind of you. We would be happy to join you and your family on shore. Give us a few minutes to dress and we will be at your service."

When they were safely in the confines of the cabin, Arzella said, "You told them I was your wife?"

"Of course. In my heart, you are my wife. These are deeply religious people, and they would not accept us otherwise. I told them that you and I married against the wishes of our families, and we have fled to find a place where we can live and raise a family in happiness." He took both her hands in his and placed them at her waist. "This story is not so far from the truth."

He removed the silver ring from her right hand. "With this ring, I vow to love you and our child for all the days of my life. Do you take me as your husband?" He placed the ring on the finger of her left hand.

"I do," she said, and then she wrapped her arms around him and kissed him.

After walking through the few streets of the village, Turan offered to show them the castle. The walk up the steep path would have been easier without the skirts, but Arzella didn't mind. It was wonderful to be on land, smelling the rich smells of sunbaked earth and thyme. And the view from the hillside over the islands grew more spectacular the higher they climbed. Alonso had given her a small journal of blank pages he had bought for doing the ship's accounts, and she'd found charcoal in the boat's stove. She'd brought her sketchbook and charcoal in a small cloth sack, and she stopped on the trail to sketch the view looking up at the ramparts.

Turan was leading them, but they had already attracted the attention of the entire village when they first came ashore. Turkish women in soft-colored skirts and simple blouses, all wearing scarves to cover their hair, reached out to touch them and chattered away in a foreign tongue. They crowded around to watch her draw. Alonso had brought his bronze telescope, and the children appeared to dare one another to run up and touch it. Half the village followed them up the trail.

A white-haired man with a long beard approached Alonso and spoke to him in their foreign tongue.

Alonso shook his head. "I don't understand."

Turan said, "He asks what brings you to Kaleköy."

"Tell him my great-grandfather, a Knight of Saint John, visited here many years ago, and he grew to love this village. His real name was Jacques de Chambray, but people called him *Le Rouge de Malte* because of the color of his hair." Alonso touched his own hair.

As Turan translated, the old man smiled and nodded, then said a few words, smiling even more widely. Turan said, "The old one here says he remembers the stories of the red-haired Knight, and he welcomes his great-grandson to Kaleköy."

Although the castle had looked imposing from afar, once they reached the walls, Arzella saw that it was not what they had been hoping for. There was nothing left but ruins. Whatever had once stood within the walls was gone. There were no intact rooms, only the defensive walls surrounding a small, open theater. There did not appear to be any place to hide his treasure, and, judging from their current entourage, to do so in secret would be impossible.

"Imagine," Alonso said. "This fortress was built over seven hundred years ago by the Knights of Saint John. The people in the village were Christians then. This was a stopping point for pilgrims en route to the Holy Land, and the castle was their defense against Ottoman raiders."

"I am glad we live in these modern times, when people no longer hate each other because of a difference of religion."

"Are you really so certain things have changed?"

"Look around you. These people do not believe in Jesus Christ as we do, but neither do they want to kill us because of those differences. We live in an age of science and reason."

"I keep trying to tell you, Arzella, though we have met many kind strangers in Asia Minor, the world has not changed as much as you would like to think."

Next to the castle ruins, she saw many odd little buildings scattered in an olive grove. "What are those strange stone monuments?" she asked Turan.

"Those are Lycian sarcophagi," he said.

"Who were these Lycians?" she asked as she turned a page and sketched the strange forms.

Turan shrugged. "They were the ancients who lived in these lands in the time of Caesar and Alexander the Great. When the Knights built the castle here many years ago, the Lycians were already gone many hundreds of years. But their tombs remain scattered all over this region."

When they began their descent down the path to the village, the sun came out from behind the clouds. The water changed from silver gray to the iridescent blues and greens of a peacock's neck and tail. Out in the water off the village, Arzella saw a half-submerged sarcophagus and a stone staircase that led down below the surface of the water.

"Why are those ruins in the water?" she asked.

"This place was once part of the Lycian city of Simena. The other half of the city was across the channel on the island of Kekova. The city sank into the sea after an earthquake, around the time of Jesus Christ. There are many more ruins of the sunken city on the island."

"You know of Jesus, then?" Arzella asked.

"Of course," Turan replied. "In all the world of Islam he is revered as a great prophet."

"Fascinating," Arzella said. "So we really aren't so different, are we?"

Turan smiled. "Not at all."

When they arrived back on the beach, Turan showed them more of the ruins of the sunken city. Children were swimming and diving off the staircase that led into the sea.

Alonso stopped walking and raised his telescope to his eye.

"Turan, you called Simena a two-part city. Is there much more to see across on the island of Kekova?"

"Yes, there are houses and a harbor all underwater and many more sarcophagi. The harbor is very well protected, and it once had room for several boats. After the earthquake, the entrance to the harbor grew very narrow. We cannot see it from here, but perhaps you can see the high red cliff that stands over the inner harbor with your looking glass. That is how you can locate the entrance."

Alonso held the glass to his eye for a long time. "Ah, yes," he said. "I *can* see it from here. Fascinating."

CHAPTER SEVENTY-TWO

Villa del Priorato di Malta
The Aventine Hill, Rome

April 25, 2014

Hawk was the last one through the chapel door. Virgil had called on the radio over half an hour ago, ordering them to convene in the church. He'd been waiting for Hawk to show up before speaking.

"You took your time," he said after the big man slid into a pew.

"Wanted to bring the fire chief's official word on the fire. It was arson."

"No shit. What a surprise."

The men sat, hands folded on their laps, staring straight ahead.

"What about the damage?"

"The back end of the carriage house will need rebuilding, but we got the cars out before they were damaged."

"What the hell happened out there?" Virgil asked.

Not one man spoke.

"You guys got skunked by some little girl?"

"We were one man down. What happened to Priest?" Jacko said.

Virgil said, "He was detained."

Dutch rubbed his hand across his mouth and spoke into his palm. "Asshole."

"Leave Priest out of this. I don't want to hear whining or excuses. I brought you men in here because I know you to be the best. And you're being paid to be that good."

Jacko said, "We can only be as good as the information we are given. We didn't know she was here."

Hawk said, "I went by the room. The way she broke out of those zip cuffs, I don't buy her as some innocent little girl."

"What are you trying to say?"

"She was out of there pretty damn fast. Who is she?"

"You're not here to ask questions. I want answers."

"We searched the grounds thoroughly. We found a chef's coat in the carriage house. It's possible she had an accomplice. Someone who came in with the caterers."

Virgil put his hands on his hips and spoke to the floor. "Goddammit." He looked up and made eye contact with each one of them individually. "How did you let him get in?"

Hawk said, "Sounds like you know who that was. Like maybe you were even expecting him. With only four men trying to cover an estate this size, you might have told us."

"Instead of spending all afternoon riding around in their Bugatti," Dutch said. "I don't care how fucking awesome that car is."

Virgil pulled in air through his nostrils and raised his chin as he stared at the men before him. He felt his face flush with heat, then he was surprised by a flash of déjà vu. How many times had Virgil silently berated the brass for not telling their men what the real situation was? Or for sitting back off the front lines, enjoying luxuries their men would never know.

Hawk continued. "If you'd told us you had a prisoner inside and you were expecting someone to break her out, we might have worked it differently. But we thought we were there to babysit a bunch of fat cats who'd come for Friday dinner."

The doors at the rear of the church opened, and Signor Oscura strode into the chapel.

Virgil nodded once in his direction.

Signor Oscura walked to the front of the church, and he said one word. "Explain."

CHAPTER SEVENTY-THREE

Basilica dei Santi Bonifacio e Alessio
The Aventine Hill, Rome

April 25, 2014

Cole took the lead in order to clear the way. The path they'd been directed to follow was overgrown with vines, and the ground was uneven. The flashlight behind them offered some light, but they were still in danger of hitting their heads on low-hanging limbs. After twenty meters, they came upon a white marble bench. Just beyond, the garden opened up, and they entered a small courtyard. The yellow light on the corner of one building was a spot that lit up the lovely fountain in the middle of the stone square.

"Stop right there."

Cole stopped, and Riley came up to stand beside him. He reached over and took her hand.

"What were you doing in the garden here?"

Cole squeezed Riley's hand, trying to convince her to let him take the lead. "We climbed over the wall from the villa next door," he said.

"Why?"

"We didn't like what the Knights were serving for dinner."

"Don't be flippant, young man. There was a fire next door to-night."

Cole was wondering what their captor had overheard of their earlier conversation, when Riley spoke up.

"My friend here did start the fire, but for a good reason. It was a diversion. I was being held there against my will, and he was trying to save me."

Their captor didn't say anything.

"It's the truth," Riley said.

The silence dragged on for a very long time. Finally, they heard the words, "Turn around."

The person standing there holding the flashlight on them was clad in black robes from head to foot, save for the white cloth surrounding her face. She was nearly as tall as Cole, and she wore silver wire-rimmed glasses on her severe, unsmiling face.

Friends of his back in Florida who had gone to Catholic schools had told Cole stories about nuns busting knuckles with wooden rulers. He had a healthy respect, even fear, of them. He was searching for what to say to her when the nun broke the silence.

"Are you hungry?"

"Sure," he said, and he was surprised to realize it was true.

The nun's mouth spread in a broad smile. At the corners of her eyes, lines fanned out like rays of sunlight. With her straight nose and her dark eyebrows, her face went from severe to lovely in a moment.

"Come with me, then. It's not far. We'll talk while we eat."

The nun took off at a fast pace. Riley pointed to the shoes under her habit. They were black high-tops.

She led them to a tiny Fiat. "I'll take you to the convent where I'm staying. There's a nice kitchen there." She climbed in the driver's-side door. "Get in," she said.

Cole pushed up the seat, and Riley squeezed into the back next to a box of books and papers. Cole had barely dropped into the front seat when the nun started the little car, threw it into gear, and took off out through the gates. Off to his right, Cole caught a brief glimpse of the piazza in front of the Knights' villa. He saw several fire department vehicles and a crowd of men milling around. From this distance, he couldn't tell if any of them were the villa's security guards.

They traveled only a few blocks and turned right into a very narrow street. After a hundred feet, the street widened, and the nun pulled the Fiat nose-in to a parking space along a high stone wall.

"Welcome to *Foresteria del Monastero Sant'Antonio Abate*—or in English, the Guesthouse of the Monastery of Saint Anthony the Abbot," she said when she turned off the engine. She held out her hand to Cole. "My name is Sister Ola."

They introduced themselves. "We can't thank you enough, Sister," Cole said.

"Come on. You've still got some explaining to do."

They followed her through an ancient stone gate into a courtyard filled with potted plants, small trees, and the overpowering fragrance of blooming roses.

She sat them at an outdoor table in the courtyard and soon returned with a tray and three cups of thick espresso. She served the coffee, then went back inside for water and a plate of olives, cheese, and salami.

"You are too kind," Riley said.

"It's the custom in my country to take care of lost travelers, and the two of you certainly looked lost when I found you at the institute."

"The institute?" Cole said. "I thought it was a church that adjoined the Knights' villa."

"Yes, the basilica is on the other side. It's quite a complex. The whole Aventine Hill is covered with old church buildings. That's one of the reasons that the National Institute of Roman Studies is located there. I'd been doing research all day, and when I went out to my car,

I smelled the fire. I decided to take a walk closer to the wall. I grabbed the flashlight from my car, and then the two of you dropped in."

Cole and Riley exchanged looks. "I think we were very lucky you found us," Cole said.

"What are you studying?" Riley asked.

"I've been doing research on John the Baptist."

Riley said, "I hear a slight accent in your speech, but I can't place it."

"I am from Jordan."

"Really? I didn't know there were Catholics in Jordan."

"Roman Catholics are not a huge percentage of the population, but there are over eighty thousand of us."

"Where did you learn to speak English so well?"

"I went to university in the US. Notre Dame. That was years ago. I played varsity girls' basketball during my undergrad years and got my degree in philosophy and theology. My family wanted me to return home after four years, but I stayed on and eventually got my doctorate. As a graduate assistant, I did quite a lot of teaching. But when I returned home, instead of teaching at the university, I decided to enter the religious life."

"Do you live in Rome now?"

"No, I just came for Easter and for the canonizations. While I'm here, I'm researching Saint John and the different ways he is depicted in the various gospels of the New Testament and in the Qur'an. For this reason, I'm also very interested in the Knights of Saint John."

"Ah, now I get it," Riley said.

She smiled and nodded. "I look forward to hearing the details of your story."

Riley looked back and forth between them. "It's a complicated story."

Cole said, "We got separated earlier today and we haven't had a chance to catch up. I'd like to know what happened to Riley, too. But we also need to find a safe place to stay tonight."

"This monastery is a guesthouse. There are no vacant rooms, due to the canonizations. However, we should be able to place each of you in a shared room. Riley can stay in my room, and I'm certain I can find a father willing to offer you shelter. You'll both be safe here."

"Thank you, Sister."

"Now tell me how you happen to be running from the Sovereign Order of the Knights of Malta."

Over the course of the next hour, they told her the whole story: about Cole's father during the Second World War, the HMS *Upholder*, the shield, the folktale about the Silver Girl, and the name of the famous cartographer that was engraved on the shield.

Sister Ola was a good listener. When Cole finished the story about the donation of books to the Magistral Library, she turned to Riley. "So you visited the library at the palace this afternoon? And what did you find?"

"Joseph Roux's sea atlas wasn't there."

"Oh no."

"It's been sent out on interlibrary loan."

"Where?"

"To the Vatican," Cole and Riley said in unison.

Riley turned to him. "How do you know?"

"When you didn't return from the library, I went to find out what happened to you."

"But someone might have recognized you."

"Riley, you were missing. I wasn't just going to sit there and do nothing. I tried to talk to the concierge, but he said the library was closed. He was giving me the bum's rush out of there when a woman came out. She wanted to give the concierge a bag you had left behind. I convinced them I was your partner, and they gave it to me."

"So you've got my phone?"

He nodded. "In the backpack. So, what happened to you?"

She told them an abbreviated version of the kidnapping, the car trunk, the catacombs, and the trip up to the villa in one of the Knights' super-expensive automobiles. She withheld the story of Diggory Priest's fate. She would tell Cole later. "Once I broke lose, I went into the church and hid. Six men came in. They called themselves Cavalieri of the Guardiani. What they were talking about is so insane, I hesitate to repeat it."

Sister Ola said, "The SMOM is a very conservative organization, but I've heard there is an even more extremist group within. That must be what this Guardiani group is."

"They talked about the shield, and how it might lead to something in their library. The guy who drove me to the villa was there. They called him Virgil Vandervoort. I think he was the only American."

"Did they say what it is they think the shield will lead to?" Cole asked.

"Not exactly. They called it the Religion. He said that the Guardiani had been charged with keeping it safe from the infidels for a long time. That's also what the legend claims. Anyway, somehow getting it back is supposed to help them in this modern version of the Crusades they've got going."

"What do you mean?" Sister Ola asked.

Riley turned to Cole. "Do you remember what your father wrote in his journal, way back in the 1990s? He said there was this chivalrous order that wanted to eradicate all Muslims and take over the resource-rich lands where they live. I actually heard the men talk about doing just that."

Cole said, "That's genocide. It's insane."

Sister Ola took a drink from a glass of water, then she adjusted the white cloth around her face. "Sadly, history has shown us that human beings do not need to be insane to commit genocide. Have you seen the anti-Arab hatred being spewed on the Internet these days?"

"I try not to read it," Riley said, "but so often it's there on Facebook or in the comment streams on news stories about Islamist terrorists. In North America, Britain, France, there is lots of hate building up."

"That is what groups like this Guardiani are counting on."

"Those people who claim we should, quote, 'nuke all Muslims' because of the actions of a few really are insane," Riley said.

"The extremists from both sides cannot open their minds to see how similar they are," Sister Ola said.

Cole shook his head. "On one side you have drone strikes on schools and weddings, on the other side beheadings and suicide bombers."

"Both are killing civilians, and that incites intense hatred," the nun said.

"Sister, do you have any idea what this manuscript might be?"

She clasped her hands together on the table and sat forward in her chair. "I pray that I am wrong. If it is what I fear, I would love to study such a manuscript, but it could be very powerful in the wrong hands."

"What is it?"

She looked directly into the eyes of Riley, then Cole. Then it appeared she had made a decision. She said, "Does either of you know much about the Bible's New Testament?"

Cole nodded, but Riley shook her head. "My French mother hated the Catholic Church, and my father was happy to indulge her parenting preferences. I'll need a crash course."

Sister Ola smiled. "As quickly as possible, then. The texts that make up the New Testament have been the subject of much disagreement dating back to Christ's time. There are few texts written in the original language spoken at the time of Christ—which was a form of Aramaic. All the texts have been translated again and again into Greek, Latin, English, and hand-copied over and over. They had to do this because the manuscripts decayed over the course of centuries. The materials they used didn't last, and of course they didn't have climate-controlled rooms to preserve them. No one can say how much these texts have changed in the copying and the translations. Then there is the question as to which texts should be included."

Riley said, "Seriously? Which texts?"

"Remember, the Old Testament was the *only* Bible before Christ. Then, the early Christians decided to add new texts, but there were many sects of Christianity. They didn't all agree. Even the famed Muratorian fragment, considered the oldest list of the books of the New Testament, is from a seventh-century Latin manuscript thought to be a copy of a text written around 170 AD. While the author accepts that there were four gospels, the names of the first two are missing—leaving only Luke and John."

"So who decided on what we have today?"

"We don't really know. Surely it wasn't just one individual. In 325, the Roman Emperor Constantine convened the Council of Nicaea to attempt to standardize Christianity, but there is no evidence they dealt with the question of which gospels would be included in the New Testament. They had other issues, like whether Christ was a man or God. Since the Romans had been pagan sun worshippers, many theologians believe that some of the results of Nicaea came from Constantine trying to appease his people. For example, although the word 'Sunday' does not appear in the Bible, the Christian Sabbath became Sunday instead of Saturday, which was the Jews' seventh day of the week. Coincidentally, Sunday was the day of rest in honor of the Roman sun god. Also, it does not say anywhere in the Bible what the date of Christ's birth was. However, the birth of the sun god was celebrated on December 25, and many Christian historians believe that was what led to the choice for Christ's birth."

Riley said, "I find myself surprised to hear this coming from a nun. I thought devout Christians believed every word of the Bible is the word of God."

"Many modern theologians see, as I do, that the New Testament is a collection of texts written by man, but inspired by God. They are testimonies written by Christ's apostles and stories about the lives of the early Christians. They are historical texts inspired by God. I happen to believe that Jesus and God are the same, but I recognize that my belief was not universal Christian belief until after Nicaea."

"What do you mean?"

"At Nicaea they were attempting to reach agreement about the question of Christ's divinity. The Roman Church maintained that Jesus was both man and God, but other sects, like the Gnostics, claimed Jesus was a man who was the son of God. Constantine voted for Jesus as God, and the Nicene Creed was composed to proclaim that as the official Christian stance. Then, in 381 AD, another meeting was held in Constantinople, and the Nicene Creed was revised to state that Jesus was the father, son, and the Holy Ghost. Again, this concept appeared nowhere in the original Greek texts of the Gospels."

"You mean they just made this stuff up?" Riley asked.

"That depends on your interpretation and faith. As I said, the gospels were copied and translated and recopied, always by hand. The possibilities for human error were great. The chance for intentional rewriting to fit the beliefs of the translator or scribe is also very humanly possible. The oldest existing fragment of the New Testament is a piece of the Gospel of John dated to the first half of the second century. There are many who believe in a conspiracy theory—not only about which gospels were included in the New Testament, but how much the included gospels may have been changed to reflect some preferred version of the events of Christ's life."

"Now you're talking Cole's language. There's nothing he likes more than a conspiracy theory," Riley said. "So there's proof that there are other gospels?"

"Yes, there were many. The Nag Hammadi gospels were actually mentioned by Irenaeus in the late second century, but little else was known about them until they were dug up in Egypt in 1945. That raises the question of what else might have been suppressed."

"And you think that this manuscript the Knights are seeking is one of those?"

"Yes, there is one which has been very controversial. It is the Gospel of Barnabas."

Riley sat up straight and said, "You're kidding. In the church tonight, when I overheard the head Guardiani guy talking? He mentioned 'Operation Barnabas.'"

Sister Ola took hold of the cross hanging around her neck and shook her head.

"What is so controversial about it?"

"The Church has always claimed that the two copies that have surfaced are forgeries. Neither of them was dated earlier than the sixteenth century. Recently, the Turks claimed to have found a copy that is between fifteen hundred and two thousand years old, but they have not allowed outside authorities to examine it or date it, so it is also being called a forgery. However, there have been whispers for centuries that there is a copy of the Gospel of Barnabas that predates any of the existing copies we have of the canonical gospels. If a complete copy were found that could be precisely dated to the first or second century, it certainly would cause outrage among Christian extremists."

"Why?"

"Because Barnabas was one of the apostles, so his would be a firsthand account. In the manuscripts that have been renounced as forgeries, the Gospel of Barnabas claims that Jesus was not divine, he was not crucified, and there was no resurrection. This gospel states that Jesus himself claimed he was a prophet, but not God. So, as you can see, if a copy of Barnabas were to be verified to be older than any copies of the canonical gospels, it could cast doubt in some quarters. And many Muslims would hail it as the true gospel."

"Why is that?"

"Because, according to the Gospel of Barnabas, Jesus himself preached that there was a greater prophet yet to come, and his name was Muhammed."

CHAPTER SEVENTY-FOUR

The Magistral Library
Via Condotti, Rome

April 26, 2014

Virgil pulled in through the gates to the Palazzo, ignoring the officious concierge. He hadn't slept well after the events of the night before. He was not accustomed to failure, and he was determined to turn things around. He'd heard Signor Oscura's words over and over in his head all night long. He'd said, "The others warned me not to hire you. They said you were too old for this sort of job."

He awoke this morning resolute: he would find Thatcher and prove to Oscura that he merited his place among the Guardiani.

Entering the opulent palace no longer gave him the pleasure it had just the day before. Only yesterday he had felt a part of this. Today, he had yet to earn it. He walked down the hall to the library, but he found the room empty. He felt the anger simmering in his belly. If he had to earn his place here, then she should, too. Where was she?

At 9:05 the librarian came through the door at the end of the hall wearing a loose-fitting brown dress and sneakers with ankle socks. She was a tiny woman—no more than five feet tall—and she carried multiple bags on both arms. She got the strap of one bag entangled with the door handle.

He followed her into the reading room. She was pulling the bags off one of her shoulders when he leaned on the reference desk and spoke.

"I need to ask you about a patron you helped yesterday."

She started like a baby awakening to a loud noise. "Oh, hello. I didn't hear you come in."

Her English was heavily accented, but he could understand her. The accent was not Italian. Maybe German.

Virgil continued. "As I said, this woman came in yesterday. She's about yea tall." He held out a hand about six inches higher than the woman's head. "In her midthirties, medium-brown hair cut shoulder length."

"No, we had no woman like that."

"Any women at all who came in requesting materials yesterday."

The librarian shook her head.

He leaned across the desk, pressing himself into her space. "You're certain?"

She took a step back. "Yes."

Virgil stood up straight, taking his arms off the counter, and simply stared down at her.

The woman's hand flew to her throat. He'd seen that same look on his wife's face when they'd argued. His ex-wife.

"There was a girl," she said.

"Describe her."

"She had black hair."

Virgil remembered how surprised he had been when he spotted her in the catacombs. Overalls and boots. Perhaps there had been a wig, too. She didn't look like the young woman on the boat.

"What was she wearing?"

"I don't know the word in English." She pantomimed straps over her shoulders. "Like a farmer wears."

"What did she ask for?"

"She was interested in sea charts from the seventeenth and eighteenth centuries."

"Any particular ones?"

"Not at first. I gave her what we had, but that didn't seem to be exactly what she was looking for."

"And what was that?"

"Just before she left, she asked if we had anything else. I told her there was only one other volume. It is called the *Carte de la mer Méditerranée en douze feuilles*, by Joseph Roux."

"Translate?"

"It's a collection of twelve maps of the Mediterranean."

"Was that what she was looking for?"

"I think so."

"And you gave it to her?"

The little woman shook her head. "I had to tell her we didn't have it on the premises."

"Checked out?"

"No. Well, in a sense. Another library had requested it, and we've sent it off on interlibrary loan."

"Where?"

"This is the third time in two days someone has asked."

"Where is it?"

"At the Vatican Library," she said.

Virgil was leaning against his car, rolling himself a quick cigarette, when the concierge called to him across the courtyard parking lot. "Signor Oscura wants to see you." He nodded toward the upstairs windows.

Virgil paused outside the executive director's door. He hated being summoned like this, but he couldn't let it show. He smoothed his black polo shirt and made certain it was neatly tucked into his cargo pants. Then he rapped once on the door.

"Entra."

Signor Oscura sat behind the enormous desk, a tiny white cup of coffee and a glass of water the only things on its surface.

"Sit down, Virgil," he said.

"I prefer to stand, sir." He assumed an at-ease stance.

Neither man spoke for more than a minute.

Signor Oscura was the first to speak up. "You took an oath."

"Yes, sir."

"You understand the impact here. We have our people inside the Pentagon, Whitehall, NATO. They are set to go. But we need more than a few beheadings to get the massive public backing we seek. We need people in the streets, crying, 'Death to Islam.' To get that kind of outrage, we need to see those Islamists claiming they have indisputable historical proof that Jesus was not the son of God. Virgil, we need the power that can only come from the Religion."

"Yes, sir."

"So what do you plan to do now?"

"I'll find Thatcher."

Signor Oscura did not say anything. He just sat there staring up at Virgil, his fingers tented under his chin. When he finally spoke, his voice was soft. "I got a phone call this morning from the Questura Centrale. A Commissario Pansa wanted information about an explosion in a catacomb out off the Via Tiburtina. He said they located one of our cars out there, parked on the street."

Virgil kept his face blank but inside he was admonishing himself for forgetting to take care of the car Dig drove out there. "I don't know what happened, sir, but I can tell you the man who checked out that car yesterday afternoon called in sick last night. I haven't heard any-thing from him since."

"I'm not happy about any of this. I expected more from you."

Virgil started to speak when the door swung inward, and the grand master entered.

"Good morning," he said in his cheery British English.

Virgil nodded and returned the greeting. Signor Oscura caught Virgil's eye. He shook his head in two small jerks from one side to the other.

"Sorry to interrupt," the grand master said, "but we need to talk about the seating for the canonization ceremony. I just got a phone call from Juan Carlos of Spain, and he has decided to come after all."

Signor Oscura offered a tight smile. "Not a problem, sir. We had just finished our business, hadn't we, Virgil?"

"Yes, sir. Good day, gentlemen."

Virgil closed the door behind him. Thank God. He'd already wasted precious time. It would be chaos at the Vatican. Of course, Thatcher and the girl marine would not have the access he had. She was good, but not that good. He should be able to get inside the Vatican Library and get his hands on the volume they sought before they even discovered the library was closed for the canonizations.

CHAPTER SEVENTY-FIVE

**Vatican City Gates
Rome, Italy**

April 26, 2014

"During my years in graduate school, I was fortunate to get a research grant to study in Rome," Sister Ola said as she downshifted the Fiat to accelerate around a taxi. "I spent six months here, but never did drive. I know the city's public transport quite well, but this time the convent offered me a rental car. They thought I would be safer. I didn't disagree because I do love to drive."

Sister Ola might have been Jordanian, but she drove like a true Roman, zipping through traffic, always with one hand on the horn. Riley was certain there would be fingernail claw marks in her door's arm rest by the time they arrived at the Vatican.

"You do realize the Vatican Apostolic Library is normally closed on Saturdays, and today is not a normal Saturday!"

"We can't thank you enough for everything you've done for us," Riley said.

"As wild as your story is, I have come to understand that there are dangerous extremists of all faiths. What I don't understand is why you two are putting yourselves at risk to stop them."

Riley turned around to look at Cole in the backseat. "It started with Cole's father, as we told you last night."

He said, "I understand that most people prefer to stay at home and believe they are safe." He put his hands over his mouth and thought for several seconds before continuing. "I can't remember when I last believed the world was a safe place. But it's what I want. For Riley; for you, Sister; for everyone. I'm just not one of those people who can sit back and leave that to someone else. I can't walk away from this fight. It's just who I am."

"Fighting evil?"

"I'm not sure I believe evil exists. I do know power exists, and men will commit horrendous acts to get more of it. This may look like the Knights are still fighting the Crusades, but I think these men are using blind faith and hate to get more power for themselves. The lands in the Middle East are too rich in oil to think otherwise."

"We won't agree on the nature of evil, but neither are we in disagreement about these men. If you can prevent them from inciting more hate in the world, I am happy to help you."

Cole put his hand on Riley's shoulder and slid it under her hair on the back of her neck. "We are incredibly thankful for that," he said.

The night before, when they had finally found their way to their respective rooms, Sister Ola had told each of them they needed to be under way early in order to find a parking place. Though they had left the monastery guesthouse by seven thirty that morning, they'd been sitting in Rome traffic breathing fumes for more than an hour. Now, Sister Ola was racing through the neighborhoods around Vatican City, trying to find a parking space.

"Look at the crowds," the nun said. "They say there are between one and five million extra people here in Rome this weekend."

The sidewalks were packed, and it was beginning to appear hopeless that they would ever find a parking spot.

"There!" Sister Ola announced as she hit the brakes.

The spot looked barely big enough for a motorbike.

The nun backed the car in, and, by inching forward and back, she squeezed the car into the space with only inches between her Fiat and the cars on both sides.

She hopped out of the car and took off at a pace that dared them to keep up. The streets and sidewalks, even blocks away from the Vatican gates, were jammed with tourists. People of all races, nationalities, shapes, and sizes were heading in the same direction. It was a festival atmosphere, and it took some concentration for Riley to remember that there were people out there who meant them harm.

It wouldn't take much work for Virgil and his Guardiani pals to figure out what they were after. A conversation with the librarian would reveal most of it. She had to assume the Guardiani would be on their tail sooner rather than later. She scanned the crowd as she trotted to keep up. It was unlikely Virgil could find them here in this crowd of millions. But the closer they got to the library, the more careful they would need to be.

They passed through a gate, and there before them were the huge white-stone columns that supported the galleries around Saint Peter's Square. Big tables on the side of the road offered every sort of touristy trinket. There were lighters, snow globes, key chains, and snuff boxes, all adorned with the image of the smiling pope. Saint Peter's Square on the other side of the columns was a brightly colored sea of humanity.

Riley and Cole followed Sister Ola to their right. Barricades meant to keep the lines orderly divided them from the masses in the square. They were nearly at the back of the square, and Riley could not see the end of the line for those waiting to get into Saint Peter's Basilica. They followed the river of people flowing past those in line, but soon Sister Ola veered off onto a backstreet in Vatican City. They passed a pair of

Swiss Guards in their uniforms with the yellow, blue, and red puffy pants, and she said something in French to one of them. He waved them through. It seemed the sister's habit and cross were as good as an ID card.

She stopped in front of a large building. "I'm going in here," she said. "I'll just be a minute."

The building was plain for Vatican City, but it would have been stunning anywhere else. Riley's knowledge of French helped her translate the sign in Italian outside. It was the barracks of the Swiss Guard.

Sister Ola emerged a few minutes later in the company of a Swiss Guardsman, only this fellow wore a much simpler blue uniform. Sister Ola introduced him as Philip Duss, the son of a friend she had met while living in Rome.

"Philip here is going to let us into the Apostolic Library. He'll take us the back way to avoid the worst of the crowds."

As they walked, the nun chatted with the young man in Swiss German.

Riley said, "It makes me feel so inadequate when I'm around people who speak so many languages."

"At least you speak French," Cole said.

Philip pulled out a ring with keys and cards, and let them into a building. The corridor inside was empty, but they could hear the sounds of people passing very close by. He led them to a side door to the library. There were no signs identifying it. He fitted a key into the lock and opened the door. The room inside was dark, but when he reached in and turned the switch, the lights revealed an all-white room.

Philip spoke to Sister Ola and pointed down the hallway, then he excused himself and said good-bye in tentative English.

"Thank you so much," Riley said.

"He said we can just lock this door behind us. The other big door opens into the Belvedere Courtyard. It's really a big parking lot. That's where the scholars come in."

Once they were all inside, Cole went to the door and turned the bolt. "Let's lock ourselves inside as well," he said. "I don't want any unwanted visitors."

Sister Ola said, "This area is for staff only." She herded them toward a door on the far side of the room. "The main library reading room is through here. Philip said the security gates are not on, so we can enter without setting off alarms."

"I had no idea it would be so modern," Riley said.

Sister Ola opened the door. "Have a look out here."

Riley stepped through the door. "Oh my God," she said. "This is stunning!"

Cole followed her, and they both walked in circles, looking around at the long, magnificent room filled with reading tables and lecterns. The elaborately painted, vaulted ceiling was two stories high, and along one side of the chamber was a second-story gallery of bookshelves and reading rooms. Twelve-foot-high arched windows let the sunlight stream in, and even without any lights on, one would be able to read easily. Books lined all the walls.

Sister Ola said, "The Apostolic Library reopened in 2010 after a three-year renovation, which brought the library into the twenty-first century. All the books are now microchipped, there's Wi-Fi, and the collections have all been digitized. There is a bombproof underground bunker for the most valuable manuscripts, and new climate-controlled consultation rooms for the researchers. Go on through the electronic gate there. We're headed for the desk at the other end."

"I hate that we can't spend more time here," Cole said as they hurried down the center aisle. "Imagine the information about historical ships and shipping."

"You might find even more in the other research institution here. The Apostolic Library contains books and manuscripts, including the Codex B—the oldest known complete Bible, dating from about 325 AD. But right next door you'll find the Vatican Archives. That's where they have all the documents and letters, including all the popes' correspondence."

"Don't tell him any more," Riley said. "We'll never get him out of here."

When they arrived at the desk, Sister Ola walked behind it and began searching the shelves underneath. "Twenty years ago, when I was here doing research for my doctorate, I often ordered up books to be brought in via interlibrary loan. They would hold them for me at this reference desk."

"I hope it's not checked out," Riley said.

"They don't allow *anything* to leave this library," she said. "Voilà. Here it is."

Sister Ola lifted out a cardboard box. She opened it carefully and removed the leather-covered album. "You know I can't let you take this."

"Don't worry, Sister." Riley took her phone out of her pocket. "We're just going to photograph the cover and pages." After she shot the cover and the title page, she folded out the first of the charts and photographed it. Each of the charts was double the size of the book when it was unfolded.

While Riley's cell phone flashed, Cole said, "Imagine—if the legend is true, this atlas of charts was used by a Knight of Malta in the eighteenth century." Cole unfolded the next chart. "There are markings on some of these pages. Looks like calculations. Maybe the location of the Religion will be marked with a big X."

"It's never that easy," Riley said.

"He must have been a corsair," Cole said. "They were essentially licensed by the grand master as pirates."

"You know the history of sailing in the Mediterranean," Sister Ola said.

"Like you, I did my time in academia. I have a doctorate in maritime archeology."

"Last page," Riley said as her cell-phone camera flashed.

Cole lifted the chart to fold it away, and he said, "Wait. There's a drawing on the inside of the back." He smoothed open the endpapers inside the leather cover, and there was a pen-and-ink drawing of a castle.

"Okay, one more," Riley said as she took the photo. "Then we're out of here."

"Can't be soon enough," Cole said.

Sister Ola replaced the leather-bound volume in the box and slid it back onto the shelf.

The three of them had begun to retrace their steps when they heard a sound like metal scratching on metal. Riley held up her hand and stopped. She put her finger to her lips.

Cole pointed to the big doorway to the courtyard that Sister Ola had indicated, at the rear of the reading room. They would have to walk past that door to get to the staff-room door they had entered through.

Sister Ola shook her head and motioned for them to follow her. They trotted back toward the reference desk, and she indicated the door behind it. "Through there is another door that will take you into the corridor leading to the Sistine Chapel."

They heard the door latch click.

"Go!" Sister Ola said.

"What about you?"

The big courtyard door swung open and more sunlight streamed inside.

"No one hurts a nun at the Vatican," she whispered.

Cole grabbed Riley's hand and pulled her through the door just as Virgil stepped into the library. She'd recognized the blond hair instantly. He must've heard Sister Ola's whispered voice, because she saw him begin to turn in their direction.

They were in another staff-only back-room area. The back door opened easily. On the other side, they were startled by the noise of the human chatter from the mob shuffling past. There was very little space between the bodies. A few individuals looked at the open door in surprise, but most had glazed eyes. They appeared to be in museum overload as they trundled toward the tour finale.

Cole pulled the door shut behind them, and they began darting through the crowd. A few people tossed irritated comments at them as they pushed their way past.

Riley never heard the door open, but she was certain Sister Ola would not be able to detain Virgil for long. She knew better than to turn around and look. Ahead she saw a sign directing them to the Sistine Chapel, and a pathway opened up for them in the crowd.

"This way," she said, pulling Cole along with her.

She vaguely remembered the time she had come to the Vatican with her parents when she was only about ten years old. She had been exhausted after the more than two hours of viewing statues and paintings and architecture. When they'd arrived at the Sistine Chapel, her mother had held the hands of her two children and told them to look up at the beautiful paintings by Michelangelo on the ceiling. Riley remembered that she and her brother were making faces behind their mother's back and giggling over the naked Adam and Eve. This time, when she and Cole squeezed through the door into the chapel, she wouldn't even have time to look up.

The chapel was a bit wider than the hallway they'd been in, so the crowd opened up a little. Cole pulled her into a run. They were halfway down the chapel when she heard a lady screech her disapproval behind them. Since they were out in the open anyway, Riley risked a glance over her shoulder.

Virgil was being far less polite than they were. He was shoving people out of his way and gaining on them.

"He's close, Cole!"

They made it to the exit onto Saint Peter's Square and pushed their way outside.

The sunlight was blinding, and they slowed to a walk for a few seconds to let their eyes adjust. Riley saw two Swiss Guards hurrying in their direction.

"Walk fast, but don't run. Guards coming on your right."

They skipped down the steps and moved into the crowd, their best camouflage. There was no room between the bodies. Riley stuck out her elbows and gently pushed people aside to make headway. She didn't dare look over her shoulder, but it sounded like the Swiss Guards had stopped everyone exiting the chapel.

"What now?" Cole asked.

"Straight ahead. Let's get out of Vatican City. That guard won't stop him for long. He'll show ID. The Knights have a direct line to the pope."

They moved through a large group of Asian tourists. Many of the ladies had umbrellas to keep the hot Roman sun off them. In their other hands, they held up smartphones, and they were shooting selfies with Saint Peter's dome in the background.

"Keep cool. He won't spot us in this crowd." Cole looked back over his shoulder. "Shit. I take that back. Run!"

CHAPTER SEVENTY-SIX

Aboard the *Ruse*
At Sea in the Mediterranean

July 26, 1798

Arzella gave the wheel a quarter turn to adjust for the big sea approaching. If she were back home standing on the ramparts of Fort Ricasoli, she would have enjoyed watching the fierce black thunderclouds building in the northeast. But she was not at home in Malta. She did not know if she would ever see her home island again.

Clouds had haunted them all along this journey home. They had left Kekova more than three weeks ago with plenty of food and water, planning to return to Malta after a reprovisioning stop on the south coast of Crete. Alonso had been successful at crafting just the right hiding place for his treasure, and he set Arzella to work engraving an enciphered key to the location on his shield. He wanted to be certain that if anything did happen to them, there would be more evidence than just the sea charts as to the location of the Guardiani's most treasured manuscript.

But windstorms and cloud cover had driven them too far south. Crete never materialized. Nor did the hoped-for rains. Alonso would bring his octant and charts on deck, prepared for any brief appearance by the sun, but the clouds never broke. They'd seen nothing but seawater from horizon to horizon for weeks. And by now, according to Alonso's calculations, they should have sighted Malta already.

Alonso appeared at the bottom of the stairs leading up to the quarterdeck. His shirt was torn and his pants hung loose around his waist. The skin on his face hung from his cheekbones like parchment, pulled taut by the weight of his scraggly beard.

"What are you doing out of bed?" she called.

He used one arm to pull himself up the stairs. "I cannot leave you alone to sail the *Ruse*," he said. "You, too, need rest."

A week ago, one of the barrels of water had turned bad. Alonso had started drinking from it while she slept, but soon his belly rumbled and cramped. He emptied the water overboard, but the damage had been done. All food and water now passed straight through his body, providing no nourishment. With little food and even less good water aboard the ship, each day he grew weaker.

When Alonso arrived at the helm, she helped him sit on the deck beside the binnacle.

"The weather worsens," he said.

"Yes," she said. "But a northeast wind will favor us now."

"I've not been able to use the octant for days, Arzella. I fear we have sailed past Malta and missed the island."

"We might not be able to find Crete, and we may have missed Malta, but it would be difficult to miss Africa."

He tried to smile at that. "The Barbary Coast. I have enemies there."

"And the world is changing. We found friends among the Ottoman Turks."

When Alonso looked up at her, the dark circles under his eyes frightened her.

"The boat has been sailing fast all day," she said. "The coast of Tunisia is our best chance to find help for you." She had almost said it was their only chance.

He pushed himself to his feet. "With that weather coming, I need to drop the foresail."

"You take the helm," she said. "Let me do it. I've seen you do it enough times."

"No, dear, this is not work for you. I'll drop it on deck. Steer her into the wind for me."

He labored down the stairs, then crossed the deck to the foremast. As soon as the bow pointed into the wind, he let fly the braces and the tackles. Then he untied the halyard. Instead of letting the sail down slowly, the line flew out of his hands and the sail began flapping wildly. The yard on the lateen-rigged sail struck Alonso across the chest and knocked him to the deck.

Arzella let go of the wheel and ran forward. Alonso lay on the deck clutching his ribs. She wanted to go straight to him, but the sail and yard swung about dangerously in the wind. She pulled down the flapping sail and tied ropes around it and the yard before it struck Alonso again. The mainsail snapped loudly as the *Ruse* lay in irons facing into the wind.

She helped Alonso to his feet, and he cried out in pain. She half carried him into the cabin, lowered him onto the bed, then lifted his legs and swung them onto the mattress.

Alonso moaned when she touched his side. Some ribs were surely broken.

"Stay in bed this time and rest," she said.

He did not answer her.

She pulled open one of his eyes, but the eyeball had rolled up in the socket. She leaned down and put her ear by his mouth. He was breathing. He was alive. For now.

She had to get the *Ruse* to land.

When the storm broke, the rain was icy cold—but it was water. She wrapped Alonso's cloak around her. The wind had flailed and tossed her hair, tying it in knots at first. Now it lay plastered to her head and dripped down her neck and chest. She was soon soaked to the skin. She opened her mouth to drink in the fresh water, even though the wind-driven raindrops stung at her face like flying nails.

The night crept up slowly. The storm had darkened the sky early, creating a false dusk that seemed to last for hours. When real darkness finally came, it was so complete, she could not see the deck of the ship.

Merely lighting the lantern exhausted her. Her arms felt alien, disconnected from her body. When she could no longer control the ship's wheel, she used a piece of rope to tie the wheel in place. That way she slept, off and on, a few minutes at a time, and when she awoke, she adjusted the course. Keeping an exact course no longer mattered. The long coast of Tunisia ran from north to south like a buttress off the African continent. It now stretched ahead to the west of them. She could not miss it.

Twice she went below to check on Alonso. He slept. She tried to force some water from the goatskin flask down his throat, with little success.

Along toward morning, Arzella awoke from a short nap, and the sky was filled with stars. The storm had blown through. The wind and seas still tossed the *Ruse* about, but the rain had gone with the clouds. She felt her clothes beginning to dry. The air felt different.

When the sky grew gray behind her, she learned why. From the top of the waves, she was able to see a dark strip on the horizon ahead. Land. As the sun rose into the sky, the coast of Africa also rose up out of the sea. The mountains surprised her. She had always thought of North Africa as a land of deserts. Yet as the big boat approached the shore, she saw trees and beaches. But she did not see what she sought. A harbor.

Arzella untied the wheel and turned the *Ruse*, putting her on a more northerly course to parallel the coast. The wind had shifted, too, and if she turned too far, the sail fluttered. She considered trying to raise the mainsail, but she did not think she had the strength to do so. Her only other choice was to tack the ship and sail away from the coast. That she could not do.

With the small sail and the poor angle on the wind, the *Ruse* no longer ate up the miles. They crawled their way north all morning, but she saw no sign of civilization. Arzella knew she needed to eat to keep her strength up, but she was too tired to seek food.

Arzella awoke when the keel hit bottom. The *Ruse* shuddered and groaned, and then with a loud *crack* the ropes holding the main-mast snapped. The tall spar fell slowly at first, then crashed down across the forecastle, smashing through the bulwarks and lodging itself in the hull.

A wave lifted the boat up off the bottom. Arzella grabbed the wheel and spun it, trying to turn them back out to sea. Seconds later the keel hit bottom again, and this time the foremast snapped the rig-ging and crashed down and broke apart, the majority of it falling into the waves. The *Ruse* rolled halfway onto her side, then a wave lifted her up and slammed her onto the bottom again.

Pushing aside splintered wood and wet canvas, she climbed down the precariously tilting steps and into the aft cabin. The decks were canted at a crazy angle, and she had to move from handhold to hand-hold. Alonso appeared half-awake as he gripped the bedclothes so as not to fall out of the bed. His eyes rolled in their sockets and his limbs flailed.

"Alonso," she said as she grasped him by the shoulders and shook him. "We must get off the boat."

He called out her name, grabbed the front of her cloak, and pulled her to him. He would not let go.

She wrestled and fought him and finally broke free. She jumped back out of his grasp.

Arzella looked around the cabin. Waves were breaking over the ship now, and water surged through the cabin door and swirled around her bare feet. Without the masts, she could no longer launch the ship's boat on her own. She and Alonso would both have to go into the water. She could swim, but in his current state, Alonso would likely drag her under. She needed some wood to keep him afloat on his own.

Hanging over his bunk was his sword. She pulled it from the scabbard, opened a tall cupboard door, and slid the sword through the gap by the hinges. She levered the door away from the cabinet and the hinges broke loose. Searching through Alonso's clothes, she found a belt and several sashes, and she used these to tie the wooden door to his chest to buoy him and to restrict his flailing.

The shield! Alonso would never forgive her if they did not take the shield with the enciphered key engraved on it. And she would need other things, too, if shipwrecked on this coast. She collected the bag she'd brought aboard from Gozo and stuffed a few clothes into it, along with shoes for both of them. She added the atlas of sea maps, Alonso's hand compass, and a flint for starting fires. She threw in her tools, their few remaining coins, and a traveler's flask she had made of silver, long ago in her father's shop. The biscuit and dried nuts she and Alonso had been eating went in, as well as Alonso's goatskin bag filled with water. She tied the travel bag closed, grabbed the shield, and started for the deck.

Then she returned, replaced the sword in the scabbard, and took it, along with Alonso's pistol and his bag of powder and ammunition. She wrapped them in his rain cloak.

Walking was difficult on the slick, slanting decks with her arms filled with such a load and waves washing about her feet. She spotted what she was after on the low side of the deck. The empty water barrel. Using Alonso's sword, she pried open the lid and stuffed all her belongings inside. She added the shield last, and said a small prayer as she pounded the lid back into place with a belaying pin. She untied the ropes that secured the barrel to the gunnel, rolled it to the gate, and pushed it into the sea.

She was happy to see it did not sink straight away, but rather bobbed to the surface. As it was in the lee of the ship, it drifted slowly toward shore. When the waves caught it shortly, it would move faster.

Arzella paused a moment to examine the waves and tried to estimate how far off shore the *Ruse* was. It looked as though they had grounded at a river mouth. The river's shoals reached farther out into the sea than she anticipated. She knew the *Ruse* to be a shallow draft vessel, so unless they had grounded on some sort of pinnacle, the water around them should not be not too deep. She should be able to touch bottom shortly after she entered the sea.

Arzella returned to the cabin for Alonso.

She could not get him to stand or walk, and he was too heavy for her to carry. Not knowing what else to do, she rolled him out of the bed, took hold of his feet, and began to drag him on his back across the tilting cabin floor. Seawater washed around him, sometimes even across his face, but he did not wake. Perhaps it was a blessing, since, with his broken ribs, the pain would have been unbearable.

When she finally got him and the door over the cabin doorsill, he slid down the slippery deck and lodged against the bulwarks. She got hold of his feet, turned him around, and dragged him to the open gate in the bulwarks. She paused to look across the water toward shore. The water was cloudy here at the river mouth, and on the shore, the beach looked like rich, dark mud. Beyond that were bright-green plants and trees. It looked peaceful there, and it was not so very far away.

She pushed Alonso into the sea and jumped in after him.

CHAPTER SEVENTY-SEVEN

Via della Conciliazione
Rome, Italy

April 26, 2014

"Cole, never turn around to look." Her voice sounded strong, even though they were running all-out through the crowd. He dodged around a lady with a stroller. When he caught up to Riley, she was still giving him what for. "He'll never spot you in a crowd from the back of your head."

"Okay, Magee. Lesson learned."

When they reached the edge of Saint Peter's Square, they entered a street and the crowds thinned considerably. It made running easier, but they had less cover.

They had a pretty big lead on him, but there was no question he was faster than either of them. Cole's backpack bounced on his back, making it even harder for him to breathe regularly. Riley was in better shape than he was, and she was starting to pull ahead of him as they dodged their way through the crowds down the street. If it came to it, he'd stay behind to take on Blondie alone, giving her time to get away with the photos on her phone.

He saw Riley skid to a stop in front of two big American guys wearing gray-colored desert camos. Cole slowed to a trot. She pointed up the street, and he heard the words "scared" and "touched me." When Cole arrived at her side, she grabbed his hand and took off running. She nearly jerked him off his feet. The last he saw of the two big guys, they'd turned shoulder to shoulder and were facing up the street.

The Tiber River was coming into view at the end of the street. They hadn't passed many businesses along the street, but the character of the neighborhood was changing. He saw what looked like a restaurant down at the corner. Maybe they could cut inside and lose Blondie while he was dealing with Riley's protectors.

Cole twisted around to look behind him. He felt Riley squeeze his hand tighter.

"Cole! I said, never look back!"

"Too late. No sign of the big guys." They were probably on the ground. Blondie was gaining on them again. "Those guys barely slowed him down."

A motorbike zoomed up behind them. They were running down the middle of the parking street that ran parallel to the main avenue. The guy on the moto beeped his little horn at them. Cole waved at him to go around. The guy beeped again, then drove up onto the sidewalk to get around them. He zipped down to the corner and stopped in front of the Versi Bistrot Bar. He swung his leg around the front of the scooter. He tossed the end of his scarf over his shoulder, then pushed the bike back onto the center stand. He walked into the bar.

"Asshole," Riley said.

Cole yanked her arm and pulled her between two parked cars and onto the sidewalk.

"Where are you going?" Riley shouted as they dodged around a wooden signboard on the pavement.

"Thank God for assholes," Cole said as he pulled her to a stop in front of the bistro bar. He jumped on the still-running Vespa and pushed it forward off the center stand. "Climb on. He's already seen us."

Riley swung a leg over the back of the bike, and Cole cranked the throttle. The dapper Italian came running out with a grease-stained takeout bag in his hand. He tried to grab at the back of the motorbike. Riley batted his hand away as Cole pulled out into traffic.

Horns blared. He veered right and crossed over the bridge with the flow of cars, then turned right down one side street and left down another. The traffic thinned as they traveled farther from the Vatican. He circled around for several minutes before he turned into a narrow alley. He made a U-turn, and they waited at the alley entrance to see if their pursuer had commandeered a vehicle of his own.

"We're going to wind up in a Roman prison," Riley said. "Grand theft Vespa."

"Hey, I think it was a better idea than getting caught by Blondie back there."

"No kidding." She climbed off the back of the scooter and wiped her face on her sleeve. "Looks like we lost him."

"So what now?"

She leaned her back against the side of the building. Her arms were crossed over her midriff, her eyes glassy and unfocused.

"Are you okay, Magee?"

She glanced at him and flashed him a grim smile. "I didn't tell you the whole story about what happened yesterday, because Sister Ola was there."

"What are you talking about?"

"When Virgil showed up in the catacombs and took me, he killed Diggory. He used explosives. Seems he really gets off on blowing stuff up."

"Can't say as I'll mourn Priest, but it makes me even more determined to stay several steps ahead of Virgil Vandervoort."

Riley pushed off the wall and brushed the dust off her hands. "I think we're done in Rome here."

Cole nodded. "We need to get back to Malta—to the boat."

"We probably don't want to fly commercial," Riley said. "These Knights are too well connected." She straightened up and pulled her phone out of her pocket. "I'll try Hazel."

She put the phone to her ear. "Hi there. It's me. Where are you?" Riley paused and listened. "What a life you lead."

Cole enjoyed watching Riley talk on the phone to her best friend. Her face always lit up.

"Rome—and I've got a favor to ask. We really need to get out of town, but don't want to use any public transport. Got any friends who live around here who might be able to help us?" She listened again, then said, "Okay, I'll hold."

"Where is she?" Cole asked.

"Sardinia—not all that far away." Riley held up her hand to let him know Hazel was back on the line. "Hang on a second." She took the phone away from her ear and pushed a button. "Okay, I've got you on speaker. Give me the address and I'll type it in."

Hazel gave her the number and spelled out the name of the street and the town. "It's not too far," she said. "Head over there. They'll be expecting you around two o'clock."

"Thanks, my friend. We're on some kind of noisy Italian scooter, and we need to get moving. I'll have to call you later to fill you in on what's happening here."

"No problem, darling. Just give that man of yours an extra hug from me. We've got wedding plans to work on, girl. *Ciao!*"

"Are you sure you got the address right?" Cole asked after the call. "You didn't read it back to her."

"Cole, I got it."

"Let's get going, then. If we get there early, maybe we can stop for something to eat."

Riley activated the GPS navigation program in her phone, and a female British voice said, "Head west one hundred meters, then turn right."

"Let's go," Riley said.

An hour later, Cole pulled the bike to a stop. Over the noise of the idling engine, he heard the voice from Riley's phone say, "The destination is on your right."

Cole looked to their right, and he saw nothing but a dirty, dusty, open field.

For the past hour, he and Riley had been arguing. There was no way some friend of Hazel's lived out here. It was arid countryside with scraggly trees, dusty homes, and dirty kids kicking soccer balls or standing at the side of the road staring at them as they zoomed past. Now, they'd arrived at a dead end. There was a chest-high chain-link gate across the road. The sign said *"Proprietà Privata."* It was easy enough to translate.

"So you still think this is the right place?"

"This is the address Hazel gave me. Sometimes Google Maps messes up and sends you to the wrong place. Who knows. But I'm sure I got the address right."

Cole turned off the bike. After riding for hours, the silence sounded loud. Slowly, as his ears adjusted, he began to hear the soft buzzing of insects and the occasional birdcall.

Riley said, "I wonder if we're supposed to go through the gate."

Cole walked over to a tree. "Excuse me. I think this tree needs watering."

Riley shook her head and walked over to the gate. She rested her arms on the top bar and lowered her head onto her arms.

When he was finished, Cole joined her.

Riley's head popped up. "Do you hear that?" she asked.

"I don't hear anything but the bees buzzing."

"Nope," she said. "That's not bees."

Riley put her hand against her forehead to shade her eyes. "There," she said. "To the west."

Sure enough, he saw it, too. The dot in the sky grew bigger and the noise grew louder. The helicopter kicked up a choking dust cloud as it landed on the other side of the gate.

Riley climbed over the gate first, and Cole followed her. The pilot leaned over and pushed the door open. He pulled one side of his big headphones off one ear and hollered, "Are you Maggie Riley?"

She nodded.

"Get in, then. Hazel says she's got champagne waiting for you."

CHAPTER SEVENTY-EIGHT

Aboard *Shadow Chaser II*
Manoel Island Yacht Marina, Malta

April 28, 2014

Hazel came up the stairs from the forward cabin looking like she was ready to dine with the captain of a cruise liner. The white, sleeveless dress with purple frangipani blossoms showed off her shapely, coco-brown shoulders.

"Good morning," she said cheerily.

Riley looked down at her own tank top and pajama bottoms and wrapped her fingers more tightly around her coffee mug. "How did you sleep?" she asked.

"Like a babe," Hazel said. She stood in the middle of the salon and turned around, examining the furnishings. She walked over to the bar and peered through at the kitchen. "I didn't really get a chance to look around much last night. This new boat is really lovely, Riley."

"And we've got Theo to thank for that," Riley said.

Theo leaned on the kitchen side of the counter and grinned.

"Good morning, Theo," Hazel said. There was something about her smile when she looked at him that made Riley suspect that Hazel's motivation for accompanying them all the way to Malta extended beyond helping with wedding plans.

"Morning," Theo said. "Would you like some coffee?"

"I'd be happy to help myself."

"He won't hear of it," Riley said. "He's got a new cappuccino machine back there, and he's been up for an hour, hoping you'll give him the chance to try it out."

"I would love a cappuccino."

"Coming right up," Theo said.

"Help yourself to a plate," Riley said. "There's croissants, fruit, yogurt. I think Theo is trying to spoil us."

"Have you all been up long?" Hazel asked her.

"I didn't sleep well," Riley said. "I couldn't get my brain to slow down. I got up a little over an hour ago, and I've been bringing Theo up to speed on what happened in Rome. We didn't have time to talk last night."

Hazel sat down with a small plate of fruit and yogurt. "Where's Cole?"

"He ran down to take a look at something in the engine room. Honestly, I think he's just gone down there to remind himself that he really does own a boat with an engine room all clean and organized like that. You should have seen what was on the last boat."

Theo said, "Not that he does all that much work in there."

"Shhhh," Riley said. "Don't tell him that."

"Too late," Cole said as he stepped through the doors to the aft deck. "I heard Theo maligning my reputation."

Theo stepped into the salon and set a frothy coffee on the table. "The truth hurts, mon. The way I hear it, you've just spent the last twenty-four hours working your way through flutes of champagne on private yachts and helicopters. And you want to claim that's work."

"While you've been back here slaving away in these deplorable conditions."

"Well . . ."

"Take a seat, man."

Theo sat in the empty chair opposite Hazel.

Cole said, "Hazel, we can't thank you enough for getting us home."

"My pleasure. In fact, the gentleman who owns that yacht and helicopter emailed me this morning that he found the whole adventure quite entertaining—sending his helicopter for you, racing down to Palermo with the yacht, and then sending us on his jet on to Malta last night. I told him you both work for an international drug task force. He made a large donation to my foundation this morning to thank me for all the excitement."

"In that case, glad we could oblige," Cole said. He tapped his coffee cup against Hazel's and said, "Cheers. But the fun's over now. We know Virgil and his friends aren't sitting around doing nothing. By now, they've already had a chance to examine the real sea atlas. And while we were on that yacht yesterday, Riley and I took a look at the photos of the charts on her phone. There are some scratchings and notes on the pages. Most of them look like calculations for navigation. The original owner of the atlas sailed all over the Med. It's going to be very difficult to know which ones mean anything. And then there's the drawing on the back page."

"You know, while you all have been off having fun, I've been busy, too," Theo said.

"Okay. What did you find?"

"I put Yoda to work. I took lots of photos of the shield. Probably more than necessary, but my aim's not so good. Yoda processed them and searched the engravings. His eyes aren't fooled by optical illusions. Whoever did the additional engravings was quite talented."

"What do you mean by additional?"

"I suspect the engravings we're interested in are almost one hundred years more recent than the original age of the shield."

"So what did you find?"

"There's an extra band around the outside edge that is of a different style altogether. In one section, the leaves actually form some almost hieroglyphic-like symbols."

"Can you show us?"

"Sure. As smart as Yoda is, there is still lots that he has yet to learn. So, while he did find the letters in the engraving, he didn't pick up on some of the symbols as separate from the design. I used my new embossing printer that now prints high-resolution graphics up to 100 dpi."

Hazel said, "That doesn't sound very high-res."

"It might not sound very high-resolution to you, but think of Braille. Blind people read those dots with their fingers. Embossing printers turn graphic designs into tactile images. I have to feel all those dots with my fingertips. I printed out what is like a 3-D relief map of the design on the shield. And this is what we found. Yoda?"

"Yes, Theo."

Hazel shook her head. "I love it."

A ghost of a smile flitted across Theo's features, but he continued, "Put the image titled *Shield* up on Display One in the main salon, please."

The monitor switched on, and a photo of the shield appeared.

"Zoom in on the letters in the design."

On the screen, they saw the engraving of a series of leaves and flowers.

"If you look closely at the stems of the vine, you will see two letters right here."

Riley stared, then suddenly she saw it. In the middle were what looked like two letters: *KK*.

"The first thing we identified were the two letters *K* here followed by the letter *S*, then what looks like the symbol for 'less than,' and then the letter *V*. Then I realized that beneath the letters *KK* were graphics that could be part of the letters. The graphics could be a series of ocean waves."

"Yes," Riley said. "I can see that."

"And can you tell what it is between the two *K*s and the letter *S*?"

Riley stood up and walked closer to the screen. "There's something there, but I can't make out what it is."

"Yoda, zoom in on the symbol between the letters *K* and *S*."

"What is it?" Riley said.

"An abstract drawing of a human eye."

"Okay, I see it now."

Cole said, "What do you think it's supposed to mean?"

"I have no idea," Theo said.

Riley looked at the image on the screen. There was something familiar about it. She pulled out her phone and began going through the photos of Joseph Roux's charts.

Hazel said, "I'm incredibly impressed with how you did this, Theo."

"Because I'm blind."

"That's a small part of it, but mostly it's the computer work. You programmed a computer to search for letters in the photo?"

"Oh, well, that. Yeah. But what I meant is that I'm better able to do some things because I'm blind."

"And you are able to search graphics yourself by using a special embossing printer? Where'd you get such a machine?"

"They do make some rudimentary ones now that are very expensive. I designed my own. Once you get used to it, seeing with your fingers works great. Your eyes simply build constructs in your mind. My fingers do."

"Found it!" Riley held up her phone.

"What?" Cole asked.

"I knew there was something in that drawing that I'd seen before. Theo, can I get the photos on my phone to display on the monitor there?"

"Sure. Are you on the boat network?"

"Yes."

"Then tap AirPlay and find the one listed as Display One."

A few seconds later, the photo of a chart appeared on the monitor.

"Look," Riley said. "This is the chart of the Greek islands, Crete, and part of Turkey in Joseph Roux's sea atlas."

"That doesn't look much like our modern charts," Hazel said.

"Yeah," Cole said. "We're spoiled today by satellite accuracy. Surveying is very difficult and time consuming. These old charts aren't very accurate by today's standards, but they were quite amazing for their day."

"You see what I'm talking about in the lower-right corner?" Riley said. "There are these strange letters. See, it starts with the letter X with a small lowercase e, then those lines and more letters?" She got up and walked over to the monitor and pointed to the symbols on the screen:

$$X^e \mid \mid XI^e = KK.$$

"It was the double K that I remembered."

Cole said, "It might be significant or it might be some navigator's doodling."

"It's definitely not calculations for navigation."

Hazel said, "What's the title of this book again?"

Riley picked up her phone again. "I can read it right off the title page. It's called *Carte de la mer Méditerranée en douze feuilles*."

"Okay," Hazel said. "So that translates to *Map of the Mediterranean Sea in Twelve Leaves*."

"Leaves?" Theo said.

"Like a table with leaves," Riley said. "It folds out and becomes bigger. All twelve of the charts in this book are on pages that are fold-ed. That way the book isn't so big, but the charts are big enough to be usable."

Hazel said, "Riley, I'm surprised you don't see this. You've not been thinking in French much lately, have you?"

"Not really. What do you mean?"

"There are twelve charts, twelve pages. How would you say *tenth* and *eleventh* in French?"

"*Dixième* and *onzième*."

"Exactly."

"Good grief," Riley said. "I should have taken Theo up on that espresso. Of course. Like we write *tenth* in English with the numerals and the little *t-h* in the corner? In France in the 1700s, they would write the letter *X* followed by a little *e* up in the corner for *tenth*. The *X* is a Roman numeral."

"So what do the two parallel vertical lines mean?" Cole said.

"My guess is it means to put them side by side. What if we put the tenth chart and the eleventh chart next to each other? What would that give us? Just a second. Let me pull up the other chart." Riley tapped the screen of her phone and a new chart appeared.

Cole stood up and walked over to the big TV screen. He pointed to a large island in the center. "I think that's supposed to be Cyprus?"

"Right. That's southern Turkey above, and Egypt is at the bottom of the chart," Riley said. "Hang on, I've got my iPad right here. Let me bring up a current chart." She tapped on the screen and brought up an electronic chart in a navigation app.

Cole said, "Yoda, place the last two images side by side on the screen."

Riley stood up and walked over to the big wall screen while hold-ing up her iPad with the modern chart. "Okay, I would say that the tenth chart here, with Cyprus and southern Turkey, ends on the left side of the page on the parallel 30° east. But the eleventh chart's right side doesn't line up as a match. It's closer to the parallel 29° east."

"So how much of the Turkish coast is missing?"

"I'd guess forty-five to fifty nautical miles."

Cole walked over to the bar and picked up the thermos of coffee. He poured himself a cup and sat on a stool. "That gap is a lot of territory to search."

Hazel said, "And you don't even know what you're searching for."

"More like impossible," Riley said.

"That's not entirely true," Theo said. "I interpret the text as saying there is something between there that has two K's in it. That's just the sort of thing a computer excels at. Yoda, find all locations on the southern Turkish coast between 29° and 30° east that have two of the letter *K* in the spelling of the name."

"Where should I post the results?"

"On the TV screen in the main salon."

The list of names appeared on the screen: Yeşilköy Köyü, Kalkan, Sicak Köyü, Gökkaya Limani, Kekova, Kaleköy, Kamislik.

"That looks like a mouthful," Riley said.

"Yoda, cross-reference those locations with the Knights of Saint John."

"Found Kaleköy."

"Yoda, translate *Kaleköy* from Turkish to English."

"Translation Turkish to English: *castle village.*"

"Castle!" Riley and Cole spoke in unison.

"Yoda, search Kaleköy."

"Yes, Theo. Kaleköy is the name of the village on the hillside beneath this crusader's castle built by the Knights of Saint John during their stay in Rhodes."

A photo appeared on the screen of saw-toothed turrets and castle ruins atop a hill surrounded by red-roofed houses. In the foreground, a Turkish yacht was moored to a dock floating in deep-blue water.

"Gorgeous," Hazel said.

"Take a look at this," Riley said. She tapped her phone, and the drawing of the castle appeared on the screen. "Yoda, can you place the last two images side by side?"

"The perspectives are not the same," Cole said, "and remember, the two images were created hundreds of years apart."

"They are still very similar," Hazel said.

Riley slid off the bench seat and headed for the coffee thermos. "Okay, that looks great, but let's think about this. Why would our Knight, who sailed out of Malta in 1798 to save this manuscript, then sail right into the heart of Muslim lands to hide something from the Muslims?"

"I think it was a brilliant move," Cole said. "Hide it in the last place they would look."

"So what now?" Riley asked.

"There's no way we can get this boat back to Turkey fast enough. I suggest you and I fly back to Marmaris and take the *Bonefish*. It looks like it's about a hundred miles down to Kaleköy. We can motorsail all night and be there within twenty-four hours of our arrival in Turkey."

"And what about us," Hazel said. "What can we do?"

"Us?" Theo said.

"Virgil and friends might have the charts," Cole said, "but they won't know what to do with them. They are going to come looking for us. I figure the only reason they aren't here already is because Hazel got us out of Italy without leaving a trace. But they'll figure we returned to Malta eventually, even if they couldn't track us. That means it's not safe for you here."

Hazel said, "We could take this boat back to Sicily. My friends are still there. I'd love to introduce Theo to them."

"You good with that, Theo?"

Riley thought his smile was going to split his face in two.

"Sounds great, Skipper."

CHAPTER SEVENTY-NINE

Adakoy Shipyard
Adakoy, Turkey

April 28, 2014

The taxi dropped them off outside the boatyard gates. After Cole paid the driver and the taxi drove off, they stood still outside, staring at the fence.

"It's difficult to believe we've only been gone two weeks," he said.

"A lot's happened," Riley said. Her phone dinged. She pulled it out of her pocket and looked at the screen. "Not again," she said.

"Your mother?"

"Who else?" She shoved the phone back in her pocket.

"Let's go," he said. He picked up their bags and crossed the road to the gate. He keyed in the combination, and they passed inside.

"Cole!" He turned to look and saw Colin, coming out of the men's head with a towel hung over his shoulder. He was carrying his toiletry kit. "How's the new boat behaving, mate?"

"It's great," Cole said. "No complaints."

"Hi, Colin," Riley said. "Are you headed out to your boat?"

"Yeah."

"Could you give us a lift out to *Bonefish*?"

"Sure thing," he said. "You off on a sailing trip now?"

Riley started to answer, but Cole cut her off. "No, we're just going to move the boat into a marina closer to town. We'll probably put her on the market."

Riley sent him a questioning look, and he made a stern face meant to get her to drop it. It worked. Cole didn't want to tell anyone where they were headed. No matter how careful they had been—clearing out of Malta with a crew list showing them on board *Shadow Chaser II*, then buying their airline tickets at the last minute before their flight while Theo and Hazel took the big boat out to sea—he knew they couldn't count on staying ahead of Virgil for long.

A few minutes later, they had hoisted their gear into the cockpit of *Bonefish* and said good-bye to Colin, and Riley was opening the padlock on the hatch by the light of her cell-phone flash.

Hot, stale air poured out when she opened the companionway doors.

"It's only been two weeks, but poor *Bonefish* already has that nasty closed-up boat smell. She doesn't like being left alone. Better open all the hatches and air her out."

"And get out of all these heavy travel clothes."

"I'll second that," she said.

Cole got straight to work going through his usual pretrip check-list. In all their miles of sailing, from the Philippines to the Med, they had worked out a comfortable system. He pulled the cover off the engine compartment to check the oil, raw-water strainer, and coolant while Riley sat down at the chart table. She checked the status of the batteries, started up the refrigeration, and turned on the navigation instruments.

"Batteries look great. The solar panels and wind generator have been doing their jobs."

"Engine oil and water look good, too." He replaced the engine cover.

"There isn't any fresh food aboard," she said, "but we've still got plenty of canned goods and staples. I'll put some beer, water, and UHT milk in the fridge." She switched on the cockpit instruments. "We going with lights or no lights?"

"Let's go with no lights for now. We don't need to show the marina busybodies which way we turn."

Riley started the engine, and, while it was warming up, she and Cole took the cover off the mainsail and readied the running rigging.

"Feels good, doesn't it?" Riley leaned back and looked up at the night sky.

"What?"

"Getting ready for a night sail."

"I guess."

"Remember that first time in Guadeloupe? We sailed on *Bonefish* over to the bay where *Shadow Chaser* was anchored?"

Cole looked at her, standing on the foredeck in shorts and a tank top, her hair loose and blowing around in the warm breeze. With her head tipped back like that, her neck looked more inviting than ever. Her body hadn't changed at all since he'd first met her. "Oh yeah, that night I remember."

She paused and looked at him. "What? You didn't put the moves on me until much later, Mr. Thatcher."

"But that night, in the moonlight with the dolphins playing around the boat—that was the night I realized how beautiful you are, Magee."

She put one hand on a hip and cocked her head to the side as she looked him over. "I don't believe we have time just now to properly reward that kind of talk, Captain Thatcher."

"Rain check, then. What do you say we drop this mooring and head on out to sea?"

"Why, that's a fabulous idea," she said.

* * *

They slipped their mooring and motored inside Bedir Island and around the flashing light on Ince Point before they turned on their running lights. They were in the shipping channel at that point, and running dark would have been foolish. They passed one little coastal freighter chugging into port and a big Turkish charter *gulet* playing loud music for the tourists dancing on deck. Then they were out of the narrow channel and out of Marmaris Bay.

The wind was light out of the northwest, which put it directly behind them. But as they motored farther out offshore, the wind increased.

"I think there's enough wind to sail without the engine," Riley said.

Cole nodded. "It's about seventy-five nautical miles until we make our turn. Straight ahead on a course of one twenty-five. Then another ten miles or so up into Kekova."

Riley unfurled the big genoa. Cole shut off the engine and set the autopilot. He checked the radar and set the alarm. He put the AIS in stealth mode. There wasn't another boat within twenty miles of them. It was going to be a quiet night.

"Ah, that's better," Riley said after she'd coiled the tail of the sheet to keep it off the cockpit cushion. She spread out on her back on the cushion and put her hands behind her head. "I needed this."

Cole loved that gurgling sound a boat made as it passed through the water just under hull speed. When she moved faster, it was more like a *swoosh*. But at this speed, it almost sounded like fingers softly playing the very high notes on a piano. Much as he loved his new boat, he would miss the sweet quiet of sailing.

"I love my dodger," Riley said, "but it does make it difficult to stargaze on nights like this. Look at all of them. Here we are on a sailboat traveling the same way the old Knights of Saint John did. In fact, when the Silver Girl sailed here with her Knight, they were probably looking up at the same stars. We're all just tiny specks. Infinitely smaller than those specks in the sky."

Cole watched her and wondered how he could possibly do right by this woman. He wanted her by his side—more than anything. But if that were to cause her harm, he wouldn't be able to live with himself.

Riley's phone pinged again. She sat up. "Okay, already. I'll read your dang messages." She pulled the phone out of her shorts pocket and slid her finger around the phone screen. "You've got to be kidding."

"What?"

"She says she's going to fly to Turkey because she's worried about me."

"How come?"

"I haven't been answering her texts or emails." She looked at him and shook her head. "I'd say we've been rather busy."

Cole stepped around the wheel and sat next to her on the cockpit cushion. "She's your mother. Of course she'll worry."

"Cole, you don't know my mother. She's just worried the wedding might get called off. We go for six years only exchanging the occasional email, but as soon as I mention I'm getting married, she latches on to me, and we're suddenly close as can be."

"She's not the only one who worries about you."

"Oh please."

"Seriously, Riley. When you didn't come back from the palace on the Via Condotti. When I saw Blondie drive you into that estate. I thought they were going to kill you."

"And you came for me."

He nodded. "When I suggested maybe we should wait on the wedding, it was because of how much I love you. Right now I would like more than anything to stop someplace, put you ashore, and send you back to Marmaris to meet your mother and take care of your family. We don't know what we're sailing into down there, and we don't even have any weapons." He leaned in closer to her. "Riley, I want you to let me finish this thing alone."

"Now that sounds crazy, Cole Thatcher."

"No, it's not. When a man loves a woman, he feels this overpowering need to protect her. Can't you understand that?"

She didn't answer right away. She rubbed her hand up his back and reached into his hair. He closed his eyes as her fingers ruffled his hair.

"Sure. I understand. But I have overwhelming feelings, too. I'm a trained marine, Cole. And you might be surprised at what can be used as a weapon on this boat. I need you to trust and respect my strengths."

"Riley, it's not that I don't trust you."

She held her finger to his lips. "I know. We're learning how to do this, how to be a couple. When do we disagree, when should we speak out. You wanted me to trust that you really saw a man I thought surely was dead. And now I want you to trust that we're better together."

"I know that, Riley, but I'm afraid for you."

"Cole, I lived alone and sailed alone for years. I'm having to make huge adjustments to this new lifestyle. Selling *Bonefish* and moving on your boat does make sense, and I suppose I'll get used to the idea eventually. But I'm still trying to find where I fit in your life." She smiled then, and he caught a devilish glint in her eye. "I mean, to be clear, you're the academic, and *I'm* the muscle."

"So you think you're stronger than I am?"

"Damn sure of it."

He narrowed his eyes and looked her up and down. "Have you ever wrestled?"

"I can take down a two-hundred-and-fifty-pound marine in hand-to-hand combat. And you, what was it? Wrestled in high school?"

"Them's fighting words," he said.

"I'm counting on it."

He turned, pushed her shoulders back down onto the cockpit seat, straddled her waist, and pinned her to the cushion. "Something tells me that was too easy."

She laughed and grabbed the front of his shirt, pulling his face closer to hers. "I thought now might be a good time to let you cash in that rain check."

CHAPTER EIGHTY

**The Grand Hotel Excelsior Malta
Valletta, Malta**

April 28, 2014

Virgil sat at a window table in the hotel bar, overlooking the harbor and the city lights of Sliema. The young woman in the chair opposite him was drinking her third apple martini. Neither of them was interested in making small talk, so he had plenty of time to think about his situation.

On the plus side, she was very young and her figure was magnificent, with the tiny waist and ample breasts, clearly enhanced by something other than nature. She was a blonde, as he had asked for, with hair cropped short just below her ears. But he was certain that the blonde hair was not natural. Like many Maltese women, her features showed the history of her island. Her almond-shaped eyes and long nose, though beautiful, demonstrated that the Arabs had been here the longest. She wore a small, tight-fitting black dress and spike heels, but he was finding it difficult to feel any interest. Maybe he really was getting old.

His wife Shawny—now she had been a real blonde. Her family was from northern Europe, and the first day he had seen her he knew he had to have her. Bonnie had inherited her mother's beauty. Someday, long after Operation Barnabas, he hoped his daughter would realize he'd done what he'd done to clean the world of filth so people like her could feel safe.

The last forty-eight hours had been hectic and exhausting, but he was satisfied he'd done his duty. As he'd promised Signor Oscura, he had found Thatcher. Well, he knew where Thatcher was, and it would be only a matter of hours before he learned what the man knew.

After he had lost them in Rome on Saturday, Virgil had returned to the Vatican Library and retrieved the book of maps. He took it back to the Via Condotti, scanned the pages, and sent them off to the Order's friend at NSA. He came back with several possibilities. First, there was the castle drawing in the back of the book. Without more data on where to look, it would be difficult to track down which of the thousands of castles around the Mediterranean that one could be. There was a reference to a location on the coast of Tunisia near Sousse, and various navigational waypoints in the waters between Malta and what the map called the Barbary Coast, as well as northward to Sicily. There was also a reference to a section of the maps that was not covered. It seemed to point to something spelled with a double K that was off the page, but the operative said his computers brought back at least ten possible locations on and off the coast. He could not determine what the actual location was without more data. *So Thatcher must have that data,* Virgil thought.

He'd wanted to leave for Malta immediately, on the assumption that Thatcher would return to his boat once he'd got the information he needed from the Vatican Library. Virgil had checked with the port captain and determined that the yacht was still in a marina there. However, there was no escaping his duties on Sunday. Every member of the Guardiani was required to attend the dual canonization mass for Pope John XXIII and Pope John Paul II, where the Knights of the Sovereign Order of Malta had better seats than many bishops. And well into the night, his duties were needed at the celebration afterward at the Villa del Priorato.

He hadn't been able to catch his flight to Malta until this morning. Upon arrival, he'd taken a cab from the airport directly to the Excelsior Hotel. When he had stepped out onto his balcony, he'd seen a big yacht powering away from the dock at the Manoel Island Yacht Marina. As the yacht turned into the channel, Virgil grabbed his small binoculars out of his kit bag. He read the name on the stern: *Shadow Chaser II*. The only person he saw out on deck was a black woman.

He immediately called the port captain. His office affirmed that the four-person crew list for departure included Cole Thatcher and Marguerite Riley. Their next port of call was to be Palermo, Sicily. Virgil contemplated renting a speedboat to intercept the big yacht, but he decided that would be foolish. He checked the Shipfinder website, and the big yacht was broadcasting her location on AIS. How difficult would it be to track them?

He called the Order's travel agency and they booked him on an early-morning flight to Palermo. Sicily made lots of sense. The manuscript likely was hidden someplace close to Malta. In the meantime, he decided he had time to enjoy the five-star hotel they had booked for him in Valletta.

The woman sitting across from him was staring at the TV over the bar. On the screen, two people were seated in chairs talking to one another. The volume was turned all the way down, but the subtitles were in Maltese.

Virgil's phone vibrated in his pocket. He pulled it out, tapped the screen, and held it to his ear.

"Hello?"

"Hi, uh, this is Colin. Is Diggory there?" The man's voice had a British accent.

Virgil was about to hang up when he thought better of it. "No, Dig isn't available. Can I help you, Colin?"

"Maybe. He gave me this as a second number to call. See, he asked me to keep a watch on the marina here in Marmaris for him. He wanted me to let him know if Cole Thatcher or his lady showed up around here. He said he'd pay me two hundred euros for a tip if they showed."

"Yes, sure, you did the right thing, Colin. Priest isn't here right now, but I'm his boss. I'd be happy to pay you for any information you have."

"He would always send me the money through PayPal. Can you do that, too?"

"Sure I can."

"Okay, I'll give you my email address."

Virgil thought, he's got to be kidding. He isn't going to talk to me until he gets paid?

"All right," he said. "I'm listening."

A few minutes later, when Colin was able to verify that the payment had gone through, he said, "Okay, I was coming out of the shitter tonight here in the boatyard."

"Where is here? What boatyard?"

"It's the Adakoy Shipyard and Marina. Where they built their fancy new boat."

"I know the place."

"Anyway, I was coming out, and I saw Cole and Riley come through the gate. They asked me to give them a ride out to their boat."

"What boat is that?"

"Her boat. A forty-foot sailboat called the *Bonefish*. They asked me for a ride in my dinghy, and when I dropped them off, I asked them if they were going out for a sail. They said no, they were just going to move the boat into a marina off town. I stayed up and watched when they left. They didn't turn on their running lights, which was odd. But through my binoculars, I could still track their boat. They didn't go to town. They turned out to sea."

"Thank you for calling, Colin. You did the right thing."

After Colin hung up, Virgil dialed a familiar number. "I need some local talent," he said into the phone. "I'm in Malta, and I need someone with access to satellite imaging." The man on the other end of the line asked him his location, then told him to hold. When he came back on, he said his talent would be arriving in thirty minutes.

When the line disconnected, Virgil set his phone on the table.

The girl across from him pulled her eyes away from the TV screen. "Do you want to go up to your room?" she asked.

He shook his head, then reached into his back pocket and pulled out his wallet. He took out several hundred-euro bills and handed them to her. "Something has come up. I've got to go. Take this for your time."

She grabbed at the bills before he was finished speaking.

"Thank you," he said. He wasn't sure what he was thanking her for.

She didn't answer. She left the bar, teetering on the high heels without looking back.

Virgil picked up his phone and checked his email again. There in his inbox were the three bounced emails that had come back when he had tried to contact Bonnie the last couple of days. Her account also had been deleted from Skype, and a search for "Bonnie Vandervoort" on Facebook revealed only a forty-year-old woman who lived in West Virginia.

The talent showed up right on time. Virgil recognized the young man immediately, though he had never met him. He wore an olive-drab army jacket over a faded T-shirt that read, "*1984* was not supposed to be an instruction manual." His jeans hung low on his slender waist, and the backs of their cuffs were frayed where he walked on them.

The young man held out his hand. "Hey, you can call me Viper." The accent sounded Eastern European, maybe Czech.

"I'm Virgil. Take a seat."

It took only a few minutes for Virgil to explain what he needed.

"Hacking into reconnaissance satellites is tricky business. They're the only ones that can track night shots."

"I don't need to know anything about how you do it. I just need results."

"Right. Don't worry. I like working for your people. When I need permission or a password, it's usually only a phone call away. Best of all, they pay well."

Virgil slid him his card across the table. "My email address is on here as well as my cell phone. As soon as you can tell me which direction they are headed, contact me. If I don't answer the phone, send me an email or text. I need to know where they're going and when and where they stop."

The young man stood up. "It's a pleasure doing business with you. Expect something in two to three hours."

After he left, Virgil ordered another beer.

When all this was over, maybe he'd hire Viper on his own. Ask him to find Bonnie. Then he'd wait and watch. He'd always been good at waiting. In a couple of years, when Bonnie was on her own, he'd see to Shawny. He could make it look like an accident.

When his beer arrived, he dialed the travel-service number once more.

"I need to change my flight tomorrow morning," he said after he had identified himself. "Yes, I want the fastest routing you can find to get me to Marmaris, Turkey. ASAP."

CHAPTER EIGHTY-ONE

Aboard *Bonefish*
Kekova Roads, Turkey

April 29, 2014

The wind had increased a few hours after daybreak, as *Bonefish* was approaching the Greek isle of Kastellorizo and the sailboat's speed topped eight knots. Riley was having a blast "pulling the strings," as she called it—tweaking the sheets and playing the vang and outhaul, all the while watching the knot meter to see if she could boost her boat's speed by a quarter of a knot or more. The wind had developed a more northerly edge, and that put it more off the boat's quarter. A broad reach was her boat's favorite point of sail.

Ahead, Riley saw another sailboat come out through the opening to Kekova Roads. It was a fiberglass boat about the same size as hers, probably a bareboat charter. The other boat put its nose into the wind with the mainsail flapping and powered straight upwind. It rose up on the little swells kicked up by the wind and then slammed into the next swell. The people in the cockpit were all bundled up in foul-weather gear when they motored past. Riley figured they were cursing at her, sitting out in the sun in her shorts and T-shirt, having a fantastic sail.

"How's it going out there, Captain?" Cole called from the settee berth in the main salon, where he was napping.

"It's glorious, and we're about to enter the channel into Kekova Roads. We'll be able to see the castle shortly."

Cole climbed up the companionway, sat next to her on the port seat, and wrapped his arms around her. He lifted her hair and kissed the side of her neck. "You're right. It is glorious out here."

Tingles ran down her back as the hairs on her arms lifted in gooseflesh. "I was talking about the sailing and the view."

"And I was just agreeing. From where I'm sitting, the view is spectacular."

Riley stood up. "Cole, it's one thing to 'knock boots,' as Theo says, out in the open ocean, but right now we have to turn upwind to make it through this channel."

"Piece of cake."

"Really? You want to take the helm and show me?"

"Hell no. I just know it won't be a problem for you."

"Okay, it's time to find out." Riley grabbed the winch handle. She pushed the button on the autopilot to start the turn and cranked in on the genoa sheet. "Head up to the bow and keep watch for rocks. I'm going to cut the corner a bit tight here."

Soon *Bonefish* had buried her rail, the sheets were in tight, and they were charging for the two-hundred-foot-wide channel. They would have to take it on the diagonal, since the wind wouldn't allow them to go straight in. She pinched her up as tight as she could, and they just squeaked through.

Cole came back to the cockpit and swung down onto the seat. "Nicely done, Cap." He pointed forward through the spray-soaked dodger. "Do you see what's just ahead?"

Riley adjusted the autopilot to put them on the chart plotter's route, then she leaned out to look around the dodger.

In the midday sun, the golden castle atop the steep hill looked magical. The jagged edges of the upper battlements stood out in stark contrast against the cloudless blue sky. The castle walls appeared to flow down the hillside to the red roofs of the village clustered at the water's edge.

Cole slipped down into the boat's interior and returned with the folder containing the pages Theo had printed out for them. It was much easier to look at the images on paper than on the tiny screen of Riley's phone. Cole flipped through the pages to find the drawing of the castle, and then he held it aloft.

"What do you think?"

The drawing was an amazing facsimile. "I think we're in the right place."

They threaded their way through the rocks, past a huge charter *gulet* boat, and dropped the anchor in about forty feet of water off the village at Kaleköy. Close as they were now, Riley could see the bright-red Turkish flag flapping from a pole over the castle. There were several small sailboats and tourist day-tripper boats tied to the docks and floating pontoons out in front of the village waterfront restaurants, but Riley preferred to anchor.

She changed clothes while Cole lowered the dinghy into the water. She always chose to dress in long pants and shirts with sleeves when she went ashore in small villages in Islamic countries. Riley believed it was a sign of respect.

Cole had the outboard running by the time she was dressed, so she locked up the boat, and they went ashore. They tied the dinghy to a half-sunk stone quay. Once on the dock, Riley looked up at the castle.

"It's amazing how little it's changed since someone drew that sketch in the back of the sea atlas."

"Well, the sketch wasn't really made all that long ago, in the total picture of things here. That was drawn just over two hundred years ago, but this castle was already seven hundred years old when the Silver Girl and her Knight visited it."

Riley asked an older woman in a long skirt and head scarf for directions to the castle. The woman pointed up a dirt track through some houses, and when they followed the directions, they found themselves at the tail end of what turned out to be about a dozen British tourists hiking their way up the steep hillside. Eventually, the path gave way to a wooden staircase. The Brits' tour guide had come ashore with them off the big charter *gulet*, and when they paused for him to point out the view of the islands in the sound, she and Cole pushed their way to the front and trotted up the stairs without them.

Riley was breathing hard when they got to the top, but it was worth it to have the place to themselves, if only for a few minutes. There wasn't much inside the castle walls except for a very worn small theater. If there had once been buildings inside the walls, they must have been built of wood and were long gone. Now the walls encased only several levels or terraces of grassy dirt.

She pulled her phone out of her pocket and started taking photos of the castle walls.

Cole walked up behind her and watched over her shoulder. "I sure don't see any obvious hiding places, do you?"

"This is really just a ruin. It looks great from far away, but there's nothing inside the walls. You think there was more to it when Silver Girl was here?"

"I doubt it. I think we're going to have to work on the second part of the engraving on the shield."

The tour guide leading the Brits arrived with his flock, and Cole and Riley moved over against the walls to give them some more room.

The wind seemed to be shifting more west. If so, their anchorage could get bumpy. She pulled up the compass app on her phone and turned to face the wind. Still north of west, but it would bear watching.

The tour guide assembled his group and began his talk. "One remarkable aspect of this location is that you have evidence of three distinctly different eras simultaneously. Of course, there are the Byzantine castle walls you see around you. The theater there was cut from the stone by the Romans before the Crusaders ever arrived here, and outside the castle walls in this direction, you will find a Lycian necropolis. The tombs you will see there are between two and three thousand years old."

Riley had never heard of the Lycians. Just as she was thinking it, one of the tourists asked, "Who were the Lycians?"

"They were an ancient people who lived along this coast and inland from Fethiye to Antalya. Ancient Egyptian records mention the Lycians as allies of the Hittites in 1250 BC. They were a hardworking, wealthy people with a distinct language, art, and culture all their own, though they were attacked by the Persians, the Greeks, and the Romans. Lycia was the last region on the Mediterranean coast to be incorporated into the Roman Empire. Follow me to the necropolis in the olive orchard outside the castle walls."

Riley followed the tourists over to a spot where she could look across the orchard. There were at least eight or ten stone tombs scattered across the ridge. Those that were intact stood about twelve feet high. They were like giant stone sarcophagi, with long domed lids perched on top. Some of them had been tipped over or the stone lids removed, but most stood intact. She could hear the tour guide telling the tourists about grave robbers who had cleaned out anything of value in the tombs by the fourth century.

Cole appeared at her side a few minutes later.

"Look at all those tombs," she said. "Seriously, two to three thousand years old, and they are still standing."

"Please don't tell me they hid this manuscript in one of those. We could never budge those stone lids."

"If we can't, I don't think they could either, Cole."

"Right."

"I've been thinking about the graphic on the shield. What if the waves meant the beach at the base of the hill beneath Kaleköy—not the castle itself?"

"Excellent! Come on. Let's go."

"Wow. You're in a hurry all of a sudden."

He grinned at her. "There are restaurants down there, and after all that exertion from sailing, I worked up an appetite."

"Riiiight," she said, drawing out the word. "It was the sailing."

The gentleman who met them at the door to his restaurant introduced himself in more-than-passable English as Lukka and explained he was the owner of the place. Riley thought there was something familiar about his name. He ushered them in to where an older lady in a white head scarf was sitting on a carpet in front of a small, round table. She held a long dowel, which she used as a rolling pin to make large circles of very thin dough. Lukka said she was his mother, and the woman nodded and smiled shyly at them. He explained that she was making *gözleme*, a traditional Turkish flatbread, which she would fill with various toppings like minced beef or lamb, eggs, or vegetables.

A VHF radio mounted on the wall suddenly emitted a loud burst of static, and then a voice called, "Lukka, Lukka, this is *Sea Rover*."

The restaurant owner answered the call, and when they switched to a working channel, the boaters wanted to make a dinner reservation. Lukka wrote the name in a book on the counter, then returned to Riley and Cole.

"I'm sorry. Please, follow me."

When he showed them to their table, they ordered a variety of *gözleme*, and he was pleased.

Before he left them, Riley pointed out to the harbor and said, "We're just learning about this region, and we saw the Lycian tombs in the necropolis up on the hill. But isn't that a tomb sticking out of the water?"

"Yes," he said, "and do you see the stairs and the stone foundations out there on that rocky islet?"

"Yes," she said. "Are those Lycian, also?"

He nodded. "Our village is built on top of the remains of the sunken city of Simena. It was common for Lycians to place the sarcophagi in the center of the living area. They worshiped their dead ancestors, and they wanted them nearby."

"What caused the city to sink?" Cole asked.

"An earthquake in the second century caused a downshift of the land in this area. Most of the city was destroyed. There are more ruins over off Kekova Island, as the city was in two parts. It's very beautiful over there, and you will want to see the hidden harbor."

"What's that?"

"It's a very small cove with high, red-colored cliffs on one side. There are some excellent examples of rock-cut Lycian tombs in that cliff face." He nodded at them. "Enjoy your meal."

"I hope you've got your wallet," Riley said.

"I don't. I'd better go out to the boat and get some money."

"Then bring back the photos of the shield, too. We need to work on this cipher. There are just too many places around here to hide something."

While Cole was gone, Riley pictured the design on the shield. The letters *KK* had waves under them, and then the eye and the letters and symbols *S<V.*

When Lukka returned to their table with glasses of tea, Riley said, "I just remembered where I heard your name before. It was the name of a man in Malta in the nineteenth century."

"My name is the ancient name for Lycia. It is not a common name in Turkey."

"It is a lovely name, though."

"Thank you," he said.

So the son of the Silver Girl, the man who donated Joseph Roux's sea atlas, was named after the ancient civilization of Lycia. That only confirmed they were in the right place. Riley was certain. Below her, wavelets were breaking upon a rocky beach scattered with local fishing boats and dinghies. The waves in the design? What of the eye symbol in the cipher, then? At what, or in which direction, were they supposed to look?

Riley pulled her phone out of her pocket to take some photos of what one could see from the beach just below the restaurant. She held the phone up and turned it on. The compass app was still selected, and she noticed that the direction she was facing was due south.

What if the *S* was for south—or *sud*, in French? Then what would the *V* mean? She remembered the cipher on the map page. Part of it was Roman numerals. What if the *V* wasn't a letter, but a number?

Riley pushed back her chair and walked across the restaurant. Lukka was nowhere in sight, but his mother was watching. Riley pointed to the radio and pantomimed taking the microphone and talking. The old woman nodded and smiled.

"*Bonefish, Bonefish*, this is mobile." She didn't think his phone was on, and she hoped that Cole had not thought to turn off the VHF.

"Mobile, this is *Bonefish*. Six eight?"

"Roger." Riley switched the radio channel and she heard Cole's voice already speaking. ". . . up, beautiful?"

"Could you bring in the sextant? I want to try something."

"That's a strange request, but your wish is my command."

"Hmm. We should stand our night watches like that every night. It does wonders for your outlook on life."

"O Captain, my Captain," he said, and she could hear the leer in his voice.

"Back to sixteen." She wanted to add "years old." But it was great to see him so happy for a change.

Cole arrived at their table carrying her sextant box at the same time their food arrived. The *gözleme* was cut into wedges that looked somewhat similar to flour-tortilla quesadillas. They had a platter piled high with them.

"My God, that smells great!" Cole pulled several pieces onto his plate. "Careful, they're hot."

Though the aroma was making her stomach growl, she had to tell him what she'd been thinking while he was gone. Riley opened the folder and took out the photo of the close-up of the engraving on the shield. Just as she'd recalled, there were the two letters K with what could be wavelets beneath them, followed by the picture of the human eye. Then the letters and symbols $S<V$.

She pointed to the double letters K.

"We already figured out that this first part might mean the beach here at Kaleköy. So what if the eye means *to look*? Like we're supposed to look somewhere."

"Okay, but where?"

"What if the S is for *south*?"

"Were they speaking English?"

"In French, Spanish, German, Italian the word for south always starts with S."

"Okay, then what do you do with the next two symbols? How is south less than V?"

"What if it isn't *less than*. What if that's the symbol for measuring an angle?"

"Okay, but what—oh, then the V isn't a letter."

"Right."

"It's the Roman numeral for five. That's why you wanted the sextant." He picked the box up off the seat and placed it on the table.

Riley flicked open the latches and opened the box. She lifted out the familiar instrument. "What sort of navigational instruments would the Knights of Malta have used back then?"

"According to the Silver Girl legend, they sailed here the year Napoleon conquered Malta. That was 1798. They actually had sextants then, but they were rare. But navigators had been using quadrants and octants to measure angles since the 1600s."

"Then this just might work. Wait here and keep eating. It'll just take me a minute."

Riley left the restaurant's open deck through a side door and walked down the steps to the beach. She took her phone out of her pocket and used the compass to line up her direction. Then she slid the phone back into her pocket and preset the sextant arm to a five-degree angle. She lifted the sextant's 7x35 scope to her eye. The line where the brilliant-blue water met the shoreline created a distinct horizon. Riley twisted the eyepiece to bring the island's image into focus, then she swung the sextant back and forth, searching for something that would pop out at her. And then she saw it. Over the top of the hills in the foreground, she saw a dark hole in a red cliff face. She remembered what Lukka had said about the rock-cut tombs in the hidden harbor.

"Cole, come here. You've got to see this."

CHAPTER EIGHTY-TWO

On the Beach
Shipwrecked on the Shore of Tunis

July 27, 1798

She dreamed of the little house by the fruit-tree orchard in Saint Julian's Bay. The house had a red roof and green shutters now, and there was a young boy playing in the yard. His soft, curly hair was the color of chestnuts. His father appeared in the doorway, and he called the boy's name. Lukka. The boy ran and jumped into his father's arms. His father was Chevalier Alonso Montras of Aragon.

The flies crawling on her face awakened her.

Alonso lay next to her. She had dragged him far up the beach to where the waves and tide could no longer reach them and cut away the cupboard door she'd tied to him. Then she had gone back to find her barrel, and she'd pushed and rolled it through the sucking, muddy sand. Then she'd gone back one last time to the waves. She'd collected ropes and canvas and pieces of flotsam she thought they might be able to use. After she'd dragged a piece of sail piled high with her treasures to the spot in the shade of a tree where Alonso lay, she had collapsed next to him and fallen sound asleep. Was that yesterday? She was not sure.

He looked so white. He'd soiled himself, and that was what was attracting the flies. She didn't know if he was alive or dead, and she hesitated before touching him. She wanted to live a bit longer in the moment of not knowing. She feared he was gone, and she felt the pressure of the tears—when she saw his hand move.

Arzella gasped and entwined her fingers in his. "Alonso, my love. I am rested now. Let us go find you help. There must be a settlement along this river."

She fashioned a sort of sled out of a section of rope and a large piece of sail. She cleaned him, dressed him, and got him to eat a few dates and walnuts. Then she pulled Alonso and all their belongings onto the sailcloth, tied the rope to two corners, and made a yoke for herself.

At first, she didn't think she would be able to move it at all. But she imagined the house in the orchard just a few steps ahead, and she pulled with all her might. The cloth slid a few inches across the sand. And then a few inches more.

All day she dragged him upriver. She kept to the sandy edges. There wasn't much water there—it was more like moist sand. The sand was more slick there, and there were fewer rocks. But if she dug, a pool would form in the bottom, and soon enough water would collect to quench her thirst and fill the goatskin bag.

The river valley changed the farther inland she traveled. Down by the sea, it had been all flat marshland, but gradually the banks rose higher. Now she was in the bottom of a gorge with rocky cliff faces on either side.

By late afternoon, she was done in. On the left side of the ravine, a tall rock pinnacle cast a shadow down the embankment. She saw what looked like a cave at the base of the rock formation, but when she climbed up to it, she discovered it was really little more than a shelf with a rock overhang. It would still provide shelter in the event it rained. She toted all their belongings up the embankment, leaving Alonso for last.

She took him by the shoulder again and shook him. He winced at the pain, but she took that for a good sign. "Can you help me?" she said.

He made no reply, but when she put one arm under him and tried to lift his shoulders, he pushed off the ground, and together they got him to his feet. It took almost an hour to get him up a hillside that she could climb in five minutes. His breathing was shallow, and often she heard a gurgling noise in his chest that reminded her of her father's last days. When they reached the ledge, she lowered him onto the bed she had made out of their clothing. He closed his eyes and lay still.

"Look," she said. "I know the climb was difficult, but from here we have a view all the way to the sea."

He opened his eyes and turned his head. He lay there staring at the sea as she worked.

Arzella made a fire with wood from their wrecked ship. She heated water in her silver pilgrim's flask and made a tea for Alonso with nettles she'd picked at the river's edge.

She shifted him so he could sit with his back against the cliff. He took a few sips of the tea when she held the flask to his lips.

"I need to talk to you." His voice startled her. Those were the first words he had spoken since the shipwreck.

"Please, don't tire yourself. We will find a doctor for you tomorrow."

He reached out and touched her hairline. "My beautiful Arzella, your hair has changed."

"Shhhh," she said. She held the flask to his lips again. "Drink some more of this tea."

He tried again to drink, but most of the liquid spilled out of his mouth. He shook his head. "I don't have much time, Arzella." His words came slowly as he labored to breathe.

"You will have plenty of time, my love."

"No, I will not return to Malta with you."

She grasped his hand and held it to her cheek. "Don't say these things."

"I cannot protect you. You might be robbed."

"The people here will be kind, I am sure of it."

"The journey will be arduous for a woman alone."

Tears wet her cheeks as she said, "I will not be alone."

"I swore an oath."

She nodded.

"One day tell our son about his father. Give him the shield."

"Alonso—"

"Promise me," he said.

"I promise."

That night, she lay curled next to him, listening to his breathing and the whistling noise made by the wind as it blew past the rock pinnacle above them. She drew his cloak around them as the night wind grew cold. She feared sleep, and yet exhaustion overcame her. When she awoke, the first rays of sun were touching the rock overhang above. When she heard nothing more than the sound of the wind, she knew he was gone.

The earth on the hillside was dry, rocky, and hard, so it took her most of the day to dig a grave with his sword. Her Alonso would rather be up there with the view of the sea than down by the river. She wrapped him in sailcloth and kissed his sweet face one last time.

"Good-bye, my love," she said aloud before she rolled his body into the grave. She climbed down into the hole and settled him comfortably, then she reached for the shield. She ran her fingers over the design she had added. She had done it for Alonso, not for the Knights. It was her best work—only a very keen eye would discover the figures she had engraved in the design. But such a valuable piece of silver might endanger her and the child she carried. She set the shield on Alonso's chest.

Filling the hole took almost no time. She tamped the dirt and placed several rocks atop the grave. She decided against any grave marker. She looked up at the rock pinnacle. That would be his gravestone. One day, she would tell her son. He could choose whether to return to find his father's grave and the secret buried within.

She packed the remainder of her belongings into a sack she'd fashioned out of rope and sailcloth and slung it over her shoulder. Shading her eyes, she looked up at the sun. There were perhaps three hours of daylight left.

At the bottom of the ravine, she turned left and began walking upriver. She rubbed a hand over her belly. There had to be a village on this river, and they would tell her how to start her journey back to Malta.

CHAPTER EIGHTY-THREE

The Sunken City of Simena
Kekova, Turkey

April 29, 2014

Riley munched on one piece and wrapped the rest of the *gözleme* in a napkin while Cole paid their bill. They motored the dinghy out to *Bonefish*, and, while Cole put the sextant away, Riley collected her gear in a backpack. After only a couple of minutes, they were back in the inflatable and up on a plane heading across the less-than-a-mile of blue water to Kekova Island.

As they neared the island, the water changed color, and soon the sea floor grew visible. They watched the water as the boat slowed. When they could first see bottom, they passed over yellow-green stones that were scattered about randomly on the sea floor. Then the sharp angles of a man-made wall appeared just a few feet beneath the inflatable. The fragment stood alone in the rubble, but just to be cautious, Cole cut the outboard and tilted the prop up out of the water. He pulled the oars out of their rubber brackets and rowed them over the shallow water.

"Look over here," Riley said.

On the other side of the boat, a large rectangle of stone walls appeared. On one side was an opening. The door. They were looking into the interior of a house in the sunken city of Simena.

Cole rowed east in the direction of the entrance to the secret harbor Lukka had told Riley about. On the shore, they now saw many fragments of walls, and higher up on the hillside stood a tomb. Cole pulled at the oars, and they kept discovering more bits and pieces of the city that had been destroyed over two thousand years before. A white staircase wound down the cliff, and they could see the steps continuing down into the blue-green water.

"People lived in these houses," Riley said. "Children played here. Mothers cooked meals and lovers made love. Generations and generations of them, and they're gone, but their houses remain. It's kind of creepy."

"That's the way it always feels when I dive on a wreck. It's almost like you feel their ghosts."

Riley put her hand on Cole's knee as he pulled at the oars. He smiled at her, then shifted his eyes to the castle. Then looked back over his shoulder at Kekova Island.

"I understand now why they call the bay 'hidden,'" he said. "I still can't see the entrance, but it must be right around here."

He'd barely finished saying the words when the opening appeared in the shore. High rocks on either side made it appear like the entrance to a miniature fjord. He tugged at one oar to turn the boat, and they slid inside the cove.

Once through the entrance, the bay opened up into a cove much larger than she would have thought. The *Bonefish* could anchor inside with room to spare, and it would be difficult for anyone to spot her unless they found the slit in the coast.

Around most of the small bay, the hillsides rose gradually, speckled with rocky outcroppings and short bushes. Closer toward the shore they saw a few ruins. Only one wall fragment was still standing, but there were several foundations, some awash in the shallows. On the hillside behind the little beach Riley saw a couple of freestanding sarcophagi like those they had seen up at the castle. But in the back-left corner of the cove, a sheer reddish-and-gray rock face rose straight out of the water to a height much higher than the surrounding hills.

"There it is," Riley said.

Three-quarters of the way up the rock face was an elaborately carved facade around the black hole of a tomb opening.

Cole said, "Now that's a brilliant hiding place. We could only see it from the beach across the way because the hill in front of it is lower."

"Think of the craftsmanship to carve that out of stone on the side of a sheer cliff."

"The Lycians aren't the only ones who used rock-cut tombs," Cole said. "You'll find them all around the Med. That one is what they call a house-type tomb. It's got the columns on both sides and the triangular structure at the top carved to look like the roof on a house. There are two carved doorways, but only one of them is an actual opening. Originally, it probably had a sliding stone door to cover the opening. If the door had been on there and closed, you probably wouldn't have seen the black hole of the opening through the sextant's scope from the beach."

"Come on. Let's not waste time."

Cole rowed them over to the small sandy beach between the ruins and the cliff face. When the hull grounded, Riley picked up her backpack while Cole pulled the dinghy up the beach. She sat on a rock and pulled her climbing shoes out of her pack.

"That cliff face is straight up and down," he said. "I can't even look up there without getting nauseated. It must be over two hundred feet high."

She glanced up at the cliff. "It's not bad. Looks like there are plenty of handholds. I'll be extra careful, though. Don't worry. I brought all my gear."

"I feel like a wuss making you go up there alone."

"Remember? It's like I said last night. I need to feel useful, too. You're the archeologist. This is where my talents come in."

She pulled her climbing harness out of her pack and stepped into it. When she'd cinched up her belt, she hung her chalk bag by a carabiner clip.

Cole said, "They did so much stonework around here because this stone is soft and easy to work. This isn't granite."

"I know."

"I wish I could do it instead of you."

"I know."

"Listen, when you get to the tomb, you'll probably find an open chamber with one or several stone couches around the edges. That was where they would put the bodies and the offerings. When you're inside, take photos. And if you have to cut or damage the tomb in any way, photograph what you're doing."

"Don't worry. I'll try not to damage anything, but if this manuscript is there, and it's stayed there for two hundred years, it's probably well hidden."

Cole pointed up at the dark opening in the cliff. "It's not like it's in the most accessible place."

"Agreed, but that wouldn't keep somebody like me out."

"You can bet it'd keep me from ever trying it. Just be careful, Riley."

"You, too. This might take a while, and we don't know if we've been followed." She took her flare gun out of her backpack and handed it to him. "This is a German Geco flare gun. It fires a 26.5 millimeter flare. Most flare guns won't seriously injure a person, but this one packs a wallop. Remember, though, you've only got one shot."

"Riley, you take it."

She shook her head. "It's not like I'm going to get jumped up there." She pointed at the tomb in the cliff off to their left. Then she stood up and slung her rope over her head. "I'll be back soon."

The terrain straight back from the beach was a more gentle slope of rocky ground, with patches of bushes and trees. She considered going up there and making her way to the top of the cliff. Then she could rappel her way down to the tomb.

But the thing was, it would be hot, dirty work in prickly bushes, and it would probably take her twice as long.

Whereas climbing the cliff face—that would be fast *and* fun.

She walked along the rocky beach until she got to where the water pressed right up against the base of the cliff. The rock face really was almost straight up.

The climb started out easy. There were plenty of hand- and toe-holds, and she made fast progress moving across as well as up, since the tomb was more in the center of the cliff. About a third of the way up, she came to a small ledge with a stunted tree and several bushes growing out of it. The tree felt strong, and she considered tying her rope to it, but she didn't like knots. They limited her options.

After taking a drink from her water bottle, she continued her climb. She didn't think she was going to need to use any bolts at all, but about twenty feet short of the tomb entrance, things got a bit more dicey.

The problem was how soft the rock was there. She had two close calls where footholds just crumbled beneath her, and she almost fell the second time. She decided she needed at least one solid anchor, so she took out her handheld drill, found a spot that looked good, and began the long process of drilling into the rock.

The good thing was that the rock she drilled into seemed solid and hard. The bad thing was that meant it took longer to drill. Finally, she got a decent bolt into the wall and hooked herself on. At least now, if she fell, she could belay and slow herself down.

It took her another half hour to make it up that last twenty feet, but she managed not to fall. When she got one hand onto the ledge, she felt the groove at the base of the entrance where the old stone door would slide. She pulled herself up and swung one leg onto the rock ledge.

The front of the tomb stretched nearly fifteen feet across. It looked as though there were two doors. And each door had three carved frames around it, with each frame getting increasingly smaller. Riley thought that style looked Hellenic, but maybe she was just thinking of the familiar facade of so many Greek restaurants she'd seen. Only one of the two doors was an actual opening, and it was only about five feet tall. She supposed the sliding door that was now long gone must have been carved to look similar, so from the ground, both would look like closed doors.

Riley bent over and stepped down to enter the dark tomb. Inside, the temperature dropped a good ten degrees. The air smelled musty and earthy but dry. It reminded her of the smell in the catacombs in Rome with Diggory. She shivered at the memory.

As Cole had described, there were two separate stone couches along the rear wall. It was quite easy to see the one opposite the door with the light from the opening, so she examined that one first. The bench was decorated with carvings of several women holding hands. The base was carved with floral designs at the two ends. She didn't see anything that looked like a hiding place.

She retrieved her headlamp out of her pack and pulled the elastic band over the top of her head. She switched it on in order to take a better look at the darker end of the chamber off to her right. While the tomb wasn't dug very deep into the cliff, it was more than fifteen feet wide inside. The darkest corner was to her right, behind the second ornamental door, which had no real opening. On the second bench were carvings of two lions. The detail was more fine. Since that area would have been more protected from sun and rain, the carvings had not eroded as much. When she shone the light on the base of the second stone couch, she held her breath. The same floral designs decorated the two ends, but in the middle was the faint outline of a Maltese cross.

CHAPTER EIGHTY-FOUR

On the Docks
Kaş, Turkey

April 29, 2014

"I need to rent the fastest boat you have," Virgil said.

He was standing inside the travel-agency office several blocks away from the new marina in Kaş, and he was losing patience with the Turk on the other side of the counter.

"They told me in the marina I could rent a boat here."

"I was just trying to show you the selections you have." The man pointed to a large laminated card on the countertop and began going through each vessel, detailing the various attributes, from seat cushions to ice makers to swim ladders. "And all our captains are very good."

Virgil interrupted him again. "I don't care about anything but speed. Rent me the fastest boat you have. And I don't want a captain. I'll drive myself."

The man shrugged and pulled a form with multiple carbons out from under the desk. "Fill this out," he said. "And we don't rent boats without a captain."

"Well, I won't fill out your antiquated forms." Virgil reached for his wallet and began laying five-hundred-euro bills on the counter. "But I am willing to pay. Are you sure you won't rent me a boat without a skipper?"

Virgil strode out the long dock, looking for the thirty-five-foot dark-blue power cruiser. Most of the other docks were populated with super yachts, while the one he'd been directed to was filled with smaller, plastic-looking sailboats. He had to walk almost to the end before he saw the sleek-looking speedboat.

He jingled the keys in his hand as he stepped out onto the finger pier, looking the boat over. He approved. He jumped aboard and unlocked the door to the small cabin. Hot air poured out. The interior looked to be nothing more than a V-berth in the bow, a head, and a small galley.

Canvas covered the front window, and he set to work removing that as well as the covers over the instruments. He followed the instructions he'd been issued for powering up the chart plotter, then turned the ignition and pressed the starter. The two outboard engines purred to life.

This shouldn't be that difficult, he thought as he hopped onto the dock to untie the dock lines. He was leaning over, unwrapping a line off the last of the cleats, when he felt cold metal press against his neck.

"Stand up slowly and hand me that line."

He knew that voice. But it wasn't possible.

"Priest?"

"Now raise your hands."

He followed instructions. The man patted him down and took his Glock.

"Climb aboard and take the controls."

"But how—"

"Virgil, Virgil." Priest nudged him with the gun, and they both stepped aboard. "You never were the brightest bulb, and now in your old age, you're really slipping."

When Virgil turned around, he saw that Priest had changed his appearance considerably since the last time they'd met. He now wore a smart haircut and fashionable black clothes. He looked more like the man who had once worked for the CIA. Except for his face.

"You left me tied with zip ties and your little bomb waiting to go off. But you didn't even bother to frisk me. You and the girl weren't gone thirty seconds before I had my knife out and freed myself."

"So you've been following me?"

"I knew you had the resources and the motivation. You'd do the work for me. You haven't even been checking for a tail. You used to be better than that."

Priest was right. Virgil silently cursed at himself. It had never occurred to him someone would follow him, and he hadn't been checking. He *was* losing his edge.

Virgil backed the boat out of the slip. He kept to the speed limit in the long harbor, but as soon as he cleared the point and could turn southeast, he pushed the throttle forward, put her on a plane, and headed for Kekova Roads.

It took them about an hour to cover the twenty miles to the last location that Viper had texted him. There had been no new texts since that last one around 11:00 a.m. Virgil recognized the castle when he entered Kekova Roads from the drawing in the back of the sea atlas. Priest had once told him that Thatcher had an uncanny talent for figuring this shit out, and it appeared to be true.

"That's her sailboat up ahead," Priest said. "I don't see the dinghy there, though. Let's go in and tie up."

As they motored into the dock, Virgil watched Priest on deck preparing the lines. He wondered if he should try to get the gun as they docked.

It was as though Priest knew what he was thinking. As they approached the dock, he came back and stood by the corner of the cabin. "Listen, Virgil. These two are slippery. You've already seen that. You and I would be better served working together than at odds. Two against two sounds better than two against one, don't you think?"

Priest jumped off and tied up the boat.

When Virgil shut down the engines, Priest returned to the cockpit. "Why don't you head up there to that restaurant and see if anyone knows where our old friends off *Bonefish* got to?" He sat in the captain's chair at the helm and put his feet up on the dash, crossed at the ankle. "I'll wait right here." He let his jacket fall open, showing the gun. "But I don't think you'll make a fuss. We want the same thing."

The Turk in the restaurant told Virgil that the couple had left in their dinghy to explore a sunken city off that island. He pointed across the water and told him about the hidden harbor.

Virgil jumped aboard and reported. "He said they went over to that island."

As they motored slowly through the cluster of anchored yachts, Priest said, "Might be best if they don't know I'm here. I like that element of surprise."

"If we're partners now, then you can give me my gun back, right?"

Priest laughed, but only one side of his face moved. "Come on, Virgil, you're a Delta. Or you were. You don't need a gun. Aren't your hands supposed to be lethal weapons?"

Virgil didn't look at Priest. He pictured Bonnie and pushed the throttle up a notch.

"Don't be mad, Virg. When we get to the island, you'll get your gun back. And you can *keep* the manuscript. I never signed on to your Knight's-crusade gig. Hell, you can even have Thatcher. I just want the woman."

CHAPTER EIGHTY-FIVE

The Sunken City of Simena
Kekova, Turkey

April 29, 2014

Cole sat on the side of the inflatable boat, rearranging the equipment in the dinghy's bow compartment. He intended to put the flare pistol away. He had to do something to keep his mind off the woman he loved up in the tomb on that cliff. Besides, the flare pistol looked too much like a real gun, with its six-inch blued-steel barrel and brown handgrip. Cole had never been a fan of guns.

He had just picked up the red one-gallon jug of extra gas they kept in the bow compartment when he heard the low rumbling of a powerboat entering the little harbor. He froze, staring wide-eyed at the entrance channel. He glanced up at the cliff and saw the climbing rope disappear up into the black hole of the tomb opening. He let the lid to the fiberglass compartment drop, picked up the flare gun from his lap, and sprinted the ten yards into the brush. He flattened himself behind a boulder, where he could watch the new arrival. He looked down and was surprised to see that, in addition to the flare gun, he was still holding the red plastic gas can. He had just run without thinking.

Maybe it was only some tourists.

The white-blond hair was visible over the top of the windshield. Or maybe it wasn't a tourist. Blondie was turning his head all around, looking over the little cove. Cole didn't think Blondie had seen the rope disappear into the tomb. It didn't seem he had noticed the tomb at all.

Then suddenly his head swiveled over and he looked up. It was almost as though someone had told him to look, but there wasn't anyone else visible in the boat. Then the man turned and looked at their dinghy. He took aim and increased boat speed.

Cole set down the gas can and tucked the flare gun into his belt in the small of his back. He pulled his T-shirt down again to cover it. The shirt was black—not the best color for camouflage in the brush. He looked at the can. Better to keep it with him than to leave it behind as evidence of which way he'd gone. Cole picked up the plastic can, bent over, and starting climbing up the hill. He spotted a freestanding sarcophagus. The top had been knocked off, presumably by tomb robbers. If he could get inside . . .

Cole crouched down in the brush and froze again when he heard the screeching noise of the fiberglass hull sliding up the rocky beach, followed by silence when the engines cut off.

A voice called out. "Thatcher! I know you're here."

He heard rocks crunch when the man jumped off the boat.

Cole ran, keeping his body low and trying to make as little noise as possible. When he reached the tomb, he saw that it had a hyposorium, or burial chamber, on the bottom, then a base, then the actual sarcophagus on top. This type of tomb would have been for a wealthy person. No wonder robbers had taken off the top. The huge, arched stone lid lay off to one side.

"Thatcher, we want the same thing. The manuscript. I can help you."

He got round the back side of the tomb, where Blondie couldn't spot him. He wedged a foot atop the protruding edge of the hyposorium, then stepped up onto the base. He dropped the gas can into the tomb, then grabbed the upper edge of the stone lip. He was able to get a foothold on the rough stone to push himself up, and then an elbow over the top. He swung his knee over, pulled the rest of his body up, and rolled over the stone edge.

He thought he would fall quite a distance, but he only fell about a foot. The tomb was nearly full of dirt. Okay, two- to three-thousand-years' accumulation of dirt. The top of the tomb was high enough that he didn't think his body could be seen from below, but if Blondie got higher up the hill, he'd see him plainly. Maybe his brilliant hiding place wasn't so brilliant.

"Thatcher!" Blondie called out again. "The Knights would be willing to pay you very well if you return their property to them."

The man's voice was still coming from someplace lower down the hill, but not by much. Cole rolled onto his stomach, pulled himself up to the end of the tomb, and lifted his head to take a quick peek over the side. He ducked back down. The man was only about thirty yards away. Fortunately, his back was turned.

Cole looked at the gas can. Maybe he should go on the offensive. He unscrewed the cap and pulled out the spout. Then he took out his pocketknife and stabbed the top of the plastic can opposite the opening. It would need an air spout. He cut an additional slit next to the opening to make sure the fluid could flow freely.

How could he get Blondie to come this way? He looked around the inside of the sarcophagus for a rock to throw, but there was nothing but hard-packed dirt and a few rotting leaves. *The spout and lid from the fuel can.* He tossed both over the side of the tomb. He heard nothing when they hit ground.

He wasn't sure if it had made a noise he just couldn't hear, or if there had been nothing loud enough to attract the man's attention.

Cole raised up to look again. Blondie was walking this way, his head down, watching his feet on the rough terrain. Cole pulled the gas can up to the stone edge of the tomb. He took another peek. Blondie had spotted the plastic on the ground, and he had zeroed in on it. He was heading straight for it with a puzzled look on his face. He was not looking up.

Cole got to his knees, leaned back out of sight, and waited. When next he peeked, the man was bending over directly beneath him at the base of the tomb. Cole stood, turned the gas can over, and emptied it over his head and back.

Blondie jumped out from under the stream of gasoline, reached into his jacket, and pulled out a gun. He raised it up and pointed the barrel toward Cole.

"Wait!" Cole yelled. "Think before you set off a spark. You'll blow yourself up."

Blondie squinted at him. His eyes hurt to look at. "You're bluffing. That wouldn't happen."

"Think. You've fired guns at night. Do you see a muzzle flash? It's not the liquid gas all over you that's the danger. It's the vapors it's giving off."

"Shut up and get down here, Thatcher."

Cole stood up. He thought, *He's not going to kill me until he gets his hands on the manuscript.* He climbed down from the top of the sarcophagus. When he landed on the ground, he looked at Virgil Vandervoort, soaked in gasoline and pointing a gun at him.

"Do you mind if I step back? I'm more worried about getting burned in the flash fire than I am about you hitting your target. Your eyes are bloodred. I'll bet that burns, eh?"

"Shut up. Where's your girlfriend?"

"She's back at the castle. She didn't come over here with me."

"Nice try. I know she's around here somewhere. And I'll bet wherever she is, that's where the manuscript is."

"If I were you, I'd head to the water and try to get some of that gas off."

Blondie waved the gun toward the water. "Okay, start walking."

The terrain was so uneven with rocks and bushes, Cole had to keep his eyes on the ground or he would fall. But his mind was focused on the flare gun under his shirt. He was worried it would be obvious to the man walking behind him. It took considerable self-control not to tug at his shirt or check to see if it was riding up.

When they arrived at the beach, Blondie walked over to the grounded powerboat and rapped on the hull a couple of times with his pistol.

"Somebody else come with you?"

Blondie smiled. "I'll be asking the questions. Where's the manuscript?"

"I don't know what you're talking about."

"Do you really think I'd need a gun to kill you?" He backhanded Cole across the face with the hand holding the gun.

Cole's arms flew out to his sides and his legs buckled. He slammed down onto the beach and the back of his head bounced on the jagged rocks. He felt warm liquid flowing across his mouth.

"Let's try this again. Where's the manuscript?"

"I don't know," Cole tried to say, but what he heard sounded like gibberish. His lips felt fat and numb.

Blondie delivered a kick to his side that knocked all the air out of his lungs and left Cole gasping and curled into a fetal position.

"Virgil!"

Cole recognized Riley's voice echoing around the small cove. He rolled over and looked up at the cliff. She was standing on the ledge outside the tomb's gaping black door. He struggled to a sitting position as Virgil spun in circles, trying to locate where the voice was coming from.

"I found it, Virgil. Up here." She put her foot against the edge of something and shoved it to one side of the carved tomb door.

Virgil's head tilted up, and he looked over Cole's head. He turned his body to face the cliff, planting his feet solidly.

"You hurt that man and I swear I'll push this thing over the edge and into the water."

When Cole saw Virgil's hands both grasp the gun, he reached behind under his T-shirt and drew out the flare gun. He was going to shout a warning, telling him not to shoot, when he saw a shadow of a smile cross the man's face. Virgil's gun started to rise.

Cole didn't remember pulling the trigger on the flare gun. The recoil knocked him back onto the rocks, but not before he heard the second explosion from Virgil's gun.

Riley. She was all Cole could think about. He was aware that something down the beach was burning, but he couldn't bear to look at it. She wasn't there on the ledge outside the tomb. He searched the rocks at the bottom, fearing he might see her. But no, there was no sign of her.

Then he saw movement on the cliff face. A long rope sailed past the rock-cut tomb, followed by a descending climber. But it didn't make sense. Someone was rappelling off the top of the cliff, from the trees above the tomb. It was a man. His feet hit the top of the carved tomb, and in one big jump he flew over the ornamental roof, landed on the ledge, ducked down, and disappeared into the black, gaping hole.

CHAPTER EIGHTY-SIX

**Inside the Lycian Tomb
Kekova, Turkey**

April 29, 2014

Riley had ducked back inside the tomb after making her threat. An instant later, she heard two nearly simultaneous gunshots. Cole! She was rushing back to the opening when rocks and dirt began falling in front of it, followed by a snaking white rope. She jumped aside just before a man slid down the rope and swung in through the opening.

"Hello, Riley."

She knew that voice. For years it had haunted her nightmares. She'd pressed herself back against the stone bench in the darkest corner. She blinked her eyes.

He stood in the shaft of light that poured through the opening, and he did not fully turn to look at her. What she could see of his face looked like the beautiful man she had once thought she loved.

"You're a difficult man to kill," she said. Her voice sounded more confident than she felt.

He was breathing hard, watching her from the corner of his eye. Riley knew he was also waiting for his eyes to adjust to the darkness.

She used the time to squat down and pick up her Leatherman and the drill bit from the rubble at her feet. She slipped the knife in her pocket, the drill bit into the chalk bag that hung from her belt.

He cleared his throat and said, "I like what you've done with the place."

She didn't say anything. *He's nervous,* she thought. Like a guy on a first date. He's fantasized about this moment so many times. Cole was wrong. This was not just another job for Diggory. This was about her.

"It's even better than the Roman catacombs," he said.

"Why?" She made her voice soft and higher pitched.

"Oh, Riley, don't play dumb with me. Your father would be ashamed of you."

"Don't you speak of him!" The words came out of her mouth faster than her brain could stop them. She couldn't let him get to her like that.

"Touchy, touchy, aren't we? You still haven't got over being Daddy's little girl?"

Riley concentrated on controlling her breathing. Okay. What do you see? Get the upper hand back.

He turned to face her, and she was shocked again by the scars and the downward pull at the corner of his mouth. One side of his face was smiling, while the other wore a perpetual frown. When he spoke, his voice was soft, like it used to be when they were courting. "I've always enjoyed the close relationship I've had with your family. First it was your brother, Michael. Brilliant young man, but so odd-looking." He held his hands up on either side of his head. "The big head and thick glasses—well, you know. That was a challenge to make it look like an accident. Couldn't leave any marks. But I've always been so good at what I do."

He was wearing black slacks and a turtleneck sweater. No belt visible. Loafers, no socks. There were white marks on his sweater where he had wrapped the line around his back to rappel down the cliff. New short haircut.

"Then Yorick." He sighed. "How well I remember the feeling of my hands around your father's neck."

He held his hands palms-up in front of his waist. The skin on his palms was red. Rope burns. Then he clenched his fists and squeezed so hard the fabric stretched tight around his right bicep.

"You've been working out," she said.

Vanity. He'd cleaned up, dressed up for her.

"After years of physical therapy, it became a habit."

She remembered the day he had killed her father. He'd tried to kill her, too. He strangled, then revived, his victims. He liked to play with them.

"I find it helps with the pain," she said.

"Shut up!" His raised his voice almost to a shout. He moved fast, covering the ground between them in seconds. He brushed aside her fists, grabbed her by the front of her T-shirt, and pulled her into the shaft of light. "Don't you ever think what happened to you in Lima was *anything* like what you did to me." He turned his face then and pointed to the scars. "This is because of you."

He let go of her shirt and shoved up his left sleeve. "And this." The arm was mottled and covered with thick ridges of scar tissue.

"And this." He pulled up the sweater to reveal the same scars on his torso. "All of this is what you did to me."

She smiled. "Remember what you once said to me about Lima? You said, 'You've already figured it out, Riley. You just can't admit it to yourself.' You're just as bad, Diggory."

"What are you talking about?"

"I didn't *do* anything to you," she said. "You did it to yourself."

He gripped a handful of her hair and drew her face close. His breath smelled sour. "It's all your fault, you stupid cunt." He shoved her down onto the stone couch.

Riley hit the back of her head on the stone wall. As she sat there rubbing it, she watched him go back to inspect the opening she'd made in the other rock couch. He picked up the large square of stone with the Maltese cross on it.

"So you found it? The manuscript?"

She pointed to the rubble on the floor of the tomb. "They dug out a hollow in the bench, then cut a piece of stone to use as a door. The cracks were smoothed over with mud. It took me a while to dig all the mud out and pry out the stone."

"And?"

"The box I found is outside on the ledge." Riley reached into her pocket and wrapped her fingers around her Leatherman.

He tried to smile, and, though both eyes glittered in the light, only one half of his face moved. "The Knights of Malta would pay a fortune for it, you know."

"For their crusade against the Muslims."

"It's just another war," he said. "Seven billion people on this planet? We need a good war now and again."

He wheeled around and dropped to one knee to reach for the box. As he slid it in front of the opening, Riley pulled out the Leatherman and opened the tool. By then he'd popped his arm back inside, and he easily snatched the tool out of her hand before she could pull the blade open.

"Weak, Riley. You don't even have a real knife with you?" He threw the tool out the tomb opening.

She looked out and saw the white rope dangling just to the right of the entrance.

"Look at this box," he said, nudging it with his toe. "Fascinating."

"There are three keyholes."

"Shall we break it open and see what's inside?"

"No!" she said.

Half his face grinned at her.

"Your archeologist boyfriend wouldn't like that, eh?"

"Fiancé," she said, and she went back to concentrating on her breathing.

"Oh, Riley. I'm disappointed in you. You've never been boring. And now look at what you've done. Marriage? That's not your style." He walked over to her and pulled her up by her hair. "I'm not happy when I'm bored."

Riley thought about free diving. When she wanted to stay underwater a very long time, she hyperventilated first. By over-oxygenating her brain, she'd learned to hold her breath for just over two minutes. Short breaths.

"That's funny," she said, breathing in and out as though she were frightened. "Because when we were lovers, I was the bored one."

He yanked her head back and stared at her throat. "You lying bitch."

"I called you a freak once. Now you actually look like the monster you are."

He wrapped both hands around her neck and squeezed her windpipe under her chin. Not too hard, though. He was playing with her like a cat torturing its prey. He didn't want to cut off the blood flow to her brain just yet.

She fought him hard enough to be convincing, then slowly she let her body go slack. Just when she felt him beginning to ease, she threw her arms up high inside his and slammed down on the insides of his elbows. His released his grip on her throat, and before he could react, she smashed her good shoulder into him and drove him back through the opening.

His feet hit the opening's rock edge, and he nearly stumbled, then his other foot hit the box, sending it skidding over the edge and knocking him off balance. Her momentum had carried her after him. When his arms flailed at her, one hand hooked onto a leg strap of her climbing harness, yanking her toward the edge with him. Riley wrenched back and seized the dangling rope with both hands, and then they both went over the edge.

The nylon rope had some stretch and give in it. They bounced, then swayed, but her grip held. Dig's weight along with her own was almost too much for her. He was trying to grab hold of something with his free hand, but whenever he reached he swung around wildly.

Riley looked down. It was his good hand on the leg cuff. She swung her free leg and kicked him in his injured shoulder as hard as she could.

He screamed and jerked, and the rope started to slide through her fists. She wrapped her free leg around the rope and that stopped the descent.

Dig's weight on the harness had dragged the waistband low on her hips, and the thigh cuff was below her knee.

Ever since her injury, her left arm had been growing stronger to take up the slack for her weak side. Now she would test that strength. She let go of the rope with her right hand and pulled the drill bit from her chalk bag, then tried to stab his hand. There was no way she could reach.

Her left hand started slipping, and she grabbed the rope with both hands again, dropping the drill bit in the process. She felt the bitter end of the rope at her ankle. She couldn't slide much lower.

She ordered herself to think. Diggory's chuffing breaths grew calmer. He was trying to get his pain under control, preparing for his next assault. She had no time.

The buckle on the front of her harness was designed not to release under pressure. But the adjustable strap that held the buckle in place was not. She let go once more and quickly lifted the plastic tab at the back of the buckle. The webbing slipped through it and the pressure on her pelvis eased.

She grabbed the rope again quickly as she felt the belt slip off her hips. She untangled her leg from the rope and hung freely from it.

When the waist belt slipped past her buttocks, the leg cuffs slid off her legs, taking her shoes—and Dig—with them. Dig didn't make a sound until his body hit the rocky shore.

Riley felt so light without his weight, she had no trouble lifting her legs up, grabbing the rope with her feet and legs, and starting to shimmy up to the tomb. It wasn't until she was able to swing her feet onto the ledge that she pried her hands off the rope. She leaned her back against the stone and closed her eyes.

"Riley." She heard a voice from below.

She crawled back to the edge and peered over. At first, all she saw was the sprawled body at the base of the cliff, a growing pool of red spreading out in the water. No way he survived that.

"Riley, here." She shifted her focus slightly to the left, and two-thirds of the way down the slope she saw Cole's white face looking up through the branches of a tree. He was on the narrow ledge, his arms wrapped around the tree's trunk. The wooden box was lodged in the branches of the tree.

"I was climbing up to save you," he said.

"I'm impressed you made it that far."

"Me, too. But I think I might need some help getting down."

EPILOGUE

**A Restaurant in Republic Square
Valletta, Malta**

May 11, 2014

The four of them had just been seated at an outdoor table when the champagne arrived.

Cole looked at the two empty seats and said, "Should we wait until they get here?"

Hazel lifted the bottle out of the ice bucket and said, "There's plenty more where this came from, and I have a few toasts to make." She filled their glasses.

Riley stood up with hers. "I want to go first. I know this week is supposed to be about us, but I want to make a toast to Hazel and Theo. I know it's early days, but Cole and I could not be happier for the two people we love most in the world."

Cole lifted his glass. "Cheers to that."

"I don't know what you're talking about," Theo said.

Riley laughed. "Come on. It's not like we didn't know. The two of you have been walking around grinning like a couple of goony birds ever since we sailed in on *Bonefish* a few days ago."

"I'll drink to that," Hazel said, and they all clinked glasses.

"I see you've started early," a familiar voice said.

Riley pushed back her chair. "Mom, welcome, and happy Mother's Day." She walked around the table with her arms spread wide.

Riley had not seen her mother since her last trip to France back in 2009, but Celeste Laurent Riley Villeneuve had changed very little. She was dressed in an elegant suit that no doubt bore a designer's name as upper-crust as her new husband's name.

They embraced and exchanged kisses on both cheeks.

Riley turned to her mother's husband. "Bertrand. It's good to see you again."

Cole embraced them, too, and Hazel followed, saying, "It's been a long time."

"I remember when you and Riley were just girls," Celeste said. "You always had such style, while this one"—she looked at Riley—"never had the eye for it."

When they were all seated at the table, Celeste leaned forward and said, "We saw your photographs on the television at our hotel."

Cole shrugged. "Yeah, well, it's not as bad as it looks."

Riley said, "They haven't pressed any formal charges yet."

"On the television news they mentioned smuggling and two men dead," Bertrand said.

Her mother nodded. "I'm glad to hear you say it's not as bad as it looks, because it looks very bad."

Riley sighed. That was classic Mother. Always worried, above all, about how things looked.

"Mom, what they're saying is technically true. While we were in Turkey, Cole and I did kill two men—in self-defense—and then we took off on *Bonefish* and sailed here to Malta, taking certain antiquities out of their country."

"Riley, if you're trying to make me feel better, it's not working."

"Don't worry. Lucky for us, we have a good friend with the Turkish *Jandarma*. We called him before we even cleared Turkish waters and told him what we were doing and where to find the bodies. Then we called the director of Heritage Malta here in Valletta, and told her to alert the authorities about our arrival. But let's not talk about that now. We're here to celebrate, and the event that's happening inside the palace here in"—she checked her watch—"about an hour will hopefully clear everything up. Anybody else hungry? Because I'm starved."

From the entrance to the Grand Master's Palace, they followed the signs that led to the Throne Room. People were filling the rows of chairs in the great golden hall while television crews set up their cameras pointing at the stage at the front of the room.

When Dr. G. spotted them, she came at a near run down the center aisle to meet them. "This is so exciting!" She took both Cole's and Riley's hands in hers. "Come, you and your party have reserved seats up front. We'll be starting soon."

Riley and the others sat in the front row while Cole followed Dr. Günay onto the raised platform. The wooden corsair's box they had brought back from Turkey rested on the center of the long table onstage, and the shield lay next to it. Several people stepped forward to admire the objects, and they introduced themselves to Cole. After a few more minutes, the museum personnel closed the doors to the room, and Dr. G. stepped up to the microphone.

"I want to thank you all for coming to our museum here in Valletta today. I'd especially like to welcome the delegations from the Bardo National Museum in Tunisia"—she pointed to a group of people and they nodded—"and the Turkish Ministry of Culture and Tourism, led by Captain Pamuk. Representing the Vatican, we have Sister Ola Momani, and we are honored to welcome Dr. Festing, grand master of the Sovereign Military Order of Malta. And finally, Dr. Cole Thatcher of the Full Fathom Five Maritime Foundation. I'm certain you all know why we are here. Without any further speechmaking, I'd like to invite our local locksmith, Pietru, to open the box for us."

The older Maltese man approached the table from the front, spread out a cloth with a set of lock picks, and went to work.

Dr. Günay continued while the man worked. "The box before us was discovered in a Lycian tomb on the island of Kekova in Turkey. It is a fine example of a late sixteenth-century corsair's box used by the Knights of Malta. These strongboxes were used to safeguard the valuables and gold coins aboard their ships. This box requires three keys to open it. Since we do not have these keys, Pietru, who works for us here at Heritage Malta, assures us he can pick any lock made before the twentieth century."

The crowd murmured softly. Within minutes, Pietru stepped back and pushed open the lid. Dr. Günay motioned to a pair of white-coated museum technicians at the side of the room. They stepped forward with an acrylic box. While the man held the box, the woman reached in with gloved hands and lifted a large, blackened manuscript out of the corsair's box. She placed it in the wide acrylic case and opened it to a random page.

The male tech closed the top of the box and set it on the table.

Dr. Günay peered through the top of the box. "At first glance, I can tell you that the manuscript appears to made of dark-stained animal skin, and the writing, which appears to be in a gold-colored ink, is certainly in Syriac, a dialect of Aramaic. For those of you who do not know, that was the language spoken by Jesus."

The noise in the room grew as the crowd murmured opinions on that piece of news. The historian waved the tech over and spoke to him. He reopened the box and showed her the front cover and inside first pages. She nodded, and he reclosed the box. "The pages of the manuscript appear to be loosely tied together. I cannot estimate how many pages there are." She paused and took a deep breath. "I am not an expert in the Aramaic language, but I have been doing research in preparation for this event. I can tell you that I recognized one word on the title page. That word is Barnabas."

Dr. Günay held up her hands for quiet as voices filled the room. "Please," she said. "At Dr. Thatcher's request, the manuscript is going to be made available to experts from all countries present and any interested Biblical scholars, in order to find a consensus on its age and authenticity. He hopes to have this manuscript become a part of our World Heritage Site here in Valletta. Thank you very much for joining us here today. Interested scholars, please see my museum director. The relics will remain on display here for the rest of the afternoon."

The audience broke into applause, then the meeting broke up. Many in the crowd surged to the front of the room to peer into the acrylic box. Riley stood off to the side, watching them, and she smiled when Captain Pamuk walked up to her and shook her hand.

"Did you bring your handcuffs?" she asked.

He returned her smile. "My superiors wish it were so."

Cole joined Riley and shook the captain's hand. "Sorry to make things difficult for you, Captain, but we thought this was the best solution. We didn't want to see this manuscript disappear again."

"I understand," he said. "But you will meet with me tomorrow so that I can take your statements? I have an investigation to conclude, and you are my witnesses."

"No problem," Cole said.

While Cole made arrangements to meet the captain the next day, Riley walked up to the front table, where people were now lined up to get a look at the manuscript. Riley moved to the opposite end of the table, to the open corsair's box, and examined the inside. She felt a hand on her shoulder.

"It is a magnificent box," her mother said.

Riley stepped aside to let her mother take a closer look.

Dr. G. joined them. "We have another corsair's box in our Maritime Museum in Vittoriosa," she said, "but this one is in much better condition. It will make a wonderful addition to our collection here at Heritage Malta."

Celeste pointed at a metal band inside the box. "Look, there are engravings on the inside."

Riley looked over her mother's shoulder. "Really?"

Dr. G. stepped in and leaned over the box. "Where?"

Celeste pointed to the letters.

Cole arrived with a penlight, and he illuminated the inside of the box.

Dr. Günay said, "It's two names. Alonso Montras and Arzella Brun, followed by the year 1798. She must have engraved it. The Silver Girl."

Riley placed her other hand on Cole's shoulder. "Hey, wasn't her son named Lukka Demontras?"

"That's funny," Celeste said.

"Why?"

"That was my mother's maiden name, and she always said she had family in Malta."

While Dr. Günay and Riley's mother put their heads together on a plan for creating the Demontras family tree, Cole pulled Riley out of the Throne Room and down the hall to a quiet bench on a balcony overlooking the palace courtyard.

"I'm ready to be done with these crowds," he said.

"Me, too. But we've still got to make it through the wedding."

"I know. I'm looking forward to the ceremony itself. I've always dreamed I'd get married on the deck of a sailing ship."

"Figures," she said. "You're the romantic in the family."

"Even I never dreamed it would be in Grand Harbour in Malta. But afterward, I have plans to whisk you away on a honeymoon."

"Really? And when are you going to share these plans with me?"

"I was thinking now was a good time."

"No time like the present."

"I want to get away from the crowds, somewhere we can be all alone and also do some great diving. What would you say to a trip to the islands of Oceania?"

"That's a pretty big territory. Could you be a little more specific?"

"Not until I do a little more research."

"Research? I thought you said this was a honeymoon."

"It is. But I've been reading about this mysterious French scientist and explorer, Jean-François de Galaup, more famously known as the Count de La Pérouse. He mounted a scientific expedition to the Pacific in 1785 with two ships, the *Astrolabe* and the *Boussole*. They sent their last reports back from Australia, then they vanished in Oceania."

"Imagine that."

"They were headed for the Santa Cruz Islands in the Solomon group."

Hazel poked her head through the balcony doors. "Here you two are. Your mother sent me to find you. She wants to talk to you about shopping for a wedding dress, florists, music, and all that good stuff."

"Can you stall her for me a little longer?"

Hazel smiled. "No problem."

After she'd gone, Riley rested her head on Cole's shoulder. "How soon can we leave?"

CHARACTERS

The characters whose names are followed by an asterisk are real figures from history.

2014 Timeline

MAGGIE RILEY – Former US Marine and solo sailor, she is the captain of the sailing vessel *Bonefish*. She is now engaged to Cole.

COLE THATCHER – A maritime archeologist who believes in conspiracy theories and is captain of the Exploration Vessel *Shadow Chaser II*.

THEO SPENSER – From the Caribbean island of Dominica, he is Cole's first mate and best friend.

HAZEL KITTRIDGE – Riley's best friend from childhood: African American, gorgeous, and rich.

DR. NAJAT GÜNAY – A renowned historian and director of Heritage Malta, which owns several museums in the islands. She is Turkish by birth but was raised in Malta.

VIRGIL VANDERVOORT – Former US Army Delta Force, he now works for and is a member of the Knights of Malta.

DIGGORY PRIEST – Former CIA agent who used to work for Skull and Bones and killed Riley's brother and father. He was once Riley's lover and caused the explosion in which she was injured and burned.

SIGNOR OSCURA – The executive director of the Sovereign Order of the Knights of Malta.

GAVINO EBEJER – A ninety-five-year-old Maltese man who served as a Royal Navy mechanic at the Lazaretto Submarine Base in World War II.

CAPTAIN DANYAL PAMUK – A captain with the Turkish *Jandarma* in Marmaris.

SISTER OLA – A nun from Jordan.

1942 Timeline

COMMANDER DAVID WANKLYN* – The British captain of the submarine HMS *Upholder*.

CAPTAIN ROBERT "TUG" WILSON* – A British Army commando with the Special Boat Unit.

CHARLIE PARKER* – A British Army commando with the Special Boat Unit.

CAPTAIN "SHRIMP" SIMPSON* – Base commander at the Royal Navy's Lazaretto Submarine Base.

1798 Timeline

ALONSO MONTRAS D'ARAGON – The youngest and last Maltese Knight to captain his own corsair vessel.

NIKOLA – Alonso's first mate, who is twice the young captain's age.

ARZELLA BRUN – The daughter of a silversmith.

PIERRE BRUN* – The most famous silversmith from Malta, he was born in France and moved to Malta to work for the Knights.

UNCLE EDWARD – Arzella's uncle, brother of her now-dead English mother.

MADAME BENIER – The widow who is renting the upstairs apartment over the Bruns' silversmith shop and studio.

GRAND MASTER HOMPESCH* – The last grand master of the Knights during their two-hundred-year stay in Malta.

ACKNOWLEDGMENTS

I would like to thank the following people: David Downing, Terry Goodman, Anh Schluep, Kjersti Egerdahl, JoVon Sotak, Alan Turkus, Alexander Ellul of Malta, Terry and Carole Hogan of the S/V *Common Sense*, Pete Peterson of the S/V *Brilliant*, Philip Duss of the S/V *Blue Bie*, Brian Barnes, Lia Barnes, Steve Gray, Tim Kling, my readers, family, and friends, and my husband, Wayne Hodgins.

ABOUT THE AUTHOR

Christine Kling has spent more than thirty years messing about with boats. It was her sailing experience that led her to write her first four-book suspense series about Florida female tug and salvage captain Seychelle Sullivan. Christine earned an MFA in creative writing from Florida International University, and her articles, essays, and short stories have appeared in numerous magazines and anthologies. Her new Shipwreck Adventure thrillers—*Circle of Bones, Dragon's Triangle,* and *Knight's Cross*—feature the adventures of a female sailor and a maritime archeologist. Having retired from her job as an English professor at Broward College in Fort Lauderdale, Christine now makes her home aboard a fifty-two-foot motor sailer, and she is cruising the South Pacific with her family, including Barney, the Yorkshire Terror, and Ruby, the Wonder Dog. You can learn more about her real and fictional sailing adventures by visiting www.christinekling.com.